Whatever Became of LuAnn?

Whatever Became of LuAnn?

A Novel

Velma Flaucher Falck

VANTAGE PRESS
New York

This is a work of fiction. Any similarity between the names, characters, and places in this book and any persons, living or dead, is purely coincidental.

FIRST EDITION

Published by Vantage Press, Inc.
516 West 34th Street, New York, New York 10001

Manufactured in the United States of America
ISBN: 0-533-14238-5

Library of Congress Catalog Card No.: 02-90071

0 9 8 7 6 5 4 3 2 1

Lost Dreams

She scattered dreams upon the sand and
watched the water lap.

Love dissolved like sugar cubes, more
painful than a slap.

Hope was washed far out to sea, all the
glitter gone.

Faith became a crumb for birds, dying
with their song.

Whatever Became of LuAnn? is dedicated to Jim Falck, my husband, who listened so patiently to each and every chapter as it was written and then rewritten.

It is dedicated, also, to Michele Bienfang, my daughter-in-law, whose encouraging words gave me the incentive I needed to seek publication. "It's wonderful! I couldn't put it down. I read until after midnight."

Words of encouragement came from these sources, also. Karen Wendling: "It's very interesting and hard to put down!"

Doris Wagner: "It's easy to read and flows very nicely."

Joyce Wendling: "It's very well written and very interesting. I couldn't put it down and hope there is a sequel."

Rose Carolan: "I enjoyed reading it. It has an interesting story line."

Whatever Became of LuAnn?

Part 1

1958

One

The passenger train rumbled and swayed, rhythmically lulling LuAnn into a stupor halfway between dream and reality. Her slim, young body rocked with the steady motion of the wheels, propelling the passenger train along its tracks. It had been hours since the hills of West Virginia were left behind. Nothing fleeting by, outside the train's windows, was familiar anymore. For that matter, nothing in her *life* was familiar anymore.

Everything that was once important had been left behind, and in its place, was confusion and distrust, sometimes even fear and panic. Now, the dreams that once centered around Tommy Maxwell could never be fulfilled. He was her first love . . . shy, with soft lips and gentle, caressing hands that could set her body on fire. Reality was in the form of her husband, Mack Hanable . . . bold and blundering, rough and demanding, whose hands made her want to scream out, "Leave me alone!" Tears she dared not weep caused agonizing pain and discomfort deep down inside. Her heart wanted to break.

* * *

The first dream began when she and Tommy were just sixteen. It was a first love for them both, slowly conceived from spending time together working on school activities and doing all the other things high school students do. Like the delicate wings of a butterfly emerging from its cocoon, newly aroused emotions and desires slowly unfolded.

In the summer, late night drives around the countryside led to passionate embraces and exploration of each other's soft, young bodies. Eventually, there was a need to fulfill their raging desires. LuAnn longed for and dreamed of that day.

It happened on the night of the senior prom after couples and groups of students left the dance at the school gym to seek greater thrills somewhere else. They selectively departed into their own worlds, searching for more sophisticated freedoms and choices. LuAnn and

Tommy drove to their favorite parking spot and made their choice . . . to make "adult" love.

The experience took place in the back seat of the Maxwell family car. When it was all over, LuAnn was confused and unsure why doing such a thing had even been considered. The intensity of the pain was terrifying, and the bleeding left her worried and unnerved. There was none of the ecstasy or romantic rapture she had expected. The love stories she read in her mother's *True Story* magazines were all lies!

"What did you expect?" was Tommy's only comment. There was no declaration of loving her forever or any of the breathless words of commitment she expected. Quite the contrary, her pain and confusion seemed to ignite an air of callous indifference in him. After that night, he avoided her whenever possible, and she missed him terribly. He was a huge part of her life for two years. Why would he desert her now?

To help finance part of her college education that fall, she took a job at the local drive-in for the summer. It kept her busy and in contact with some of her classmates, and yet, she was by herself much of the time. The two years she spent with Tommy had left her on the outside of their circle.

Her mother, Fern Soppee, insisted she become a teacher, just like her older sister, Jane. Whatever their mother wanted, Jane had no problem doing, but LuAnn was different and she found it hard to live according to someone else's expectations and desires. Shouldn't her life be her own? So, in an effort to avoid clashing with Jane and her mother at home, she kept to herself most of the time.

When Tommy didn't come around to the house anymore, she was terribly lonely, tired and depressed. To make matters worse, nearly every Friday and Saturday night, he showed up at the drive-in with a bunch of friends, or sometimes, with a girl. The raging and uncontrollable emotions within her allowed for little contentment and little sleep. The loneliness and a sense of shame were devastating and consuming. She wondered if the pain would ever go away.

* * *

When Mack drove up to the drive-in and parked in LuAnn's serving area, she was desperate for some attention. Here was a man dressed in Army uniform . . . handsome, dashing, and in control of the world. His dark hair and dark eyes would make any girl's heart flutter . . . and it did . . . LuAnn's.

In fact, she was very much out of control. She undid the top buttons of the green uniform and boldly flirted with him. As she put the tray in place, she leaned forward, giving him a full view of cleavage. Regrettably, there wasn't much to show, but he got the message, and rewarded her with a big smile and a dollar tip. "I'll see you later, Honey."

The incident seemed of little consequence until two weeks later when he parked in her area again. It was nearly closing time, and he ordered two burgers and two shakes. When they were delivered to his car, he asked to take her home. "I'll be waiting right here," he winked. It made her feel a bit uncomfortable . . . but what the heck.

The attention excited her. She finished up two other cars and used the restroom. After making an attempt to wash off the smell of burgers, onions, and fries, she ran a comb through tangled ash blonde hair and sprayed on some perfume taken from her shoulder purse. She yanked the apron off, and she headed for the car. Knots were in her stomach; she had never been so reckless. Always before, after work, she walked through the alleys and across the streets towards home by herself.

She edged into the passenger seat and slammed the door. A weak smile touched her lips, and she immediately, looked out the side window, avoiding his gaze. A dull ache caroused her insides, and nervous fingers played with strands of hair. He turned on the lights, put the car in gear, and aimed for the city park down by the river.

"So, your name's LuAnn Soppee." He looked at her from the right corner of his eyes realizing . . . here was someone very young and vulnerable. "Guess you're surprised I know your name, huh? Well, I've been doing my homework." Getting no response, he went on. "I also know you were on the honor roll all through high school, and you were a cheerleader among other things. More recently, you broke up with your boyfriend. Pretty tough . . . right?"

She was startled to think he knew so much about her . . . rather flattered, too, in a way. Stammering, she answered, "Y . . . y . . . yes, you're right, about everything." His reference to Tommy was hard to take, and it took effort to control her response. She cleared her throat and swallowed hard. "I guess I should ask your name," her eyes darted in his direction.

Gaining courage, she turned to get a view of his profile. In the dim light, he seemed more rugged and older than she had thought previously. Muscles flexed as he steered around the curves in the park, and his jaw jutted strong and determined. What was she doing here with this stranger? The situation was becoming increasingly threatening. Despite the show of false bravery, her hands and legs were shaking. Reluctantly, a chill ran through her, and she fought the urge to throw the door open, jump out, and run.

He pulled the car up at the side of the drive and stopped on the river's edge. The headlights were turned off, and the still dark night engulfed them. A slim piece of moon and a dull lamp high on a utility pole were the only light. "Me, I'm Mack Hanable, from Iowa, and just about to be discharged from the Army. Here, have a shake and burger." He reached into the sack and shoved them at her.

The food she served all evening didn't look very appetizing and smelled worse, but, not wanting to appear ungrateful or upset him by rejecting his offer, she unwrapped the burger and bit into it. They ate in silence. When they were finished, he suggested a walk down by the river. He seemed to be OK . . . just a lonely soldier out for the weekend. *Why not?*

As they walked along the riverbank, he talked about himself. "I was raised by a great aunt and uncle on a small farm near Cedar Rapids. My mother deserted me when I was seven years old. She ran off with another man. My father left shortly after that . . . just disappeared. None of my grandparents wanted anything to do with me, so I ended up with Great Aunt Ruby and Great Uncle Charles. They had no children of their own and were willing to give me a home. Great Uncle Charles died two years ago, so that leaves me with Great Aunt Ruby as my only known relative."

As LuAnn listened, she began to relax and even enjoy his companionship. Then she told her story. "I'm the younger of two girls. My sister, Jane, is twenty-three. My mother and father always seem to favor her for some reason. Sometimes, I wonder if they wanted a boy when they had me, so, for that reason, I'm a disappointment. Anyway, I'm convinced Mother, especially, would be happier if I left. She and Jane have so much in common. They don't seem to need me around.

"But still, Jane is arranging for my entrance into college . . . finding scholarships and that sort of thing. She just finished her first year teaching second grade at Grafton Elementary School. She has a serious boyfriend, Chester Wright. In four more years, he will have a doctorate in Internal Medicine. Pretty impressive, huh? I'll be getting my degree in education at the same time." She had someone to talk to again, and fears and apprehensions slowly dissipated.

They linked arms and walked back to the car. All his intentions seemed honorable. He drove home and escorted her up to the house. Ceremoniously, he took her hand and kissed it. "Is it all right if I pick you up tomorrow night, too? I feel like I've known you all my life." He had a nice smile, showing white, straight teeth and a dimple dented his chin. Life was moving on, and she was part of it.

The next two weeks flew by with candy and flowers delivered to the drive-in on a daily basis. He was there waiting when she got off work Friday and Saturday evening. She was ecstatic and in love, overwhelmed, possessed, and needed. Three weeks later, after their usual walk by the river, he suggested they get in the back seat of the car. She didn't hesitate, even though there was a gnawing at her insides.

His love-making was intense and demanding. She didn't feel cherished or content, but her disappointment was rationalized. The situation was difficult, the first time and everything. She excused his roughness as being inexperience and fear of rejection. Things would get better. She knew what rejection felt like, and the thought of being rejected again . . . even by him . . . was too much to bear. She could please him.

When the evening was over, he walked her to the house. Holding her at arm's length, he murmured, "I love you." Her heart lurched and she pressed close to him. This was the dream . . . something deep and exciting she could lose herself in. A car went past with a blast from the horn. Cheers of, "Wheee! Whoopee!" came from the open car windows. She supposed some of the kids out riding were jealous.

Every night, they ended up in the back seat of the car. Pregnancy occurred to her, but the possibility seemed irrelevant. She wondered why she felt no guilt . . . perhaps because she didn't think anyone cared, anyway. Or, maybe, she just didn't care about herself!

By the first of August, Mack was preparing for his discharge. LuAnn didn't consider how his leaving would affect her. Her college plans were materializing, and tuition money for the first quarter was paid from her tips. She had something to look forward to.

By the middle of August, just two days before Mack was to be discharged, and two weeks before she was to start college . . . LuAnn knew for certain . . . she was pregnant. There were options. She could let Mack leave without him knowing and find a way to have the baby adopted after it was born. Of course, that meant she would have to live at home with her parents while attending the first and second quarter of college. Then, she could drop out, have the baby, and begin school again the next fall. She didn't consider how the news would affect her family. She really didn't care.

Then, she wondered if, perhaps, Mack would be happy about the baby and want to marry her. He had no family to go back to in Iowa, except his great aunt. She decided to tell him. He deserved to know.

"We'll be married the day I'm discharged. The Justice of the Peace here in Grafton can tie the knot for us. The day after, we can leave for Iowa on the train." He had it all planned, as though the pregnancy was anticipated.

Iowa was a long way from West Virginia, and LuAnn felt excited and apprehensive at the same time. Mack drove her to the college, and the tuition money was refunded. With the rest of the money saved from the summer, she had three hundred and twenty-five dollars. It was a small fortune. The days ahead looked good.

They drove home to break the news of their marriage plans to Fern and Clifton. Her parents didn't have to be told she was pregnant, they decided. Still, Fern made her usual declaration, "I hope you don't *have* to get married!" This comment was always made, no matter who she was referring to. Didn't anyone ever get married out of love? LuAnn was certain, in spite of being pregnant, she was marrying out of love.

After Mack left, she began packing clothes and other belongings. Suitcases piled up outside the bedroom door. At ten o'clock, the phone rang. "Hi, LuAnn, long time no see. How're you doin'?" Her heart soared to the top of the Empire State Building and plummeted to the sidewalk below. It was Tommy. "We should get together and do something one of these evenings before you start college."

Where was he all of this time when she so desperately needed him? How dare he call when her life was reeling off in another direction without him! She struggled to make the right response. Despite everything, she started to shake and her hands trembled as the receiver was cradled to catch every word and every breath. The love she had for him was still overwhelming, even though everything she did, all summer long, was in defiance of him . . . even getting herself pregnant! His call had come too late. She had to get on with her life. She and Mack were going to have a baby.

Fighting the torrent of tears that were welling up, she replied flippantly. "I'm doing just fine, Tommy. I'm getting married tomorrow and will be moving to Iowa the next day. Thank you for asking." She hoped he didn't detect the tremor in her voice.

"Isn't that pretty fast? I mean . . . we just graduated three months ago. Who is this guy anyway? He seems to be in a big hurry to get you away from here." There was sincere concern in his husky voice, but she chose to ignore it.

"We are very much in love! Besides, what I do isn't any of your business! I wish you well, Tommy. Good-bye now." She hung up the phone and burst into uncontrollable sobs. An hour later, she washed away the tears with cold water and continued packing. Regret wrapped itself tightly around her . . . but she couldn't let it shackle her, too. After a restless night, she arose and prepared for her marriage to Mack.

Determined to make the most of the situation, she put on her best dress . . . a yellow dotted Swiss with a large satin sash tied in the back . . . worn only to church on Sunday. Her parents had given her pearl earrings for graduation and a watch on a gold chain to be worn around her neck. These completed her wedding ensemble. She wondered if Mack would have a wedding ring for her. She had none for him.

Before leaving for the court house, Fern handed her a bouquet of mixed flowers picked from the garden and Jane placed a single rose in her hair. Dad squeezed a roll of bills into her hand. "Put this away in case you need it. It's yours, you don't have to tell Mack you have it." There was a tone of apprehension and warning in his voice.

She did as he said. The money was secured in a small coin bag at the bottom of her shoulder purse, beneath the cosmetics. There was no sense of guilt, and without question, she felt safer and more in control of her destiny. Doubts began to sting and smart, like a hive of honey bees disturbed. If only someone would tell her not to go through with the marriage . . . but no one did. The Soppee family drove to the court house together.

LuAnn went into the women's restroom. In one of the stalls, the money was retrieved from the bottom of her purse and counted out. There were five one-hundred-dollar bills. Along with the money she already had, she felt very rich. She took all but one hundred dollars of her own money and put it with what her father had given her. The seven hundred twenty-five dollars was placed in the sanctuary at the bottom of her purse.

Mack arrived at the court house dressed in civilian clothes . . . a blue suit with a white shirt and a blue tie. It was the first time she had seen him wearing anything other than Army clothes. He looked so handsome . . . and it was for her. Her doubts evaporated. There was a small bulge in his jacket pocket, she hoped it was a ring. Jane pinned a rose to his lapel and kissed him on the cheek. An embarrassed grin was his 'thanks.' They filled out the required information for the marriage license, and Clifton and Jane acted as witnesses. Mack pulled a ring from his pocket and with the words, "I do," took LuAnn as his wife.

LuAnn Marie Soppee, age eighteen, and Mackenzie Linn Hanable, age twenty-five, were married by the Justice of the Peace in the court house located in Grafton, West Virginia, August 28, 1958.

After the brief ceremony, the five of them went to a local diner for the wedding meal. Suitcases and boxes were transported to the Grafton Hotel where they would be spending the night, and, with tears in her eyes, LuAnn courageously said good-bye to her family. She was Mrs. Mackenzie Hanable, and she would soon be a resident of Iowa. In due time, she would be a mother. She had a future to plan. She wiped the tears with the back of her hand and took Mack by the arm.

* * *

After the flood of tears the night before, she had tucked Tommy away in the bottom of her heart, much the same as she tucked the money in the bottom of her purse. She could bring out his memory if she needed him. She could also bring out the money if she needed it.

Mack had made the reservations for them at the hotel. Here they would spend their wedding night and wait until it was time to catch the train the next morning. He had sold his car and it would be picked up by the new owner at the station.

* * *

Soon after lunch, the newlyweds packed most of LuAnn's belongings into Mack's car and they went up to their room. He stripped off his suit and lay down on the bed. With a smirk on his face and lust glowing like coals in his black eyes, he began to torment his wife. "Do a striptease for me, Baby." He had never talked like that before. "Come on, Baby. What's the matter? You're not going to hold out on me, are you?"

Shame swept over her body, but she slowly unbuttoned the dress and carefully hung it on a hanger, reminding herself that she was his wife now. She stood in the middle of the room feeling self-conscious in her bra and can-can slip.

"Take off the can-can." She did. This left her standing in bra, panties, garter belt and hose. She had never been on display for him like this before, nor had she ever actually been in bed with a man.

"The bra, Honey. Take off the bra." She reached behind her and released the hooks, letting it fall to the floor. She didn't look at him. She couldn't. But she didn't wait to be told what to do next either. Instead, she slid off her panties and unhooked the garterbelt, skimming the hose down over slim, shapely legs. Denying any emotion, she stood and waited. With a satisfied grin, he held out muscular arms, and greedy fingers beckoned. Her whole body burned with a mixture of shame and anticipation. She began to savor the sensations, and she lay down beside him with desirous expectations.

Precipitous hands grabbed, and fingers dug into her arms like the jaws of a steel trap. His mouth bit, chewed, and sucked at her velvety flesh. "You're mine now, Baby, and don't you ever forget it. Old Mack knows what to do with a pretty, young thing like you." Sensuous sensations turned to electrifying pain as her body was ravaged.

The ceiling above turned into a revolving carousel with horses of every color going around and around, up and down. Tommy was pulled from the bottom of her heart, and he took her hand, as she dismounted from the large black steed. His face rippled through the tears as they rolled down her checks and onto the pillow. He would never understand why she was here with Mack. Neither did she.

Finally, he was satisfied, and it was over with. There was no mention of, or inquiry to, her well being. She felt dirty and violated, but she rationalized that it was her own fault. She didn't have to be here. It had been her own choice. Without comment, they showered, dressed, and went out for dinner. The same scene was repeated that evening and again the next morning. She wondered if all marriages began this way.

When they went down to breakfast, the desk clerk raised his eyebrow and winked. She felt naked and exposed, but supposed she would get used to being married. Probably every new wife had the same thing to go through. She would learn how to deal with her husband's needs and emotions; teach him to be gentle and kind. That was her only choice now.

The hour's drive to the station was made in silence. LuAnn lay her head back on the seat and pretended to be sleeping. Finally, the departure time was announced. "Here comes the train, LuAnn! We're off for Iowa! It's sure going to be good to see Aunt Ruby!"

° ° °

Indeed, here they were headed for Iowa. The rhythm of the train lulled LuAnn into a discontented sleep. Her purse was clutched protectively with both hands, the strap over her shoulder. In a dream, someone was trying to pull a screaming baby from her lap, wrenching it away from her. The hands were unyielding and imperious, resembling a steel trap. She clung tightly and tried to scream, but no scream came. Panic overpowered the dream and she abruptly sat upright in the seat. Startled eyes popped open, fast enough to see Mack's hand pull away from her purse. "Did you have a good sleep, Honey?"

She felt nauseous, and needed to use the restroom desperately. The nausea had started a few days earlier, and she tried to ignore it, but it was getting worse. She heard of women being sick with pregnancies, but she didn't think it would happen to her. She always figured it was 'all in their heads.' "I . . . I . . . I guess I did. Do you know where the women's restroom is? I really need to use it." He pointed towards the back of the Pullman and stood up for her to get out of the seat. He squeezed her buttocks as she brushed past him.

She pushed open the door marked 'women,' thankful that the space wasn't already occupied. She hurriedly pulled down her panties and sat on the cool rim of the stool. The wastebasket was close enough to yank over, and she vomited into it. As her stomach wretched, she wondered how anyone's life could change so much in just a few short months.

Cold water was splashed on her face, and she cupped her hands for a sip, to rinse out her mouth. She cleaned up the area with paper towels from the dispenser and covered the vomit, hoping to prevent the smell from saturating the small area. Red eyes and a pale face stared from the mirror. With trembling hands, she opened the clasp on her purse. A bit of powder and lipstick from the cosmetic bag helped.

When she returned to the seat, Mack was dozing, so she cautiously stepped over his legs. She pulled out the magazine that had been tucked into the seat beside her and skimmed through the pages of the *Ladies' Home Journal.*

At suppertime, the newlyweds sat at a table in the diner with a view from the southside of the train. Small towns and large farms streaked past the windows. Occasionally, black and white wooden arms came down at the intersections, and cars waited while they whizzed past. "We're going to eat in style! Nothing's too good for my bride. Get anything you want." LuAnn chose a salad and a glass of milk from the menu. The prices were exorbitant. She hoped it would stay down. Mack ate his steak and baked potato with gusto. They ate in silence. Darkness set in during the meal.

When they returned to the Pullman, their seats were converted into a bed. Curtains were drawn, and the couple prepared for sleep. LuAnn made another trip to the rest room, taking her night bag along. This time she managed to wash most of her body and apply fresh deodorant. Her teeth were brushed with vigor. When she returned to their compartment, she put on pajamas and brushed her hair. Mack was in the men's room for what seemed like a very long time. She hid her purse beneath the pillow and slept through the night without being disturbed by her husband.

Early the next morning, they changed trains in Chicago. They were on the last lap of the journey. They would arrive in Waterloo before noon. Great Aunt Ruby was driving there to meet them, and they would be staying with her until Mack found a job and a place for them to live. LuAnn was still feeling nauseous, but she didn't vomit up the breakfast of toast and hot chocolate. Perhaps if she chose foods carefully, the disaster of yesterday could be avoided.

The closer they got to their destination, the more excited Mack became. LuAnn really couldn't blame him. It had been over three years since he had been in Iowa or seen his aunt.

Two

The passenger train rumbled and swayed past the miles of ripening corn fields, pastures with lazy streams running through their midst, and herds of milk cows with heads down nuzzling the grass with their noses. From her seat in the Pullman, LuAnn's gaze searched longingly for the hills of West Virginia. The August sun beating down on the plains gave her a smothered feeling of unrelenting heat, one she had never before experienced. She wondered if there would ever be any more hills covered with cool shade trees and paths that led into arbors fragrant with flowering shrubs.

She began to think of her family. Jane would be in her room at school preparing for the new year to begin. Her mother would be making early preparations for dinner so she wouldn't have a lot of cooking to do in the heat of the afternoon. Dad would be at the post office diligently sorting the mail for the carriers, a job he has held for the past twenty-five years. She couldn't speculate as to what Tommy might be doing. The only thing he ever talked about was running his own business some day. Most likely, he would soon be off to college somewhere, so he could do just that. The sooner she forgot about him, the better.

° ° °

At the same time LuAnn was contemplating her dad's job at the post office, he was thinking about her. He seldom paid attention to the thousands of letters that passed through his hands every day, but today, one of the letters fell to the floor. He stooped to pick it up, and for some reason, the return address drew his attention. MACK is all that was written in large, scrawling letters. Curiosity wasn't to be ignored.

Of course, tampering with anyone's mail could mean a fine and expulsion from the job, but inquisitiveness permitted him to hold the letter up to the light. There appeared to be just one folded page. The cheap, see-through envelope gave him privilege to a bit of the letter's contents. *'Hi Honey . . . excited about the baby . . . in Korea . . . nine months or more . . .'* Turning the letter over, Clifton Soppee could make out a bit more through the envelope. *'See you later, Honey. Hugs and kisses from Old Mack.'* The letter was addressed to Miss Mary Lou Bailey, 109 Second Street Southeast, Grafton, West Virginia. Clifton Soppee sent the letter on, but he registered the name and address in his head and later that morning, he wrote it on an office pad and placed the sheet of paper into his shirt pocket.

* * *

The train was slowing down. The panorama was quickly changing to hills and shady masses of trees. Mack came hurrying back to the seat. Excitement radiated from his face.

"The Mississippi River is coming up! Don't miss it! It's really something to see! After we cross it, we'll be in Iowa!" Indeed, the scene was breathtaking, and LuAnn was thrilled with what lay outside the confines of the train window . . . a bit of West Virginia dropped into the middle of America.

There was a brief stop at the station in Dubuque, and then, with the blowing of the whistle and the lurching ahead of the cars, they were once again on their journey. There had been a strong impulse to exit the train in that picturesque town by the river. How romantic it would be to leisurely explore the countryside and to make a life for herself and the baby. Of course, that was all fantasy. She was Mrs. Mackenzie Hanable now and she dared not forget it.

Mack's apparent excitement sent him leaping up from his seat every five minutes or so, "I need a cup of coffee from the diner. Do you want anything?" She knew better than to drink coffee, but she told him a glass of orange juice might be nice. He handed it to her with a shaking hand and headed, once again, for the men's room. His excitement seemed to be turning more into apprehension, and sometimes LuAnn thought she detected an aura about him that approached fear.

The train made a brief stop in Manchester. Mack grabbed her arm and roughly ushered her to the station platform. "We need a breath of fresh air." Then he pushed her back on the train and hurried her back to their seats. His energies sent him pacing up and down the isle, a caged animal looking for a means of escape. As the train slowed and stopped in Independence, he flopped into the seat beside LuAnn. "There's something I need to tell you!"

Certainly . . . he needed to explain the restlessness that was dominating them both since switching trains in Chicago early that morning. "I told you we would be staying with Aunt Ruby for a while. Well, the truth is, Aunt Ruby doesn't know about you yet, and she may be pretty upset that I got married without talking to her about it first. Of course, there really wasn't much of an opportunity, and when I called to tell her to meet me in Waterloo, well, that wasn't a good time either. So, maybe if you stay on the train for a bit, let me go ahead of you, so I have a few minutes with her by myself, she might accept the situation better. Can you do that for me?" His dark, pleading eyes studied her face.

LuAnn tried to comprehend what Mack was saying to her. She wasn't really going to be welcome in this other woman's home? Well, she would have to make Aunt Ruby like her. She would make a good impression. That had never been a problem for her. She had always done well in school and was chosen cheerleader all through high school. She presented herself well in school plays and at speech contests. How could meeting Aunt Ruby be much different?

Without commenting, she hugged her purse close, picked up her night bag, pushed past her husband, and headed to the women's room to freshen up. Standing at the mirror, she looked at herself . . . really looked at herself . . . for the first time since she and Tommy broke up. Before then, considerable attention had been given to her appearance. But with Mack, regretfully, she hadn't really cared.

The reflection in the mirror was evidence of this. Fine, blonde hair hung limp and dirty, a mangy cockerspaniel in need of grooming. Her face was pale and in need of makeup, and her eyes were dull and lifeless, a product of nausea. Spots from spilled orange juice stained the pale beige and white print fabric of her sundress. This person wouldn't make a good impression on anyone, let alone Aunt Ruby.

Where to begin? First the hair, she took a comb, ran water over it, and pulled it through the tangles. No time to shampoo, and no way to do that anyway. She rubbed and fluffed until her hair began to take on some life, and then she rummaged at the bottom of her purse for bobby pins and wound strands into pin curls. Soap from the dispenser was used to wash and rinse away the oily accumulation from her face. Fresh powder and lipstick were applied.

Lastly, she tackled her dress. Cold water and a vigorous rubbing took out the orange juice, and a wet paper towel, brushed lightly over the rest of the frock, freshened the fabric. She scrubbed under her arms and applied deodorant. The reflection in the mirror was more familiar now. With bolstered confidence, she was about to step out onto the stage. "Aunt Ruby, may I present LuAnn Marie Soppee Hanable." Impudently, she jested and curtsied to the reflection in the mirror before returning to their seat.

Mack clutched his night bag. The train was preparing to stop in Waterloo, their destination. He clumsily reached for her hand. "You know I love you. Stay on the train as long as you can, OK? I'll meet Aunt Ruby by myself. When I think the time is right . . . after I tell her about you . . . I'll motion for you to come over to us. OK?"

Baffled by his show of insecurity, she leaned over and kissed him lightly on the lips. She had never taken the initiative before, and he drew back . . . startled. She realized how little they really knew of one another.

He rose clumsily from the seat before the train came to a complete stop and headed doggedly towards the exit. With a slight turn, he nodded and waved as though she were a mere acquaintance he had met on the train.

LuAnn slowly drew the bobby pins from her hair and dropped them into her purse. Using the window as a mirror, she pulled the comb through her hair. The conductor came through the car and offered to carry her night bag. It was time to get off the train, so she followed him to the exit. The security of his hand, as he held her arm to dismount the steps, reminded her of Clifton Soppee, and a wave of homesickness gripped her senses.

At noontime, the hot, August sun was stifling on the platform of the station. She hurried over to the shade of the station house. With her hand used as a shade, she searched around to locate Mack and his aunt. He was still standing by himself. LuAnn was about to walk over to him when a tall, big-boned, and unsmiling woman came from around the building and approached him. Her hair was graying and wrinkles creased her strong features. She wore a blue figured dress and a black, straw hat with a bit of veiling over her eyes. Her black shoes and purse gave the impression of just having arrived from a funeral. There was a slight limp to her walk. Her demeanor was handsome and striking . . . in a formidable way.

LuAnn expected to see a demonstration of affection and joy, but that didn't happen. Instead, the woman seemed to be taking charge of the situation in her own way. Mack was shaking his head in agreement, and Aunt Ruby seemed to be doing most of the talking. They looked down the platform and located the luggage. The pile was huge . . . since it contained most of LuAnn's possessions. A questioning look appeared on Aunt Ruby's face . . . and it was time for Mack to do some talking. He methodically gestured like a wooden puppet on it strings and adamantly explained his situation. Disconcertingly, LuAnn was too far away to hear what was being said . . . and she had never cared for mime.

Finally, they shifted their attention in LuAnn's direction. Mack beckoned to her. She lifted her head and walked onto the stage to give her best performance. She could be this new character now . . . Mack's wife . . . and play her role to perfection.

With a smile on her face, she held her hand out to Aunt Ruby. Although her hand was ignored, her determination wasn't diminished. She still remembered the words in the script. "So glad to finally meet you, Aunt Ruby. Mack has told me so much about you, how you mean so much to him." There was a momentary flicker of warmth from the steely, gray eyes.

Without comment, they all walked over to the pile of luggage and loaded it into the car. When it was all packed into the Ford, there was just enough room left for LuAnn to fit into the back seat. Aunt Ruby took the front seat on the passenger's side. "Mack, you can drive us home!"

* * *

The drive to Cedar Rapids took them along curving roads and through many small towns. The countryside was dotted with farmsteads setting amidst the corn fields. There were occasional fields of beans, and pastures of cattle. Warm air rising from hog lots filled LuAnn's nostrils with their putrid odor. She hoped she wouldn't get sick. She wondered if Mack had told Aunt Ruby about the baby. She doubted he had. LuAnn's presence in Aunt Ruby's life was probably as much as she could handle for one day.

The ride seemed to last forever. It was after one o'clock before Aunt Ruby suggested they stop in the next town for something to eat. They pulled into a drive-in, and LuAnn got out to use the restroom. The giggles and chattering of the girls preparing the trays sent a wave of nostalgia coursing through her. Would she ever feel that giddy and free again?

The meal was eaten in relative silence. LuAnn's attempts to start a conversation were unproductive, so she finally just settled into eating the food. Aunt Ruby gave Mack a ten dollar bill, and he handed her the change before digging into his pocket for some quarters that were flipped onto the tray for the girl car hop. "Thanks, Honey." She was poignantly reminded of how all this had gotten started.

° ° °

LuAnn closed her eyes and ears to everything around her. Occasionally, she heard the murmur of voices in the front seat, but her mind drifted back to Grafton. Jane would be finishing up her day. Dad was about to head for home after his day at the post office, and Mother would be putting the final preparations into dinner. She wondered if Tommy thought about her after their conversation on the telephone. She hoped so.

The car slowed up and made an exit from the pavement onto dirt. The bumpy road and the dust that began seeping through the floor boards brought LuAnn out of her reverie. They must be getting close to their destination, her home for several weeks to come. Mack had explained, "I can't just leave Aunt Ruby right away after being gone for so long. She needs help with some of her affairs, especially since Uncle Charles is gone." LuAnn had understood his reasoning at the time, but since meeting Aunt Ruby, she doubted the woman wasn't capable of making her own decisions. In fact, she would probably insist on it.

The fields turned into acreages with horses rather than cows in fenced areas. The houses stood much closer together. Some had barns; others had garages or other small sheds. Most of the homes were well-kept with gardens and patches of flowers. A few yards contained remnants of better days. Old cars, old appliances, and furniture decorated the lawns. Weeds seemed to take precedent over grass. With a sense of dread for the worse, LuAnn wondered what category Aunt Ruby's house fell into.

The car slowed up. "Stop at the mailbox, Mack!" He pulled over to the side of the road. Aunt Ruby rolled down the car window and reached into the third mailbox in the row of seven. She pulled out a small bundle of letters and papers. LuAnn's thoughts briefly flew to Grafton, as she envisioned her father doing his work. Mack turned the car up a curving lane, and the older woman placed the mail in her lap and began leafing and sorting through the array.

Ahead of them was a small house, painted gray with white trim. Two upstairs windows looked out over the front of the house. A closed-in porch ran nearly full-length across the lower front. What appeared to be a tool shed set off to the right. The door was held open by a wooden stake driven into the ground. Further off to the right was, obviously, a chicken house. Out in front, a few black and white speckled hens were pecking around in the dirt. A lone rooster threw his head back and crowed a hoarse welcome. Two skinny, gray cats scurried away from the front porch steps as though they weren't welcome there. A deserted barn and corncrib were further to the east . . . some distance from the house. Their shadowed interiors were defined with silhouettes of old machinery, a tribute to the past fifty years of farming.

To the left of the house there was a rather expansive yard containing promises of spring flowers that would appear on peony and lilac bushes and white blossoms that would appear on bridal wreath. To the back of the lawn, a garden flourished with borders of bright perennials surrounding cabbages and ripening tomatoes held up on sturdy poles. There were rows of carrot tops, and vines ran helter-skelter with green lumps of squash, pumpkins, and watermelon clinging tightly. A pile of compost occupied the back corner near a row of evergreen trees. It was apparent that Aunt Ruby cared about her property.

With a sense of adventure, LuAnn opened the car door and placed her feet securely on the ground. If this was to be her home . . . for a while at least . . . she was going to accept the fact and get acquainted with the new surroundings.

Aunt Ruby and Mack went to the back of the car and opened the trunk. As they brought out the many bags . . . using a hanky from her purse . . . LuAnn wiped off the thin layer of dust that had seeped into the trunk. All the time, the purse was kept close to her side. There was no doubt Mack was curious about the purse's contents, and she wondered what to do with the money now that she was here. She couldn't continue to carry it around with her.

Aunt Ruby led the way into the house by entering the door to the closed-in porch. She stopped at the front step to retrieve the house key from beneath the kerosene can setting by the doorway. To LuAnn, that was a strange place to hide a key. Surely, it was the first place anyone would look. *A country thing, no doubt.*

The narrow porch was stacked with old newspapers and magazines, along with some buckets of cobs and boxes of split wood. LuAnn reasoned there must be a fireplace, but when the next door was opened, they were in the kitchen, and there set a huge iron cookstove taking up most of the wall space on the west side of the room. To her relief, there was also a small bottle gas stove, much like her mother's, not far from it.

The kitchen seemed to be the main room in the house. A large table occupied the center and was surrounded by six sturdy-looking chairs. An old cupboard was set against the north wall and a doorway led into the pantry. There were newer built-in cupboards and counters with a sink, along with the refrigerator, on the east wall.

A door led to the right off the kitchen. LuAnn could see towels hanging on a rack. That must be the bathroom. To the left was another door leading to the living room. To the back of the living room was a small bedroom, apparently Aunt Ruby's room. Another doorway off the living room led upstairs to the hallway and two bedrooms. She followed along as Mack carried their bags up there. The whole house seemed to be spotless and kept in immaculate order. She began to relax.

He led the way to a bedroom on the west side of the staircase and then had second thoughts. "This has always been my room, but look at the other room. If you like that one better, we'll use it." She looked into Mack's room and saw that it was very much a man's room . . . very much still a boy's room . . . in fact.

She looked into the other room. It was more to her liking. "Why don't we put our belongings in your old room . . . for the time being . . . and sleep in the other bedroom. That way, we can take our time unpacking and finding a place for everything." He offered no objections. "How does Aunt Ruby feel about my being here?" she asked in a hushed voice. They had all communicated so little, that she wondered what was going on.

Mack chose not to answer. "Take your time unpacking. If you want to get a little exercise, you can go out and explore the farmstead. I'll be helping Aunt Ruby with the chicken chores, and the lawn needs to be mowed." He went back down the stairs.

The purse, with its treasure, was still snug under her arm. The keys to her luggage were pulled out, and one of the suitcases unlocked. A jacket was removed and hung on the back of a chair. The purse was snuggled into the suitcase, and it was locked once again. She put the key on the chain around her neck with the watch . . . that should take care of her problem for a while. Satisfied, she went down the stairs and acquainted herself with the bathroom before leaving the house.

The trees to the west of the lawn gave shade to the garden area in the afternoon. She walked out there first and was amazed at the size of the tomatoes. Some of them were red and ready for picking. She chose two of the ripest and snapped them from their vines. She would prepare them for their supper. That would surely please Aunt Ruby. With a tomato in each hand, she walked among the grove of evergreens. The murmuring of the wind through the branches reminded her of the day her class had spent at the Roanoke State Park. That was when she and Tommy were high school juniors. She received his first kiss beneath the evergreen boughs.

Her thoughts were interrupted by the sound of a lawnmower tractor. Mack was sitting on a green and quite new machine driving slowly, but steadily in her direction. She held up the tomatoes for him to see, giving him a smile of satisfaction. He pulled the machine up beside her and reached for the tomatoes. "I'll tell Aunt Ruby I picked some tomatoes for our supper. You better stay away from her garden, she's pretty particular when it comes to her gardening." He sullenly tucked the tomatoes inside his shirt and turned the tractor back towards the house. She watched thoughtfully as he stopped by the front door, dismounted from the lawnmower, and entered the house.

Aunt Ruby emerged from the chicken house carrying a pail. LuAnn wasn't about to give up. She hurried across the lawn and approached her with a cheerful smile. "Is there anything I can help you with? I really like to be busy . . . and helpful."

The pail of eggs was set down and Ruby looked LuAnn straight in the eyes for the first time. "I will let you know if and when I need any help. I have been doing my own work all my life. I don't know why I would need any help from you now." She picked up the pail and scuttled off towards the house. A pronounced limp indicated otherwise.

Resigned to Ruby's rejection, LuAnn walked towards the deserted buildings beyond the chicken house. Behind the old barn, she found a well-worn path and decided to follow it. Weeds towered above her, but she pushed them aside and went on. In due time, she came upon a small lake with an old dock and a boat submerged in the water next to the shore. She supposed Mack had come there many times as a youth. She continued along the path that wound around the lake. Eventually, it came out in a neighbor's backyard.

There was an elderly man and woman sitting in lawn chairs on their back porch where the shade engulfed them and the breeze stirred, cool and welcoming. A cold, icy pitcher of lemonade set on a small table between them. An extra glass set there as though waiting for her. LuAnn didn't hesitate, but she walked across the lawn and approached the couple. "Hello, I'm Mack Hanable's new wife, LuAnn. Do you know Mack or Ruby Dutcher?"

They smiled greetings and held out their hands. Finally, someone acknowledged her existence. "We're Milford and Maude Trout. Glad to meet you." Smiles lit up their wrinkled faces. "Yes, we know them both, but we don't see much of them anymore . . . since Charles died. Milford and Charles used to go fishing in the lake . . . you look hot! Would you like some lemonade?" Maude offered.

LuAnn hadn't realized how thirsty and uncomfortable she had gotten pushing her way through the weeds. But now, the thought of lemonade, made a drink seem almost a necessity. She gratefully accepted a glass from Maude.

"Will you be staying long, or are you just here for a visit?" Milford wanted to know.

LuAnn wished she could answer that question, but she hardly knew herself. "Well, Mack is out of the Army now, but he has some business and chores to help his Aunt Ruby with. I understand they're liable to take several weeks. Perhaps, I'll get to visit with you a bit while we're here. Did I come far?" She sipped the lemonade and held the cold, wet glass to her sweating forehead.

"You've walked about half a mile. The street in front of our house leads into Hiawatha. It's just a small town with a post office, bank, drug store, and grocery store, as well as some other small businesses. But the community is growing as local farmers sell off their land to developers," Milford expressed pride in the community.

Now she knew what she could do with her money. Hiawatha had a bank.

Three

The walk back to the Dutcher farm gave LuAnn time to mull over plans for the next day. It was apparent that Aunt Ruby didn't really want her around, so most of the day would, most likely, be her own responsibility. She glanced at the watch hanging on the chain around her neck. The hands were approaching five o'clock. She supposed dinner—or supper—as the mid-westerners called it, would be around six o'clock. If that was the case, she still had an hour.

Ten minutes on the path easily took her to the small lake. She slowed her pace to a leisurely stroll and took in the surroundings. There was a small, sandy beach just off the path. The water's edge looked crystal-clear and inviting. She removed her sandals and walked through the warm sand. Setting the shoes down, she pointed hot thirsty toes . . . testing the water . . . one foot at a time. It was amazingly fresh and cool—spring-fed, she supposed.

Suddenly, she was very aware of her body's irritating discomfort. Tangled hair clung in sweaty, stringy, tendrils around her face and neck. When she shook her head, weed seeds and chaff fell into the shallow water at the lake's edge. Her skin was clammy, and there were numerous small red scratches all over her body, left by the weeds she had pushed her way through. Bumps were rising on her arms, legs, and neck . . . mosquito bites. The sun dress, worn for two days now, was soiled with a multitude of spills and damp with perspiration.

The chain was carefully removed from around her neck, and the watch was placed into a sandal. Unabashed, she waded into the water hip-deep and sank with grateful relief into the cool water. Then, she tipped her head back, stretched out, and languished. The chill of the water was scarcely felt as it penetrated and clarified her tangled consciousness.

The past two days had been dreamlike and, at times, a nightmare. Why had she continued in this venture and not turned back at some point? She supposed it was the stubbornness to make things right, inherited from her grandmother. At least, that's who Fern Soppee always credited it to. "You're just like your grandmother!" had been directed at her accusingly by her mother more times than she could remember. She loved her grandmother, so what's so terrible about being like her?

With determination to give credence to her grandmother and to the decision she had made, LuAnn reluctantly raised her body from the mind-purifying water and pushed through the tranquil ripples towards the shore. Now, she understood why John the Baptist deserved so much credit. She felt renewed, as though just baptized, bodily and spiritually.

She stood and let the water run from her hair and over her breasts. The dress clung and wrapped itself around her scratched and insect-bitten legs. She took wads of the fabric in her hands, twisted and wrung out the skirt. Flipping it outward, grains of sand flew in every direction. She raked slim fingers through the tangled hair, and the hot sun began its drying process immediately.

There was a swishing noise coming from the direction of the barn. She looked up from the seclusion of the little beach. The despised weeds were swaying and toppling over. She stood transfixed, wondering what was coming her way. Suddenly, Mack emerged. He was vigorously swinging a scythe, and his tanned, muscled body shone with sweat. She watched appreciatively as he finished clearing the weeds from along the edge of the path. He looked good. "Mack!"

Her voice startled him. He almost looked embarrassed to realize she had been watching. Then, his expression answered hers, smile for smile. "I watched you take off this way. When I saw how tall the weeds are, well, the lawn can wait until tomorrow to be mowed." His eyes roved over her entire body taking in the transparency of the wet clothes. "It looks like you've been swimming." He seemed more relaxed than he had been in the past two days. Perhaps the physical exercise and just being back home were helping his state of mind. "Wait just a minute!"

LuAnn stood in amazement as he ran down to the beach, quickly skimmed off his jeans and headed for the old dock in his underwear. He hesitated momentarily as he tested the rotting boards, paused at the dock's edge, and dived into the depths of the water. Her fantasy saw a little boy running across the dock, pausing, and then diving into the depths. Was it Mack as a child? Perhaps, it would be their own son, some day. He laughingly emerged, swam a short distance, and then walked out of the water towards his jeans. He pulled them up and held out his hand to her. "We'll have a good time tonight, Baby, after Aunt Ruby is asleep." She was looking forward to some time alone with her husband. They had much to talk about.

Mack led the way down the path towards the house, and LuAnn quickened her pace to keep up with him. They passed the barn and then the tool shed almost at a run. He left the scythe there and entered the front door of the house at a lope. He immediately looked at the clock. They had just five minutes before supper.

LuAnn ran a comb through her hair and shook out the nearly-dry skirt of her dress.

Mack splashed cold water over his face and arms, and dried himself on the way to the table. She had been correct with her assumption, Aunt Ruby left little to chance or choice. "Supper will always be at six o'clock. If anyone wants to eat, they had better be here at that time."

Three plates, glasses, and sets of stainless steel were in place on the table. Aunt Ruby dished up scrambled eggs with bits of ham, green beans from the garden, and newly fried potatoes. The tomatoes LuAnn had inadvertently plucked from the vines, had been washed, sliced, and placed in the green tomato dish. If tomatoes were to be placed on the table, they were to be put in that particular dish.

She learned more of Aunt Ruby's commandments during the meal. If anyone was late for supper, they had to wait until everyone else had finished. Only then could they eat.

The doing of the dishes and cleaning up of the kitchen would be left to the tardy one. She supposed that was fair enough. It seemed strange, however, that the table couldn't be set until just ten minutes before six. She wondered if the same rules applied for breakfast and dinner, at noon, as well.

LuAnn could scarcely wait until the meal was over. She was so in need of a hot bath and shampoo. The mosquito bites were itching terribly, and her dirty scalp put her mind in a fog. Aunt Ruby rose from the table, "Mack and I will be taking the paper to the yard. You, LuAnn, will be doing the dishes and cleaning up the kitchen." Apparently, relief from her misery would have to wait until the chores were finished.

Aunt Ruby gathered up the newspaper. "Come, Mack, you can catch up on some of the news" He obediently followed his aunt to the front door. They picked up chairs from the enclosed porch and carried them out to the lawn. LuAnn went to the living room window and watched as they settled themselves where the breeze was sure to find them. Aunt Ruby handed Mack some of the newspaper and the two went about their business.

Of course, she wanted to help with the work, but she resented being ordered around like a little child. Oh well, hopefully that would change when Ruby got used to her being part of the family. She looked at the job before her. There was not only the supper dishes to do, but the breakfast dishes, as well. After scraping them off, she located the dish-washing detergent. It was the same kind her mother used, and it was kept beneath the sink. Those two things were a small comfort. Perhaps the two worlds weren't so different after all.

She was nearing the end of the task when Aunt Ruby came back into the kitchen. Her eyes scanned every corner of the room, evaluating what LuAnn had accomplished. Neither of them spoke. The older woman went to her bedroom and came back carrying night clothes. She went into the bathroom and shut the door. For the next half hour, LuAnn heard sounds of running water, teeth being brushed, and the toilet flushing.

When Aunt Ruby finally emerged from the bathroom, she once again looked over the kitchen with a critical eye, said nothing, and headed to the bedroom. LuAnn offered a feeble, "Good night." The woman gave no indication of having heard her.

LuAnn ran up the stairs and retrieved night clothes and toiletries. A quick survey of her belongings offered assurance that the suitcases had not been disturbed. She hurried down the stairs and entered the kitchen just as Mack came in the front door and headed for the bathroom. She sat down with a groan and tried very hard not to scratch the mosquito bites that were driving her crazy. The wait would be longer yet. But to her elation, Mack flushed the stool and came out immediately.

"My dip in the lake sure felt good this afternoon. I think I'll go for a real swim. I'll be back before long. See you upstairs." He patted her on the backside and headed for the door.

"Don't forget your swim suit."

"Honey, I skinny-dip! Nobody's out there this time of night. You'll have to come with me sometime." With eager anticipation, he shot out the door like a child.

Relieved, LuAnn entered the spacious bathroom and locked the door behind her. At last! A deep breath was drawn and released. She unbuttoned the bedraggled sun dress and let it fall to her feet. She had to peel off her bra and panties. Sand and seeds came with them. She gathered up the clothes and smelled them. *Awful!*

She wondered how Aunt Ruby did the laundry. The room was very large, and behind a narrow partition set a washer and dryer. *Whoopee! Praise God!* There was detergent on the wooden shelf above. The clothes were placed into the washer, detergent added, buttons pushed, and the hum and fragrance of cleanliness soon filled the room.

She eyed the large bathtub and searched for bubble bath or bath salts, but none could be found. The water was turned on, and with a joyful surge, the stream of anticipated relief came splashing out. A bar of Lux soap, a wash cloth, and a towel were retrieved from the shelf above the washer and dryer. Water rose slowly in the tub while she scrimmaged around in the toiletry bag for shampoo. With preparations completed, she thankfully stepped into the tub and slowly sank down into the luxury of warm water. Never again would a simple bath be taken for granted.

She was in no hurry, so every portion of her exhausted and abused body enjoyed the leisure and comfort of the warm soapy lather. Dirty hair was vigorously scrubbed until her scalp tingled appreciatively. The faucet was turned on, and she got on her knees to let fresh water wash away the dirty suds. Then, she lay back to soak and dream. She didn't emerge until the clothes in the washer had gone through the rinse and spin cycle.

Ceremoniously, the stopper was pulled out, and soapy water escaped through the drain. Mesmerized by the swirling, sucking action, she slowly and carefully dried with the nearly-new large yellow towel. The bath water had done its job, so now it could escape. Ridiculously, she envied it and wondered where it went. Subconsciously, inquisitive hands ran contemplatively over her stomach.

With a deep sigh, she reached into the toiletry bag and found a comb and brush. She took them to the sink and ran warm water over them, a little shampoo, a good rinsing, and they were ready for use. She combed, brushed, and towel dried her hair and then pin curled the bangs securing them with bobby pins. She desperately needed a hair cut and perm. Deodorant was smoothed under her arms and clean pajamas were pulled on. Then she brushed her teeth, relishing the pepperminty taste.

The clothes were taken from the washer and thrown into the dryer. Once again, buttons were pushed. They would be dry in the morning if she chose to wear them. She had plans for tomorrow, and may not have time to do any unpacking. She placed the bag of toiletries on the shelf above the washer and dryer, hoping they would be out of Aunt Ruby's way. Then, she turned off the bathroom light. The lamp on top the utility pole in the yard flooded light through the windows and illuminated the kitchen and stairway. There was no need for more. She carefully ascended the stairs to the bedrooms, hoping to be alone for a while longer.

Mack wasn't back yet. He must be taking a long swim. She unlocked the suitcase, where her purse was stashed, and found everything just as it was left. Perhaps she was being too cautious, and yet a deep sense of precaution nagged at an inner sense. If she was being paranoid, so be it. The suitcase was locked again, and the chain and key were hidden beneath the mattress on her side of the bed.

She was trying to get settled into the unfamiliar bed when Mack came into the house. He entered the bathroom and turned on the shower. Within minutes, he was crawling in bed beside her, still warm and damp from the shower, and smelling like aftershave. She had no way of knowing he had been watching her during most of the bath routine. Naturally, the striptease and all the sensuous body positions that followed had excited him. He reached for her. "I'm back, Baby. Give Mack a big kiss." As they made love, his hands explored every fold and crevice of her flesh. This time, consideration and tenderness were shown. Her body had appeared so soft and fragile in the bathroom light. LuAnn joyously responded and prayed, *Dear God, let everything be OK.*

* * *

The next morning, the rumble and roar of the lawnmower awakened LuAnn from a peaceful sleep. Mack was mowing right beneath the bedroom window. *Good, he was busy this morning.* She wondered where Aunt Ruby might be and went to look out the window of the west bedroom. Sure enough, the woman was stooping over the squash vines in the garden, pulling out weeds and tossing them aside as they were located.

LuAnn retrieved the chain, with the watch and key, from beneath the mattress. The watch said eight o'clock. Good! She could easily be at the bank by nine-thirty. She hurried down the stairs to the bathroom, freshened herself up and removed the clothes from the dryer. For the third day in a row, she put the same ones on.

In the kitchen, Ruby and Mack's breakfast dishes remained on the table. A box of cereal was there, as was a clean bowl, spoon, and glass. LuAnn opened the refrigerator. There was milk and juice on the middle shelf. She quickly fixed some breakfast and then remembered, the last person to eat, when late, does the dishes and cleans up the kitchen. She set about doing just that before brushing her teeth and putting on makeup.

Upstairs, she unlocked the suitcase and retrieved her purse. Just to make sure, she dug to the bottom and extracted the coin bag. There were still the seven hundred and twenty-five dollars. She took twenty-five dollars and put it into her billfold. It would be needed until she could find a job. With one hundred dollars, she would open a checking account. She couldn't rely on Mack meeting her needs, and certainly not Aunt Ruby.

Eventually, she would need to find a doctor, but perhaps not right away. Except for the bit of nausea, the baby was not a reality as of yet. She hurried down the stairway. It was past nine o'clock.

Mack and Aunt Ruby were still in the yard and garden. Thankfully, the air was cooler today. Apparently, there had been some light rain during the night. Everything looked clean and fresh, and the smell of freshly mown hay rose up from the lawn. A faint scent of fish wafted on the light breeze blowing over the lake towards the yard. It was a pleasant morning to be out and about.

With shoulders squared, head held high, and the purse clutched tightly at her side, LuAnn walked over to the area where Mack was mowing. She waited to be seen. Tender feelings from the night before coursed through her veins. After making another run past the chicken house, he pulled up beside her and cut the engine down. He reached out a slightly greasy hand and playfully chucked her under the chin. "Good morning, Sleepy Head."

"I'm going into the bank to open a checking account." She waved the one hundred dollar bill. Perhaps that would be enough to satisfy any curiosity as to why the purse was being clung to so tightly. "I may even look for a job. That way, you and Aunt Ruby won't have to worry about my needs, and, perhaps, I can contribute a bit to the household expenses." A bright smile enunciated her sincerity and intent.

* * *

That sounded good to Mack. He didn't have any idea how he was going to support a wife and baby. During the three years in the Army, he had sent Aunt Ruby a little money to keep for him. But it wasn't much. He had theorized . . . if he had to put in time . . . he was, at least, going to enjoy himself. He had done just that. Nearly every penny had been spent . . . most of it to have a good time with some woman.

The letter from Mary Lou had, at first, sent him reeling. However, after a little thought, he doubted the family would make an effort to locate him. No doubt, she would be sent off someplace to have the baby. It would be given up for adoption, and she would get on with her life of privilege. They were wealthy . . . so they had the means to do anything they chose. He dismissed that whole situation as being irrelevant.

Here was LuAnn, though, and he had to deal with her and the baby some way. There really needed to be someone in his life besides Aunt Ruby, so he had made a resolution to treat his wife better. She really wasn't a bad sort.

He missed Great Uncle Charles. The old man had made an effort to treat Mack right. *If we have a baby boy, maybe I'll name him Charles.* Thoughts raced through his mind with the steady roar of the engine as he propelled the lawnmower around the yard.

* * *

With a light kiss on the lips, LuAnn said, "Good-bye." She started across the yard and down the path winding around the lake. She was grateful that the weeds were cut down. Meadow larks were singing, and monarch butterflies flew around and about in lazy flight. Grasshoppers hurled themselves chaotically across the path. It was a glorious morning.

She began to hum a senseless tune, and then she began to sing, "I went to the garden alone, while the dew was still on the roses . . . " She couldn't remember the words very well, but she began to recall the last time she attended church services with her family. It was the Sunday before prom night, and she had worn the yellow dress.

She wondered if Aunt Ruby was a churchgoer, and if she and Mack would be required to go with her. Today was Friday, so she would have the answer to that question soon enough.

With a few more stabs at the chorus and an effort to whistle back at the call of an exuberant bird, she was soon in the Trout's backyard. She decided to knock on their door, just to say, "Good-morning," and headed cheerfully for the back porch.

Before she was halfway across the lawn, they came out to greet her. Milford and Maude sparkled in the sun with their very white hair, wrinkled faces, and twinkling eyes. Neither of them, being large of stature, stood barely as tall as LuAnn at five foot three inches. "My, you look pretty this morning! Are you on your way into town?" Milford inquired.

"Yes, I'm going into the bank. Is it far? I also need some things at the drug store." That wasn't entirely true. She hoped the druggist could recommend a doctor. She knew it wasn't wise to wait too long into her pregnancy before getting medical advice.

"Why, no, dear, the main part of town is just a quarter of a mile to the north of our driveway. It won't take you long to get there." Maude offered this information . . . followed by some advice. "Don't stay out in the sun for long though. That wouldn't be good for you or the baby. You are expecting, aren't you?" She scarcely waited for an answer. "I could see it in your eyes when you were here last evening." LuAnn had heard that some older women have an uncanny knowledge of when a woman is pregnant, but this was phenomenal. She was hardly aware of the condition herself. "Perhaps you could have dinner with us this noon," Maude added with a smile.

LuAnn jumped at the chance to sit at the table with this dear couple. She had told Mack she may not be home in time for the noon meal. "I would love to!" She waved "Good-bye" and started around the house to the street going into Hiawatha.

The buildings of the small town were plainly visible up ahead, and it wasn't long until she was standing on the sidewalk out in front of the bank. She sat down on the wooden bench just outside the door of the building and contemplated, again, what she wanted to do. In hope that the right decision for the future would be made, all the conceiveable possible situations and circumstances were filtered through her brain. Finally, clutching the purse even tighter, she entered the bank.

Having come in from the bright sunlight, she squinted, and her eyes gradually adjusted to the dimness. The lobby was small and sparsely furnished with a single worn wooden table and two chairs pushed up to it. On the table, three lead pencils protruded upward from a tin can painted yellow. A rumpled note pad lay beside it. A ceiling fan rotated from the high ceiling overhead, moaning with each turn. Years of grime clung to the blades. The plastered walls were painted beige. There was only one teller's window, and she walked up to it. The brown linoleum-covered floorboards creaked beneath her slight weight. "I would like to open a checking account please." She placed the one hundred dollar bill in front of the teller. The stone-faced oldster nodded her blue-gray head and passed back the required paperwork, along with a ball-point pen. LuAnn filled in the blanks and signed her name, *Mrs. LuAnn Hanable.*

She had a strange feeling of having lost part of her identity. In fact, she had. She had lost her last name. Her mother always wrote *Mrs. Clifton Soppee,* not even claiming her own first name. LuAnn couldn't do that. The teller handed her a check book with her name in it and the amount of the deposit. HIAWATHA STATE BANK was written in gold letters on a green, leather cover. She ran her fingers over the lettering.

The one hundred dollar bill was whisked away into the teller's cash drawer. "Thank you, Mrs. Hanable. Can I do anything else for you?" The teller mustered a smile, not really expecting any more business from the young woman.

"Well, yes, there is, but you may think this is a strange request. I have seven hundred dollars that I would like to put into a savings account. However, is it all right if I put it in my maiden name along with my father's name? It's really his money. Also, I would like the bank statements sent to my father." At first, she was extremely nervous to be discussing the issue with the teller, but then, seeing the blank look on the woman's face, realized she could not really care what a customer did with their money. It was none of her business. LuAnn pulled the wad of bills from her purse and spread them out on the counter, flattening out the creases as she did so.

The account was set up, and she wrote out his name and address: *Mr. Clifton Soppee, 806 Primrose Drive, Grafton, West Virginia.* The teller recorded the information and handed the account book to her, "There you are." LuAnn stared at the flat little document and wondered what to do with it. She pursed her lips, frowned, and thought hard. The post office, of course! That was the logical place to keep it. She would get a box there in her maiden name, along with her father's name. A smile lit up her face, and she turned to the teller. "Thank you so much!"

The post office was just across the street and down a block. It wasn't much larger than the bank and just as dreary looking. However, the postmaster issued overt friendliness, especially after LuAnn explained that her father, also, worked for the U.S. Postal Service. LuAnn paid the three dollars rent, and, after placing the account book into the box, the key was strung on the chain around her neck.

Postcards were purchased, and notes written to her parents and Jane. She had noticed Aunt Ruby's address, Rural Route 2, Cedar Rapids, Iowa. That was used as the return, but she, also, informed her family of the box in Hiawatha, number 18, and of the 'secret' savings account in the Hiawatha State Bank. Without doubt, they would understand her actions. The post cards were dropped through the slot.

Now she had one more thing to do . . . go to the drug store. Deacon's Drug Store was up the street from the bank and around the corner. When she walked into the building, the pungent smell of medicines and perfumes overwhelmed her. Nausea prompted her teeth to clinch and her hands to message and hold her stomach. She wandered up and down the aisles, swallowing hard, and trying to gain composure before approaching the pharmacist. The business she was conducting in this new, little town was making her very nervous. A wave of homesickness suddenly hit her and felt like a smothering blanket.

When she saw an elderly man wearing a white smock come from the door of the back room, she knew that was her cue. She swallowed hard and approached him with a cheerful smile. "Hello, I'm Mrs. LuAnn Hanable . . . Mack Hanable's wife." She wanted to be sure he knew she was married. "I'm new in town, and I seem to be pregnant. Can you recommend a doctor?" She twisted the ring on her finger, waiting for his answer.

"Well, I'm Dr. Lou Smith. I have a small practice here in town. I'm kind of filling in for the pharmacist today. My office is just behind the post office. I could see you on Monday if that suits you, say ten o'clock?" That was certainly easy.

With all of the business taken care of, LuAnn set off for the Trouts'. The sun was high overhead, and the walk was a hot one. There was little available shade along the way, and she was thankful to be greeted at the front door with an ice-cold glass of lemonade. The easy chair in the living room was graciously offered, and she gratefully accepted.

"Dinner is almost ready. Do you like fried chicken and mashed potatoes? I hope so, they're one of our favorites." LuAnn assured Maude there wasn't anything she liked better. After the meal, the two women washed and dried the dishes while Milford put them away. The three of them retired to the living room, and Maude got out the family photo albums.

The Trouts proudly pointed out their three children. "The two oldest . . . boys . . . live in California. We try to take a trip out there once a year in the fall . . . going by train all the way. Our daughter, Francis, lives on the other side of town. She has a beauty shop at the back of her house. Her only child . . . a daughter . . . Karen . . . just left for college. She's been a widow for five years."

When the words 'beauty shop' were spoken, LuAnn became quite excited. "Do you think Francis could give me a hair-cut and perm?"

"Well, let's just ask her." Maude went to the telephone and dialed her daughter. "She can do it tomorrow afternoon. Is that OK?" It sounded fine to LuAnn. She would be there at one o'clock, somehow. Maude gave her directions to the shop and Francis' telephone number. "Just in case something comes up." She slipped it into her purse.

She looked at the time. It was already after three. "I must be going. Perhaps I'll see you on my way to the beauty shop tomorrow. Thank you so much for everything." She ran out the back door and across the lawn towards the path that took her to the lake and on to Ruby Dutcher's home.

Four

At ten minutes to twelve Ruby Dutcher took three plates, three glasses, and three sets of tableware from the cupboard and arranged them on the table. She set out the butter and milk from the refrigerator and went to the bread box for a loaf of bread. She filled her own glass with water and placed it back on the table.

At five minutes to twelve, Mack came in from the yard. The mowing was finished, and after dinner, he would trim the weeds from around the buildings. There was a tangy odor of grass, sweat, and gasoline issuing from his body, and he needed a shave. He hurriedly washed up in the bathroom and sat down at the table. Ruby dished up the hamburgers, fresh fried potatoes, corn, and green beans. She sliced up a large, red tomato into the green dish and set it on the table. Then she seated herself.

She glanced up at the clock, "Humph! Your wife doesn't remember very well! . . . Does she?" A thin smile spread across her tight lips. She leaned across the table and stacked up the third table setting before settling back into her chair. If LuAnn came now, she would have to wait until the two of them were finished eating. Mack hungrily helped himself to the food on the table, but his mind was back ten years before.

* * *

The cow, Betsy, was having a hard time delivering her calf, and he had spent the morning trying to assist her. At the age of fifteen, he hardly knew what to do, but just before noon, the efforts of them both paid off. A fine bull calf was produced, and Betsy was doing just fine. With a mixture of pride, joy, and relief churning around on his insides, he ran over to the stock tank by the windmill and cleaned up. Blood and membrane swirled through the stagnant water. He shook his hands to dry them and then went behind the shed to relieve himself. It had been a very long morning.

When he entered the kitchen, the clock read twelve-o-five. Ruby and Charles were filling their plates. Mack's dishes were stacked. He went into the bathroom and cleaned up. Then he sat in silence waiting for the other two to finish their meal. His guts ached from hunger and the stress of the morning. No one even asked about Betsy and the calf. Anger at the unfairness of the circumstances surrounding the 'punishment' raged deep within. A look from Uncle Charles said, 'I'm sorry about this.' But he had learned many years before not to defy his wife's commandments, so he said nothing in Mack's defense.

Even then, she was still treating him like a rebellious, irresponsible child. Out of necessity to survive, any such behaviors had been squelched long before. After Uncle Charles' first heart attack, Mack took over more and more of the responsibilities around the farmstead. But that carried no weight with Aunt Ruby. She refused to give anyone room in which to maneuver their own lives.

* * *

Mack ate the fresh apple pie and, thoughtfully, went back to the work outside. He should really learn how to defend his wife and himself. What would Aunt Ruby be like when the baby came? He was beginning to doubt if he could afford a home, and they might be living with her for a long time. Her disregard for others had always torn him apart. The worst part was the helplessness that he felt. How do you weave a tapestry for living your own life using only broken threads that someone reluctantly hands you?

* * *

Ruby got up from the table, wiped her hands on her apron, and went into the bedroom. A small safe was hidden in the corner behind a rack of clothes. She knelt down and turned the dial, right to two, left to two, right to four, left to four, zero, and the door pulled open. She gathered up a batch of envelopes containing documents and opened them one at a time, skimming over their contents, refreshing her memory.

There were a large number of savings bonds guaranteed by the United States Government, totaling fifty thousand dollars. Stocks in AT&T and Quaker Oats totaled seventy-five thousand dollars. A stack of five hundred dollar bills counted out to twenty-five thousand dollars. Ruby and Charles had done well financially during their lives together.

The inheritance from their parents had been kept in that safe in the form of cash for a good many years.

* * *

Her father had been scrupulous, hoarding every dollar made. Charles' father had done likewise. Neither parent had trusted banks, so when the depression hit in the thirties, they remained virtually unscathed.

Just before Charles died, he and Ruby decided to trust the United States Government, and so they had purchased the bonds. AT&T seemed secure, so money was invested with them. A lot of people ate oatmeal. Quaker Oats seemed a safe bet.

* * *

Ruby laid the documents out on the worn chenille bedspread. Much thought had been given to her situation. Since there was no one else . . . she had to confide in Mack. Why had he brought a wife home with him? The girl was definitely an impediment. Of course, she would draw up a will leaving everything to him, but what would happen after she was gone? What would he do with the estate? If it could be helped, LuAnn wouldn't get any benefit from her hard work!

Ruby left the bedroom, determined to settle the issue. "LuAnn! . . . LuAnn!" No answer. Good! The girl still wasn't back! She went out the front door and looked around. Mack was down by the windmill swinging the scythe back and forth. Weeds tumbled to the ground. Admittedly, he had learned to do some things competently, and . . . perhaps, she should commend him. On the other hand, as long as he kept trying to please her . . . well . . . the easier it was to keep him under control.

She walked, determinedly, across the yard towards him. Her hip was getting worse all the time, and it was very irritating to have to favor it. She clenched her teeth and tried hard not to limp as she headed his way. A portrayal of strength and power was important.

When he saw Ruby coming towards him, determination in her gait, Mack leaned the scythe against the water tank, and, with a hairy bare arm, wiped the sweat from his forehead. Having shed his shirt, itchy bits of grass and weeds clung to the hair on his damp, bare chest. What now?

He felt like a trapped gorilla about to be prodded with the zoo keeper's stick. Most likely, she was upset because LuAnn was still gone, and a wave of smoldering defiance surfaced. However, he was wrong!

"We have some business to discuss! It's best we do it without LuAnn being around." She pierced him with steely gray eyes. The prod found its mark, but, as yet, it didn't hurt. "We need to go into the house, I have some things to show you." He washed off at the stock tank and obediently trailed behind and into her bedroom. Remarkable! He was in that room only twice before that he could remember. It had always been off limits. His curiosity was mounting by the second, but he waited for Ruby to speak.

One at a time, she ceremoniously picked up the contents of the envelopes and showed Mack the small fortune. Then she spoke. "Everything is in my name now, but I will be contacting my lawyer to see how my estate can be left to you. I don't want that girl . . . LuAnn, to get anything if I can help it." Mack was astounded. He thought Ruby was just skimping by . . . living off the money real estate developers paid for the twenty-acre plots she was selling off. "Right now, I have an offer of one hundred thousand dollars for the forty acres containing the lake. I'm holding out for fifty thousand more. My lawyer, Mr. Allbright, says it's worth at least that much."

Mack swallowed back years of resentment and attempted to appreciate everything she was disclosing. Of course, Aunt Ruby would be gone someday, and, apparently, the estate was of utmost importance to her. That was understandable, but he didn't want to be left with nothing else. He needed LuAnn. That was becoming more and more real to him. But, that was something Aunt Ruby would never understand. From every indication, there was never a necessity to have anyone else in her life. In his view, she was a solitary sentry posted permanently at life's prison gate.

Perhaps, if he got acquainted with the lawyer, Allbright, he could figure out how to handle the situation. Right now, he needed to appease her. His excitement daren't show. "You've done well, Aunt Ruby. I'm glad for you. Just let me know when you need me, and I'll help you in any way I can." She placed the envelopes back inside the safe and showed him the combination. They both left the room. Mack went back to cutting weeds. His mind raced from one scenario to another.

* * *

LuAnn circled around the lake and through the barn yard. As she hurried past the chicken house, a hen scratching in the dirt, squawked, fluttered its wings and flew off, creating a small flurry of dust. She didn't see Mack anywhere, so she went into the house. In the kitchen, she saw the remnants of the noon meal, everything sitting as Ruby and Mack had left it. The kitchen was waiting for her to clean it up.

She had planned to get some clothes unpacked. Someone had been emptying out the closet in the east bedroom, and, apparently, it was meant for her use. But, right now the kitchen had to take priority. The plates were quickly scraped, and the left-over food was taken outside and dumped into a bowl for the cats. She wiped off the table and started on the dishes. Fifteen minutes later, they were finished, and the counters were wiped clean.

Upstairs there was a note laying on the rumpled covers. MAKE THE BED. It was another one of Aunt Ruby's commandments. In her rush that morning, she hadn't given the bedroom any thought. The sheets and bedspread were quickly straightened. One suitcase was drug in from Mack's old bedroom, and she began to unpack clothes. It was obvious everything needed to be pressed.

She scoured the house looking for an ironing board and iron. The bathroom would be a logical place to keep them . . . near the washer and dryer . . . but they weren't there. With a sense of adventure, she stuck her head into Ruby's bedroom. The room was small and crammed with a clothes rack and boxes. The black hat and purse set on the dresser amidst opened mail and small containers of various shapes. The essence of lavender and mothballs tickled her nose . . . and she sneezed. There was a feeling of discomfort just standing there, so she turned and went back upstairs to search the closets. Nothing there, so she went back to the kitchen and investigated every possible nook and cranny. Still nothing!

Of course, the porch! She had probably walked past the ironing board a dozen times. Indeed, she had. There, it set propped up in the corner. A small corner cupboard held the steam iron. She lugged them upstairs and began the task of taking one item at a time from the suitcase, ironing it, and hanging it in the closet.

By five-thirty, she had taken care of most of the clothes that needed pressing. Then she plopped the one holding underwear down on the bed, and opened it. Her church dress lay on top with the can-can slip. The garments were smelly and terribly wrinkled. She sat on the edge of the bed and buried her face in the soft, yellow fabric. Had it been only four days since they stood in the chambers of the Justice of the Peace in Grafton, West Virginia? Or was that in another life? She looked at the ring on her finger. It was real.

Tears surfaced, as she remembered buying the dress . . . because Tommy had liked it so much. She had worn it to church on Easter Sunday and every Sunday after that until school was out. That was a long time ago . . . and so far away. Tears of regret and loneliness for the past soaked into the fabric. A tribute to Tommy? Another effort to wash him from her soul? With acceptance of the present, the dress and soiled underwear were gathered up to be laundered.

When she reached the bottom of the stairs, Aunt Ruby was there in the kitchen preparing supper. She would not apologize to the woman for being absent at noon. No matter how hard she tried, she had never been able to please her own mother, so why should she try to please Ruby Dutcher? Still, the woman deserved courtesy.

"Some of my clothes are really soiled and need to be laundered. Will you be needing the washer and dryer for a while?" Ruby waved towards the bathroom with a 'don't bother me' look about her.

LuAnn locked the door behind her. The settings on the washer were selected, and, as the tub filled, Ivory Snow was added. The clothing was put in and the lid closed. So much for that! Now what? She looked into the mirror and saw a tear-stained face. It was apparent she had been crying, so the washcloth, used the night before, was used to sponge off her face. The night bag was still on the shelf where she had left it, so the comb and brush were used to arrange her hair before unlocking the bathroom door and facing Ruby once again.

It was ten minutes to six o'clock, and Ruby was taking the table settings from the cupboard. "You can put these around." She set the utensils on the table, and LuAnn willingly complied. She stood quietly and waited for further directives, but none came. Mack walked into the house at five minutes to six o'clock and cleaned up in the bathroom. They all sat down to supper at six o'clock.

Aunt Ruby looked at LuAnn and then at Mack. "Mack and I will be driving into Cedar Rapids tomorrow. We have business to attend to . . . Perhaps you would like to buy my old Ford, Mack. I have been considering the purchase of a new automobile. You can have the car for four hundred dollars. That's less than list price. Think about it and let me know." Having said that, Ruby helped herself to the food on the table.

* * *

Mack had been wondering what to do about a car. In a few months, the weather would be very cold, and LuAnn couldn't keep walking everywhere she wanted to go. Iowa winters could be pretty hard. After Aunt Ruby was in bed tonight, the two of them could go skinny-dipping in the lake. He would talk to LuAnn about it then. If she found a job, maybe she could help pay for it. "That sounds like a good idea, Aunt Ruby. I'll let you know tomorrow."

* * *

LuAnn didn't have a driver's license. Dad had let her drive a few times when they were out looking for wild flowers along the country roads. Her mother was trying to start a nature plot in the corner of their backyard, so she and Dad went exploring the countryside. She was sixteen then. Shortly after that, she became more interested in Tommy than in taking rides with her father. Now, she hoped Mack would teach her to drive. There was skepticism in her thinking.

* * *

The two young people were occupied with their thoughts, while they finished eating their supper. As soon as the meal was over, Aunt Ruby and Mack, once again, gathered up the newspaper and took their lawn chairs outside.

LuAnn tackled the dishes. However, she was in no hurry. It was rather amusing that whether she was to the meal on time or not, she ended up doing the work in the kitchen. A quizzical smile touched her lips, and she began to hum a nonsensical tune in rhythm to the dish washing. She was really glad to be helping, and if that was meant to be punishment, well, she could certainly handle it.

About halfway through the work, she heard Mack come in on the porch. He had asked Aunt Ruby where he might find a roll of black tape to repair some bare wires out in the tool shed. She sent him to the small cupboard in the corner of the porch.

When LuAnn went out to feed the cats, he still sat there, like a small child, with tears running down his cheeks. A rope was in his hands, and a sad, dazed expression covered his face. Startled, she could only stare and turn away. The food was dumped out for the cats, and she went back into the house, ignoring the hunched figure in the corner. Hoping to spare him any embarrassment.

* * *

The little seven-year-old boy in Mack was remembering what that length of rope had been used for. When he first arrived to live with Charles and Ruby, he was wild with anger and fear. Both of his parents had deserted him in a matter of months. When the social worker found him alone in the old trailer house down by the river, near Littleton, he was dirty, hungry, and very confused. After weeks in an orphanage, he was taken to live here with Great Uncle Charles and Great Aunt Ruby.

He had been hungry for a long time, for both food and love. The first night there, during supper, Ruby set down her 'commandments.' The little boy had not been able to take so much in all at once. The second day, he was late at suppertime. His dishes were piled up at his place, and Ruby reminded him that he would have to wait until she and Charles were finished eating.

The fear of being hungry, again, overwhelmed him, and he grabbed a piece of bread and crammed it into his mouth. Ruby squeezed his cheeks between thumb and pointer finger until the food was dislodged. Anger consumed her, and she screamed, "Sit down!" With the piece of rope from the cupboard, she bound his hands to the chair behind him. After Ruby and Charles were finished eating, she untied the rope, and the couple went out to the yard to read the newspaper. "Don't forget to do the dishes when you finish your supper."

Of course, the order was absurd, and Charles had known this. So, after fifteen minutes, he went behind the house to 'use the toilet.' But, instead, he sneaked into the house and hurriedly helped the little boy do up the dishes and tried to explain away Ruby's anger. Then, he went back outside to sit with his wife.

The first five years on the Dutcher farm, Mack was tied to a chair several times a week for circumstances often beyond his control. By the age of twelve, he had grown to Ruby's height, and his body was muscular and wiry. Tying him up didn't work anymore, but she still made him wait to eat if he was late for a meal, and he did a lot of dishes.

Soon after he graduated from high school, he went to Waterloo and worked at the John Deere plant, pushing a broom around. Charles started selling off twenty acre plots from the farm, so there was less and less work for him to do around there. After four years, he decided to put in the three years with the Army. After being gone all that time, he thought the pain Aunt Ruby had put him through was over, but obviously, it wasn't. It still gnawed at his guts.

* * *

After finishing the work in the kitchen, LuAnn went upstairs to wait for Mack. She didn't know what else to do, so she found her bathing suit and tried it on. Maybe he would like to go swimming. Unsure of the situation, she waited around upstairs and went through some pictures and other possessions brought from Grafton. She had scarcely looked at the 1958 year book, because she and Tommy were together in it, and the hurt was just too great. She closed her eyes and curled up, hoping to alleviate the pain.

* * *

Impatiently, Mack started shaking her. "Wake up, LuAnn! We're going to the lake, OK? Aunt Ruby's asleep, so just follow me." Sleep was instantly forgotten.

The two tip-toed from the house. He grabbed her hand, and they ran down the path in the mellow light cast by the moon. When they reached the lake they were out of breath and giggling, like two kids who had just pulled a fast one on their parents. In truth, that was how they felt.

At the lake's edge, Mack took LuAnn in his arms and gently kissed her on the lips. He reached behind her, and slowly unhooked the top of the swimsuit. It dropped to the sand beneath their feet. His eager hands skimmed over her buttocks, and the bottom of the suit was skillfully removed and let drop. He stepped out of his own. Their bodies glowed seductively, mystiquely in the moonlight. He lifted her and walked chivalrously into the water . . . two nymphs playing. Enchanted and seduced by the night, LuAnn clung to him longingly and passionately.

When waist deep, he lunged, and flipped her up and away, unceremoniously, dumping her into the cool water of the lake. The shock of the plunge sent her gasping for air and coughing out water. Mack swam off towards the dock, his laughter echoing eerily off the surface of the lake.

LuAnn was not a good swimmer. She panicked as her arms flailed wildly, and her feet searched for the bottom of the lake. The grittiness of sand underfoot finally assured her. Shaken . . . all romantic feelings were gone, and she hoped Mack wouldn't come back to bother her. Cautiously, she pushed her way through the water back to the shallow edge of the shore.

Mack emerged from the night, a sea monster, ghostly in the moonlight. "You don't like water much, do you?" Unconcerned, he didn't wait for an answer. "What do you think? Should I buy the car? It's a real good deal, and to be truthful, I don't have much money. It should do us until I get a job. In fact, I guess I'll need a car to look for work." He didn't actually speak to her, but instead, directed his voice out to the lake.

"Whatever you think. You know what you can and can't do." No enthusiasm could be mustered. Her mind was on other things. "Do you want to tell me what was happening on the porch after supper? It kind of scared me. . . . You and Ruby both frighten me sometimes, you know."

He shrugged, as though unconcerned, and looked at her from the corners of his eyes. "It probably wasn't as bad as I remember it. . . . " He recounted to LuAnn his life with the Dutchers. Then he concluded, "Aunt Ruby has a mean spirit, and I've never seen anyone penetrate it, but there must be a reason for her being that way."

Compassion for a little boy overpowered reason and caution, and emotions soared anew. LuAnn straddled his lap and put eager arms around his neck. There was a need to comfort him. Making love on the edge of a lake was a strange and wonderful experience.

* * *

The next morning, Ruby and Mack left for Cedar Rapids shortly after ten o'clock. LuAnn assured them she would be, "Just fine." The next hour was spent investigating all the nooks and crannies of the house. She opened drawers and cupboards and examined their contents. She found the safe in Ruby's room and decided to stay out of there. She didn't need to be accused of stealing anything.

She located the pots and pans and decided what they could be used for. Using one of them, she cooked up a large pot of soup made from hamburger and a mixture of vegetables. It tasted savory to her. She ate some for dinner and put the rest of it into the refrigerator. Perhaps Ruby would think it was good enough to eat for supper.

At twelve-fifteen, LuAnn put her purse over her shoulder and started the walk around the lake, and on to Hiawatha. On Main Street, she found the small, yellow house with green trim, the home of Francis and her Beauty Shop. The entrance sign pointed to the rear. She opened the gate to the white picket fence and followed the sidewalk.

She was greeted at the door by a smiling face, looking much like Maude, only younger. LuAnn guessed the woman was somewhere in her forties. There were pictures of her daughter all around the shop. *Her name is Karen, and she's going to college, majoring in education.* LuAnn burst into tears.

Five

Ruby and Mack spent the morning driving around Cedar Rapids to the various car dealers. Each vehicle that seemed to be a possibility was thoroughly examined inside and out. Despite having asked for his opinions, it soon became apparent to Mack and to the salesmen, that whatever appealed to him wasn't going to appeal to her. Finally, resigned to this fact and feeling like an inadequate child, he gave up on giving any advice and agreed with whatever she said. Whatever . . . just keep her happy!

Then, shortly before noon, they went into the Chrysler dealer's showroom. Immediately, a salesman with shiny black shoes, an expanding waistline, and a Cheshire grin approached them. "Good morning, Mrs. Dutcher! Have you come to pick up your new Chrysler? It's all ready for you, just a little paperwork to be completed." The grin didn't, even momentarily, leave his face. Here was a happy man!

Ruby pierced him with her steely eyes and nodded solemnly in agreement, the black straw hat bobbing precariously atop the stately gray head. "But . . . we won't be taking it until later this afternoon. However . . . I would like Mack to see it now, and then we can get the paperwork completed. I want his name on the title as well as mine. Do you understand, Mr. Tuttle?"

Aunt Ruby was full of surprises. They had spent over an hour and a half debating over other vehicles, surely causing some degree of annoyance for the salesmen, and now it comes to light that she has already purchased a new Chrysler.

Mr. Tuttle nodded vigorously to indicate that, indeed, he understood whatever Ruby had to say, and then he clicked his heels and led the way across the red marbled showroom floor to a sleek, black automobile regally occupying its space near the front window. It glistened in the fluorescent lighting, putting the shine on his shoes to shame. The door on the driver's side was opened with a flourish, and a gallant motion indicated that Aunt Ruby should get in. She chose to ignore the act of chivalry.

"Mack, you try out the driver's seat. I'm going over to the passenger's side." She hustled around the front of the automobile, brushing Mr. Tuttle aside. Black shoes clomped on the marbled floor, and the black purse swung defiantly from her arm. With the other hand, the hat was pushed more firmly onto her head.

Mr. Tuttle, still wearing the Cheshire grin, hurried after her and grabbed the door handle to, once again, assist her into the vehicle. She paid little heed to his actions and wriggled her stoical frame into a comfortable position in the seat. "Hmm!" was the only comment, but apparently, it met with her approval. "If you like it, Mack, we'll go to the office with Mr. Tuttle and take care of the paperwork." What was there not to like?

Papers were quickly gathered and placed in front of Aunt Ruby. After reading them over carefully with Mack, she signed them, and the title was handed across the desk to her. She scrutinized the document through her bifocals, got out her checkbook, and wrote out a check for three thousand, two hundred and fifty dollars. Mack was in awe, even though, by now, he knew Aunt Ruby could well afford it, and he was certain she hadn't lost her power of reasoning or anything like that. *So,* he concluded, *why not enjoy this new revelation and take advantage of it, should the opportunity arise?*

He began to wonder how to play his part at the lawyer's office. There was definitely a crack in Aunt Ruby's steel armor. The appointment was for two o'clock that afternoon, so he still had a little time to think about it before then.

As they left the showroom, Ruby walked passionately around the Chrysler, a jaunty swing to her hips, and trailed her fingers possessively over the glassy-smooth surface before exiting the building. She squinted into the noontime sunlight reflecting from the many car windows in the lot, clutched her purse tightly, and climbed back into the 1952 Ford. The familiarity of the old car seemed good to Mack, and it would soon be his. He patted the hood appreciatively before opening the door and taking his place at the wheel.

With degrees of inner satisfaction, Ruby Dutcher and her great nephew headed for a proper noon meal at Smulekoff's.

* * *

Francis ushered LuAnn to the customer's chair by the sink. She pulled a stool up beside her and sympathetically patted the trembling young shoulders. "Would you like to talk about it, Honey?" The woman had seen her own daughter through many a tearful session, so she had some idea of how to begin. She reached around to the well-worn, green counter top behind her and handed LuAnn a box of Kleenex. "Here, wipe your eyes and blow your nose. I can wait." She busied herself with preparations for the hair-cut and perm, keeping a concerned eye on her new customer. The young woman sitting in the chair looked about as miserable as a human being could be.

Finally, she handed back the box of Kleenex and spoke, "Do you have a bathroom? I would feel better if I could wash my face off. It was pretty hot walking out there in the sun." Francis pointed towards the back of the shop. LuAnn stood up on shaky legs. She felt nauseous. Closing the door, she dropped to her knees and vomited into the stool. The stool rim's label mocked her, *Tuffy*. Yeah, sure! With a wet paper towel, she sponged off her face and neck, as tired, bloodshot eyes were closed tightly to the bedraggled image in the mirror.

Deflated and discouraged, she looked forward to sitting down and being fussed over for a while. She took a deep breath and opened the bathroom door. A brave smile was mustered, and she settled back into the chair, determined that the many smells permeating the beauty shop wouldn't get the best of her again. "OK . . . all set. I'm all yours! Do what ever it takes."

If she could talk to this woman, perhaps a brighter perspective of the situation could be painted. With a daughter of her own, Francis seemed to be the best council available.

"Do you really want to know why I made such a fool of myself? I mean, you must get tired of listening to people's troubles." She nervously twisted the tail of her shirt into a knot and then tried, unsuccessfully, to smooth out the wrinkled fabric.

"Anytime you're ready to talk, Honey, I'm ready to listen. I'll just start cutting. I'm thinking that something on the shortish side would work best for your fine hair." LuAnn nodded in agreement. Strands of hair were measured and the crisp sound of snipping shears filled the silence.

She began to relax, and old memories poignantly surfaced. When she was younger, her mother had trimmed her hair. However, a few years ago, she became more sophisticated and particular about her appearance. She had insisted on going to the beauty shop like the other high school girls. They had something in common to talk about. Now, she missed those hands running through her hair.

"I'm pregnant!" She suddenly blurted out, hardly aware that the words had surfaced. The shears kept snipping away. "I don't even know why I'm here, in Iowa. I mean . . . I know why I'm sitting here . . . I need to have my hair fixed." The shears just kept snipping.

"What do you think? Is that going to be short enough?" With her fingers, Francis squished hair up towards the scalp and turned LuAnn's face towards the mirror. "With the curl in, it will be about up to here."

LuAnn took a quick look and then turned away. "Oh, sure. That's good! You know, I used to think it was all in a woman's head when she got sick, but it isn't. I can testify to that now! My mother said she had to spend several days in the hospital when she was pregnant with Jane. She's my sister, a second grade teacher. This is her second year teaching second grade. That sounds funny, doesn't it?" There was a nervous, little giggle. A lump stuck in her throat. "Then, there was Tommy."

"What do you think, a medium curl, or a tight curl?" Francis was holding up two boxes, one blue, and one yellow. LuAnn couldn't make the decision and shrugged her shoulders. "We'll go with the tight curl, your hair probably doesn't hold a perm very well." Francis put the blue box back into the cupboard and placed the contents of the yellow box on the table at her side. She chose an array of rollers and started sectioning off strands of hair. "Who is Tommy? A special friend?"

For the next forty-five minutes, LuAnn told her all about Tommy, right up to their last telephone conversation the night before she married Mack. It felt good to talk about him. She needed to talk about him. Francis seemed to understand and offered no advice or criticism as the account rambled on. Instead, she dampened strands of hair, put on papers, rolled, and secured each curl, covering the entire scalp. She soaked the curls with lotion and handed LuAnn a towel to catch the runoff. Then she offered one tidbit to consider.

"I think every girl figures her first love is the love of her life. In time, she realizes that isn't necessarily so. Real love happens over time, sometimes taking many years of commitment and hard work. Real love recognizes responsibility for the people around them. Those first feelings of passion are wonderful, but they are usually just that. I would give Mack a chance. He has a lot to learn, too."

LuAnn contemplated this for a bit and then asked, "Can you tell me anything about Ruby and Charles Dutcher? It seems to me they really messed Mack's life up." She related the events of the night before. Francis covered the dampened curls with a plastic bonnet and set her timer for twenty-five minutes.

* * *

Her recollections went back to the first time she saw Mack. It was late one evening, about eleven o'clock. The moon was full, and the June air was heavy and warm. She and Karen happened to be spending the night with her parents. Ray, her husband, was out of town on business. At first, she thought the strange sound, coming from outside, was a Siamese cat prowling the neighborhood. A cat's cry often sounds like that of a child. Being restless herself, she stepped out on the back porch.

There, huddled in the shrubs beneath the window, was a very frightened little boy. She asked him what he was doing there, and he said he was hungry. She took him into the house, washed his face and hands, and fed him bologna sandwiches, peaches, and milk. Francis noticed red marks around each wrist, they looked like rope burns. When she asked him what had happened, he said Aunt Ruby had tied him to a chair because he was late for supper. When he had a chance, he ran away. He had been hiding in bushes and weeds around the lake all evening, afraid to return to the Dutcher farm. His body was dirty and covered with mosquito bites and weed scratches.

Using a flashlight, she had held the boy's hand and walked him home. Ruby and Charles had been preparing for bed. Francis heard the end of their conversation through the screen door, and apparently, they had been looking for him. Ruby was saying, "He'll get hungry and show up sometime. We'll look again in the morning if he hasn't come back yet."

She had knocked on the door but didn't wait to be admitted. Instead, she barged into the house, still holding his hand. They were told where she found him, that she had fed him, and that he should be bathed and put to bed. "A seven year old boy needs to be cared for, not abused!" She was very adamant in her opinion, but doubted it had much influence on the situation.

* * *

Francis' story was disheartening and enlightening, and it supported what Mack had already told her. The weight of the world came pressing down upon her, and contemplative stillness settled in around the beauty shop. She would have to make some decisions. The atmosphere in the Dutcher household was smothering, and now she knew why. She couldn't depend on Ruby and Mack. Their own relationship was precarious. They had nothing to give to her. By the time her hair was set, dried and combed out, a plan had formulated in her mind. She had to be able to take care of herself, and the first thing she needed to do was to find a job.

Before leaving the shop, one more issue was brought up. "Do you know any place where I can find work, Francis? I was really good in school, and I learn quickly."

"Sometimes the drug store is looking for someone, especially now that the summer help is back in school. You might try there." Francis handed LuAnn a mirror so she could see the results of their three hours together. Very pleased, LuAnn paid her, and they ambled over to the door of the beauty shop. Francis patted her back reassuringly.

"You're going to be just fine and you just stop by anytime you're in town, OK? Good luck with finding a job. I'll keep my ears open. Check back with me if you don't find anything. OK?"

She walked down Main Street and entered Deacon's Drug Store. The regular druggist, a rather tall, slim, young man in his early thirties with reddish hair and freckles, was clerking. DANIEL CUMMINGS, PHARMACIST identified him on the name tag. LuAnn wandered along the well-stocked shelves and located the shampoo and bubble bath. She waited until the other customers left before going to the checkout. After paying her bill, she made the inquiry. "I was wondering if you need help . . . if you're looking for someone to hire. I'm looking for a job. I really need a job."

Daniel looked at this attractive, young customer, and an appreciative smile spread across his face. With the new development going on, he had more business than he could handle by himself, and he really needed a young woman's expertise for ordering cosmetics and perfumes. His customers were getting younger and asking for items that he had little knowledge of. He showed LuAnn around the store and hoped she could start work on Monday. "I have an appointment with Dr. Smith in the morning, but I can start Monday afternoon." Smiles of acceptance were exchanged between two happy people.

* * *

Ruby's lawyer, O.B. Allbright, was late for their appointment. Mack was glad. He had a little more time to mull over the events of the past week. His life had changed more drastically than he could ever have imagined. First his marriage to LuAnn, and then the disclosure of Aunt Ruby's wealth. He didn't want to alienate Aunt Ruby, and, at the same time, he couldn't bear to lose LuAnn. There must be some way to reconcile the two.

He may as well be direct with her. He reasoned that, at her age, she needed him more than he needed her. He didn't have to allow the bullying to continue. "You know LuAnn and I are expecting a baby . . . don't you?" He tried out this new courage and strategy while sitting outside the lawyer's office.

"Of course I didn't know!" she yapped at him. "What makes you think I would? For heaven's sake! I'm not the girl's keeper!" Sparks flew from Ruby's angry eyes. Not a good start!

* * *

A woman's pregnancy was the last thing she wanted to think about. It was a sad reminder of the summer she was seventeen years old, and she and the neighbor boy had discovered one another. By Christmas of her senior year in high school, she was pregnant. The lethargy and nausea had drawn her mother's attention. A trip to Dr. Smith's office had confirmed her mother's suspicions. Another trip to a back-street office in Marion had put an end to the pregnancy.

A few days later, the then young Dr. Smith had been called to their home to stop the bleeding. Her mother had explained it as a miscarriage. However, Dr. Smith had known better. In an effort to maintain the deception, her mother told everyone who would listen that Dr. Smith was a 'quack.' The abortion kept her from ever having any children, and that was probably a good thing, because Mack had been more than she bargained for.

* * *

Undaunted, Mack pressed on. "You may not like LuAnn, but I doubt if you would like any woman brought into your house. She's a fine person, and I intend to do all I can to keep her. You can do as you please with the estate, but if you expect either of us to stay around, you'll treat us both fairly." Mack had never confronted his aunt with such determination before and wondered if the bluff would work. He was shaking inside and out, but he hoped the insecurity didn't show. He looked at Ruby unwaveringly. "And I mean it!" He was relieved, at that moment they were called into the lawyer's office. She wasn't given a chance to respond.

Ruby rose stiffly from the seat and stomped off towards the open door. With purse in hand, the hat was, once again, mechanically nudged into place. With Mack following behind, they entered the office of O.B. Allbright.

He was an older man, probably just a few years younger than Ruby. He was shorter than her, heavy-set, and slightly balding with an air of confidence and authority bordering on military . . . the mess sergeant in disguise. He waved the two clients to chairs and produced several folders of documents. "You wish to bring your will up-to-date, Mrs. Dutcher, but may I first show you the last offer for the forty acres containing the lake?"

Papers were laid out on the desk between them. "I don't believe you'll do any better for quite some time." He placed a contract in front of her. "Joe Weatherby wants to develop the property. He's offering one hundred, seventy-five thousand. I really think you should accept it."

Mack was grateful for the diversion from a discussion of the will, and after some time devoted to the particulars of the offer and several phone calls, Ruby signed the contract.

When they left the lawyer's office, the will had been drawn up, leaving everything Ruby Dutcher owned to Mackenzie Linn Hanable, great nephew, and his issue. There were other stipulations, but that was 'it' in a nutshell. It would be in the best interest of them both to find ways in which to 'get along.'

Back at the Chrysler dealership, Ruby handed Mack the title and keys to the Ford, and he dug four hundred dollars out of his jeans pocket. Ruby led the way back to the Dutcher farm driving her new black automobile. Mack followed behind in the 1952 Ford. He didn't think he could enjoy the new Chrysler any more than that old car.

* * *

LuAnn had a new job to look forward to. She liked Daniel Cummings and the way he interacted with the customers. With his robust and friendly personality, no wonder he had a good business. She would do her best to make it even better.

Having gained a new sense of confidence, her steps were quick and easy going back to the Dutcher farm. She expected Mack and Ruby would be home by now, so she was happily surprised and relieved when they weren't there. Without fear of being in someone's way, she primped and posed in the bathroom mirror, arranging and re-arranging her hair.

At five-thirty, she courageously decided to get supper ready. She took the pot of soup from the refrigerator and set it on the gas stove burner turned low. Out in the garden, she found a cabbage and chopped and peeled off the outer leaves into the compost pile. Using the butcher knife and cutting board, she fixed a cabbage salad with marshmallows and nuts . . . something she loved. She put bread, butter, and plates on the table and bowls for the soup. She filled the water glasses and found soup spoons at the back of the utensil drawer. It was six o'clock. Supper smelled delicious, but Ruby and Mack still weren't home.

At ten minutes after six o'clock, she heard the Ford drive up and the engine cut off. The hum of another motor still remained in the air. Curious, she looked out the door as Ruby stepped out of a beautiful, black automobile. Mack held the door for her and waved at his wife. "Hi! . . . Look at what Aunt Ruby bought today! It's a beauty! . . . Isn't it?" LuAnn stood and stared, not sure of what the proper comment might be. "Maybe we can take a ride in it later, if Aunt Ruby doesn't mind." His voice had a defiant ring to it. "Come here and look at this!" He beckoned vigorously.

LuAnn stood in wide-eyed amazement. Then, she walked slowly out into the yard. After scrutinizing and admiring the vehicle, Ruby brushed a light film of dust from it with her handkerchief. The three of them walked to the house and entered the kitchen. Ruby stopped short and opened her mouth, but no words came out.

"I hope you haven't eaten yet. The soup is really pretty good. I'll dish it up." LuAnn hurriedly began ladling soup into the bowls. Ruby took her purse and the documents into the bedroom. In a few minutes, they were seated around the table enjoying supper. Mack looked at LuAnn and winked.

When Ruby was finished eating, she went into the living room, picked up her Bible and went to the yard to read. No newspaper came on Saturday, so the Bible took priority for that evening. Mack helped LuAnn with the dishes. Then, he boldly got the keys to the Chrysler from Ruby's purse in the bedroom. Together, they crossed the yard to where she sat.

The keys were nimbly tossed and caught in the palm of his hand as they walked.

"Will we be going to church tomorrow, Aunt Ruby? Do you mind if I take LuAnn for a ride into Marion?" He held up the keys and jingled them. "We'll get some ice cream . . . and we'll bring you back something if you like."

The Bible was momentarily laid down on her lap. She looked up at them from above the lenses of her bifocals. "Yes, we'll be going to church. The service starts at ten o'clock." She picked the Bible back up. "Take LuAnn for a ride if you like. You can bring me back a cherry milk shake . . . since we didn't have any dessert for supper!" The needle thrust had missed its mark; LuAnn was oblivious to the insinuation.

Fifteen minutes later, they pulled into the drive-in feeling very privileged to be driving such a magnificent vehicle. It definitely stood out amongst the old beat-up jalopies. The order was placed, and Mack handed the car hop an extra dollar bill.

"Like your hair, Honey." His fingers brushed the curls around her face. He tipped her head back and nuzzled his face in her hair, enjoying the smell of the new perm. "If Aunt Ruby lets me drive the Chrysler, you can drive the Ford. I paid for it this afternoon, so it's mine now." He finished up his banana split and started up the engine. "Just listen to this baby purr." They headed back to the Dutcher farm with Aunt Ruby's cherry milk shake in an orange sack situated on the seat between them.

Six

Sunday morning, after a breakfast of scrambled eggs and toast, LuAnn and Mack donned their wedding clothes, and at nine-thirty, the residents of the Dutcher home were ready for church. They walked out the front door with Ruby in the lead, followed by Mack and then LuAnn. After Ruby had locked the door and put the key beneath the kerosene can, the threesome headed towards the new Chrysler. Because there was no garage, it was still sitting out in front of the house beside the old Ford.

After yanking Mack's handkerchief from his pocket, Ruby tried to use it to brush away the light accumulation of dust and some bird droppings that were splattered on the hood. Her efforts were of little consequence, and, with a heightened degree of irritation and disgust, the cleaning cloth was dropped to the ground. Ruby rapidly brushed her black-gloved hands together. "Ick! Something has to be done about this!" She hustled over to the passenger side of the vehicle.

Mack eyed his new white handkerchief that now lay on the ground in the dirt. He scowled, shrugged his shoulders, and obligingly opened the two doors for the women. Like a clucking, old setting hen, Aunt Ruby wriggled herself into the front seat. Using the mirror on the visor, the veil on the black hat was adjusted, and she folded work-worn arthritic hands primly in her lap. LuAnn had the back seat all to herself.

Once they were out on the highway, Mack turned to his aunt with a proposal. "If I clean out all the old machinery from the barn shed, there would be a place to keep your new car. What do you think?" LuAnn noted a take-charge ring in his voice.

There were no objections, and Ruby even agreed. "I suspect you're right. Maybe some of that old stuff could be sold to the Amish over by Independence. That's what I've been thinking. We'll run an ad in the *Gazette* this coming week. I'll call it in tomorrow." As an afterthought, she added, "That is if you can have everything ready by the end of the week."

"Well, yeah! Sure!" Mack looked at LuAnn in the rearview mirror and winked.

Having made the decision, Ruby settled down further into the front seat and brushed her hands over the soft gray leather of the interior. Imagined dust was blown from her finger tips. She was wearing a rose-red dress with the black accessories, and she looked less formidable than usual. LuAnn was surprised at the woman's choice of color for attending church services. Perhaps, there was something risqué about her after all.

She wondered what Ruby meant by, 'the Amish' and would ask Mack after church. Right now, she was going to enjoy the ride. The skirt of her yellow dress was spread out over the seat. She crossed her ankles, and leaned back against the soft leather . . . silky smooth and smelling new. With closed eyes, she imagined how Cinderella must have felt when transported to the ball in an elegant coach. Of course, Cinderella wasn't pregnant. The silly thought made her chuckle, and a smile of contentment touched her lips.

When the automobile pulled into the parking lot of the Open Bible Christian Church, many of the arriving members turned their heads to take a second look. One young woman, in particular, was about to step inside the church, but she paused at the doorway. A quizzical look touched her brow. Who could be driving such a beautiful vehicle? Sumptuously, Mack stepped from the driver's seat, and she blinked, frowned, and stared in wide-eyed disbelief.

Thoughtfully, she hesitated for a moment and then hurried over to the automobile. Mack was opening the door for Ruby. "Mackenzie Hanable! Is that really you? You've been gone for so long! At first, I hardly recognized you!" His arm was grabbed by two strong, clutching hands with long, red fingernails. "You do remember me, don't you?" Her perfect teeth flashed behind full, crimson, pouty lips, and her breasts and face were pushed up close to him. A flood of warmth and perfume rose to his nostrils. Dark, smoldering eyes searched into his own. In spite of himself, a hot lust washed over his suddenly sexually-alert body.

* * *

Of course, he remembered her! What he remembered most is that she had never seemed to want to know him. In fact, she had never spoken to him before in all the years they attended the same church and high school. At that time, she was a curvy teenager, cute and flirtatious. With her dark, curly hair and smoldering, dark eyes, all the boys were wild about her, including him. She could have any guy she wanted, and she did. But she had never wanted Mack Hanable, not Ruby Dutcher's great nephew. Why? Because there was no way he could have measured up to her expectations.

* * *

Now, he found it humorous how being twenty-five years old, single, thirty pounds overweight, and within reach of a new Chrysler, could change a woman's attitude so much. Curiously and with a slight smirk, he acknowledged her presence. "Why . . . hello, Kate, you're looking . . . a . . . looking . . . healthy." He pulled back, and his eyes roved over her body, bringing a flush to the woman's plump but beautiful face. He dislodged his arm from her grip. "Of course, you know my Aunt Ruby." He nodded in the older woman's direction. Ruby pursed her lips, nodded, and smiled stoically. He reached for the handle to the back car door and opened it. Very gallantly, he took LuAnn by the hand and helped her to the blacktop surface of the parking lot. "This is my wife, LuAnn."

Kate watched as a beautiful, young woman with blonde curly hair, blue eyes, and wearing a yellow dress, stepped from and stood beside the shiny, new automobile. The blue eyes sparkled with amusement. She was enjoying the interchange between the two old classmates. Without further comment, Kate nodded curtly and hurried away. Her buttocks rippled under the knit skirt of her red suit. Mack and LuAnn looked at each other and burst into laughter . . . two impudent little children with a shared secret. Ruby eyed them coolly. "You realize that is Joe Weatherby's daughter, don't you?"

* * *

LuAnn enjoyed participating in the church service. A peacefulness that she hadn't experienced in a long time began to penetrate each pore of her body. During the singing and scripture readings, her clear voice joined those of the other members of the congregation. Then Pastor Yokum began his sermon, "Through the Eye of a Needle." He lamented on the difficulties that life gives us. He ended up being very adamant concerning the wealth that people accumulate. "It is easier for a camel to go through the eye of a needle than it is for a rich man to get into Heaven."

On their way out of the church building, Pastor Yokum grasped Ruby by the hand and clung to it for what seemed like a very long time. "I see you have a new automobile, Ruby. You'll have to give me a ride in it sometime." Ruby nodded her head in agreement and released her hand. "Good day, Pastor Yokum."

They drove into Cedar Rapids for Sunday dinner at the Red Herring Restaurant. Ruby silently contemplated raising her weekly offering from two dollars to, perhaps, four or five. She's not sure just how wide and how high the eye of that 'needle' is.

* * *

Sunday afternoon was always a time for Ruby to relax, take a nap, or read. This Sunday, she decided to catch up on reading the *Successful Farming* and the *Farm Journal*, The magazines still came regularly, even though no farming has been done on the Dutcher place for the past two years. Since the sale of the forty acres of lake property, all that remains of the farm is the twenty acres the house and buildings set on. Nevertheless, she located the magazines, picked up the lawn chair, and went to sit in the shade of the west grove.

With Ruby so occupied, Mack wanted to take advantage of the situation. "Do you like to fish, LuAnn? This is a great day for fishing!" He figured this could be his last opportunity to use the lake before the developers take over. "Let's put on our jeans and dig some worms. Can you wash out that bean can in the trash to put them in?" They went upstairs and pulled on some of Mack's old jeans and shirts. The idea of fishing wasn't very appealing to her, but she hated to disappoint him.

They procured a tined potato fork from the garden and went out in back of the old barn to dig. Here the ground was cool and moist, making for easy digging and an abundance of angleworms. The can was soon filled with dirt and bait. He found the old fishing poles over head in the tool shed. They weren't much, but they would do. There were no reels on them, but he knew a good spot where they could just unwind the string and 'drop' the hooks into the water.

With Mack leading the way, brandishing a machete to clear a path, they walked around the south edge of the lake and started east. LuAnn hadn't been around that way before. Nor, apparently, had anyone else in a long time. The trees and bushes were thick and prickly, and it was unpleasant pushing through the weedy growth. The poles had to be held high over their heads to keep the lines from getting tangled up. Even then, the way was difficult. In her opinion, fishing wasn't a good idea, but she said nothing.

Finally, Mack stopped near an old tree that had partially uprooted and blown over into the lake years before. Still alive, the trunk was large enough to walk out on over the water, and the leafed branches afforded perfect seats and shade. LuAnn took off her sandals, knocked out the dirt and chaff, and left them on the lake's edge. Catlike, she followed her husband and selected a secure, comfortable perch between two branches. The can of worms was set between them. He baited her hook and then his own. They let the strings unwind into the water. It wasn't long until they were pulling in bullheads that were then strung onto a cord stringer.

LuAnn wished she could enjoy it just a little bit, but the hungry mosquitoes managed to find the flesh on her arms even through the long sleeves of the shirt. They seemed to find her ankles appetizing as well, and she unrolled the cuffs on the jeans. The couple had spoken very little, but LuAnn finally asked, "What are we going to do with them?" She hoped her irritation wasn't evident.

"They'll be fed to the cats."

In an added effort to deflect the discomfort, she turned her mind to other things. "I'm really excited about my job." There was no response, so she continued. "By the way, did I tell you I have an appointment with Dr. Smith in the morning? I thought I should find out for sure if I'm pregnant." There was a tug on her line, and she pulled in yet another bullhead.

Mack held the fish in his hands, and, for a moment, he looked at her quizzically. Then rage flared into his dark eyes. "What in the hell are you talking about? You're telling me you don't really know if you're pregnant!" He gave the hook a quick jerk to dislodge it from the bullhead's mouth. It came loose, and the line flew upward to whip around the branches of the tree. "Shit!"

Stunned by the overt reaction, she stammered, "I mean . . . sometimes cancer and things like that can make women feel the same way . . . I just read that in a magazine." She ended lamely. What must he think of her? Just two weeks ago, she told him she was pregnant. Now, she's telling him perhaps she isn't? Still, she's certain that she is. What good would explaining do?

Mack was burning inside. *If this girl is trying to pull something over on me, she'll wish she hadn't. I'll kick her butt out of here so fast, her head'll spin*. "We'd better get back to the house! We have more fish than the cats will eat already!"

LuAnn was ready to leave. Mack was angry, and, besides the pesky mosquitoes, her rear was numb from sitting on the rough bark of the tree trunk. She stood up and rubbed the backs of her legs and thighs. Mack leaned over and picked up the can of worms. Like a bullet, he hurled them far out into the lake, can and all. When he brought his arm back, a hard blow hit LuAnn's shoulder and knocked her off balance. Startled, she gasped, grasped the nearest branch, and clung tightly. Even then, her feet slipped, and she dangled out over the water. With a great surge of effort, she swung back to the tree trunk and sat down. Panic smothered her senses, and her lungs gulped for air. Trembling with fear, she was afraid to move.

Mack picked up the poles and the stringer of bullheads. Then he scurried down the trunk back to shore. Not looking back, he yelled at her, "You'd better watch what you're doin', LuAnn! It's deep down there!" He was soon out of sight, back through the passage he had hewn through the brush and weeds a short time before.

She was dazed from the pain and the fear of falling. Surely she was misinterpreting what just happened. Yet, Mack showed no concern for hitting her, and his last comment was unnerving. With shaking legs, she crossed the log to the security of the lakeside and slowly pulled on her sandals. The walk back to the house was made slowly and deliberately. She hurt too much to think rationally. She just needed some time to herself.

Mack had taken off at a near run. By the time LuAnn reached the barnyard, he and Ruby were in deep conversation out by the chicken house. "We'll know tomorrow, if that quack, Dr. Smith, knows anything." Mack didn't care if LuAnn heard him or not.

Discouraged and choking back tears, she went upstairs and gathered clean clothing. Back downstairs, she went into the bathroom, and started running a tub of warm water. Dirt, dust, seeds, and weeds clung to her clothes and hair, and she smelled like fish and perspiration. Perhaps, she could clean out her mind while she cleaned her body.

Of course, Mack had every reason to be angry. What did he know about pregnancies? Even less than she did, no doubt. Still, if he loved her, why would it matter if she was pregnant or not? Was that the only reason he had married her? In truth, it was the only reason she had married him.

She threw the fishy-smelling clothes down into the basket by the washer. Then she stepped into the bathtub and scrubbed vigorously. After bathing, she put on clean under clothes, shorts and a blouse, tied a scarf around her pin-curled hair, and went outside to look for Mack and Ruby. She wasn't going to let them think she was fearful of anything they might do. They were out by the garden looking over the squash.

"Aunt Ruby, I would be glad to start supper, if you like." She looked from one to the other and defiantly stood her ground.

"Why don't you just call me Ruby? I'm not your aunt, you know. Some scrambled eggs and peaches would be plenty after that huge dinner we had after church." She pulled one of the squash from its vine. "We can start eating these now."

With a powerful look of defiance, LuAnn challenged Mack. "I'll wash our fishy clothes after you clean up." She walked across the lawn and into the house. He followed her, went into the bathroom, and turned on the shower. She got the supper ready, and at six o'clock, the three were seated around the table.

Quite unexpectedly, Ruby suggested that, perhaps, they should say grace before eating. Grace had not been said since Charles died. "Mack, you can do that for us. You remember what Charles used to say, I'm sure."

In a halting voice, at first unsure of the words, he began, "Bless us, Oh Lord, in these, Thy gifts, which we are about to receive. From Thy bounty, through Christ, Our Lord. Amen." When he finished, he looked from LuAnn to Ruby and a bit of a gleam lit up his eyes.

* * *

Monday morning, the twenty-ninth day of August, 1958, LuAnn's pregnancy was confirmed. She would give birth to her first child sometime in early April. Doctor Smith gave her a thorough examination and found her to be in excellent health. It shouldn't hurt her to work at the drug store for as long as she felt like it.

She immediately loved working for Daniel Cummings. He was pleasant and considerate and happy to have her. When he realized she hadn't planned for the noon meal, he phoned his wife, Becky. She would bring some sandwiches for them both. After this, she would remember to take a sack lunch. Her hours would be from ten until five, Monday through Friday.

Becky Cummings was a small, bubbly, brunette. Shortly before noon, she arrived with their two-year-old, red-headed twin boys towed in a wagon. The twins were just as cheerful, friendly, and outgoing as their parents. She didn't stay for long, because the twins were into everything in the store if let out of their confinement in the wagon. "Oh, she keeps busy, all right," Daniel Cummings agreed.

LuAnn began thinking of her own child. She wondered what he would look like, Mack or Dad. Maybe a bit of both. But then, maybe it would be a girl and look more like Jane or her mother. She supposed it was too soon to get a letter back from her parents, but tomorrow she would take time to check the box at the post office. She missed them all dearly.

That evening, LuAnn waited until after the dishes were cleared away, and the kitchen was cleaned up. Ruby was in her bedroom, and Mack was at the kitchen table repairing a broken electric cord on the toaster. "I was right. Our baby is due the first part of April. I hope you want it as much as I do." She hoped he would apologize for hitting her and nearly knocking her into the lake, but he didn't.

Mack reached out and patted her on the behind . . . something she hated. The act seemed demeaning. "Sure, Baby, sure, I'm glad. I don't know anything about having a kid, but I guess I'm going to learn." He pursed his lips. "Say, I've been thinking. Your old man is a postal worker, isn't he? How did he get his job? Did he take a test or something?"

LuAnn didn't have a clue. She shrugged her shoulders. "Dad has just always been sorting mail at the post office. That's what he does." Then she added, "Well, I guess we could find out if we called him." Her heart quivered with anticipation. It had been her desire to call Fern and Clifton when they arrived, but, after meeting Ruby, she didn't want to do anything to further upset the household. Now there was a good reason, so she didn't have to feel guilty.

"OK, go ahead," Mack shook his head in the affirmative. "I'll just sit here at the table while you put the call through."

She went to the phone and dialed the long distance operator. "Give me Grafton, West Virginia, please, 277-8377." She waited while the line buzzed on the other end. "I hope they're home," her voice caught.

"Hello," it was Fern.

"Hello, Mom. This is LuAnn! How are you? . . . How is everyone?." She paused for her mother's replies. "Yes, I'm doing just fine, too. Is Daddy there? I need to ask him some questions."

Clifton Soppee was on the line immediately. Her card had arrived that day. He had intercepted it at the post office, and he had questions to ask. "Are you all right, LuAnn? Really all right? If you have to be careful about what you say, just answer yes or no." He continued with questions and advice. "If you need us, call us collect at any time, no matter where you are."

"I have a job in the drug store, and Daniel and Becky Cummings are so nice. I've met an elderly couple, too, the Trouts. I even got a new perm from their daughter, Francis." Mack gave her an icy stare and started to get up from the table. "How did you get your job with the post office, Dad? Did you take tests or something?" By the time their conversation ended, LuAnn had the information Mack needed.

"Oh, Dad, can I talk to you and mother both for a minute. I want you both to hear this. OK, ready? You will be grandparents in April." There was silence on the other end of the line. She realized it was too soon to tell them. "Mom? . . . Dad?"

Finally, Fern took a deep breath. "We'll be there for you when the time comes. We'll get tickets just as soon as you're more certain of the date. We love you."

Dad got on the phone one more time. "Give me your telephone number. We'll be calling you at least every other week. 634–7787, got it. Bye, Honey."

"Well, what did he tell you? Do I have a chance to work for the postal service or not?"

"You need to go to the library and find out all you can about civil service jobs, requirements, and tests." She shrugged her shoulders. "You study, and then take the tests. If you score high enough, you'll be eligible for a position when one opens." That sounded reasonable enough.

"I can do that! Thanks, LuAnn! I'm gonna get myself a good job!" He set the repaired toaster back on the counter and walked outside. He needed some time by himself to think.

In spite of everything, LuAnn couldn't get Mack's lack of compassion out of her mind. Tomorrow, she would leave the house early enough to stop and see Maude and Milford before going to work. She could use their advice and encouragement.

She figured out the amount of her weekly earnings at two dollars and fifty cents an hour, seven hours a day, five days a week. That would be about eighty-seven dollars. It seemed like a staggering amount of money. She could give Ruby some for her share of the expenses, save some to buy her own car, and still have a little left for personal needs.

Mack planned to get up early the next morning and drive into Cedar Rapids. He had never had much use for libraries before, but he did now. He was determined to get a job as quickly as possible and a good job, too. He didn't need people talking about his wife supporting him or anything like that. He didn't need to hear any complaints from Aunt Ruby either. He would go to the library in the morning, be back by noon, and spend the afternoon hauling old machinery out of the shed.

He thought about Kate and the other girls who figured they were too good for him. Well, he would show them all. Even LuAnn could be kept in line when it was necessary. Eventually, he would inherit all of Aunt Ruby's money. Then he could do as he damn well pleased. Nobody could push him around anymore. That night, in his dreams, he was trying to carry a bushel of money through the eye of a needle while riding on the back of a camel.

That night, after making love, LuAnn fell asleep picking petals off of daisies. "He loves me. He loves me not. He loves me. He loves me not."

Seven

Mack's mind wouldn't stop churning, and, so, he spent another very wakeful and restless night. His body lay rigid and exhausted beside LuAnn, but his brain wouldn't stop its relentless probing long enough for him to sleep. So many changes in such a short time. So much to do. So many decisions to make. Even Kate Weatherby's image wouldn't leave him alone and emerged periodically. When the rain started early Tuesday morning, it was definitely a relief . . . from the heat at least.

He stealthily drew back the covers on his side of the bed, slipped out, and went down the stairs. Aunt Ruby had already lowered the windows, so he used the toilet and went back up to the bedroom. He stood silently . . . on guard . . . and looked out the window facing east towards the deserted farm buildings. He stood as a sentry at dawn, watching over the one part of Uncle Charles' life that the old man had managed to claim as his own, his machinery . . . and, so, he had kept it all. Now, it was up to Mack to dispose of it, and emotions he couldn't understand tore at his insides.

The afternoon before, the old farm machinery had been pulled from the back of the barn shed, and corncrib, its refuge for many years. Out in the yard, the rows of old horse-drawn and tractor-drawn implements stood rigid and black in the downpouring rain . . . disciplined brigades of soldiers ready to advance towards the enemy. Their silhouettes were lit up by bolts of lightning . . . artillery firing in the distance.

Mack had managed, with some difficulty, to get most of it hauled into the yard and arranged in an orderly fashion for the sale. Today, there would be ads running in the Independence and Oelwein papers. By this time tomorrow, they had to be ready for the anticipated buyers, and the rain would help. It would wash off the accumulation of dust, bird droppings, and cobwebs. With a sense of some relief, he walked over to the south window and focused on the Chrysler. He was reminded of the tanks at the Army base, not a pleasurable memory. Clammy cold sweat broke out on his skin.

* * *

His thoughts drifted back to the months he spent with Mary Lou Bailey. He had met her on a Saturday at the grocery store in Grafton. While driving around the town, he had decided that he was hungry for some Twinkies. He pulled into the parking lot of the Piggly Wiggly, and, after strolling the aisles for a time, he had encountered her by the rack of snack cakes. They both reached for the same package at the same time, and his hand brushed hers. She wrapped her fingers around the prize, smiled in a tantalizing manner, fluffed out her long brown hair, and sauntered off down the aisle between rows of cereal and bags of sugar and flour.

The jeans she was wearing were the tightest he had ever seen on any woman's behind. As she walked, full hips gyrated, and he was turned on. So, he followed her out of the store and grabbed the seat of the bicycle as she was about to peddle away. "Where you off to, Honey?" That's what started it all, and he hoped his letter had finished it.

* * *

A week ago, he had written her . . . explaining that his platoon was taking off for Korea. So, at that time, there wasn't anything he could do about the baby. It was written in the hotel room in Grafton the morning of his marriage to LuAnn. He had even driven to the base to mail it, making certain the postmark looked convincing. He was back at the hotel room just in time to get dressed in a new suit and tie.

* * *

Mary Lou knew very little about him. He had seen to that. So, he figured there was nothing to worry about. All he ever let her know was he is from the Midwest, and that seemed to appease her. It was amazing how little it took to satisfy some women . . . just as long as you didn't get hooked up too close to them . . . that is. If you did, then they started expecting things of you . . . and she was getting that way.

Money was no problem in the family. He had figured that much out . . . so they could do whatever it took to protect their 'little girl.' She didn't have to be his responsibility . . . but maybe he had messed up by not marrying her. With their standing in the community, it's possible there could have been great things in the making for him. Too late for that, now. He had allowed himself to get hooked up with LuAnn . . . at least for the time being.

Not to worry, though, because, now, Kate Weatherby seemed to be a possibility. She really came onto him out in front of the church. Her father, Joe, bought the lake property, and, with her, he could still have access to it. Something to think about. If LuAnn didn't work out . . . Kate might be a consideration.

* * *

He looked over at his sleeping wife. A small flicker of affection touched his heart. For a moment, he felt weak and vulnerable. He didn't like feeling out of control that way. Nevertheless, he had to find a way to get her to work this morning. She couldn't walk in the rain, but if he took her at ten o'clock, there wouldn't be time to do research at the library. And . . . damn it all! He needed a job!

She had said something about visiting the Trouts. Maybe he could leave her off there. If it was still raining at ten o'clock, they could take her in their car, if they were still driving. They must be pretty old by now though. Oh well, that was the best he could do. The rest was up to her. He was getting tired of thinking.

Mack woke her up and explained the situation. She stretched lazily and smiled appreciatively. Then she reached up and wrapped grateful arms around his neck. "I'll just give the Trouts a call to make sure it's all right with them." She kissed him and went downstairs to start the day.

She found their number in the telephone book and dialed. "Of course, you may come. You don't even need to ask. For goodness sake! We're always here. Just come when you're ready."

* * *

The rain was pouring down when the Ford pulled up in front of the Trout's home just before eight o'clock. LuAnn threw a jacket over her head and ran for the shelter of the porch. Water squished in her sandals and splashed up her legs. Milford was watching for her and held the door as she hurried inside. There was a chill in the rain, an indication of autumn approaching.

"Land sakes, Child! We were wondering what you would do this morning. We saw you go by yesterday. We heard you started your job at the drug store." Maude took LuAnn's wet jacket and hung it on the back of a kitchen chair. "Would you like some hot cocoa or something?"

LuAnn flipped the skirt of her dress, shaking off drops of water. "It should dry by ten o'clock." She sat down at the table and accepted the hot cocoa. "I hope it's not raining when I have to leave. I'd really hate to ask you to take me to work."

"Well, we most certainly will, but why don't you just plan to take our car? It's old, but it works like a charm," Milford offered.

She admitted to not having a license or even knowing how to drive. "I really need a car of my own, but that will have to wait until I put some money away. Do you know of anyone that could teach me to drive? I don't think Mack would have the patience. Anyway, I don't want to put any more pressure on him. He seems to have enough on his mind right now. He's trying to find a job." The less she expected of him, the better.

Maude got up from the table and beckoned for Milford to follow her to the living room. LuAnn heard their hushed, monotone voices coming from the next room. In a few minutes, they came back into the kitchen. Their faces radiated with pleasure, like two children who have just discovered their Easter baskets.

"LuAnn, how would you like me to teach you to drive? You can use our car, and when you get your license, we'll sell you the car if you want it." Milford's offer was overwhelming. "We're about to the end of our driving days. We would ask just one thing from you . . . that you will take us to our doctor appointments . . . and things like that."

Of course, she accepted their generous offer, and it was arranged for her to be at the Trout's home every morning by nine o'clock for the driving lesson. As though on cue, the sun started to shine, so she and Milford went out to the garage. "We may as well get started!" He backed out the old 1950 Chevy. They parked in the driveway, and for the next hour, he patiently explained all the basics of driving the stick shift.

LuAnn sat in the driver's seat and started the engine several times. The gear shift was tried out. She was getting the hang of it. When it was time to go to work, Milford took his place at the wheel and drove down the street. He stopped in front of Deacon's Drug Store and let his pupil out.

* * *

Mack's morning at the Cedar Rapids Library was productive. He had all the materials and information he needed, in hand, to prepare himself for the Civil Service Exam he would be taking to work for the U.S. Postal Service. The years he had spent in the Army were to his benefit. At last, he felt in control of his future.

* * *

In the afternoon, Mack and Ruby worked at final preparations for the sale. She decided to get rid of the old cook stove, so he made a sign to hang on the front door. Those who were interested could go inside. Together, they decided, "It won't be moved unless it's sold!" They cleaned out the cellar and attic, finding many items certain to appeal to the Amish. Stone crocks, washtubs, a wringer washing machine, tables, chairs, and old dishes were set out in front of the house. Another rain shower came up and washed the pieces free of dust and cobwebs. Ruby considered it a blessing from God, giving His approval. Mack was just happy that the shower was saving him some work cleaning up the old junk.

By late afternoon, they were ready for the sale, so he decided to pick LuAnn up from work. He reasoned that the path around the lake would be wet and muddy. Besides, he wanted to talk to her without Aunt Ruby being around. At five o'clock, he was sitting in front of the drug store when she came out. He beeped the horn and leaned across the front seat. "Hi, Honey. Did you have a good day?" He was anxious to talk about his.

LuAnn wondered how to answer his simple question. It was hard to know if he was really interested or not, but, there must be some reason he was there. "My day was fine, Mack. How about yours?" She listened. "That sounds good, Honey. I'm truly glad for you."

They drove into the yard, and she took in the array of old machinery and household items. "You really have been busy, all right!" They walked along the rows of implements, and Mack explained what each piece had been used for.

Then, they looked at the assortment of household items. Some were quite unique, and she was fascinated by them. In her opinion, some of the dishes were just too pretty to sell and wondered about buying them for herself, but decided against it. Ruby would wonder where she got the money. The shoulder purse still contained ten of the twenty-five dollars she had kept, but she wouldn't get her first pay check until the end of the week.

Ruby had supper ready, and they sat down at the table. Mack anticipated the events for the next day. "I imagine we'll have buyers by seven o'clock in the morning. Regardless of the weather, you're going to have to walk into work, LuAnn. We can't leave with people here."

She was certain Milford would come and pick her up. Besides, he would be getting the car out for the driving lesson anyway. Perhaps this was a good time to tell them about the lessons and Milford's offer to sell her the car, but she thought better of it. With the excitement of the sale tomorrow, they probably wouldn't be interested anyway.

* * *

The next morning, by eight o'clock, the sun was shining, and the atmosphere surrounding the Dutcher place was hectic and festive, reminding LuAnn of a carnival she had once attended. The yard was full of black hats, black bonnets, beards, and long, plain-colored skirts. Most of the Amish arrived in cars with English (as the Amish called them) drivers. Many came in trucks, apparently expecting to take home a number of items. Each new arrival seemed intent on doing business.

Mack and Ruby rushed from one area of the yard to another in an effort to keep up with the buyers. The cook stove was the first item sold from the house. It took six men to load it into the back of a pickup truck. The first of the implements to leave the farm were the horsedrawn corn planter and the corn plow. Ants on an anthill couldn't have been any busier. Mack went into the house twice to put money into the safe. Ruby's apron pockets were stuffed with small bills that she periodically dumped out on her bed to be counted later.

LuAnn talked to some of the young women who were toting babies on their hips. The women spoke perfect English to her, but used a different language to communicate among themselves. German? Dutch? It really didn't matter. It was a pleasant experience, getting acquainted with the Amish.

At eight-thirty, she reluctantly left for the Trouts. The lesson went well, and Milford let her drive up to the drug store. She hopped out of the car and began her third day at work.

It was a very busy day, with students buying supplies for the new school year. The older students came in, flashing five dollar bills, determined to get the most for their money. The younger ones came in with their parents or older brothers and sisters. She had forgotten how important the color of a pencil or notebook is to a small child. By the end of the day, it felt good to be going home.

She hurried along the path around the lake, wondering if the yard would still be full of Amish. As she walked around the barn, the last of the machinery was leaving in the back of a stock truck. A pickup was loaded down with the washing machine and tubs. Two teenage boys sat on the side of the truck box with their long hair blowing in the wind. When the pickup drove away from the yard, they waved their hats, and she waved back. Mack went into the house to place the last of the machinery money in the safe.

There were still three Amish women doing serious business with Aunt Ruby. A gray-haired female driver with a bored look on her face sat waiting for them in an old station wagon. Ruby looked totally fatigued and she finally relinquished. "All right, you can have what's left for ten dollars." She accepted the bill and put the last of the dishes into a box. It was placed into the car's trunk, and the women got into the vehicle and drove from the yard.

With a huge sigh, Ruby sat down on the front porch . . . legs sprawled out . . . with varicose veins protruding. "Thank God that's over!" Her hair hung limp around her face, and her dress' blue checked bodice was soaked through with perspiration. The pockets of the matching apron, stuffed with bills, puffed up on her lap as though she was trying to conceal two large loaves of bread. The starch was all gone out of her. LuAnn had never expected to see her look so bedraggled. A wave of compassion for the woman floated over her.

Mack and Ruby had been too occupied with the buyers to have a real meal at noon, and they were nearly sick with hunger. A day of oatmeal cookie snacks isn't very satisfying to the stomach. LuAnn herself had put in a hard day. She courageously offered a suggestion. "If you two are as tired as I am, I think we should drive into Marion and eat at the drive-in." There were no objections. Hamburgers, onion rings, fries, and shakes tasted like a banquet.

* * *

While LuAnn was in the bathroom preparing for bed, Mack and Ruby counted out the money in her bedroom. The machinery brought two thousand and fifty dollars. The household items brought four hundred and eighty. "I'm going to give the money to you, Mack." She started stuffing it into one of her hat boxes. "You worked hard getting the sale ready. I couldn't have done anything without you." He was astounded at her confession.

"Besides, I don't need any more on my income tax!" She was discovering that money can create its own problems. She also had some advice to give. "I think you should open a checking account. Just make sure it lasts until you get a job! There won't be any more handouts!" She pushed the lid on the box and thrust it at him.

"Thanks, Aunt Ruby. I'll pay you back some day. I really will." He went up to his old bedroom and placed the box at the bottom of the closet. Tomorrow, he would open a checking account in Hiawatha. Since most of his cash was gone, he would keep out a couple of hundred. It would sure feel good to have some real cash in his pocket again. There was no need to tell LuAnn anything. She would have her own money when she got paid. He slept peacefully that night.

* * *

The driving lessons went well, and the weeks passed without LuAnn saying anything about them to Mack. Maybe he knew, and maybe he didn't. He was so busy studying for his examination that very little attention was paid to what she was doing. A reserved peace settled over the household.

At the end of September, Milford drove her into Cedar Rapids. She passed both tests easily and walked out of City Hall with a new driver's license. With an air of confidence, she drove back to the Trouts with Milford in the passenger seat.

"Well, LuAnn, the car's yours now! How much money do you have saved for it?" He pressed the keys into her hand.

"Well, I've just saved one hundred and seventy-five dollars, and I know that isn't enough." The keys were handed back to him.

"Then, that's how much I want for it." He again pressed the keys into her hand and got out of the car. He closed the door and waved her off. "Just stop to see us when you have time. Maude likes to take rides into Cedar Rapids occasionally. Just don't forget about us." He looked after her as she drove away, a satisfied smile etched on his face. His job of growing old had just been made a little easier. He couldn't have given a piece of his past to a better person.

LuAnn drove down the street and parked in front of the Hiawatha State Bank. She owned a car! She really owned a car! . . . Almost, anyway! She walked into the bank and withdrew the money from her account. She drove straight back to the Trouts. "I think you forgot something." She opened the front door and handed the bills to Milford. "See, I'm back already!"

"Just a minute! I had the title changed over to your name some time ago. Let me get it. I'd loose my head if it wasn't attached." He came out of the bedroom and handed her a piece of paper. "Keep this in a safe place. It's important. Don't forget to buy some insurance!"

She studied the title and placed it into the zippered compartment of her purse. "I won't forget! I'm late for work! See you later!" She drove up the street and parked. Entering the drug store, she waved her hand at Daniel. "I got my driver's license!" She placed her purse beneath the counter, and got busy arranging the cosmetics display.

* * *

At five o'clock, LuAnn drove the mile around the side road off Main Street, steered the Chevie up the lane, and parked beside the Ford out in front of the Dutcher house. Ruby and Mack came to the screen door. When she stepped out from the driver's seat, a puzzled look registered on Mack's face. A look of disgust clouded Ruby's features. LuAnn smiled brightly. "How do you like my car?"

"Where in the hell did you get that? I thought you couldn't drive!" Mack glared at his wife accusingly.

"Mr. Trout has been teaching me," she told him cheerfully. "I got my license this morning." She proudly raised her chin. "He sold me his car. He's decided not to drive anymore." She looked from one to the other, defiantly.

"Why in the hell would they do you any favors?" Mack's voice was rising. Ruby was enjoying the exchange between her great nephew and his wife.

"They are kind and compassionate people! That's just the way they are. It seems to me they showed you kindness and compassion when you needed it many years ago. They are no different now." She walked past them and into the house.

Upstairs, she took off her skirt to get some relief from the tightening waistband and pulled on her largest pair of slacks. She lay back on the bed. Well, that was another hurdle. She didn't care how her words affected them. She had spoken the truth, and as Pastor Yokum said last Sunday: "The truth shall set you free."

* * *

Mack stared at his aunt. His black eyes penetrated until she turned away. They both knew what LuAnn was referring to. Apparently, the Trouts and LuAnn had been talking, telling each other more than any of them had a right to know. "Some people just talk too much!" Ruby hissed.

For him, it was easier to just deny what had been said. "Pregnant women tend to become emotional, Aunt Ruby . . . I read that . . . don't worry . . . I'll straighten her out later." He walked out towards the lake, and Ruby went back into the house to finish preparations for supper.

Eight

LuAnn planned to spend the weekend shopping for maternity clothes. The only thing she could get into at all anymore was one pair of good slacks, and she was relieved that Mr. Cummings didn't mind when she showed up for work dressed in them and a loose shirt with the sleeves rolled up belonging to Mack.

On Friday, she no more than walked into the drug store when Becky shoved through the door behind her, red-faced and disheveled. She was pulling the big coaster wagon with the twins in it. This time, she not only had the boys, but they were squeezed in among bags and boxes of clothing. Perspiration stood out on her brow. "Phew! That's quite a load to haul for four blocks."

Earlier that morning, Daniel had offered to take the clothes down to the store in his car. Typically independent, Becky insisted on delivering the clothing herself. "I want to be sure LuAnn really wants them!" Besides, it felt good to get out of the house, even though it meant hassling with the boys.

"What in the world are you doing, Becky?" LuAnn's inquisitive look went from the frazzled woman to the load of kids, boxes, and bags. "Do you need help with something?"

The boys had scrambled from the wagon, and LuAnn quickly grabbed one little hand that was already squeezing a chocolate candy bar. The soft center was oozing out between little fingers "Is this Larry or Jerry? I can never tell them apart." She wasn't having much luck prying the fingers from their firm grasp, and she looked at his mother beseechingly.

"Give Mommy a bite, Sweetheart." Becky crouched down to the little boy's eye level and opened her mouth. "Feed the baby bird." He held the candy bar out, and she took a small bite. "Hmm, good boy! Now, give LuAnn a bite. She's a baby bird, too." The candy bar was, again, thrust out to LuAnn's reluctantly-opened mouth, and, at this juncture, Becky jerked it away. Larry wailed and, with determined, chocolate-covered hands, he grabbed at the legs of his mother's new blue linen slacks and rubbed his face on her pant leg. LuAnn watched the distasteful scene unfold.

Thankfully, Daniel was in control of Jerry, keeping a firm grasp on the whining little boy who was determined to eat a package of bubble gum. He first tried, without success, to scratch Daniel's face with his stubby fingernails, and then he alternately kicked, squirmed, and straightened his little body into a poker.

Becky picked up Larry and held him in a vise-like grasp as well. He freed one arm, grabbed her hair, and pulled with all his might, a determined scowl on his face. "Stop that!" Becky administered a sharp slap to his hand. He let out a scream. The wailing became piercing. "I had better leave! LuAnn, I brought my old maternity clothes for you to try. I'm not planning on needing them again! Just use whatever you want." She was yelling to let herself be heard above the children's screams.

Daniel pulled the wagon out to the sidewalk in front of the store. He opened the door of LuAnn's car and put the bags and boxes into the back seat while hanging onto Jerry with one arm. One at a time, he firmly placed the twins back into the wagon. "Now you stay in there until Mommy gets you back home, or Daddy will spank your backside! Hear me?" He shook a persuasive finger at the two boys. They looked back at him with big, brown eyes and solemn, tear-streaked faces.

Becky took off down the street at a trot. The wagon jerked and rumbled over the sidewalk. She hoped to go fast enough to keep the boys seated by making them fearful of getting out. It seemed to work. They clung to the sides of the wagon with tight fists. Their heads bobbed back and forth, up and down, as the wheels hit the cracks. Daniel watched them go around the corner. So far, so good.

LuAnn picked up the remnants of the candy bar and a package of gum that had been chewed on. "Tell Becky, thanks, will you, Mr. Cummings?" She went to work on the shelves of school supplies, wondering what was in store for herself as a parent. Some of the items had already been pawed and mulled over so much that they had to be trashed. Kids could sure be a pain.

At that moment, she felt the little one inside of her rouse for the first time. Startled, she wondered what was happening. Then there was a fluttering sensation, and she sat down to take it all in. When Daniel finished with the customers at the drug counter, the baffled young woman inquired, "Mr. Cummings, do babies kick and move around before they're born?"

He looked searchingly into her eyes. "Why, yes, LuAnn, they do." He selected a small pamphlet from behind the counter and handed it to her, *So You're Going to Have a Baby!* "Here, you had better read this!" He was always amazed at just how little young people knew about reproduction. No wonder they got themselves into difficult situations.

* * *

Saturday LuAnn tried on all the clothes from the bags and boxes. Anticipating the cold weather ahead, she chose the warmest ones. She laundered and ironed smocks and skirts with holes cut out in the front, ridiculous in appearance, but apparently necessary. If she wanted something different, she would buy it later.

Her checking account was slowly growing, as was the baby, but there would be a crib to buy, as well as clothes, and diapers. She looked through the J.C. Penney's catalog trying to get used to the idea of having a little person to take care of. Perhaps she could order a few things, but Mack needed to be involved with some of the decisions too. *It's his child as well as mine.* He needed to be reminded of that fact.

* * *

Mack and Ruby drove into Waterloo that morning. She would like to have gone with them, but the clothes were of more importance. Besides, she liked time to be alone. She put a call in to Clifton and Fern to let them know how she was doing. "I bought the Trouts' car, and I have my driver's license!" They wanted to meet the Trouts when they came out in the spring. "Oh, I'm handling everything just fine, and do you know what? The baby has started kicking!"

* * *

At five o'clock, Ruby and Mack still weren't home. LuAnn put on a black skirt with a hole in the front and a green smock. Self-consciously, she studied the reflection in the mirror and brushed inquisitive hands down over a slightly bulging stomach. Something she had no control over was growing inside of her. She was anxious to hear what Mack would have to say about the change of fashion. Perhaps the impending arrival of a baby would seem more real to him now.

At five-thirty, the Chrysler purred its way up the lane, and the motor was turned off. The two car doors were opened and shut with a solid slam, and LuAnn waited for her husband to come into the kitchen. He looked at her, and a big grin spread across his amused face. "Hey, the little mama's getting too fat for her clothes! . . . Huh?" He pushed up close behind her and patted her fanny. From the dish on the table, he took a piece of celery and chewed at it on the way up the stairs to their bedroom.

Tears were choked back. Crying would have to wait until later. Right now, the crude and insensitive remark wasn't going to get the best of her. Supper preparations were completed, and, at six o'clock, the three of them sat down at the table. "Well, how was your day?" She looked from Ruby to Mack. Neither of them answered, so she tried again. "Did the drive into Waterloo go well?" A sense of embarrassment hung in the atmosphere. Regardless of her shape, the condition wasn't going to change right away. They may as well get used to it.

After the dishes were finished and the kitchen was cleaned up, she gathered night clothes and went into the bathroom. The water in the tub was turned on full force, and she let herself have a good cry. Finally, feeling clean on the outside and drained of frustration on the inside, she crawled into bed. Maternity clothes monopolized the hangers in the closet.

* * *

Apparently, she had gotten Mack's attention, because he boldly confronted his aunt. "Aunt Ruby, we're going to need some space for the baby bed. There would be room in the hallway upstairs, just outside our bedroom door, if all the boxes up there were moved. Can I put them somewhere else?"

"I'll start going through them this next week." Seemingly, she was resigned to the circumstances. "I suppose it should have been done a long time ago, anyway." Most of them contained possessions once belonging to her mother or Charles' mother. They had been sitting stacked along the walls of the hallway ever since Mack could remember.

During the next weeks, the boxes disappeared a few at a time. True to her word, Ruby spent part of each afternoon going through one or two of them. These were the legacy of two families left behind. With her prodding fingers, flattened baby shoes and bonnets were encouraged to take back their shape, only to be thrown into the trash box to be taken outside to the burn barrel. Long white baby dresses with eyelet lace at the bottom, wrinkled, torn and yellowed, were smoothed out, examined and added to the cast-offs. Some items fell apart as they were caressed, and Ruby's heart fell apart with them. She was a baby once, long ago, and she allowed tears to be shed for that baby. Tears were also shed for the baby that had been forced from her body before its time. Once again, she relived the agony.

There were hat pins and broaches, bloomers and corsets, of which all were rusted and yellowed. There were rumpled long-skirted dresses of satin and lace and large and small hats with tattered feathers, bows, lace, and veiling. There were shorter-styled dresses, straight and beltless, which had been worn by the Flappers. A tight smile touched her lips. She had been one herself. The short, white dress of satin and lace had been worn when she married Charles. That was a long time ago. A bit of tenderness touched her heart. He had been gone for two years, and tears were finally allowed to fall in his memory . . . a current of relief, flowing through the dry ravine of her emotions. Every day, the burn barrel blazed up with fiery extinction and then settled into whiffs of spiritual smoke, heavenbound.

Two days before Halloween, she struggled on the way down the stair steps with the last box of trash. Tired, hip aching, but elated that the job was finished, she stepped on an old ragged shirt that had fallen from a previous load. Her shoe got tangled up in it, and she toppled helplessly down the last six steps. There she was, broken and dazed, a rejected old doll that no one cared about anymore. Her head had hit against the door frame, and a three-inch gash dripped blood. Intense pain radiated from her hip, and she couldn't move. Her screams for help echoed through the empty house. Then, silence, with only the syncopated ticking of the clocks for company. She lay at the foot of the stairs with a broken hip for two hours, because no one could hear her lonely pleas for help.

Mack walked around the circumference of the lake, his vaporized breath spewing out ahead of him. By now, most of the leaves were blown from the trees, and, with each stride, they scrunched beneath his feet. A few evergreens stood out amongst the skeletal branches of the deciduous. Taking his time and with an eagerness to remember, his eyes took in every tree and bush. At times, he stood at the edge of the lake just to watch its ripples and to listen to its sounds. To him, the lake had been the best part of the Dutcher farm. In the spring, Joe Weatherby would have control over all the activities in that area. Even if he was allowed to go there, it wouldn't be the same. He would be a trespasser.

Before going back to the house, he loped down the lane and, with anticipation, eagerly reached into the mailbox. His heart drummed in his chest, and his head felt light and foggy. Today, the letter he had been waiting for was there amongst the papers and magazines. It was hurriedly ripped open. With elation, he read its contents. The job of mail carrier in Marion was available . . . if he wanted it. "Yes! Oh, God, yes!" was yelled out repeatedly on the way to the house, while a clinched fist of victory struck at the air overhead. "Aunt Ruby! Aunt Ruby! Guess what?"

* * *

It seemed to take forever for the ambulance to get there. A note was left for LuAnn telling her what had happened. She shouldn't expect him for supper. Mack followed after the emergency vehicle en route to the hospital in Cedar Rapids. His elation had been short-lived. *Why does everything have to happen to me? How am I supposed to take that job now? Can't I plan on anything?* Self-pity and anger enveloped him.

When LuAnn arrived home from work, she found Mack's note and, also, the crumpled letter he had received from the Civil Service Department informing him of the job opportunity. She felt certain Ruby's fall would discourage him from taking the position, but there had to be some other solution.

* * *

She would be in the hospital for approximately six weeks. Together, they formulated a plan. Mack would start the job in Marion and then see what needed to be done when Ruby returned home. They would figure out something when the time came.

On the weekend, LuAnn scrubbed and waxed the upstairs hallway. The floor and walls were filthy where the boxes had been sitting. The walls would have to be painted. She washed the one window at the top of the stairs and then decided to drive into Cedar Rapids to the Ben Franklin Store to buy new curtains and some paint. Perhaps a visit to the hospital to see Ruby would be appropriate, but she decided against it. It would feel better to wait and go with Mack after church on Sunday. With just a twinge of guilt, she went about her business and was glad she and Mack would have six weeks to themselves.

* * *

"The smell of the hospital is so, well, so medicinal," was LuAnn's observation as they walked down the hallway. In one of the rooms, Ruby lay still and white in a narrow bed. Her whole left side from the waist down was encased in a plaster cast. A catheter ran from under the sheet to a bag attached at the side of the bed. She was totally helpless, *Probably for the first time in fifty years*, LuAnn thought. They should have brought some flowers, but Mack hadn't suggested it, and she didn't want to propose something that made him feel uncomfortable. Besides, flowers cost money, and he hadn't started his job as yet. That was reason enough.

"I'm so sorry about your accident, Ruby." LuAnn spoke compassionately. "I feel partly responsible since you were cleaning out the hallway for us. If there is anything I can do for you, let me know." Ruby turned away and made no answer.

* * *

Mack would start his job November twelfth. He would need to arrive at the post office early in the morning to sort out the mail for his delivery route. He would place the mail into a large, leather bag and deliver it by foot to the residents of Marion. There would be three stops along the way to refill the bag from depository boxes. He should finish up the route by four o'clock in the afternoon. He was fitted with warm, winter uniforms. It would be Christmas in just six weeks, and he could expect the mail bag to get heavier and heavier as the holiday approached. He was anxious to get started . . . to get in condition for the heavier loads. The job paid well, and the money from Aunt Ruby's sale was nearly gone. Unexpected repairs to the old Ford had taken a good share of it.

* * *

Severe weather set in early. The day after Thanksgiving, a huge snowstorm ravaged its way through Iowa. When the wind went down, Mack shoveled the lane out at four o'clock in the morning. Then he shoveled, pushed, and ground his way into work. *The mail must go through.*

LuAnn put on new boots, scarf, mittens, and a fur-collared coat. The snowplows were out, so she was able to make the short drive to the drug store.

Shortly before noon, an ambulance's siren wailed mournfully on its way down Main Street. There were no customers in the store, so Daniel and LuAnn went outside to the front of the building and huddled in their coats while the frigid north wind pushed against their backs. The Trout house was a good ways down the street, but LuAnn felt certain that was where the emergency vehicle stopped. Milford had been outside shoveling when she drove past earlier.

Silhouettes, dark against the snow, rushed to the front door of the house, and minutes later, a stretcher was brought out with a blanket-covered shape on it. Her heart plummeted into the depth of her chest. "Oh, God! No! Don't let it be either of them! Please, God! No!" But later in the day, a customer came into the drug store with the news. "Milford Trout died of a heart attack this morning. Did either of you know him?"

* * *

It was ten degrees below zero the day of the funeral. LuAnn met Francis and Karen at the Trout home, and she rode to the funeral with them and Maude. A sorrow akin to black velvet hung heavy over the day. It was the first funeral LuAnn had ever attended, and it was for someone she had grown to love and respect deeply.

This was her first opportunity to meet Karen, and she was sure they could be friends. She just wished the circumstances were different. "Perhaps we can get together during Christmas vacation," Karen offered. "I would really like to do that. Grandpa thought so much of you, and you are so good to Grandma."

"Yes, we'll plan on it!" She hoped Ruby's condition would allow time to follow up with those plans. As far as she knew, no arrangements had been made yet for taking care of her after leaving the hospital. It would be unbearable if Mack insisted she quit working at the drug store, so she could take care of Ruby.

* * *

For the next two weeks, LuAnn stopped at the Trout home every other day before going to work. She knew Maude would be lonely, and

Francis started working on her customers very early in the day. She needed someone to look in on her before Francis was available.

When Karen got home for Christmas vacation, they made plans to go into Cedar Rapids for shopping and a movie on Saturday. It had been months since LuAnn had spent a day with another young woman. As much as she loved Maude and Francis, the companionship of someone her own age was exhilarating.

* * *

Ruby was to come home the day before Christmas. She could sit up in a chair just fine and get around with a walker. She was doing okay, her recovery would just take time. At Mack's insistence, LuAnn drove to the hospital to bring her home. He didn't want to take time off from work, and she would be discharged in the middle of the morning. LuAnn didn't need to go back to work until after New Year's Day, so the task fell on her.

She had never driven the Chrysler before, and her hands clung nervously to the steering wheel all the way to the hospital. Ruby was wheeled out to the car and placed into the front seat by two aides in white suits. They closed the passenger-side door, placed a walker in the back seat, closed that door, and waved them off. If she started to complain, LuAnn feared there would probably be an accident. She put the key into the ignition and hoped for the best. But, Ruby sat passively in the front seat, saying nothing all the way home. LuAnn made no effort at conversation either and just concentrated on getting her there safely.

The drive to the Dutcher farm went just fine, but no one had considered how Ruby would get from the car to the house, once she got there. She sat immobile in the front seat while LuAnn stood outside by the car door and, frantically, tried to figure out a way to move her. Besides Ruby being a dead weight, LuAnn's stomach was in the way, and their winter coats were another cumbersome barrier. To add to the problem, the temperature had started to drop, and the wind was whirling light snow through the air.

LuAnn tried to be nice. "Ruby, put your legs around this way!" They both tugged and pushed to get them to the side of the seat. She put her arms under Ruby's and tried to lift her to a standing position. The old woman offered no resistance, but gave no help either. Finally, her impatience dictated the approach. "Get up, Ruby! You've got to help me! Put your arms around my neck! You can't just sit there!" The wind blew icy on

LuAnn's legs, and her body was hot with the effort. Perspiration stood out on her forehead, and the old woman's breath came in puffs . . . moist, warm and rancid against her cold cheeks. She turned away, feeling nauseous.

"One! Two! Three! Now, Ruby!" After several attempts, she managed to raise from the seat and plant her feet on the ground. The walker was retrieved from the back seat and situated in front of her. There was a slow push and hitch all the way to the porch. They managed the two steps in the same manner, with LuAnn's arms around Ruby's middle and a push up. By the time the kitchen was reached, they were both exhausted and shaking. Thankfully, they sank into chairs, unable to go any further. LuAnn hoped the cramping she felt in her abdomen didn't mean anything. "Will you be all right, Ruby? I have to go lie down for a while."

* * *

After that ordeal, LuAnn knew one thing for certain. She couldn't help Ruby in her recovery. Ruby knew that too. So, the three of them sat in the living room that night and discussed their options. Finally, Ruby consented to finding an LPN to start helping with her recovery the day after Christmas. "I suppose I can find the money somewhere."

Mack called the hospital explaining their need. The hospital staff had already told Ruby she would need assistance other than her pregnant great-niece. They had a woman lined up and ready to take the job. "I hope they send a decent person that doesn't snoop around my house. I just hate snoops." She gave LuAnn a steely glare.

* * *

The only thing that looked like Christmas, in the Dutcher house, was a small tree that LuAnn had set up and decorated for the table in the living room. Its lights shone brightly on the few packages beneath its boughs. Everyone had been so consumed with Ruby's care and other activities, that Christmas had seemed like a long ways away. But it was here now, and there was no more time to prepare.

LuAnn wished they could go to the midnight church service in Marion. So, after Ruby was settled into bed, she expressed the desire to Mack. Feeling a bit guilty for what she had gone through getting Ruby home and into the house, he agreed. "Well, there's no doubt she will sleep now. Sure, let's get ready and go."

They walked into the church at eleven o'clock and sang carols with the rest of the congregation. Mack had an acceptable tenor voice and joined in. Now that he had a job and life was going better, there was something to sing about.

Her mother had written to say they would be calling Christmas morning. Jane and her fiancé, Chester Wright, would be there, so she could talk to the whole family. Life just kept moving on . . . just as there was no stopping the growth of the baby she was carrying. She had no way to control any of it. But God does, and He will provide for her just as He did for Mary on the first Christmas Day. With the love of the Christmas season all around them, LuAnn hugged Mack's arm close to her.

Nine

Mack's blatant disrespect and rejection of Kate Weatherby, outside the church, had enraged the woman. She wasn't used to that kind of treatment from anyone . . . let alone from the likes of Mack Hanable. To her, he had always been a 'nothing,' not someone to give consideration to or to take seriously. In her selfish mind, the fact that he was married should have no bearing at all. After all, what was LuAnn to her?

Kate's flirtatious aggression and disregard for others had always ended with her desired results . . . and that was whatever happened to please her at the moment. If or when the situation she created became boring or too hard to handle, she could find a way to escape. It was a game she had played most of her life, and the other players were destined to strike out first. Why should Mackenzie Hanable be any different?

* * *

When she was a little girl, Joe Weatherby had loved her beguiling ways and often encouraged them. The way she looked at him, pleading with seductive big, brown eyes, produced the desired results; a new doll, a new bicycle, or some other passion of the moment. If she alluded to tears, he would hold and caress her soft, young body or indulge her with some other trinket. In return, her gratefulness was bestowed upon him in the form of hugs and kisses. It was their game.

As she grew older, she learned that rejecting him could produce great rewards. When she threw a tantrum, Joe would endeavor to appease his daughter, and there seemed to be no limits. These tantrums, among other things, gave her a mink coat when she was a freshman in high school, diamond earrings as a sophomore, a tour of Europe in her junior year, and a new Corvette for graduation.

She had barely been able to earn a business degree at *Stephen's College for Women*, but that held little significance for her future. There was a job in her father's real estate office whenever she wanted it. Joe and

Clare Weatherby had hoped their daughter's four years at a women's college would give her a broader view of the world, help her to understand a woman's role in society, grow up and become responsible. Too late, they realized that a spoiled child grows up to be a spoiled adult.

In reality, she had spent a great deal of time studying other women students, learning ways in which to take advantage of them. She planned to be the winner. Competition unnerved her. It was no surprise when, by the end of her first year in Weatherby's Real Estate Office, she managed to get rid of the most effective and dedicated woman realtor working for the company. A few documents misplaced and a few funds transferred to Irene White's account created enough doubt of the woman's honesty to justify Joe's firing her. Kate insisted on it. "I don't want to be working in an office with an embezzler!"

Deep down in the recess of his conscience, Joe was aware of the truth, but he couldn't bring himself to confront his daughter with it. Instead, he put a call in to a friend in Waterloo at the Hope Realty Company, highly recommending Irene White. He told Irene there was a job waiting there for her if she chose to take it.

Irene felt only remorse for the predicament Joe Weatherby had gotten himself into. She had witnessed enough of Kate's tantrums and manipulation to know he had no control over the girl. Clare Weatherby was no stronger than Joe when it came to their only child. She feared for what could lie ahead for the family and for Weatherby Real Estate, for that matter. Nevertheless, she had packed up her things and moved, leaving her home to be sold. Joe had assured her of a good price.

It wasn't long until other problems began to surface. By the end of Kate's second year at the office, two married men had left their wives and families. After they lost their jobs, she found a great deal of pleasure in dumping them. She was getting bored, and looking for her next victim when Mack drove into the church parking lot.

The men she had picked before were wealthy, and they lavished her with gifts, large and small. She was looking for more of the same, but Mack Hanable intrigued and puzzled her. Until now, he had seemed to be extremely poor. His clothes were shabby, and there was never any money in his pockets. Curiosity was a torment . . . but not for long. In her position at the real estate office, there was privilege to client's financial records. A few phone calls and small lies confirmed what she knew all along. Mackenzie Linn Hanable was virtually penniless. Still, she couldn't get him out of her mind. He was a handsome hunk, and what about that new car? That must represent something . . . hopefully a change in his financial position.

Unaware of his daughter's consuming interest, Joe Weatherby began discussing the purchase of the Dutcher lake property and its future development with some of the contractors in the area. As soon as Kate caught wind of this, she was in her father's office prodding him for information. "Daddy, why didn't you tell me we own the Dutcher lake property? Did you buy it from Ruby? How much did you pay for it?" The amount was significant but not impressive. Still, perhaps she could find a way to get some of the money back for herself.

* * *

The information disclosed by her father hadn't satisfied her. So, she found other ways to probe further into the family's background. Pastor Yokum was a willing informant when she stopped by to inquire about Ruby Dutcher's well-being after her 'terrible fall down the stairs.' "Perhaps she could use some assistance?"

"How kind of you, Miss Weatherby, but Ruby has plenty to keep her going. Charles left her well off. I suspect a large endowment will be left to the church someday." A look of pious pleasure illumined his face.

That was all she needed to know, and Kate began to formulate a plan. The look of amusement and scorn on Mack's face as he looked her over out in the church parking lot had infuriated her. She wasn't used to that kind of mockery. She would see to it that he repented . . . along with that smug, little wife of his.

After leaving Pastor Yokum's office, she propelled the Corvette homeward and came to a skidding stop out in front of her parents' home. The car's door was yanked open and then slammed behind her. The entrance door of the huge colonial house was flung wide and then closed with a crash. The sound of her heels on marble clicked and echoed down the hall, then, thudded on carpet up the stairs and down the hallway into her bedroom. Again, another door was slammed behind her. She stood with clenched fists, breasts heaving, and scornfully looked around her. Her dark eyes fell on the pink canopied bed. With disgust, one by one, she picked up the accumulation of dolls and teddy bears adorning the lace spread and hurled them towards the fireplace that monopolized the opposite end of the room. Porcelain heads cracked and shattered. Beady eyes stared at the ceiling or at the floor.

Every piece of clothing was angrily and impatiently stripped from her body and flung to the floor. Seams ripped, and buttons popped. Then she stood trembling before a full-length mirror. With critical eyes, she did a truthful assessment. Reflected was the fat body of a twenty-five year old woman, looking more like a middle-aged mother of six. The cute chubbiness and curves of her teen years had turned into ugly sags and rolls. Something needed to be done about that. Her hair was good, but a shorter style would be more slenderizing and chic. A look of contemplation replaced the look of anger.

She would begin the plan by losing weight. With Kate, plans often became obsessions . . . if the incentive was good. In this case, it was good enough for her. So, she had one of the secretaries in the office take a full-length picture of her wearing the same knit dress she had worn to church on that "day of scorn." It was posted on the refrigerator in the Weatherby kitchen. "Don't you dare move it! Where are all the fruits and vegetables around this place? Get rid of it! It's fattening!" Demands were issued, and tempers flared. By Christmas Eve, Kate had lost twenty pounds. She had a new shorter hair style and a new wardrobe.

* * *

After their encounter in the parking lot, Mack hadn't seen Kate in church again. Apparently, she had been humiliated enough to stay away. The idea of Kate Weatherby being embarrassed by someone brought a satisfied chuckle to Mack. The score had evened out a little bit. Still, he wondered about her.

* * *

On Christmas Eve, Mack's attention was focused on the new face and body in the choir. Something about her seemed familiar, and he couldn't take his eyes off the woman. *She was gorgeous! Chic! Stunning!* Beautifully manicured hands held the music at an angle partially covering her face. He found his senses aroused. *Damn it!* Then she slowly lowered the sheets, as though doing a strip tease. She looked directly at him, winked flirtatiously, and gave him her brightest smile. It was Kate . . . the Kate he had longed for as a lovesick teenager . . . only much, much better. Their eyes locked, and he couldn't look away. There was no awareness of LuAnn hugging his arm tightly against her body.

* * *

Kate was elated. She had his attention. Now for the next part of her plan. She had to be in a position to make contact with him on a regular basis. It was time to move out of her parents' home and into a house of her own, and she knew the one it would be. It had just gone on the market, a smaller two-story colonial located at the end of Mack's delivery route on Walnut Avenue in Marion. The day after Christmas, she would make an offer, one that couldn't be turned down.

The church service ended, and Mack tore his eyes away from Kate to look down at his wife's dumpy shape. *Not much to attract a guy.* He told himself. LuAnn smiled sweetly up at him. *Why does she have to be so damned nice?* A momentary stab of guilt touched his conscience, but he looked back towards the choir loft in time to see Kate exiting through the side door. A wave of excitement ran through his veins.

* * *

Two weeks later, the wind was blowing frigid particles of frozen rain against Mack's cheeks. He was nearing the end of his delivery route. It would be a relief to get home today, have a hot shower, a hot meal, and crawl into a warm bed. He was beginning to find something comforting in snuggling up to his pregnant wife. Her body was warmer and softer, like a mother cat nursing her kittens.

He mounted the steps to the porch of his last stop, flipped the lid of the mailbox, and placed an accumulation of flyers into its interior. He knew that most of what he delivered today would go out with the trash tomorrow. That was okay with him, as long as he got paid for doing his part.

Across the street, a crew of four men were unloading a moving van and hauling the furniture through the front door of the colonial home. They wasted no time in their struggle against the wind and sleet. Ear flaps were pulled down, and their voices rose over the wailing tempest only to be lost in its fury. The house had been empty for only a few days. A FOR SALE sign had never even gone up out in front. He guessed he would soon know who the new occupants were.

* * *

By the middle of February, Mack was making routine stops at the last house on the delivery route. Kate was more than happy to warm him up before walking back to the post office with the empty mail bag. He had delivered some "occupant" fliers the first day she was living there. As he flipped up the lid of the mailbox, the front door opened, and a warm eager hand with long red fingernails and sparkling with fires from diamonds and rubies was placed on his arm. The fire in her eyes matched . . . hot and seductive. "Aren't you cold, Mack?" she purred. "Come in and get warmed up." Sensuous perfume saturated his brain. The invitation couldn't be turned down. After that day, he left the Dutcher place earlier in the morning and got home later in the afternoon.

* * *

For the next several weeks, LuAnn gave little attention to Mack's schedule. Her own work day was as much as she could handle, and there was much more to think about. There were six weeks to go before the baby was due. Mr. Cummings would allow for as much time off as she wanted, and if she decided not to go back to work, that was OK, too. Becky decided she needed a change from caring for the twins. She found suitable day care for them and looked forward to helping out at the drug store.

Ruby's LPN was still stopping by every day to give physical therapy to the woman and to help her with bathing. Her hip had not healed properly, and she would need continued assistance for quite some time. The housework and much of her care was up to LuAnn. Mack gave them no consideration at all. He was barely there in time to eat his supper, and then he would shower and go to bed. Sometimes she heard him get up in the middle of the night and drive away.

It had been a lonely situation for quite some time. Ruby kept to herself except to use the bathroom or eat supper. Mack scarcely spoke to either of them. What good would it do to confront him? He didn't like confrontation. No one in the Dutcher household had even gone to church together since the first part of February. Ruby wasn't capable of going, Mack wasn't interested in going, and LuAnn was too tired to go.

She would quit work in two weeks. That would give her three weeks to prepare Mack's old bedroom for her parents to use when they visited. A folding screen was set up in the hallway to partition off an area for the baby's bed and chest of drawers. So far, she had made all the necessary purchases herself. If it was a boy, Becky had more clothes than any one baby could ever use. She would be happy to give them away. Other needs could be bought at the drug store at a discount. The time would be filled with preparations.

* * *

"She means nothing to you! She can't give you what I can! Don't you see that? Daddy will help you get started in real estate. You can make a lot of money, and it's such fun meeting all those different people." Kate just never gave up. "You're so handsome! You could sell to any woman, and more women are beginning to invest their money in property. Think about it, Honey, or I might have to start looking for another man that really loves me." Her harping began to get on Mack's nerves. What had he gotten himself into? He had no intention of leaving LuAnn. She took such good care of him. Still, he kept going back to Kate for more.

* * *

Then one afternoon in early spring, Mack stepped into the front hallway of the colonial in Marion, expecting a cozy hour by the fireplace before going home. But instead, Kate greeted him with a savage attack. She had been brooding about their relationship all day, and her dark eyes shot sparks of hate and anger. With both fists, she pounded on his chest. "You son of a bitch! Is that wife of yours so important? Or is it that baby she's going to have? I saw her today. I stopped by the drug store this morning to see her. Should I tell her about us, huh? If you can't, I will." Her screams grew shriller and shriller.

Reactively, he stepped back and quickly grabbed her wrists in a powerful lock to hold off the attack. Her nails raked the left side of his face, and blood trickled down his cheek and around the blue shirt collar.

"Bastard! How dare you! You nothing!" She kneed him in the groin, and he slumped to the floor in agony. "Just look at my wrists! You've bruised me! I'm going to call the police!" She backed away and reached for the phone on the hallway table.

"No, no, Kate, anything you say! I could lose my job!" Then the realization dawned. That's exactly what she wanted. If he lost his job, he might be destined to go to work for Joe Weatherby. He crawled over to her and wrapped shaky arms around her strong, shapely legs. "See, Kate! . . . I'll do anything! . . . I love you! . . . I'll do anything!"

Her rage turned to scorn, but she put the phone down. He obediently limped after her over to the fireplace. She went to the bathroom for a wet washcloth, a towel, and Band-Aids. Lovingly, the blood was cleaned off, and Band-Aids were put over the wounds. "Poor baby!" She kissed him on the forehead. "You can go now. Just remember what you said. 'Anything,' right?"

* * *

The scratches were explained to LuAnn. "Some branches were hanging down, and I wasn't paying attention to where I was going." He didn't need to explain further, but he had to get rid of Kate some how. By now, he realized that she would make hell out of anybody's life. Either that, or he had to get away from her. Maybe that was it. He had gotten away from Mary Lou. Hadn't he? So, he could get away from Kate, too. So, maybe he would put in for a transfer. He doubted that Kate would follow him to another town. She was too dependent on Joe's real estate firm to risk leaving it. That's what he would do, and in the meantime, he would try to pacify her. He didn't want another outburst like the one he had just encountered. Maybe a dozen roses delivered to her office would keep her happy for a while. He would take care of it first thing in the morning.

* * *

Mr. and Mrs. Soppee arrived the day before the baby did. After twelve hours of labor, LuAnn delivered a seven pound baby girl. The mother was delighted, but the father seemed to be preoccupied. "Isn't she beautiful, Mack?" A shrug of his shoulders was the only response. "What shall we name her?" He didn't care. She could pick out any name she wanted. "Then her name is Joyce Marie."

Her parents made up for Mack's lack of enthusiasm. They couldn't get enough of holding their first grandchild. While she was at the hospital, the house was cleaned throughout, and all the bedding was changed. For two weeks, Fern prepared the meals and did the laundry while LuAnn concentrated on being a mother. The Cummings came and brought three diaper sets with ruffles. Francis and Karen brought a sweater, bonnet, and bootie set. Maude gave the new mother a baby book and a rattle. Mack remained aloof and unresponsive to his wife and new daughter.

"Mack is acting so indifferent! LuAnn, why don't you and the baby just come home with us? I don't think he would really care." Clifton Soppee expressed deep concern.

"He just has a lot on his mind right now. He'll get used to being a father." LuAnn never gave up easily.

* * *

But after Clifton and Fern left, she was filled with a deep sorrow and feeling of despair, unlike anything she had experienced before. Perhaps it was a natural let-down, something like what was felt after Christmas and other holidays. She would get over it. She was probably just lonely. Joyce slept most of the time, and Mack was seldom around. Ruby kept to herself in her bedroom or in the living room. She wouldn't even hold the baby. LuAnn was even thankful when the LPN stopped to see Ruby. She had someone to talk to for a few minutes.

* * *

When little Joyce was a month old, Mack asked LuAnn and Ruby to sit down in the living room. He had something to discuss with them. "I've taken a job with the post office in Independence, Aunt Ruby. I've located a house for LuAnn and me, and we'll be moving the end of May. That's just two weeks from now. You'll have to decide what to do. I think you should sell the house and buildings and move into an apartment, but you have to decide for yourself. I don't think you can stay out here alone." His news left few options for Ruby and none for LuAnn.

Ruby contemplated Mack's news. "I've been thinking of moving to an apartment myself, but I figured you and LuAnn would be staying here. Now, I'll have to sell the place. Oh well, I'll call Weatherby's Real Estate tomorrow. Everything comes to an end sometime." Too worn out to be concerned, she leaned back and closed her eyes.

"Aunt Ruby, I was thinking of Well's Real Estate myself. I've heard good things about them." Mack's retort was brisk with a hint of panic. He hoped to keep Kate from knowing his intentions until it was too late for her to do anything foolish. He had been pacifying her with flowers and an occasional piece of jewelry for the past month. The pretense was wearing him out and gnawing at his guts.

"Well, I suppose that's all right. It will be up to you to do the work involved." Ruby conceded to the suggestion without opening her eyes.

Now LuAnn knew what had been on Mack's mind for so long. Of course, the change in living arrangements was exactly what they needed. She had misjudged him. She would miss the Cummings, Maude, Francis, and Karen, but she could drive to see them. It wouldn't be that far. Moving would mean quitting her job, but the idea of leaving Joyce with a sitter was difficult to comprehend, even though Becky had, reluctantly, offered to care for her. She was enjoying the work at the drug store and her newfound freedom away from the twins.

* * *

The ensuing days were spent going through cupboards and closets with Ruby deciding just what she would need and what she would discard. Boxes were stacked in the living room and kitchen . . . one pile for Ruby, the other for Mack and LuAnn to take with them. They could also have any of the furniture they wanted. Ruby's apartment was furnished.

LuAnn and Mack drove to Independence one Sunday afternoon, to see the house he had rented. It was small and old, but in good repair, and it was adequate for the three of them. They would, at least, have their own home. On the twenty-ninth day of May, Ruby was delivered to her apartment in Cedar Rapids. On the thirtieth day of May, the moving van was loaded with most of the furnishings from the Dutcher house, and the Hanable family started their life in Independence.

The daily routine was peaceful at last. Ruby was sitting comfortably in her furnished apartment, not far from her doctor and the hospital. Mack made several trips back to the Dutcher place, "To get it ready for selling," but he finally settled into the new position with the post office in Independence.

Nothing was said about LuAnn going back to work, and she didn't mention it. Mack seemed to have conceded to the situation. "I suppose I can give you half of my paycheck. Half for you and half for me." *Hell!* he reflected to himself, Some weeks he had spent that much on jewelry for Kate. LuAnn knew she would have to budget tightly, but she would manage.

* * *

In the middle of June, the headlines in the *Cedar Rapids Gazette* read, LOCAL WOMAN MISSING. LuAnn got a phone call from Francis. "Did you ever know Kate Weatherby? I understand she attended your church. The paper says she's missing. Some people figure she ran away with a new boyfriend . . . but I don't know. She wasn't the kind to give up her position with the real estate company. She had it made there . . . and she liked nice things. She wouldn't just up and leave that beautiful new house she recently bought either. Didn't Mack know her?" Francis had heard rumors about Mack and Kate Weatherby, but she had never told LuAnn about them. She still didn't. "Maybe you should get a paper and read about it."

LuAnn was compelled to follow her friend's advice. Joyce was put into the stroller and wheeled down to the drug store, where she picked up the paper from the newsstand. From the front page, the beautiful face of Kate Weatherby looked back at her. She took the paper home and thoughtfully read the article.

That evening, she showed Mack the paper, and he intensely studied the picture, and read and reread the account of Kate's disappearance. The paper was shuffled around, folded, and laid down, only to be picked up again. With a sense of discomfort, she studied her husband's face, trying to understand his seemingly ardent concern. He finally pronounced with conviction, "I'll bet somebody killed her!"

"Why would you say that?" LuAnn fired back at him. A sense of panic gripped her, but she didn't know why. "You know how she liked men! Maybe she just decided one of them was worth leaving it all for!"

"No . . . not Kate! That couldn't happen! She would never give up anything for a man! She wanted everything any man had to offer! Then . . . that wasn't enough." Mack's voice rose and then trailed off. He got up and went into the bathroom. The shower ran long and hot. Steam condensed, and water trickled down the window pane and mirror. It was an attempt at purifying his soul.

Part 2

1968

Ten

LuAnn and her two children were sitting on the living room floor, an atlas spread out before them. She was excitedly explaining to Joyce and Jason the route the bus would be taking which would eventually get them to Clarksburg, West Virginia, where the three of them would be picked up by Grandma and Grandpa Soppee. "We'll start right here in Independence, and then we'll go east through Manchester and Dubuque." Her finger traced along the highway. "When we get here to Dubuque, we'll head towards Chicago. See, here, along this highway. We'll go through Galena, Freeport, and Rockford, and then we'll be in Chicago." Her finger hopped along the highway pointing out the towns on the route. "Chicago is a really big city!"

"Then we'll stay for two days with Aunt Jane, Uncle Chester, and Carmen and Roy!" Joyce excitedly finished up the little allegory she had been hearing almost daily for the past week. Her mother couldn't get enough of the account. "Aunt Jane is a teacher, and Uncle Chester is a doctor. Carmen is seven, and Roy is five. They live in a great big house in a very wealthy neighborhood." The little girl's excited rush of words finished out the story. Only this story wasn't one of the fairy tales she loved. It was real!

"You forgot the part about the two dogs and the horses!" Jason chimed in. That was the part he liked the best. Black Labrador Retrievers. He had seen pictures of them. Brown Shetland ponies. He had seen pictures of them, too. He went to the small table in the corner of the living room and pulled open the drawer. He gathered up a handful of well-worn pictures and spread them out on the floor along with the atlas. There were a dozen or more of Jane and her family, home, and animals, having been sent to them over the past eight years. "I'll get to ride the horses! Right?"

"They aren't horses, dummy! They're ponies! Horses are bigger!" Joyce set her brother straight. He was only a year younger, but sometimes she couldn't seem to make him understand just how things really are. Then again, sometimes she wondered if he deliberately acted dumb just to bug her.

"OK, now where do we go? Jason, show us." His finger pointed to Gary, Indiana. "What's next, Joyce?" Her finger went to Fort Wayne. The kids took turns pointing out Dayton and Columbus. After Zanesville and Cambridge, they moved to Wheeling, West Virginia. "Now, where do we go?" Two fingers plopped down on Washington, Pennsylvania, and there was a race to see who could find Clarksburg, West Virginia. It was a tie.

"This is where Grandma and Grandpa will pick us up!" Two excited voices finished up the narrative. Giggles filled the room. LuAnn reached out and pulled the children close to her. The baby smell had left long ago, but that essence still filled her senses. The soft vulnerable warmth of their bodies set a protective flame burning deep inside her. Joyce was a miniature of her Aunt Jane with brown straight hair and bright green eyes. Jason looked very much like Mack, with dark brown hair and brown eyes. The three fell back onto the floor in a heap. Monkeys at play.

⚬ ⚬ ⚬

The last day of school was just two days away, and the day after that, LuAnn and the children would be starting their trip to West Virginia. LuAnn hadn't been "home" since she graduated from high school and married Mack ten years before. When the invitation to her class' ten-year reunion arrived, she knew it was time to go back.

Through the years, she had felt a need to stay close to Mack. Whatever demons were haunting him had, in a way, haunted her, too. But, she, at least, had the support of her parents. Every year, Fern and Clifton Soppee made two trips to Iowa to see for themselves if their younger daughter was as OK as she led them to believe through telephone calls and written correspondence. They always returned to Grafton with doubts nagging at their senses. Yet, ultimately, LuAnn had refused to have her life any other way.

Mack had no one except LuAnn and the children. His Aunt Ruby had gotten continually more fragile and dependent, and now she was spending her final days in a nursing home. Ruby was demanding of Mack's attention, but she had never wanted LuAnn and the children around. The situation remained divisive. Mack needed someone to care for him, and LuAnn had done so, willingly, for ten years now. But she was wearing out, and the trip back 'home' was probably just what she needed.

* * *

Mack would soon be coming home from the post office. She gathered up the atlas and pictures and instructed Joyce and Jason to go to their rooms and do their homework, or read, or whatever would keep them out of their father's way. He never seemed to enjoy the children and often treated them as though they were an unwelcome burden. LuAnn had realized, very early in their marriage, that Mack lacked the capacity to nurture his children. After Jason's birth, she had driven to Deacon's Drug Store and asked Mr. Cummings about birth control pills. He and Becky had been her advisors for many aspects of her life.

* * *

Maude Trout had been a substitute grandmother for the early part of the children's lives. During the summers, LuAnn, Joyce, and Jason spent many mornings and afternoons in the Trouts' backyard watching the developers bulldoze trees and rocks and piles of dirt. The children were mesmerized by the noise and activity as the big machines worked their way around the lake and right up to the yard in which they were sitting. Karen married after graduation from college, and during the last year of Maude's life, her baby played happily on a blanket spread out on the grass. They all watched the new homes being constructed around the lake, envious of those who could afford to build on the Paradise Lake front. After Maude's stroke, Francis accepted the role of grandmother to all three of the children. She moved into Maude's house, and expanded the beauty shop in her old home. Most of what she did now was the management aspect of her business. She relaxed and enjoyed the role of grandmother.

* * *

Joyce and Jason were three and four years old at the time. The children were playing with two neighbor kids in the back yard. LuAnn asked Mack to look out for them while she walked to the A&P to get some eggs. Mack stepped out the back door just in time to see the neighbor kids and his own two picking up handfuls of sand from the sand pile and throwing it at one another. Their behavior and giggles irritated him.

"What in hell do you kids think you're doing?" He stalked out of the house and grabbed Joyce and Jason by the back of their necks. Raged at the other two, "You kids get the hell home!" Squeezing hard, he shoved his own through the kitchen door and into the house. "Goddamned kids, don't you know anything?" Another shove placed the terrified children into chairs, whereby he commenced to tie their hands behind them with pieces of clothesline rope. "You kids are worthless. Do you know that?" Their struggles caused the ropes to tighten up and cut into their wrists. Mack stood staring at the children, rage pouring from every pore of his body. "Damn kids!"

LuAnn heard their wailing nearly a block away. "Oh my God!" She ran the last block, the eggs juggling precariously in their cartons. The vision of the terrified children and their fearful, tear-stained faces still haunted her after five years. But the look on Mack's face was even more disturbing. All of the demons he had been carrying within him seemed to have been unleashed. His eyes focused on another realm of reality, one that she had no knowledge of. She bordered on hysteria herself, but managed to hold together long enough to resolve the situation.

She stood at a distance, afraid his wrath would be turned on her, too. *"MACK! MACK! GET OUT OF HERE AND LEAVE US ALONE! NOW! GET OUT!"* The Satanic-like features and narrowed, smoldering eyes gradually "cooled" into an empty expression. He stared, incomprehensibly, at LuAnn and stalked out the kitchen door. His car pulled away from the house with a roar and stripping of gears. A shower of pebbles and dust were torn up from the street and spewed from behind each rear tire. An angry lion had been released from its cage.

Blanched and shaken, she talked soothingly to the children. "Daddy's just upset. Don't worry. He won't hurt you again, Mama will take care of you." Her own heart was racing. She hoped that was true. Gradually, their sobs subsided, turning into occasional gasps. She untied them and led them into the bathroom. Warm water and bubble bath calmed them down further, as she washed away the fright along with the sand and tears.

This could never happen again, and she came up with a plan to make certain it didn't. "Let's pack our suitcases and go stay with Grandma Maude tonight. Shall we? I'll give her a call and make sure it's OK with her."

They had never stayed with her overnight before, so when LuAnn made the request, Maude knew something was very wrong. "Of course, you can come. Is anything the matter?"

"I'll explain later!" LuAnn got them all ready as quickly as possible and left a note for Mack. It spelled out her demands. 'You will never lay your hands on the children again in any threatening manner. You will never speak to the children again in a hostile way. You will seek psychological help from the mental-health professionals.' With a heavy heart, she drove to the Trout home in Hiawatha. They stayed with Maude for the remainder of the weekend without hearing anything from Mack.

Sunday evening, he arrived at the Trout home with a dozen red roses and promises to do whatever LuAnn wanted. He had never given her flowers before, and she felt moved by his peace offering. He told the children a new swing set was in their yard, and they should come back home to play on it. "How do you feel about that, Joyce? Daddy says he's sorry. Jason, what do you think? Daddy wants us to go home." Children are very forgiving, and they wanted their own house back. Besides, until then, he always impressed upon them the lack of money for a swing set, and now they had one.

"Mack, you go back home now, and we'll think about it for a few days." She needed to be convinced he took her seriously.

Even then, she went against the advice of Maude and Francis. "You're making it too easy for him." However, she followed up on one of their suggestions. She needed to get a job. "Just in case the situation becomes intolerable." With her dependence on him, she was left in a very vulnerable position. The savings account in Hiawatha was slowly being depleted. She was withdrawing a little from it every month since the money Mack provided was never quite enough to meet their needs.

* * *

He held to his promise, and their family life settled into an acceptable routine. Although he spent little time with the children, there was no more abuse. He was certain the dozen or so visits to the psychologist's office had given him 'helpful insights.' She was grateful for his efforts. Eventually, her inquiries landed her a job at the new day care center located in the First Presbyterian Church basement. An added benefit of the position was free day care for her own children.

Still, the past five years had been extremely hard. Her work days started at eight o'clock and ended at five o'clock. She was barely able to make it home in time to get supper on the table by six o'clock. Then she had all of the housework to do in the evening, but she survived it, and, in the process, had learned something about herself. *I can be as tough as the situation requires.*

° ° °

As soon as school was out, her work at the day care center would end. Next fall she would start classes at the Hawkeye School of Technology. She wanted to take up business and interior design, so she could start her own interior decorating shop. But right now, she was looking forward to going back to West Virginia for a whole month's vacation away from the responsibility of pre-schoolers, a home, and husband.

Mack hadn't outwardly approved or disapproved of the trip. He knew she meant to have her way in this venture, so he remained silent. As the day of their departure drew closer, LuAnn had the feeling Mack's fuse was growing shorter and shorter. So, she made certain he was given no reason for an explosion. Supper was precisely at six o'clock, and the children were fed before he ever got home. She gave him plenty of undivided attention.

The departure date and hour was consciously set at a time when Mack would be at work. Nothing he might do was to prevent their leaving. Francis was driving up from Cedar Rapids to take them to the bus station, and to make certain they got off safely.

° ° °

When Mack got home from work on Tuesday, he sat down and ate his supper. He took a short nap in his favorite chair in the living room, got up and left the house, not to return until eleven o'clock or after. This was repeated for the next two evenings, so LuAnn's fears of an outburst did not materialize.

He hadn't told his wife that Aunt Ruby was near death. He didn't want her to change her plans. He needed time to be by himself as much as she did . . . probably more. He even hoped the next month would be long enough for him to take care of the impending business his aunt's death would impose upon him.

° ° °

Francis arrived shortly after eight o'clock, and the bus was leaving at two o'clock. She hoped Joyce and Jason wouldn't be underfoot, so she could have a frank talk with LuAnn. Thankfully, the kids were encouraged to stay outside. "You're going to be sitting for a very long time, so why don't you run around now while you can?" She helped LuAnn pack a canvas bookbag full of small games, paper, and crayons, so they would have something to entertain themselves with on the bus. With each item packed, LuAnn became more excited . . . and apprehensive. It was hard for Francis to interrupt her reverie.

"Do you think anyone will know me at the high-school reunion?" She looked into the mirror and studied her face. "I don't think I've changed that much, do you?" She stood on tiptoes and studied her shape, sucking her stomach in flat. Her hair had darkened, but Francis had put some highlights around her face with the last perm. They both thought the effect was rather striking. "See my new outfits? I spent my last two paychecks on them. Are they worth it?" She held up two new pant suits and a dress for Francis' approval. At mid-morning, she finally collapsed into a kitchen chair.

Francis grasped the opportunity. "How have you and Mack been doing? You know, I've been seeing him around the Dutcher place lately. Do you know why it hasn't been sold by now? It's been what, nine years, since Ruby moved out?" LuAnn's manner changed from exuberance to sober contemplation, but she pushed on. "He always seems to be looking around . . . like he's lost something. I even walked over to talk to him once, but he just said that he 'misses the old place.' Joe Weatherby is putting pressure on him to sell. It's a real eyesore to that wealthy community around Paradise Lake."

"I hadn't thought about that kind of pressure. I know Mack has been acting strange lately . . . like he's ready to blow up or something. I've kept the kids away from him as much as possible . . . and he has been gone a lot . . . But, I guess I'll deal with any problem when I get back. I just want to think about my trip now," LuAnn sipped a glass of juice.

"Talking about when you get back, LuAnn, I think you better just stay out there. I have that feeling, too, like something is about to blow up around here. Everybody that comes into the beauty shop has the same notion. Something is about to happen. Ruby's on her death bed, you know, and you admitted Mack sure is acting strange."

At that point, the children traipsed into the house, thirsty and pleading for a drink and something to eat. Orange juice and a peanut-butter sandwich were handed to each of them. "How much longer, Mom? Isn't it time to go yet?"

"You're right. Go get your showers and put on your traveling clothes. We'll be leaving in an hour." LuAnn finished up the chores in the kitchen, making sure that Mack's supper was ready for him in the refrigerator. After that, he was on his own. Since he didn't seem to know how to cook, he would probably eat most of his meals in the café downtown. She would leave that up to him. "I guess I'd better get myself ready!"

Francis drove LuAnn and the children to the bus depot. They waited for about fifteen minutes before the bus pulled in. LuAnn clung tightly to the tickets and looked anxiously around her, half expecting Mack to show up at the last minute and insist they stay home. That didn't happen. The bus pulled up with a sign reading DUBUQUE AND POINTS EAST. Francis gave LuAnn and the children hugs and placed a paper bag into the hands of each of them. "You may want these for your supper. Buses don't always stop long enough to get a proper meal." LuAnn hadn't given that aspect of their travels a thought.

"Francis, you are the best person in this whole world. I hope I can pay you back some day." A few tears slid down her cheeks. "I don't know what I would do without you."

"Just take care of yourself, and remember what I said. You should just consider staying out there until Ruby's gone and Mack gets himself settled down again. I don't like the feel of what's going on at the Dutcher place. I hate to say it, but Mack's behavior is just plain weird."

LuAnn touched Francis' cheek reassuringly, "Now don't you worry." The three boarded the bus and settled themselves into their seats.

Eleven

Mack hurried along his mail route with optimism and zeal. There was a spring in his step that hadn't been there for a long time. There was a reason for the enthusiasm. It was the last time he would be delivering mail by foot. He had put in for a rural route, and the request was accepted. His legs were beginning to feel the punishment that nine years of trodding sidewalk put on them. Starting a week from Monday, he would be driving his Lincoln out into the country and making deliveries to the folks north and west of Independence. His new route included the Amish community, and he kind of liked those folks. They had a tendency to keep to themselves, and so did he.

He had a week off to meet with the lawyer, O.B. Allbright, to take care of Aunt Ruby's final business. She was no longer lucid, and now everything was up to him. For some reason . . . he didn't mind that. Any day could be the last for the old woman. For some reason . . . he didn't mind that, either.

His Lincoln would serve him well for quite a few more years. He bought it five years ago, trading in Aunt Ruby's Chrysler and the old Ford. It wasn't hard to convince himself that he deserved something plush to ride in, after walking around town all day . . . day after day. Now, he figured the roomy Lincoln was just the right vehicle for delivering on a rural mail route. For the past month, his brain hadn't stopped churning and planning for his next move. Now, he was about to take action.

After finishing up the route, he slid behind the wheel, started up the engine, and headed for the dirt road leading north out of Independence. While scouting out the new route a few days ago, he had seen a FOR SALE sign out in front of a farmstead over towards Otterville. He liked the idea of finding a place out in the country. The little house he and LuAnn had been renting for the past nine years was in much need of repair. With the money from Aunt Ruby's estate, he could most likely buy a place free and clear.

The Lincoln barreled along the curving, dirt road and passed several buggies with Amish families in them. The big car's wheels churned up dust clouds that obscured the view of the buggies until the light westerly breeze could blow the dirt away. The drivers had to stop the horses until the air cleared, and they could see the road ahead of them again. Mack was oblivious to their discomfort.

He had other things on his mind. His eyes searched for the farmstead with the sign out front. He finally found what he was looking for. The property was being offered for sale by Hope Realty Company of Waterloo. The contact to call was Irene White. He wrote down the information from the sign on a small notebook and put it into his pocket. He pulled into the farm yard and stopped the Lincoln. The place looked deserted. In that case, he decided to get out and look around. No one could object to that, certainly. He circled around the house first and then the nearby out-buildings, making mental calculations of their condition and size.

By his appraisal, the house looked to be relatively new and certainly large enough for his family, while the out-buildings were quite adequate and kept in good repair. To the west of the building site, the Otter Creek wound its way through acres of wooded land. He had missed the lake, and he liked the idea of being near water again.

So it was decided, right then and there, that Joyce and Jason should have the opportunity to go fishing just as he once had. At the thought of the two children, a twinge of love touched his heart, and he pledged, resolutely, to respond differently to them from now on . . . to be more of a father. Out there in the country, he could be. When Aunt Ruby was gone, there would be more opportunity to concentrate on his family. Driving from the yard, there was a feeling of certainty that the place would soon be his.

He found the supper LuAnn had prepared for him in the refrigerator and decided to shower before eating. After that, he had to drive to Cedar Rapids Care Center to visit Aunt Ruby. The evening would be long and late again. There was a sense of relief that his family was on their way to West Virginia. There would be no one else to consider for a while, no one else to please. That felt good. Anyway, they would be in Chicago around ten o'clock that night, and if LuAnn did call, he wouldn't be home.

He whistled while showering and then stopped long enough, after shaving, to take a satisfied and conceited look at himself in the mirror. The sideburns and longer hair added considerably to his dark rugged good looks. At thirty-five years of age, some of the younger women on his route had been making a play for him. He guessed he couldn't blame them.

Apparently they were bored . . . staying at home with kids all day. More than one had offered him a hot cup of coffee on a cold, blustery day or a glass of iced tea or lemonade when the temperature was in the nineties. But he always reminded himself of the mail route in Marion that had led him to the home of Kate Weatherby, and he wasn't going to take a chance on a repeat of that experience! He doubted there was a woman alive who wasn't after something from a man. He turned from the mirror and headed for the kitchen and the supper in the refrigerator. *LuAnn sure takes good care of me.*

° ° °

The receptionist at the care center stopped Mack at the desk. "Mr. Hanable, I'm sorry to be the one to tell you this, but your aunt passed away about five o'clock this evening. We tried to reach you, but there was no answer. Her body has been taken to Hoover Funeral Home, as had been requested. We suggest that you call them in the morning to make final arrangements." Miss Jennings offered her hand to Mack in condolence. "We are so sorry. We'll miss her." Mack nodded his head, turned, and walked out the front door. A huge grin spread across his face. He was free to get on with his life . . . his plans. *Praise God!* He got into the Lincoln and, without consideration as to why, headed towards the Dutcher place.

There was still a good hour of daylight. He would look, once more, for the missing keys and locket. He knew that after nine years, the search for the items was hopeless and ridiculous, even obsessive, but he couldn't help himself. He had to keep looking. If he ever found them, perhaps he could get some peace . . . bring the nightmare to a close.

° ° °

Kate Weatherby, of Weatherby's Real Estate Company, was furious when the multiples landed on her desk nine years before. Wells Real Estate had gotten the listing. How dare the Dutcher place be put into the hands of Wells Real Estate! Mack was her 'catch,' and no one had the right to disappoint her. Just where would he go if the place was sold? If his intent was to leave her, well, as far as she was concerned, he didn't have that right either. It was his obligation to consult her first.

She immediately tried to phone the Dutcher residence. The operator informed her that the phone was disconnected. Having to see for herself, she drove out to the place. No one was around, and it appeared to be completely deserted. The door to the house was locked, so she resolutely cupped her beautifully manicured hands against the dirty window panes and peered inside. Every room was empty. Even the curtains had been taken down. Did Mack really think he could get away with this? Every muscle and organ raged as she got back behind the wheel and slammed the door. The Corvette roared off . . . back down the lane.

Back at the office, Kate made phone calls to the right parties. Posing as an interested buyer, she eventually got all the information that was needed. She even managed to get the Hanable's address in Independence . . . as well as the place of Mack's employment, and the location of his mail route.

* * *

Just days after his unexpected exodus from the Dutcher place, Kate drove the streets of Independence until she spotted her prey, with the heavy mail bag hanging over his left shoulder, whistling and striding confidently down Third Avenue North East. As he crossed the street heading for the next house on the route, she wheeled around him and stopped abruptly, cutting him off with the Corvette.

Startled . . . not expecting the combative intrusion . . . adrenaline poured through his system, and he immediately reacted in defiance and challenged her. "What in the hell do you think you're doing, Kate? Get out of here! Don't you get it? I don't want anything more to do with you!" Despite the brave demeanor, he began to tremble.

Leaving the Corvette parked vertical across the street, she sprang from the vehicle. Her dark eyes glowed . . . a ravenous panther in pursuit.

"Just get back in your car and get out of here! Leave me alone!" Mack kept walking, taking care of his job.

With strength of the damned and no intentions of giving up . . . she pounced. Fingernails dug in . . . clenched fists pounded . . . kicks were delivered . . . oaths were screamed.

People up and down the street looked out their doors wondering what in the world the commotion was all about. The situation was critical, and he frantically searched for a solution. In defeat, he raised both arms up to surrender.

"OK . . . OK . . . Kate! Look, if you'll just leave now, I'll meet you at the lake tonight, say, eleven o'clock. We can talk then. Better yet . . . park on Main Street in Hiawatha, and I'll meet you there." With a lop-sided grin that always appealed to her, he persisted. "We can walk over to the lake together." The romantic overtone that he strove to impart, was meant to entice her. As further insurance, he added what he hoped would be a seductive wink. "How does that sound, huh, Baby?"

Perplexed, she backed away. "You better be there, or I'll be down here looking for you!" With clenched fists, she stepped towards him. "Don't you know you can't leave me and get away with it?" A venomous smile dripped from full, pouty lips. "We love each other too much for that to happen!" She slammed back into the Corvette, and, without looking back, sped away.

Obsessed by the challenge and writhing with frustration and anger, Kate drove back to Cedar Rapids. By the time she got to the office, Mack's worth was being critically analyzed. Perhaps, after all, there was no profit in pursuing him. Why bother with anyone that inaccessible? Besides, any money available was really 'just peanuts,' and she had never been particularly fond of peanuts. Still, she wanted the listing for the Dutcher place, so all efforts would be directed to that aspect of their relationship. One more thing to wrangle out of him.

* * *

They met on the Main Street in Hiawatha shortly after eleven o'clock. The night was still and the street deserted. Feeling certain Kate would rapidly tire of a long-distance affair, Mack decided to play the game a little longer.

The lights of the Corvette dimmed, and he stepped out from the shadows of Deacon's Drug Store. Regally, he opened the car door and gallantly offered his hand. She accepted, and they walked side-by-side, brushing shoulders, towards the shadows of the trees in Trouts' back yard. In spite of himself, her full, shapely figure, clad in black pants and shirt, aroused him. As a measure of precaution, his hands were thrust deep inside his pants' pockets.

After leaving the darkness of the trees, they felt their way along the path in the moonlight. He knew every step by heart. Their breathing was deep, and there was an occasional gasp when a foot was misplaced along the path. Otherwise, the only sounds were the forlorn call of lonely night birds and the gentle stir of water-scented air whispering through the trees and brush. Eventually, they came to the barnyard and their stride slackened.

"I want to look at the house, Mack. I've never seen where you lived. It must be a charming place, out here in the country." Seductive fingers crept up his chest beneath his shirt. "Do you have your key? Show me, please?" She smiled innocently and the plan unfolded. "I think I have a buyer for it already. But, I do wish you had listed the place with me. After all, a single girl needs as much help as she can get."

"That sounds fine with me. I have my key, and there's a flashlight in my car. I left it parked at the end of the lane and walked over to meet you. Wait right here by the house." He was apprehensive and wondered what she had in mind . . . probably a sex orgy of some kind. Well, he could put up with that one more time, too . . . if necessary.

The flashlight was retrieved from the glove compartment of the Ford, and they entered the house. Moonlight flooded through the curtainless windows, and their hollow foot steps echoed through the empty rooms. A ghostly presence was felt, and sweat broke out on Mack's forehead. Reluctantly, he escorted Kate throughout the downstairs . . . shining the light here and there at her request.

"We have to go upstairs, Mack. I insist that we go upstairs." Appeasing her once more, they mounted the steps to the second floor. A little moonlight filtered through the hallway window, and, mysteriously, there was a soft, mellow glow coming from the bedroom Mack and LuAnn had shared. "In here, Mack."

When they entered the room, the flames from a vast array of candles, sitting on the floor, flickered and danced in the air coming through the opened windows. Handcuffs, ropes, and a whip lay on the floor beside a blanket and pillow. Mack froze and stared in disbelief. "What the hell!"

"This is the ultimate, Darling!" Kate grabbed the flashlight from his hand and threw it to the floor. The clatter resonated like cymbals let drop, and its light went out. "We don't need that anymore." Candlelight burned in her black eyes, as she commenced to unbutton his shirt. Her passion-heated body pressed close. "I was here earlier, Darling, and I got our little love nest ready. I have a key, too. Realtors have access to keys, you know."

His terror was darker than the night. When he gained his senses, adrenaline coursed through every vein, and she was shoved aside as he lunged through the doorway. "Come on! We're getting out of here!" She stood silhouetted against the eerie light of the flickering candles, Satan stepping from the pit of hell. "I'm telling you to come on! Get out of here! This is my property! Leave! Now!" His voice rose to a higher decibel with each command.

His knees buckled unwillingly, but he staggered to the top of the stairs and grasped the railing. From behind, demonic arms wrapped around his body in a steel vice, as fingernails raked and dug in an effort to locate fleshy eye sockets. "Damn you! Leave me alone!" He turned and grabbed for the groping, persistent hands. She shoved, and they fell one over the other, tumbling to the bottom of the stairs.

Dazed and sore, Mack got to his feet. "Come on, give me your hand." With shafts of moonlight coming through the windows as illumination, he reached down to pull Kate to her feet, but sharp teeth clamped into his arm. "You scheming bitch!" He reacted with a powerful backhand across her face.

Staggering, he crossed the room over to the door and threw it open. Moonlight streamed in, and he could see blood dripping from Kate's nose. "I'm sorry I hit you. Come on, let's be two civilized human beings about this. I'll wait to sell the house . . . if that's what you want . . . I'll wait to sell until I can change the listing over to you." He struggled to establish control over body and voice.

Pushing to her feet, Kate screamed. "That might do!" Lunging towards the door, she suddenly turned. "Here, take your cheap jewelry back!" She dug into her pants pockets and commenced to throw fistfuls of jewelry into the dark corners of the kitchen. "You no good bastard! Why couldn't you go to work for Daddy? We could have had it so good!" Earrings, bracelets and rings bounced off walls and went pinging into the sink and against the cupboards. When the pockets were emptied out, she staggered out the door into the moonlight. Seemingly defeated, she sank onto the front steps, head hanging down between her wide-spread legs.

Gathering his wits, Mack used the reprieve to dash back upstairs and extinguish the sputtering candles, muttering, *Damn woman! She could've burned the place down!* Then, he followed outside after her and locked the door. Wanting to get the night over with, he pointed towards the barn, "That way! We go that way!" Precaution was taken to stay behind her, to be aware of her every move.

Suddenly, she sprinted off into the black shadows of the barn. The demon beast was seeking its dark habitat. Mack kept on. All was quiet as he ambled down the path towards the lake, eyes alert for movement. From the moonless depths surrounding the barn, a black form charged menacingly towards him with a piece of wood held tightly in both hands and raised to strike.

"Damn you, woman!" He reached out to protect himself from the blow, and his hand grazed her neck, getting tangled up in the chain of her locket, the first piece of jewelry he had given to her. It broke from her neck, and the locket and chain went flying off into the darkness. *To Kate from your lover Mack* was etched inside the heart.

"Ouch! . . . You Son of a Bitch! . . . That hurt!" Her knee came up to hit him in the groin, but the action was anticipated. Deftly, he dodged and pushed her aside. His contemptuous laugh tantalized her rage. "You'll be sorry! You'll be sorry!" Her screams echoed from the surface of the lake, as she, once again, raced off and down the path. Footsteps echoed and then were silent. The stealthy, wild beast prowled out there somewhere in the moonlight.

Mack was already sorry. He didn't think he could be any sorrier for having fallen into Kate's lair. Right now, it was best if she just kept going. There was no doubt she could get back to her car all right. He would focus on something else. The house needed to be cleaned up. With a sigh, he turned and headed back down the path.

Only a dozen steps were taken when he heard heavy breathing over his shoulder. He turned just in time to duck the blow of a fifteen pound rock. She came at him with the fire of hell blazing in dark, wild eyes, and blood and sweat trickling from her nose into her mouth and around her neck. Her face was streaked and smeared, twisted and eerie in the moonglow. A vampire? A demon? One of Satan's messengers?

With tremendous force, he shoved the creature aside, and she fell sprawling. Her head hit a large rock that protruded from the ground. There was a sickening sound, as a jack-o'-lantern splattered on Halloween. Her body twitched, and there was a deep agonized moan. She lay very still with blood oozing onto the rock from the back of her head. Dazed and in disbelief, he stood and stared for several minutes. There was no more movement . . . no sound. A peaceful feeling of relief and acceptance gradually seeped through him. Their battle had finally ended.

He tried to think. He had to think. What was he to do now? In the stillness of the moon-drenched night, he sat down beside the lifeless body . . . head in hands . . . trying to gain composure. A cool breeze suddenly blew up and rustled the leaves of a nearby tree. Night birds called to one another, and frogs croaked contentedly at the water's edge. The normalcy helped to clear away the chaos bombarding his brain. No one would believe it was an accident. He didn't stand a chance against the powerful Weatherbys and their attorneys. He wasn't even sure she was dead . . . maybe just knocked out.

Regardless, he went back to his car and got two lengths of rope from the trunk. He picked up two cement blocks from the side of the barn, and there in the moonlight, on June 12, 1959, Mack tied Kate's wrists together and her ankles together, attached cement blocks to the ropes and dumped her body off the end of the dock into the deep, dark water of the lake.

The house had to be cleaned up, but right now, he had a bigger problem. Kate's Corvette on the Main Street of Hiawatha put her near the Dutcher place. He had to get her car away from there, and it was already after two o'clock in the morning. Were the keys left in the car, or had they been in her pockets? She had emptied out her pockets in the frenzied trashing of the jewelry, so maybe they were someplace in the kitchen. Time was getting critical, and he knew where the spare was kept, so he took off running. He had to get his plan underway.

Racing with time around the lake, sweat poured from his body . . . smarting his face and saturating his clothes. For once, he was thankful for the Army's relentless training. All was silent and deserted on Main Street. The keys weren't in the ignition, so the spare was taken from the ashtray. Using side streets and alleys, he drove the Corvette into Cedar Rapids. It was a conspicuous car, bright yellow with chrome wheels.

His destination was the southeast side. With luck, it would appear that the car was stolen, and the police would assume the person who stole the car was, also, responsible for Kate's disappearance. He finally found a suitable location behind an abandoned house with an old wooden fence around it. Fingerprints were wiped off with his shirt.

It was a good seven miles back to the Dutcher place and his own car, so he took off running down alleys and across lawns. It was nearly sunrise by the time he reached the destination. Needing a shave . . . dirty, and exhausted . . . he looked like a transient to anyone who may have seen him.

He went back into the house. To his relief, there were just a few drops of blood on the floor so his shirt was removed and they were wiped away. Upstairs, he gathered the candles and placed them in the blanket. The wax was scraped from the floor with his jackknife. Downstairs, he gathered up the jewelry and placed it in his pocket. He ran, full-speed, down to the lake and threw it out into the water with all the strength he could muster. The blanket and its contents were placed into the trunk of the Ford to be disposed of later. Finally, he drove to a pay phone and called LuAnn. "Ruby was sick last night, so I decided to stay the night in Cedar Rapids. I've had a hard night, but I'll be home soon."

As Mack drove out of Hiawatha, the rain started pouring down. It was only then he thought about the blood on the rock and the trail of blood leading to the dock. *Praise God!* He didn't have to go back. The rain would take care of everything outside. That afternoon, when the rain stopped, he went back to check. Sure enough, all traces of blood and footprints were gone, but the keys couldn't be found, and the locket was nowhere to be found either.

* * *

For nine years, he had periodically scoured the house and yard without either of them showing up. It was time to let the nightmare go, to put the past to rest. With Ruby's death, he was certain he could do just that.

So, instead of driving out to the Dutcher place, he stopped at the Dairy Queen and treated himself to a hot fudge sundae. It was time to get on with life.

* * *

On June 13, 1959, Maude Trout went outside, early in the morning, to enjoy the beginning of a new day. Something shining in the grass drew her attention. She left her seat in the swing on the back porch and walked across the lawn to investigate. It was probably a gum wrapper, but she decided to find out. A little exercise never hurt anyone. She stooped over and picked up a set of keys. On the ring was a gold medallion with the initials KW engraved on it. *Hmm, that's strange, but then again, a lot of people cross through the back yard going one place or another. I'll just keep them and see if anyone stops to inquire about lost keys.* Maude took the keys into the house and threw them into her junk drawer in the kitchen. The old lady immediately forgot about them.

⁂

On June 15, 1959, LuAnn drove to Hiawatha to visit Maude. Just before leaving for the drive back to Independence, she decided to walk over to the lake and the Dutcher place. Once the construction was started, she wouldn't have access, and the equipment was already being put into place.

As she rounded the corner of the barn, a glint of something in the sunlight caught her eye, probably a piece of broken glass. But it wasn't broken glass. It was a gold heart locket, and a broken chain laid nearby. She opened the locket, and her heart froze. The inscription read, *To Kate, from your lover, Mack.*

So that's why Mack was gone so much! To be with Kate Weatherby! Because Kate hadn't been attending church services since Christmas Eve, LuAnn thought she was probably involved with some man. In fact, it looked like she was! With her husband, in fact! LuAnn put the locket and chain into her pocket. She would need time to think the situation through before confronting Mack. It could just drive him away, and maybe she didn't want that to happen.

At home, the broken locket lay at the bottom of her underwear drawer for nine years, concealed in a small jewelry box, placed into a small plastic bag.

⁂

When Kate's car was found hidden behind the wooden fence, surrounding the yard of an abandoned house, there was no need to confront Mack. Apparently, the abduction occurred on her way home one night, and no body was ever found. The police conducted a long and intensive investigation, but nothing ever came of it. The case remained open, but Kate was gone. One way or another, Kate was gone. The woman was of no consequence anymore, but the locket was still kept hidden beneath the underwear. For some reason, she could just never dispose of it.

⁂

After Maude's death, Francis cleaned out her mother's house. The junk drawer in the kitchen contained a set of keys with the initials KW engraved on a gold medallion. *That was odd.* She didn't know anyone with those initials, but she decided to put them back where she found them. You just never know, perhaps her mother had a good reason for keeping them.

Twelve

LuAnn chose seats that were across the aisle from each other. The canvas bag, containing activities for Joyce and Jason, and the knitted bag, containing needlework for herself, were placed on one of them. She hoped it wouldn't be necessary to give up the fourth seat to a passenger. Joyce agreed to sit beside the bags and let Jason sit beside their mother. "You can trade seats at one of the stops if you agree to do so." She wasn't going to put herself in the middle of any conflict that may arise between the two children. She worked hard at teaching them compromise, and most of the time, her efforts paid off.

At this point, the bus was only half-occupied. LuAnn glanced at her watch. Just one more minute, and they would be on their way. She looked out the window and waved at Francis, who was standing on the sidewalk, determined to see them off safely. They blew kisses to one another, and she sat back down in the seat. The bus driver took his position at the wheel, adjusted his cap, and prepared for the drive east.

Suddenly, a young Amish mother and her daughter stepped into the Greyhound. The woman thrust two tickets towards the driver. "We made it, Susie! Praise God! We made it!" Her head nodded towards the driver, seeking affirmation.

"Yes, you did, Mam . . . do you have suitcases?" The question was cordial, having been resigned to receiving last minute boarders years ago.

"Yes, sir, we do. We're sorry to be late."

Perspiration was creeping out from under the woman's black cap and running down the sides of her flushed face. A large, white handkerchief was pulled from an apron pocket and dabs were taken at her brow. She was a pretty woman, probably very near LuAnn's age, with curly brown hair showing around the edge of her cap.

The daughter appeared to be around eleven. Brown curls were escaping from under her cap as well. Since they were both wearing a black cap and black shoes with a light blue apron over a dark blue dress, she was a miniature of her mother.

The woman looked around the bus to see which seats were available. She chose the two directly in front of Joyce, and they hurriedly seated themselves. Nervously, she rose and looked out the window to make certain the driver was loading their suitcases and parcels. When she saw that her husband was monitoring the procedure, she sank back into the seat and sighed. With a reassuring smile and nod, she reached over and lovingly patted her daughter's arm.

* * *

LuAnn recognized her immediately. It was Sarah Yoder. LuAnn had been buying eggs from her mother-in-law for the past five years. Martha Yoder always did the egg selling. She had fallen from the hayloft years ago, and the inability to seek prompt medical attention for a broken leg, had left her slightly crippled. As she aged, the handicap worsened. However, she still managed to collect the eggs, clean them, and put them into the cases for selling, most of which were sold to a steady stream of faithful customers, LuAnn being one of them. Sarah Yoder helped out as well. She made sure the chickens were fed and watered. She watched for any sign of sickness among the hens, destroyed the infected birds, and dispensed medicine as needed into their drinking water. During those five years, LuAnn had learned a few things about the egg business.

* * *

She wondered what circumstances put Sarah and her daughter on the bus. To her knowledge, the Amish seldom traveled anywhere at a great distance, especially the women. They were noticeably disheveled and nervous, so it wasn't a good time to initiate any conversation. Perhaps it was their first time on a Greyhound passenger bus. There was a chuckle at her thoughts. It was her own first time anyway!

The driver closed the door and the bus pulled away from the depot, drove a half block to Main Street, took a right turn, and made its way through two stop lights. It passed the hospital and was soon rolling along through the countryside. The first stop would be in Manchester. After that, it would just keep going unless a red flag was pulled down at the stop indicating a passenger wished to board. Otherwise, if no passengers wanted off, the bus would keep going until it reached Dubuque.

All those who boarded in Independence were soon asleep from the lullaby motion of big tires on concrete and the monotonous roar of the motor. Excitement and apprehension gave way to a peaceful rest.

* * *

Dubuque was their first real stop . . . twenty minutes for loading and unloading passengers and their luggage. By this time, the rest rooms were a necessity. The brief interlude gave LuAnn a chance to approach Sarah. "I believe you're Sarah Yoder. I get eggs from Martha." She waited for some sign of recognition.

Slowly, a smile spread across the Amish woman's face. "Oh, yes, of course. I remember you. Are you on my bus, too? Where are you going?"

"I'm going to Grafton, West Virginia, to visit my parents. I haven't been there in ten years, but I'll be visiting my sister in Chicago first. I haven't seen her in ten years either. She's a teacher." It was satisfying to share her happiness. "Where are you going?"

"My daughter, Susie, and I are going to Lancaster, Pennsylvania. It has been ten years since I've been home, too. We just got word from my mother yesterday that Father is quite ill. He had a heart attack and is in the hospital." Tears began to well up. "Henry told me I should go home. He wanted Susie to go with me . . . so my parents could see at least one of our children. We have four more, you know . . . but we decided one was enough to take on such a long trip."

LuAnn felt a twinge of guilt for her happiness. She gave Sarah's hand a gentle squeeze, and the two women walked towards the bus. Joyce and Jason had made friends with Susie while the children waited for their mothers. "Mom, can Jason and I sit clear to the back of the bus on the bench seat? There's room for three back there if Susie wants to sit with us? Please Mom?" Joyce pleaded with her eyes . . . giving full expression to the puppy-dog look LuAnn found so hard to deny.

"That sounds fine with me, but Mrs. Yoder will have to decide if the arrangement is all right for Susie. Is this something Susie wants to do, or is it all your idea?" LuAnn knew her daughter well. She looked questioningly at Susie and then at Sarah.

"Do you want to, Susie?" Sarah asked.

She shrugged her shoulders . . . a shy smile on her face, "I guess so."

"Well, then if that's settled, we may as well sit together, too. That is . . . if you want," LuAnn suggested to Sarah. The seating arrangements were reorganized just before the bus filled up.

The children occupied themselves with activities from the bag for the remainder of the long trip into Chicago. Stops in Freeport and Rockford gave them twenty minutes to stretch their legs and use the rest rooms. They shared parts of the lunches Francis had provided. She had been very generous, so there was plenty to go around.

By the time the Hanables left the bus, the two women and their children had become friends. They would try to reconnect on their trips back home at the end of the month, probably in Washington, Pennsylvania.

* * *

Jane wondered if she would recognize her sister. It was ten years since LuAnn married Mackenzie Hanable and ran off to Iowa. She had gotten periodic reports from their parents, but without seeing for herself, that didn't mean much. Parents so often overreact to their children's situations. As a mother herself, she knew this to be true. She wondered if LuAnn would recognize her. She had gained nearly twenty pounds, and there were streaks of gray near her temples. Crow's feet were beginning to show up around her eyes, and makeup did little to disguise them.

She had turned down Chester's offer to go with her to the bus station. She felt the need to wait there by herself . . . to be alone with her sister for a while . . . to get reacquainted. In many respects, LuAnn was a stranger. The two were never close . . . not even as children.

So, she stood and waited while the night closed in on the city. Lights came on, and shadows filled the corners and crevices of the waiting room. When she walked, dirt grated on the worn floor beneath her feet. There was a noticeable stench of garbage cans that needed to be emptied and toilets that needed to be cleaned. From somewhere came the faint aroma of greasy popcorn. The fumes of gas and oil intermingled with it all. A few other people quietly milled around, restless and bored; some sitting on benches, yawned and fidgeted . . . apparently waiting for the same Greyhound to arrive. She felt uncomfortable and a bit frightened. Airports seemed much more secure.

Finally, the huge bus pulled into its parking space, and people began to emerge. A slim, young woman stepped down to the sidewalk dressed in a smart-looking pant suit and carrying a knitted bag along with her shoulder purse. *LuAnn always carried a shoulder purse.* Two children followed after her. The girl, looking very much like herself twenty-five years ago, carried a canvas book bag. The boy, with shaggy dark good looks, had to be Mack's. "LuAnn! LuAnn! Is that you?" Jane wound her way towards them pushing through the crowd of people.

The three somnolent travelers turned towards the cheerful voice. Relief spread over their faces, and smiles lit up their eyes. They had made it! They were really in Chicago, and Jane was there to meet them! The sisters looked each other over . . . as sisters would. Tears ran down their cheeks, and they embraced, unwilling to let go. Finally, LuAnn pulled the two children over to them. "This is Joyce, and this is Jason. Say hello to your Aunt Jane."

"Hi!" was echoed in unison. The children allowed her to pat their heads and caress their shoulders and backs. Then Jason looked around with a quizzical expression on his face. "Where are Uncle Chester, Carmen, and Roy?"

"They're probably in bed and asleep by now. You'll get to see them in the morning." She chucked him under the chin. How could anyone look so much like his father? "Let's get your luggage. We have over an hour's drive ahead of us."

The four of them claimed the suitcases, loaded themselves into Jane's station wagon, and began the drive down the busy streets towards the Highland Park residential area. It was after midnight when the tired trio settled into the guest rooms at the home of Dr. and Mrs. Chester Wright.

* * *

Mack was up before sunrise on Saturday morning. He was anxiously waiting to put calls into the Hoover Funeral Home, O.B. Allbright, and Irene White. He would call them in that order. Breathing deeply, he paced around the kitchen, a hungry gleam in his eyes, a tiger in its cage about to be fed.

Feeling stifled by the confines of the house, he shoved through the living room and barged out the front door. He circled the yard and went through the back door into the kitchen, where he poured another cup of coffee. With cup in hand, he strode out the front door again.

The lawn needed mowing, but it would have to wait. He went out to check the gas in the mower's tank when the phone rang. It was probably LuAnn. She said she would call when they got to her sister's in Chicago. He decided not to tell her about Aunt Ruby's death. Why bother her with that bit of news? "Hello . . . great Honey . . . just fine . . . sure, I am . . . say hello to the kids . . . have a good time, now . . . see you in a few weeks." He looked at the clock and dialed the funeral home.

° ° °

When all the calls were completed, he had an appointment with Irene White out at the Harris farmstead near Otterville at ten o'clock, an appointment with Hoover Funeral Home for three o'clock, and an appointment with O.B. Allbright at four o'clock.

He decided to drive out to the Harris farmstead right away. He wanted to get a genuine feel for the place before the realtor was there to distract his attention in any way. According to her, there were forty acres offered with the buildings. Much of it was wooded. The Otter Creek ran through the west twenty acres. There were five acres of pasture. The house and buildings were set on five acres, and ten acres was tillable should he want to plant it into something. His mind raged, unchecked, and his excitement grew.

° °

When Irene White wrote the name *Mack Hanable* on the note pad, something seemed to ring a bell. She had heard that name before, but then, so many names passed by her on a daily basis, that she didn't give it another thought.

She pulled into the Harris farmyard shortly before ten. Her perspective buyer was already there. His big black Lincoln was parked near the kitchen porch, and it looked as though it belonged there. This was one of her favorite properties. The price was out of range for most people, but it appeared that Mack Hanable might be able to afford it. She reached over to the passenger seat for the keys to the house and slid out of the old, beat-up station wagon.

Mack came striding . . . with a military gait and intent . . . from around the back of the barn . . . shoulders squared and head held high. Much to her surprise, he was wearing fatigues and combat boots, . . . not what she had expected. Mustering up a degree of enthusiasm, she waved and flashed a cordial smile. "Hello there! I see you beat me here!" With a spring in her step, she walked towards him. As they approached one another, the significance of his name occurred to her. She had seen him, only briefly, once before, but the occasion and his rugged and dark good looks had left an impression.

* * *

It was hard to forget the impression that Kate Weatherby had left, too. That's where she had seen him with Kate Weatherby, at a realtor's convention in Des Moines. At the time, she wondered what Kate had in mind for him. During her years with Weatherby Real Estate, Irene had watched as she maliciously played games of seduction that ended up destroying men and their families. She had inquired of others, as to who he was, thinking the young man needed some helpful advice. All anyone knew was "His name is Mack something, maybe Noble, or Hanable, or something like that." Most everyone felt certain he was married and, probably, had children. That was the type Kate chose . . . the most vulnerable. When she mysteriously disappeared, Irene had felt a sense of relief for him and any others Kate could get her claws into.

* * *

Now she offered her hand. "I'm Irene White, and you're Mr. Hanable . . . I assume." He nodded. "I imagine you want to see the house first. Come along." She led the way to the side facing towards the road. They mounted two cement steps and then crossed the broad, wooden porch that extended across the front of the house. Their footsteps rang hollow and lonely outside the deserted home. She inserted the key into the lock.

They entered a small foyer, and the sense of desertion followed them inside. "There is a closet here." She opened the door. "That makes it nice for guests coming in from the front." She smiled. "There's a place for boots and coats." She closed the door. "This way is the living room. It's really quite spacious." She gestured with an experienced hand. "The picture window lets in the afternoon light. Through here is the dining room." She led the way. "As you can see, there is plenty of room for seating." She continued, "Then the kitchen has lots of counter space. And look at those beautiful cupboards!" She again gestured and looked at him for a comment. None. "There is a large pantry over here." She opened the door and closed it. "Then there are two bedrooms on this floor . . . down this hallway . . . and a large bath." She led the way. "There are two more bedrooms upstairs . . . and another larger bath." Again, she led the way.

They wound their way through the house with Mack non-committal . . . only nodding his head, 'yes,' in agreement, occasionally. Their echoing footsteps and her solitary recital began to wear on her nerves. At the end of their tour, Irene inquired, "Well, Mr. Hanable, what do you think?" By this time, she was feeling certain he was 'just a looker' and not an enthusiastic one either. She waited for any comments he might have to offer.

"How much do you want as a down payment, Ms. White? I believe the property is listed at one hundred and twenty-five thousand. Will a check for twenty-five thousand do?" He had already made up his mind to purchase the property even before going through the house. With nearly thirty thousand dollars in his account, the check was good.

"That will do nicely, Mr. Hanable." She swallowed hard and tried not to appear surprised. "I will write up the contract. Which bank or loan company do you prefer to go with? I can help you secure financing for the remainder."

"That won't be necessary. Just give me thirty days, and I can have the rest of the money." Most of Aunt Ruby's assets were already in his name. He anticipated no problem.

"This is highly unusual, Mr. Hanable. Let me run this past Hope Realty, and I'll get back with you by Monday afternoon. For now, you've bought yourself a farmstead." Irene drove from the yard with a signed contract, a check for twenty-five thousand dollars . . . and a lot of doubt in her mind.

* * *

By three-fifteen that afternoon, the final arrangements were made for Ruby's burial. The preliminaries had been made six months ago while she was still in control of her faculties. There would be a graveside service Monday morning at ten o'clock, conducted by Pastor Yokum.

* * *

At four o'clock, O.B. Allbright ushered Mack into his law office. "You understand, I'm sure, that most of Ruby's estate is gone. The last three years in the nursing home depleted most of her assets." He studied

Mack's face before going on. "All that remains of her estate is the Dutcher place in Hiawatha. With my encouragement, she hung onto that piece of property, anticipating the increase in value over time. Six months ago, Weatherby Real Estate offered her two hundred thousand dollars. Ruby accepted the offer with the stipulation that the property would remain in her name until the time of her death. Upon her death, a check for that amount would be placed into an account bearing your name, Mackenzie Linn Hanable." O.B. Allbright paused, waiting for Mack to comment. What was there to say?

He went on. "Here is the bank book bearing that account." He handed Mack the slim, black document. "You are to be given sixty days following Ruby's death to remove anything of importance from the residence. However, legally, the property is now in the hands of Weatherby Real Estate. Do you have any questions?"

Mack took the book, studied its contents, and satisfied that it was all in order, put it into his pocket. He swallowed hard. "Will there be any more expenses connected with Ruby's care or burial or anything like that?"

"Most of the expenses were anticipated and allowances were made for them. I will prepare a financial statement for you in the next two weeks. It is possible that a few thousand dollars will still be available to you. I will let you know. She had also paid my fees in advance, if that is a concern of yours." O.B. Allbright folded his hands on the desk, and a satisfied expression enshrouded his jovial features.

Mack had trusted his aunt's lawyer for the past ten years. He had no cause to doubt the man's trustworthiness now. Besides, there was two hundred thousand dollars in his pocket, and he couldn't fault that.

"What does Joe Weatherby plan to do with the property?" Suddenly, the reality hit him. The man would be around the place . . . a lot. Maybe he would find . . . no! He brushed off the panic . . . no! . . . He wouldn't let that nightmare saturate his brain again! *Forget it Mack!*

"Why, I believe he plans to dredge out the western bank of the lake . . . back into the Dutcher property. He has never allowed any building on that side . . . apparently with this project in mind. The expansion will make room for about a dozen more homes with a lake front. He's an ambitious man . . . you know."

* * *

Mack convinced himself there was nothing more to worry about. It was time to celebrate. Before leaving the city to drive home, he pulled into the Red Lobster parking lot. Within minutes, the largest lobster in the tank was pulled out and being prepared for his dinner. He never had lobster before, or even tasted it, but it was the most expensive item on the menu, and he intended to get anything that struck his fancy. The most expensive wine was brought to the table, and the meal was finished with a rich dessert.

The bill came to over one hundred dollars, and he left the waiter a fifteen dollar tip. Mackenzie Linn Hanable was in the money! Monday, he would own a choice piece of property. He would give the landlord notice, and by the time LuAnn and the kids got back, he would be able to usher them into their new home.

Thirteen

Saturday morning, June 1, 1968, LuAnn woke up to a warm sun shining through the lace curtains of one of the guest bedrooms of the Wright home located in the Highland Park area of Chicago. With sleepy eyes, she surveyed the surroundings. She was here. She was really here! Lazily . . . she stretched, enjoying the soft caress of the white, silk sheets against her skin. Satin-covered pillows, reminiscent of peppermint candies strewn on a bridal table, were stacked haphazardly at the foot of the canopied bed covered with an antique lace spread. A swag of the same pinks, blues, and yellows was elegantly draped over the tops of the curtains. The wall across the room was papered in the same floral hues. The remaining walls were a soft yellow. The floor was covered with a thick, plush carpet of a pink rose color. The furniture, in a soft gray tone, complimented and energized the pastel colors.

She didn't have a clue as to the style or period, but was keenly aware of the comfort felt by being surrounded with such elegance. She coveted the privilege of waking up to such bliss every morning. All women should have that opportunity, perhaps not with such elegance, but certainly with a sense of style. If she was ever going to be an interior decorator, there was a great deal to learn.

Adjacent to the bedroom, there was a bath. What a luxury . . . not to have to walk down the hallway to get there and then to be in competition with two children or a husband besides. She slid out from between the sheets and ran her hand over the smooth sensuous fabric, once more. Then she walked across the room, enjoying the petal softness of the plush carpet under bare feet. Back to reality . . . she opened the beat-up suitcases and removed familiar clothing needed for the day.

A glance at the clock indicated the morning was already half gone, but she wasn't going to be in any hurry. Last night, baths had been rushed just to get the day's travel grime washed away, but this morning, time wasn't going to be a dictator. She intended to enjoy every minute the comforts provided. Invitingly, the bath was meticulously coordinated with the bedroom in style and color. A mental note was made of this and filed away for future consideration.

Scents floating from the room were intoxicating, causing her nose to twitch inquisitively. She was as happy as a rabbit in the garden patch about to sample the produce, and, unashamedly, she indulged in the extravagant array of sensuous-smelling soaps and shampoos. Each crystal container was uncapped and the fragrance issued was passed beneath her nose to be scrutinized. When the choices were made, she stepped into the shower. For fifteen minutes, soft, bubbly water played seductively over her hair and skin. She hummed softly and fantasized that this would be a mermaid's ultimate experience. Reluctantly, she shut off the water and stepped to the bathroom floor. After drying with one of the large, soft, yellow, towels, a bottle of lavender lotion was chosen, and its contents was spread slowly and lavishly over her body.

As she stepped into a blue chambray sun dress and began pulling it up over her breasts and shoulders, the voices of children came up to the bedroom window from the yard below. She drew the curtains aside and looked down towards the spacious lawn. There was a handsome, slightly gray-haired man, Chester, no doubt, leading two dark brown ponies. One of her children sat on each of them. Two other children, Carmen and Roy, of course, ran alongside, shouting out their knowledge of horsemanship to the new equestrians. The dogs followed at their heels, tongues hanging out and canine smiles on their faces.

The scene was wonderful to behold, and a smile played on her lips. Movement of the curtains drew Jason's attention, and he looked up at his mother. "Hi, Mom! Get down here! See what we're doing!" He waved an energetic arm, and a huge grin spread across his beaming face. Joyce, too, looked up at her mother and smiled but, apparently, was feeling too sophisticated to wave back. Chester took note of LuAnn's presence and gestured toward the children mounted on the ponies. A nod of his head indicated, all was well.

There was a light knock on the bedroom door, and it was pushed open a crack. Certainly, it was her sister, impatient to get the day started. "Come in, Jane."

Her head poked through the narrow opening. "Good morning, sleepy head. Let's get going! We've got things to do today." Enough time had already been wasted. "Chester is staying with the kids, and you and I are going shopping. I'll bet you've never even heard of Bloomingdales. We'll have lunch at Caesar's Palace. You do like Italian food, don't you?" There was no opportunity given for comments or objections. "The dress you have on is just fine." Her eyes did a quick scan over LuAnn's body, as only an older sister's eyes can do.

"We're going to get you something really classy for that upcoming reunion of yours. More than likely, you don't even *own* a mini skirt. Well, we'll do something about that! Now, hurry up, little sister! I'll give you ten more minutes." With that, the door was closed, and she went back down the hallway to finish getting herself ready. Jane was still good at issuing orders. A smile tantalized LuAnn's lips, in spite of herself. She was beginning to feel right at home.

* * *

By the time the weekend was over, the Hanable family had been thoroughly entertained. LuAnn had bought a new dress. She had been wined and dined at three of the most popular restaurants in the Chicago area, and on Sunday, the families had attended St. Peter's, the largest and most beautiful church imaginable. Besides doing those things, she had studied every nook and cranny of the Wrights' spacious home. Joyce and Jason were well acquainted with their cousins. They were even happily sore from their waists down and begging for a pony when they got back home. LuAnn stopped trying to convince them there was no place to keep one. She let them hold onto their dreams. She had a few of her own.

* * *

The Greyhound bus left the Chicago depot at four o'clock Monday afternoon, and LuAnn and the children rode all night. There were stops in Columbus, Ohio, and Wheeling, West Virginia, where they changed buses. There was another change in Washington, Pennsylvania, and an hour layover before going south to Clarksville, West Virginia. The three slept most of the night and aroused themselves only to make the necessary bus changes. At the Washington layover, LuAnn and the children freshened up. She was glad to have the hour to get rearranged and to compose herself. Finally, with a sense of relief, they pulled into the Clarksburg bus depot. Here, they were picked up by LuAnn's parents.

* * *

Her first thought was how much her parents had aged since seeing them last Christmas. In five more years, Clifton Soppee would retire from the post office with a good pension. With a lurch of her heart, she hoped he would last that long. However, Ruby's resilience over the past nine years had surprised her, too. She wondered, briefly, how the elderly woman was doing. Mack seldom talked about her any more.

Hugs and kisses were exchanged. The luggage was collected and stashed inside the automobile's trunk. Then, the five of them piled into Clifton's new Ford Custom. "How about a little tour of the town, Honey? There's been a lot of changes in the past ten years." His eyes lit up with anticipation of doing something for his younger daughter.

LuAnn didn't think she and the kids could tolerate any more touring right then, but she didn't want to hurt her father's enthusiasm or his feelings. He had been very supportive of her over the past ten years. "Well . . . uh . . . "

Her mother, immediately, came to their rescue. "For heaven's sake, Clifton! What is the matter with you? They've been riding around for nearly a day now. Your tour can wait until some other time! Right now, they need some good food and a place to run around and get the kinks out!" Clifton propelled the automobile homeward.

* * *

Just two years before, an empty lot near the Soppee home had been turned into a neighborhood park. Joyce and Jason soon made friends of the other children who played there on a daily basis. Every morning, from nine until noon, a summer recreation program was led by two college students. There was a new swimming pool on the other side of town. Clifton hauled LuAnn's and Jane's old bikes out of the garage . . . and after two evenings of tinkering they were rideable. Every afternoon a half dozen bikers from the neighborhood, Joyce and Jason among them, zig-zagged their way down side streets to the pool. The weeks ahead were no problem for the children. They were finding plenty to do.

* * *

For LuAnn, it was a different story. In the ten years since she was gone, most of the people whom she considered friends in high school, had moved away, or were working . . . or busy raising children. She felt they wouldn't want to be bothered. By the end of the first week, she and

Fern had talked themselves out. Her mother's prattle, over insignificant issues had always been an irritation that was hard to endure.

An effort was made to help with the garden, but that was to no avail. She had always hated gardening. Who wants to get dirt under their fingernails? Nearly every night there was a call put into Mack, but most of the times, he didn't answer. Of course, he wasn't going to sit around waiting for her to call. Still, she wondered what he was doing. She was feeling sorry for herself and wished the summer would pass quickly, so she could get started on the classes at Hawkeye School of Technology. Seeing Jane's and Chester's beautiful home made her more determined than ever to get on with plans for a business in interior decorating. Out of boredom, the second week in Grafton, she offered volunteer assistance to the recreation program at the park. Then, at least the mornings were filled.

* * *

As the fourteenth day of June approached, she began to get butterflies. Scheduled for that Friday evening was a social gathering of the 1958 class and their spouses or "significant others." The gala would be held at the new country club. For the first time, there was a sense of real panic, as she envisioned walking, unchaperoned, into the dining/ball room. What would people think of her?

The black lace mini-skirted dress Jane thought appropriate for such an occasion was critically scrutinized all over again. How could she, so foolishly, have allowed her big sister to persuade her it was worth squandering one hundred dollars on? Perhaps it seemed right to her, there in Chicago, but LuAnn felt certain such a dress would be out of place in Grafton. But after considering other options hanging in the closet, they seemed dowdy in contrast, and the one dress shop downtown offered so few choices. Apparently, she was stuck with it.

The cocktail hour was scheduled for six o'clock, with dinner at six-thirty, followed by after dinner speeches and commentaries by class members. Early Friday morning, the black lace was tried on once more . . . this time with the black hose and pumps that were purchased in Grafton to complete the outfit. With a critical eye, she looked into the mirror and was astounded at how tasteful the ensemble appeared. "You'll knock 'em dead!" had been Jane's comment. She was right. Now all that was needed was a black evening purse. Perhaps Fern would have such a thing. She did.

At six o'clock, LuAnn walked out the front door of the Soppee house and slid into the driver's seat of Cliftons' Ford . . . determined to have the time of her life. Courageously, she drove into the parking lot of the country club and maneuvered into one of the few available spots that were left. It was a considerable distance from the front door. Feeling conspicuous but determined, she stepped gracefully from the car. The new heels made her legs appear even more shapely, and she was aware of that fact. She tossed back her lightly sprayed hair, straightened the black hose and smoothed down the black lace dress. Then, she clutched the black handbag, closed the door of the automobile, and headed, with quick steps, for the entrance to the club.

The door was opened and held by a stranger who projected a slight degree of familiarity from the past. Was it the smile? Never mind. She stepped into the entryway, her heart pounding. Surely, it would bust right through the lace bodice. Her eyes quickly scanned the surroundings. A banner read WELCOME CLASS OF '58! There was a tremendous urge to turn and run, but before she could, a cool hand reached out and touched her arm. "Please register over here and get your name tag." Willowy legs carried her over to the small registration table.

With a shaky hand, her name was written. *LuAnn Soppee Hanable, Independence, Iowa,* then, a waiter with a tray of drinks appeared at her side. The name tag was fastened to the side of her purse, and a drink was selected. Jane had told her, "Don't spoil the effect of your dress with a name tag. Put it on your purse." So, that's what she did. As for the drink, what should she do with it? She didn't have a clue as to what it was.

Just a sip and the bubbles nearly prompted a sneeze, but it gave her a bit of courage. At least her hands were occupied. Her eyes skimmed the crowd of perhaps seventy people. She picked out three of the girls who had been fellow cheerleaders, one of them being Mary Lou Bailey. Gaining courage, she walked over to her. "Hi, Mary Lou, do you remember me?" She read the name tag, *Mary Lou Bailey Carpenter.* "Carpenter . . . Carpenter . . . let's see . . . oh, yes . . . Jeff Carpenter! Did you marry Jeff Carpenter?"

* * *

For years, Mary Lou had felt cheated and humiliated when Mack Hanable didn't return from the Army to marry her. All of her letters to his military address had been returned unopened. But, after all the heartache and frustration surrounding the rejection, her life had turned out better in the long run. This, she knew for certain. It hadn't mattered to Jeff Carpenter that she was a single mother. It hadn't mattered to Mary Lou's parents either. She was their only child, so when they had learned of her pregnancy, they were not too displeased. They encouraged her to keep the baby, to forget about Mack Hanable, and to concentrate on getting her education. They would help care for their grandchild. It had all worked out.

By the time she graduated from college, Jeff was coaching the Grafton boys' senior varsity basketball team. He had gone from a gangling, clumsy, and shy high school kid to a talented, charming, and enthusiastic sports director and coach. Mary Lou and Jeff found themselves working in the same school system, and the two hit it off immediately. They were married at the end of her first year of teaching at the Grafton Elementary School. In fact, she had taken Jane's place when she married Chester and went off to Chicago to be a doctor's wife. Jeff adopted little Billy, and the marriage was successful by anyone's standards.

* * *

Mary Lou knew LuAnn had no knowledge of Mack having fathered her son, and there was no need to tell her now. From all reports via the grapevine in town LuAnn had not faired too well with Mack either. So, now she could openly welcome her back into town without any feeling of regret for the past ten years. "So good to see you, LuAnn. Apparently, you remember my husband, Jeff Carpenter." A tall man with muscles rippling under his sports jacket, took her hand and nodded.

"LuAnn! Of course! You know, just the other day someone was asking about you!" His deep voice resonated throughout the room. A few heads turned in their direction. "Oh yes, it was Thomas Maxwell. We ran into each other in Charleston and were discussing the upcoming reunion. He wanted to know, 'Whatever became of LuAnn?' I told him Mary Lou might know . . . did he ever call you, Honey?" Jeff turned to his wife. She shook her head in the negative, and he turned back to LuAnn. "Say, you used to date old Tommy, didn't you?" A grin spread across the big man's face. His eyes briefly looked past her.

Why did he have to go there with their conversation and so soon? "Well . . . yes . . . I did. What is he doing now?" In spite of herself, her voice caught. "I haven't heard about him in years!" She hadn't wanted to deal with the issue of seeing Tommy, but she bravely pursued the subject. "Perhaps he's here tonight?" Her eyes scanned the crowded room.

"He sure is!" From behind, a pair of strong hands grasped her shoulders. The voice and sensation of his touch were only too familiar. Even the scent of All Spice entered her senses. "As for what he's doing, how about finding a cozy, little corner . . . and he'll tell you." Thomas slowly turned the bewildered young woman around to face him, and he looked quizzically into her eyes, one eyebrow raised. The handsome face was matured, but otherwise, hadn't changed at all.

LuAnn's heart lurched, and she started trembling. *Oh dear God, no! Why do I have to feel this way*. She mustered every ounce of strength and flippantly consented. "Tommy! Or, is it Thomas now? I would love to catch up on the last ten years with you. Why don't you introduce me to your wife, or 'significant other,' and she can join us." His hands were brushed away, and she maneuvered to a more comfortable distance. "Perhaps this table over here."

"I'm afraid it's just me." He shrugged his broad shoulders and spread out two strong, slightly calloused hands. "No woman seems to want me." He jested back with a tantalizing grin, and a devilish gleam sparkled in his deep blue eyes. "I was thinking more of a table out on the patio. It's a beautiful evening." He took possession of her by the arm and escorted her gently but matter-of-factly out through the patio doors into the soft summer night.

At that point, much to LuAnn's relief, dinner was announced, but Thomas wasn't deterred. "You will be sitting at my table, by the way. I had a little pull with the planning committee. And another thing," he leaned down and whispered to her, "You are the most gorgeous woman in the room." The warmth of his breath in her ear sent her already foggy head into a dizzy spin. They made their way into the dining room, and she sank, thankfully, into the chair he pulled out from the table.

As the dinner progressed, LuAnn managed to grasp and slow down the runaway emotions that kept surfacing. Once, she excused herself and went to the women's lounge. While there, she scolded herself in the mirror, took several deep breaths, and found some gum in her purse to chew. After that, she began to relax and enjoy the festivities.

Laughing came easily while in the company of Mary Lou and Jeff . . . who were also seated at their table. It had been a long time since she had enjoyed any occasion so much. She had almost forgotten how to have a good time. Eventually, she was convinced that the behavior of others shouldn't be taken so seriously. After all, she wasn't a teenager any more and, so, should lighten up and handle situations with more sophistication . . . just enjoy the moment. But most acute and painful was the awareness that, for the past ten years, she had been a virtual social dropout. With Mack, there had been very little socializing or joy in their lives.

By the time dinner was over and the speakers were introduced, it was no surprise that Thomas was one of them. The committee had chosen three class members to share their experiences over the past decade. The other two speakers were Mary Lou and Jeff.

The couple spoke freely and openly of their recollections and perceptions during their high school years . . . of their immaturity and the mistakes they had made. They gave witness to how their choices in the ensuing years were affecting their lives. All the credit for their successes was given, "To the praise and glory of God and our Savior, Jesus Christ."

LuAnn had never before heard such a confession of faith, and she was overwhelmed with emotion. She dabbed at persistent tears and tried to understand the meaning behind them. It was embarrassing . . . to say nothing of what was happening to her makeup. It was impossible to look at Thomas.

Then, Captain Thomas Maxwell of the Charleston Police Department was introduced. He related to former classmates how, after his little ten year old sister's abduction in 1960, his major was changed from business to law enforcement. For six years now, his career has been devoted to solving cases involving missing children. He shared his belief, "Jesus Christ is working in me and through me. To date, Amy's case has not been solved. However, I haven't given up. It will be solved in God's time." The assembly of former classmates and guests sat mesmerized by the presentation.

By the time toasts were made, the atmosphere was relaxed and festive once more. The band began playing, and partners took to the floor. "Would you like to dance, LuAnn, or should we try for the patio again?"

She didn't know this person at all anymore. His life had taken so many turns without her. She had never even known of Amy's abduction. Why hadn't her parents told her? He hadn't gone into any details, probably assuming everyone knew them. Or perhaps, they were just too difficult to relate. There were many questions to ask him.

"Let's try for the patio." It was apparent she couldn't handle the emotions that were certain to arise when being held in his arms on the dance floor. “Shall we?” Ignoring his arm, she sprinted off, a slim silhouette in black.

The fresh cool air provided comfort, and unwelcome emotions were challenged and controlled. “I didn’t know about Amy, my parents didn’t ever mention it. I’m very sorry.”

LuAnn had always been such a sincere person, and the extent of her caring was still obvious to Thomas. Ten years ago, it was just that quality that had scared him to death. Now, he found this same sincerity and concern very appealing. In his line of work, such emotions were welcomed and honored.

They settled into chairs at a wrought iron table to the far end of the patio. A soft breeze carrying the sweet scent of roses floated around them. A flicker of candlelight danced from the holder at the center of the table. The moon was full and easily located in the clear, star-laden sky.

Thomas studied the face of the young woman sitting across from him. “You heard about me in there. Now tell me about you, LuAnn. What is life like in Iowa? You said you have two children. What are their names?”

He wanted to know more about her. She seemed very familiar, and yet, so very different. *Unsure of herself,* he decided. Once . . . long ago, she was quite the opposite . . . determined and carefree. Her portrayal of characters in school plays had been engaging and convincing. She was one of the spunkiest cheerleaders. Back then, her plans were to be a teacher. Somewhere, over the years, the confidence and spark had gotten lost, and he was determined to find out why. It was obvious the evening was difficult for her. Her eyes had hardly met his. He wondered if he had anything to do with the course her life had taken. A familiar tinge of guilt grabbed at his insides. He wanted to know.

“Catch me up on the past ten years, LuAnn. Your ten years. What have they been like?” His eyes searched into the blue depth of her soul.

“Are you sure you really want to know?” Her eyes lowered, and fixed on the surface of the table. Slim, nervous fingers turned the evening purse over and over on the black lace in her lap. Finally, gaining courage, with a deep sigh, her head lifted. “Well, some have been good and some not so good. Isn’t that the way life is?” A smile twitched on her lips, and tightly intertwined fingers came to a rest on the table top.

She commenced to tell him about Ruby Dutcher and the Trouts, about Francis and her daughter and grandchild. She told him about Joyce and Jason and her plans to be an interior decorator.

Then, finally, she told him about Mack. That was the most difficult part. How do you explain someone you barely know yourself? You can't! The harder she tried . . . the more she knew that to be true. Eventually, she came to the realization that Mack didn't really know himself . . . so how could she know him? She related the abuse he had suffered from Aunt Ruby, and that he had gotten psychological help at one time . . . at her insistence. As she talked, previously confusing issues began to clear up in her own mind. Then, she concluded, "You see. Life has just been very difficult for him."

As the narrative unfolded, Thomas began to see the characteristics of an abusive person in the portrayal of LuAnn's husband. When it appeared that the tale had been brought to a conclusion, he asked the question that was utmost on his mind. "Does Mack abuse you and the kids?"

"He hasn't for a long time." There was a forced smile, and her gaze dropped to the table top once again.

Fourteen

The morning following the gala at the country club, LuAnn prepared fried chicken for the potluck picnic to be held at the Grafton City Park. The children would be participating in this part of the reunion weekend. The new park was constructed with the latest in play equipment and foot paths leading in every direction to the surrounding woods and lakes. The swimming pool was built adjacent to the park area, so there would be plenty of activities for everyone. Jeff and Mary Lou Carpenter were instrumental in the development of the new recreational facility. Their names were engraved on a bronze plaque and attached to the wall of the new shelter.

LuAnn hummed softly as the chicken sputtered and crackled in the frying pan, and the tantalizing aroma filled the kitchen. Her mind, reluctantly and yet passionately, went back to the evening before when emotions ebbed and flowed so naturally and with such familiarity. She and Thomas had talked candidly for most of the evening, strolling along the patio of the country club, or sitting at one of the small tables.

* * *

That morning, her feelings were as restless as the sea, as they searched for the stability of the shore, and, yet, crumbled at the very edge of that which they were seeking. Nature was taking its course, as Tommy disappeared with the ebbing tide, only to be brought back to her thoughts again as Thomas. There was a new creation in him showing strength and endurance . . . definitely a man now . . . well beyond the "Tommy" she had known ten years before.

He possessed the ability to understand what was being communicated between them, even when she didn't. Perhaps, too much of her personal life had been divulged, but keeping confessions confidential is part of his job. So, she had held nothing back. He was told, in great detail, about her puzzling relationship with Mack . . . how it had started . . . the disappearance of Kate Weatherby . . . and of finding the locket with the inscription, *To Kate, from your lover, Mack.*

Mostly, he had been noncommittal, even when she bordered on being accusatory toward him concerning their own past relationship. He knew that it was important for her to express pent-up feelings honestly, so she had rambled on . . . and from time to time, he had encouraged her with a gentle question or comment. At approximately eleven-thirty, she had reluctantly ended the evening. "I'm afraid if I stay any longer, I'll turn back into my rags at midnight." He had escorted her to the car, and watched as she drove off.

* * *

The chicken was cooked and browned, so it was placed into a Pyrex casserole. She called Joyce and Jason from the backyard, where they were pulling weeds from the rows of carrots under their grandfather's supervision. "Come on, kids! It's time to get ready! Don't forget your swimsuits!" The three quickly cleaned up, donned their shorts, and were out the door on their way to the park.

The Ford was maneuvered around the twisting streets. In just minutes, they pulled into the parking lot, and everyone scrambled out. The kids were off with a whoop, having spied some of their friends already on the play equipment. LuAnn headed for the shelter with the casserole in hand and a spring in her step. She hadn't felt so exuberant and lighthearted in years. It was a beautiful day, one to be enjoyed for every minute of it, regardless of the challenges!

Thomas walked towards her, a huge grin covered his face, and eager hands were held out to take the casserole. They lightly brushed hers as he did so. "Hmm, smells good. You're looking bright and chipper today." He placed the dish among the other contributions brought for the meal. "You know, I haven't met your kids yet. Will you point them out to me?" He took her hand and they sauntered towards the playground.

She should withdraw her hand from his grip, but there was no inclination to do so. They stopped at the edge of the sandy area, and her eyes searched for the two familiar figures. "There's Joyce . . . the one in the red shorts and white blouse, standing at the top of the slide." She pointed out her daughter. "There she is going down! Did you see her?"

"Yeah . . . I see her! Beautiful, like her mother! Now, where is Jason?" His gaze swept over her as she searched for her son, pride and love radiated from her very soul. He wondered what it would be like to be a parent . . . trying to find a part of yourself.

"There he is! Over by the monkey bars! See. The one with the dark hair and the green shirt. . . . No, that isn't him either . . . I could have sworn that was him . . . only, he didn't wear a green shirt today, his is blue. . . . Well, let's see. OK, there he is on the swings, the one that is pumping the highest. He always does that, and it scares me to death." She felt confused and ridiculous. She hadn't known her own son! She looked for the other boy that she had mistaken for Jason. She found him . . . and realized the two boys could pass as brothers.

Thomas realized the same thing. Jeff and Mary Lou's son and LuAnn's son could, indeed, pass for brothers . . . because in reality . . . they were brothers—half-brothers. He wondered if LuAnn was ready for the truth. He watched the puzzled expression on her face as her eyes shifted from one boy to the other, but she made no comment. Instead, she was very quiet. He would discuss the matter with Jeff and Mary Lou before getting into that one. Mary Lou might be the one to tell LuAnn, if the truth needed to be told.

A whistle shrilled from the direction of the shelter and the gathering of two hundred or more started forming two lines. Their attention was brought back to the reality of the present. Paper plates, napkins, and plastic utensils were gathered at the beginning of the line. Drinks were picked up after the plates were filled. Children sought out their parents for assistance, and grimy fingers clung to the edges of overloaded plates.

"Joyce, Jason . . . this is Mr. Maxwell. He and I went to school together . . . a long time ago." LuAnn motioned for the children to get in line ahead of them.

They gave Thomas a quick glance, "Hi." The food was far more interesting to them. With plates filled, they looked for a place to sit down. "Hey Mom, how about over here?" Jason and Joyce headed for a table where four kids were already seated with their parents. LuAnn and Thomas followed along.

"Whatduyasay, Tommy? I didn't know you were a family man!" The father seated at the table was Eddie Smith, a big, burly man with shaggy hair and in need of a good shave and some deodorant. They both remembered him as being a bully and the instigator of many a classroom disruption. "And if this ain't LuAnn . . . then it sure must be her double! My! My! Sit down! Sit down!" He looked from one to the other, a decided smirk on his face, and made an elaborate motion with his arm indicating the empty seats.

"I assure you, Eddie, there is only one LuAnn. These are her children, Joyce and Jason. They seem to know your children already. This must be your wife." Thomas nodded towards the bedraggled-looking woman seated at the table. She was still wearing a house dress and apron. Her already graying hair hung in tendrils around her damp face and neck. Thomas' compassion went out for the woman, but he wasn't going to let Eddie make further inference to any impropriety concerning his relationship to LuAnn. He eyed Eddie and waited for him to comment.

"Well, well . . . she ain't my wife, but she might be someday. This is Marlene. Marlene Hillman." Eddie's face reddened, and he turned his attention to the food on his plate, shoveling it in and chewing with gusto. He seemed to swallow with difficulty. His eyes flitted anxiously around the group of people, never quite landing anywhere. "Guess I need some dessert now!" Suddenly, he rose from the table and left, not to come back.

LuAnn sat across from Marlene and engaged her in small talk . . . the weather . . . the children . . . the new park, and the swimming pool. She was a thin woman and decidedly nervous . . . surely looking older than her years. There was a bruise on her neck and one on her arm. Not once did she look directly at LuAnn or Thomas, but, occasionally, a smile flitted across her lips when the children were referred to. "Yes, they are good children! Their ages are eight, seven, four and three."

It wasn't long until all of the children got up from the table to leave. "You kids have to wait for an hour before going into the pool, just to be on the safe side," LuAnn advised them. They left the table scowling, but a few minutes later, they and half a dozen others were exploring the trails that circled around the park.

"Are you going swimming, LuAnn, or will you take a hike with me? Jeff and Mary Lou are acting as lifeguards, so you don't need to worry about the kids." Thomas got the answer he was hoping for, and when the kids were safely in the pool, they struck out into the direction of the woods. It wasn't long until they were engulfed by the pungent smell of damp earth, evergreen trees, budding shrubs, and fragrant wild flowers. The path was narrow, scarcely wide enough to walk side by side.

* * *

For a time, they walked in silence. LuAnn was wondering how to broach the subject of Billy Carpenter's parentage. She had been mulling around the ages of her children and the age of Jeff's and Mary Lou's son, and what she was speculating was possible. There was no way she was the first woman Mack ever made love to, and she knew Mary Lou was dating a military man earlier that spring in 1958. She even referred to him during her testimony the evening before. Of course, no name had been given.

Then came the realization that it didn't really matter one way or another. In spite of their years together, she had never acquired an emotional attachment to Mack. But she still needed to know the truth. She finally stopped along the path and turned to her companion. She pulled his arm and blurted it out. "Thomas, who is Billy Carpenter's real father?"

Her question had been expected, and his words were selected carefully. "That depends on what you mean by 'real father,' LuAnn. Jeff Carpenter has been caring for Billy since he was three years old. He adopted him, and he loves him. That's a 'real father,' as far as I'm concerned. Jeff and Billy are lucky to have each other. Jeff isn't able, physically, to have a child, because of a bad bout with the mumps. It's a good match, it seems to me."

He hoped the conversation could turn to something else. Taking long strides, he continued up the path, but LuAnn wouldn't give up. Determined, she plunged after him and clumsily caught her sandal on an exposed root in the path. With a gasp, she reached out and grabbed his arm. Strong fingers dug in and held on. She wanted an answer.

"Sorry! Guess I better slow down. Are you all right?" His arms went around her protectively, and he held the warmth of her for a moment before reluctantly letting go. The smell of her, so close, sent his emotions reeling. He would deal with whatever she had to say. "Go on, LuAnn, what do you want to know?" He continued down the path.

"From my calculations, Thomas . . . Billy could be Mack's child. Maybe I'm being paranoid, but Jason and Billy look so much alike . . . enough alike to be brothers. Besides, I would be kidding myself if I didn't admit Mack was fooling around with others before he started fooling around with me." She stopped in the path, squeezed Thomas' arm, and looked unwaveringly into his eyes. "If you know . . . tell me . . . please."

He searched the pleading face looking up at him and reached inside his own soul. "OK, you have a right to know. I hoped Mary Lou might tell you sometime . . . but I can see the truth can't wait. The Bible says, 'The truth shall set you free.' It's for sure you deserve that freedom. Yes, Billy is Mack's child. He knew Mary Lou was pregnant at the time he married you . . . and left for Iowa. Apparently, he figured that 'out of sight . . . out of mind,' and in a way, that is exactly what happened. Jeff and Mary Lou are very happy. They hope Mack never reappears and wants a part of Billy's life."

LuAnn felt tremendous relief. Another mystery concerning her husband's past was unlocked. She could understand him better, forgive him for the pain he inflicted on her and the children. Tears slid down her cheeks, and she buried her face in Thomas' t-shirt. "Mack has such a heavy burden to carry. I think I understand him better now. I'm sure if it wasn't for the pressure from his Aunt Ruby, he would make different and better decisions for his life."

"LuAnn, are you thinking straight?" He grabbed her by the shoulders, and it was all he could do to keep from shaking her. "What about the pain he inflicted on Mary Lou, and you, and the kids, and who knows how many other women and children?" His anger began to escalate. "He was an adult, for crying out loud, when he got you and Mary Lou pregnant!" He shook his head, dropped his hands, and strode away. It always amazed him when the victims of abuse could come up with so many excuses for their abusers. The abusers didn't have to be responsible and take care of themselves. Their victims willingly did it for them!

She ran and caught up with him. She must make him understand. "Thomas, he needs me! He needs the kids! He's never had anyone he could count on. Please understand! I'm not condoning what he's done . . . but he's had his own reasons; his own demons to overcome. Tell me you understand."

"LuAnn, I deal with people like him every day. He's an abuser! Abusers have no conscience. If they did, they couldn't do the things they do." He turned her towards him.

"Promise me one thing. If you ever find yourself afraid of him you'll get away. Go someplace. Fear is a pretty darned good indicator that something is very wrong. If you need help get it! Let me or *somebody* know . . . OK?" His billfold was pulled from a back pocket, and he handed her a business card. "Here's my card. Put it someplace safe. Do you have a safe place? If you don't, find one."

"Well, I started an account in the bank in Hiawatha soon after our marriage . . . with my father's name on it. Dad didn't think I should let Mack know. He had doubts about him, too. The statements are sent to

Dad, rather than to me. I have a post office box there, too. Dad sends me copies of my statements. Then . . . I . . . tear them up." Her voice trailed off . . . realizing how strange it must all sound.

He studied her in amazement. "Then you *are* afraid, aren't you?"

"I suppose so. But most of the time I don't think about it." With determination, her head was raised up a notch. "I've learned to get along. Maybe after I get my education, things will be different. I have two children to consider, you know."

"I have to leave tomorrow right after the breakfast, LuAnn, but I will keep in touch with you. Give me your box number in Hiawatha." He pulled out another card and wrote the information on the back. "We had better get going, the kids will be getting out of the pool." He held out protective arms, and she was enfolded in a warm and gentle embrace. His lips brushed her cheek. For fear of wanting more, he released her and started down the path towards the pool.

* * *

That evening, it was all Thomas could do to refrain from leaving the motel room and driving over to the Soppees'. But he had inflicted pain on LuAnn once . . . and he would never do that again. She was already dealing with enough. So, instead, he opened up his briefcase and leafed through the file of missing persons. The front of the file contained those of children, and the back of the file contained those of young adults. He always kept the file with him. Occasionally, a word mentioned, or a name given, would be a clue to one of the cases. Thomas looked at the card with LuAnn's box number on it in Hiawatha. What was it she said about finding a locket? And the name in it? Kate? The last name? Weatherby. Yes, that was it. He began leafing through the back files.

It was there. Weatherby. He scanned the report. It was from Iowa! His excitement heightened. He read it carefully and deliberately. Katherine (Kate) Weatherby disappeared June 12, 1959. Her car was found hidden on a vacant lot in southeast Cedar Rapids. No keys were found, and any fingerprints were wiped from all surfaces. There were no witnesses. No body was ever found. What was it LuAnn had told him was inscribed in the locket she found? *To Kate, from your lover, Mack.* That put Kate in the vicinity of Hiawatha at some point. What was the name of Mack's aunt? Ruby . . . Ruby something. He would ask LuAnn in the morning at the breakfast.

He deliberately hadn't told LuAnn that he takes time off from the Charleston Police Department if the leads to a missing persons case warrant his attention. In such cases, he works with other law enforcement agencies or simply makes himself available to the families of the victims.

With the information she had related to him concerning the Weatherby case, he felt justified in contacting the Cedar Rapids Police Department. He would, at least, see if there was an interest in reopening the case, and he started scribbling notes. He felt strongly that, given Mack Hanable's attraction to women and his relationship with Kate Weatherby, the man was highly suspect.

Thomas examined his own motives carefully. Was he finding his attraction to LuAnn so strong that he would try to find an innocent man guilty? No, he was too good an officer for that. He had to keep her out of the whole thing . . . find a way to protect her and the children if necessary. He knew when pressure was put on a guilty party, that person often took their anger, fear, and frustrations out on those around them . . . blaming their families for the circumstances they found themselves in. He wanted to make certain that didn't happen. He also knew she could end up hating him, but that was a risk he would have to take. There were a lot of details to work out, but he was certain his hunches had merit. He hoped circumstances would allow him to follow up on them.

* * *

The next morning at breakfast, LuAnn was noticeably bubbly and vibrant . . . probably too much so. More like her old self, she shashayed around the tables in the dining room, making sure each former classmate was greeted. She was convinced that too much time had been spent with Thomas and that she was missing out on getting reacquainted with the others. However, she graciously moved through the serving line with him and the Carpenters and happily gave Thomas the name he needed, "Ruby Dutcher." She dared not be honest with herself and admit how painful his leaving was going to be.

Mary Lou insisted she should spend some of the next two weeks with her. "We have much to talk about, and, perhaps, the children should have a chance to get acquainted." Especially since she was now aware of the circumstances concerning Billy's birth. *Some day, the children will need to be told.*

After breakfast, LuAnn walked out to Thomas' car with him. A piece of her heart was being ripped out, once again, but he couldn't know that. "It has been wonderful seeing you again, Thomas. Please take care. Don't worry about me and the kids. We're going to be just fine." She hoped her smile was convincing.

He touched her chin, aware of its trembling, and tipped her head back. He kissed her softly on the lips. "You're some lady. Take care, and keep in touch." He settled into the Firebird and, with a roar, drove off towards Charleston. She looked after him and then went back into the restaurant to join the others. She was determined not to let the overwhelming sense of loss get the better of her.

* * *

The next week and a half passed quickly. Old high school classmates began calling the Soppee home asking for LuAnn. Many special memories were relived. Three days before their departure, Sarah Yoder telephoned. "You asked me to call you. We're leaving Lancaster Thursday morning at eight-thirty . . . We'll be in Washington at three-thirty, I hope you can meet us there. We so much would like to have your company for the remainder of the trip." Her voice was hesitant, almost apologetic.

"Oh Sarah, I'm so glad you remembered to call! My parents said they could take us to Washington to meet the bus whenever you would be there. We'll be there on Thursday, for sure! How is your father doing?"

"Father is recovering as well as can be expected. Mother is doing well, too. I'll tell you all about it when I see you. I must go. Good-bye for now. Don't forget . . . this Thursday at three-thirty." There was a click and the line began to hum.

By the time Thursday arrived, LuAnn, Joyce, and Jason were busting to leave for home. Mr. and Mrs. Soppee delivered them to the bus stop in Washington, and they said their tearful good-byes. Yet, for all of them, there was a sense of relief that their lives would soon be getting back to normal. Sarah and Susie greeted them with beautiful, welcoming smiles, and the mothers and children settled in for the long trip home.

* * *

When they got to Chicago, LuAnn called Jane to let her know they were there and doing well. She also called Mack. He sounded extremely happy to know his family was nearly home. "I have a big surprise for all of you! Sure, I can meet you at the bus station early Saturday morning."

With a heavy heart, she felt regretful and apprehensive . . . as though she were leaving one world and entering another. What was it Thomas said? "I like to think of life as being one great adventure. God gives us diversity for reasons only He knows. Trust Him." Tears welled up, as she recalled, once again, every moment they had spent together. As she tucked his memory away, she whispered to her quivering heart, "I will love you forever, Tommy." Then her mind was set to what lay ahead.

* * *

Mack waited impatiently at the bus depot in Independence. His wife and children had been gone for nearly a month, and he was mighty tired of trying to fix his own meals or eating them at the café. The kitchen was scroungy, and the ring in the bathtub was one solid mass of grime. The sheets had never been changed, and dust covered everything. He decided not to worry about it . . . because in just a few days, they could start moving into the Harris farmstead. No . . . he corrected his thinking . . . the Hanable farmstead!

Life was going pretty well for him. His mail route out in the country was a welcome change. Sometimes his legs were swollen in the evenings, but he was learning to take care of that problem, too . . . by occasionally getting out of the Lincoln, walking and stretching, and using the ditches and lanes for a rest stop when he needed one, rather than trying to hold it all day. He kept his legs elevated in the evenings while watching television. That's where he usually ended up spending the night.

Saturday morning, he took special care to get a haircut, to shave, and take a shower, and he even used deodorant and put on clean clothes. There wasn't many left in the closet, and he supposed he should have done some laundry. LuAnn and the cleaners always kept his uniforms in immaculate condition for town deliveries . . . but who was going to see him out in the country among the Amish? So, what the heck!

He hadn't been near the Dutcher farm since his aunt's death, and he never wanted to go there again. There was no need for that. With his own place now, he could make sure his family had everything there is to enjoy. Among other things, he planned to dredge out a little pond to be fed by the Otter Creek. He could stock it, and it would be a great place for the kids to go fishing. He glanced at his watch for the hundredth time, and the Greyhound bus turned the corner and headed down the street towards the depot.

* * *

Joyce and Jason hopped down from the bus steps. With sleep-deprived eyes, they looked at their father. Jason piped up first. "Hi Dad! That was sure a long trip home. I'm hungry. Can we get breakfast someplace?"

"Sure! Are you hungry too, Joyce? I'll just bet you are. Where's your mother?" Mack looked towards the door of the bus.

LuAnn took a few seconds to comb her hair, powder her nose, and apply fresh lipstick. She must put on her best face, not only for Mack, but for her own state of mind as well. Having done so, she stepped out of the bus and was immediately crushed in a passionate embrace. Mack held her face between the palms of his hands and kissed her hard on the mouth. "I've sure missed you, Honey. Do you want some breakfast before we go home?"

Fifteen

Mackenzie Linn Hanable had never paid a household bill in his life. Aunt Ruby had always taken care of the bills on the Dutcher place. It seemed to be the woman's job. He had never heard Uncle Charles complain; maybe he hadn't dared. Anyway, when the family moved to Independence, he had started giving LuAnn half of his paycheck . . . figuring half for her and half for him. That seemed to work out all right for both of them, and with her half, she tried to keep the household bills paid.

Very early in their marriage, it became apparent that the mention of money could send Mack off on a barrage of verbal assaults. So, LuAnn had learned to manage well, and when a financial need that surpassed her half arose, her own earnings were used, rather than approach him with the issue. Each month, this happened more often than not, and, most of the time, she really didn't mind. To her, it felt good to contribute to the family.

Five years working at the day care center had allowed for enough money to be saved to finance the trip to West Virginia and the expenses of the next two years at Hawkeye School of Technology. No money had been taken from the account in the Hiawatha State Bank except for rare emergency reasons, like the repair of her car. Mack had never even wondered, verbally, anyway, where the money had come from to fix the transmission.

* * *

Before leaving to go east for the ten year class reunion, some decisions were made. The rent would come due on the first of June . . . and the utility bills . . . telephone bill . . . and the garbage and sewer bill would follow right behind. The cupboards and freezer were pretty bare. Her first inclination was to pay the bills ahead of time, or to leave signed checks, so he could pay them from the household account. But, then she wondered if he didn't need a shot of reality. So, she left without making any arrangements for the bills to be paid, and the checkbook was placed securely in the bottom of her purse.

* * *

The first shot of reality, for Mack, came on June 2, when the landlord called. "Mr. Hanable, I was wondering if your wife is sick or something. She didn't stop by yesterday with the rent check as usual. If she's got a problem, tell her I can wait a few more days, but I will need it by the fifth . . . OK?"

Mack did some rapid mental calculations. He knew they couldn't be moved out of the house until the middle of July. LuAnn and the kids wouldn't even be home until around the first. Damn! That meant at least two more months' rent!

"My wife's gone. She's visiting her family in West Virginia. How much is it? Let's see, that's sixty-five dollars. Right? I'll be over with a check." He nearly hung up before the landlord could remind him that the rent was now one hundred and twenty-five dollars.

"Well, I'll be damned! If I had known I was paying that kind money for this rundown old shack, I would have moved out a long time ago." He slammed down the receiver and went into the bedroom to get LuAnn's checkbook. It was always kept on top of the chest of drawers, but it wasn't there! "Well, I'll be damned!" He repeated again. "She must have taken it with her!" He rubbed his chin thoughtfully. Now what?

Then, he begrudgingly ripped a page from his own book and scribbled out a check for the amount. Not remembering the landlord's name, the recipient line was left blank. With the check held tight in hand, irritation grew as he propelled the Lincoln out of the drive and tore up the street. Gravel and dust sprayed out behind, and he headed to the east side of the river. Gaining some composure, he slowed down the speed and suddenly wondered if the landlord still lived in the same house. He did, and he was waiting out on the front porch sitting in a new metal rocker with the price tag still hanging from it.

The guy sure looks old, Mack thought. For an instant, he felt a pang of guilt for having been so sharp with him over the telephone. Leaving the Lincoln, he approached the porch, and, to get the man's attention, deliberately coughed twice. The second time being louder than the first.

Apparently, he hadn't seen nor heard the car pull into the drive. But, now, he abruptly rose from the seat. "Mr. Hanable! It's nice to see you again. I'm sorry if our conversation had upset you. You see, I've had to increase the rent every year just like everyone else. I assumed you knew that."

Mack shrugged his shoulders. "I suppose so." With an exaggerated snort and huff, the check was handed over. "You can fill in your own name." Since they would soon be leaving, he wanted to tell the guy 'where to get off,' but decided to wait until the July rent was due. That was soon enough, and LuAnn could inform him that they would be leaving. She could take care of that.

He drove home slowly and, reluctantly, deducted the amount of money from his account balance, leaving one hundred and twenty-nine thousand, six hundred and forty-three dollars, and fifty-five cents. That wasn't the last check he had to write either. By the time the month ended, his account was six hundred dollars less than that. Hell! He had spent over seven hundred dollars just on himself!

At that time, he began to wonder what the expenses would run on the farmstead. They were bound to be significantly more than at the house in town. Another sour taste of reality . . . LuAnn wasn't going to help out anymore. Hell! She had quit her job! And, she was going to school! That meant she would be an even bigger expense! One by one, fears and apprehensions were built throughout the weeks his family was gone.

* * *

Breakfast was eaten in a hurry, because everyone wanted to get home. That is LuAnn and the children did. Joyce and Jason bubbled over with accounts of their trip, hoping to get their father interested . . . but the most he said was, "Is that so? Is that right? You don't say so?" His mind was elsewhere. When the waitress brought the bill, he looked at the total and handed it to LuAnn. "I ain't got that kind of money on me! You've got the checkbook! . . . Don't ya?" He stood up and waited for it to be produced from her purse.

Instead, she took out her billfold and flipped through its contents. "I have sixty-five dollars that I was planning to buy groceries with this afternoon. We'll just have to do with a little less, I suppose." Smiling wanely, she picked up the bill, walked over to the cash register, and handed the man a twenty dollar bill. "Let's get home. I'm in need of a bath and a change of clothes. I feel like I haven't cleaned up in a week."

"Hell, LuAnn, I was planning on showing you the surprise. Nobody seems interested in the surprise I told you about. It's not far from here." He looked from one face to the other, but no one showed any excitement for the proposal. "Well, I suppose we should go home first and at least get the luggage out of the trunk." They all piled into the Lincoln for the short drive.

Joyce and Jason sat on the edge of the back seat, getting more and more excited as they neared home. Their eyes bugged, and their necks craned for a look at their house. Jason saw a friend from across the street, waved, and yelled, "I'm home, Scott!" The car pulled into the driveway, and the kids scrambled out to race with Scott to the swing set in the back yard.

LuAnn got out and stretched. "It sure is good to be here!" Their home wasn't much to look at, but right now, to her, it was the best place in the world. Mack opened the trunk and they grabbed suitcases in both hands and lugged them towards the house.

With each step, Mack was visualizing the mess that was left for LuAnn to clean up. Maybe he should have given a little more effort to keeping the house tidy while she was gone. He set the suitcases on the porch and pushed the door open.

She stepped into the kitchen, and the condition of their home hit with the impact of rotten garbage being hurled in her face. The countertops and table were covered with dirty dishes and pans, spilled food and hungry ants. The stove and sink were covered with dirty dishes and pans, spilled food and hungry ants. The floor was littered with empty boxes and cans, crumbs, spilled food and hungry ants. Dish towels and dish rags were molding where they had been left. The place smelled like a sewer.

She stared in shock and astonishment . . . disbelief that any place could be made into such a pigsty in one short month. Anger began to rise from toes to head. Ready to explode . . . her body trembled, and she swallowed hard.

Tears welled up, and she blindly stalked through the house to access the condition of the other rooms. The bathroom was so filthy; it would need to be cleaned before a shower could even be taken. The bedroom smelled of soiled bedding and clothing that lay in piles around the room, and dust rolled up on the floor and covered the furniture. The living room was in the best shape. The biggest mess was around the recliner, where sticky pop cans, empty wrappings, and a multitude of crumbs were left to attract still more ants. Thankfully, he had closed the doors to the children's rooms, and they needed only dusting.

He stood in the doorway of the living room. "Well, shit, LuAnn, if you had stayed home, there wouldn't be this mess! What do you expect of me after working all day? Besides, we won't be here much longer anyway." He cocked his head to one side and mustered a smile. "That's the surprise. We're going to be moving out into the country just as soon as we can get things packed up."

The little boy excuses and the little boy pleading had lost their affect. People do grow up and assume responsibilities. She faced him with an icy stare of contempt and wiped the tears away with the back of a clenched fist. "So, what do we do until then? I can't live this way!" Her hands flew out with vengeance in all directions. She wanted to pound on him with her fists, and it was all she could do to keep from attacking him.

Instead, she charged into the kitchen and pulled a can of Raid from beneath the sink. With vigor and determination, she strode back into the living room and sprayed its putrid-smelling vapor over the mess. An attack on the kitchen followed and the black pesky ants were left curled up into tarry little balls. The gaseous fumes intermingled with the odor of garbage that already permeated the house. All the doors and windows were yanked and shoved open.

He stood silently watching, not sure just how to handle such a display of wrath, and not offering any help either. "Just get out of my way. OK?" With a commanding scream, the spray can was pointed directly into his face.

"Damn woman!" Deftly, he wove around the debris in the kitchen and kicked the door open. It slammed shut behind him. "Jason! . . . Joyce! . . . Come here! . . . Right now! I've got a surprise for you! Your mother doesn't care about it . . . but you're going with me! . . . Right now!" He bellowed the orders military-style, so all the neighborhood could hear. Scott went scuttling home.

The other two children ran like jack rabbits over to their father. "Get in the car!" The back door was flung open, and his head jerked in its direction. They got in, and it was slammed shut. With a grinding of gears, the Lincoln shot down the street. The horn blasted at a car about to pull out from a neighbor's driveway. He headed for the country.

* * *

LuAnn located trash bags in the kitchen drawer, and yanked one open. The debris in the living room was picked up and, unceremoniously, crammed into it. It was vigorously shaken down to make room for the attack on the kitchen. Dirty dishes were eyed with distaste, and those stuck with egg yolk and other yuck were thrown into the bag. Anything salvageable was stacked beside the sink, all others were trashed. Pans encrusted with rust and stuck or burnt food were trashed, and casserole dishes exhibiting stuck or burnt food were trashed.

The more that was thrown into the bag . . . the more exhilarating and satisfying the sound of breaking dishes and clanging pans reverberated in the kitchen. Most of the wares had come from Ruby Dutcher's kitchen, and with each item that crashed into the bag, there was a smashing of Ruby's and Mack's selfish disrespect for her and the children. A torrent of tears were continually brushed away, but she kept at it: the cleansing of a tired body and soul.

Finally, there were three large trash bags filled and tied, and they were lugged out to the porch. She grabbed the broom and swept up the ants, crumbs, and dirt from the floor. The salvaged dishes were left soaking in the sink while the counters, stove, and table were scrubbed with scouring powder.

Towels were collected from the bathroom, and a load of laundry was started in the utility room. The smell of soap and the persistent churning of the agitator became a balm to frazzled nerves. The crazed tempo subsided, and persistent diligence took its place.

After scrubbing out the tub, shower and sink, she started in on the floors. The kitchen floor was mopped, and then the living room was vacuumed. Dirty clothes and bedding were collected from the bedroom and piled around the utility room to be laundered later. The bedroom was vacuumed and dusted. The living room was dusted. The children's rooms were dusted. Their suitcases were placed on the beds to be unpacked when they got home.

* * *

After four hours, a very tired, sweaty, and dirty body was dragged into the bathroom. With clean clothes in hand, the door was locked, and water was run into the tub. Nothing was going to get her out of the bathroom until she was good and ready to get out. At twelve-thirty, the Lincoln pulled into the driveway, and the kids feet pounded over the planks on the porch. The screen door opened and closed with a bang. "Mom, we're home! You won't believe this!"

"I'm in the bathroom, and I can't come out yet! You're just going to have to wait!" She allowed thirty more minutes to dress, fix her hair and put on makeup. When she exited from her sanctuary, the three of them were sitting in the living room, heads in hands, waiting for her to join them. "So, what's all the commotion about?"

"Dad, can I tell her?" With sparkling eyes, Jason looked at his father. Mack nodded, and the boy continued. "Mom, we've got a farm! . . . A real farm! . . . Dad even said we can get two ponies, just like Carmen and Roy!"

"Yeah! And don't forget about the woods and the creek!" Joyce chimed in.

"What are you talking about?" LuAnn studied the children, trying to understand. "Mack, is this true?" She implored him for clarification or denial. "We can't afford that!"

She was thinking of a husband who, just hours before, denied his ability to pay for their breakfast. With the money he gave her, the bills had scarcely been paid for the past nine years. "You must be out of your mind!" Had he discovered her money in the Hiawatha State Bank and figured they could use that? Or, was he making more money than he let on? She had never seen a paycheck. Her mind searched for some rationalization.

"LuAnn, sit down! I've got something important to tell you. Aunt Ruby died while you were gone, and the Dutcher place was sold. I had enough money to buy us a place in the country north of town, out near Otterville. The kids are real excited about moving. I hope you will be, too. If you aren't, we'll be going anyway." He nodded towards the kids. Mack stood up and looked down at his wife. "If you want to see it, I'll take you now. We can get some groceries on the way home. It won't hurt if dinner's a bit late."

Without looking at him, she stood up on legs of wood, too tired to argue. Brushing past him, she went into their bedroom to get her purse. The family settled into the Lincoln, and she laid back on the seat, closed her eyes . . . and tried to clear a cluttered and confused mind. She immediately fell asleep.

Just minutes later, she was being shaken awake. "We're here, Honey! Wake up! Just look at this! Here, I've got the key to the house." He shook her again, more vigorously. "Come on!" The driver's side door was opened and slammed shut. Impatiently, he strode around to open the passenger side door. Joyce and Jason were curled up on the back seat sound asleep. "We'll leave the kids here."

He took ahold of his wife's arm. With a great deal of effort, she put aching legs beneath a tired body and lifted up from the seat. Groggy from the unfinished nap, she slowly began to take in the grandeur of the scene. The woods with the creek in the distance sparkling through the branches of the trees and the picturesque old barn were all beyond anything she could have imagined. Then she turned to look at the house. It wasn't large, but it was quite beautiful.

"Mack, it's wonderful, but can we afford it? There's so much to keep up." She followed him through the front door. All of the rooms were freshly painted, and it was ready for new occupants. Her brain gradually awakened, and she began to visualize their old furniture in such a house, but she dared not mention buying anything new at this time. Besides, when she became more knowledgeable about decorating, through the classes at Hawkeye College, she could make appropriate selections, a few at a time. "It's lovely, Mack, just lovely. What are your plans for moving?"

"We can start tomorrow! Tomorrow's Sunday. I can work at it all day. After that, I'll have to do the moving after work, but the evenings are long enough to get two or three hours in. You really like it, huh?" A satisfied and proud grin spread across his face. "I guess we better go and get some groceries now. The kids were complaining about being hungry an hour ago."

* * *

The A&P was packed with grocery shoppers, and the check-out lines were long. LuAnn was thankful Joyce and Jason were still sleeping in the back seat of the car, and Mack had stayed with them. As tired as she was, it would be very difficult to contend with everyone right now. She hurried as fast as possible. The bags were loaded into the trunk, and they were on their way home. With careful planning, the supplies should last them for two weeks. Monday, she would drive out to the Yoders for a couple dozen eggs.

She began to think about living on the farmstead. Sarah Yoder would be living only two miles further up the winding road. Joyce and Jason would even be able to ride their bicycles there. It could be a beautiful life, but she still wondered where the money to support such a lifestyle would come from.

⁂ ⁂ ⁂

It was well after three o'clock before dinner was prepared and eaten . . . and the dishes were cleaned up. LuAnn insisted that Joyce help, and then she directed both of the children to empty out their suitcases and to put their clothes away. Normally, she would have done those tasks herself, but reality was dawning. If she was going to get the education she was aspiring to, she would need some help and cooperation from her family.

⁂ ⁂ ⁂

All day Sunday, LuAnn and the children concentrated on the bedrooms. They cleaned out closets and dresser drawers. The end results were two more bags of trash from each room. Since getting anything new for the house wasn't a reality, they decided to refinish the furniture. Joyce wanted hers painted red, and Jason wanted his painted brown. LuAnn agreed, "Good choices! I'll get the paint tomorrow." For the furniture in her and Mack's room, she settled on a bit of sanding and a coat of varnish.

The plastic bag, containing the box with the locket in it, remained at the bottom of the underwear drawer. She sat for several minutes, holding the small package, contemplating what to do with it. Her decision was to slide it back into its hiding place.

Mack reluctantly sorted through the junk in the garage. LuAnn reminded him, emphatically, that it was mostly his. "Don't you even begin to think I'm going to do it! That's your mess! I just cleaned up one of your messes in the house, and I'm not about to clean up another one!" There was no argument from him.

⁂ ⁂ ⁂

Monday morning, LuAnn, Joyce, and Jason made a trip to the hardware store. The materials needed for the painting and refinishing jobs were purchased and loaded into her little Volkswagen. Then, they headed for the Yoder farm. They were excited about the move, and wanted to share the news with the Yoders. "It's really a beautiful place, Sarah. You must know the one I'm talking about. It's about a mile east of Otterville."

Sarah acknowledged that, indeed, she knew the place. She had some exciting news of her own. "Henry and his brothers, Perry and Lester, have been offered the materials on an old farmstead in Hiawatha. They can have any of the wood and other things just for tearing it down. There are good oak floors and woodwork in the house. There should be enough lumber for us to construct a new kitchen. The barn has enough good lumber in it to construct a new chicken house for our egg business. They've already started tearing down the barn," Sarah's smile radiated with excitement.

"In Hiawatha . . . you say? Do you know the name of the place?" Somehow, LuAnn was certain she was talking about the Dutcher place.

Sarah confirmed her intuition. "The Dutcher place, it's called. Do you know it?"

"Sarah, that's where Mack was raised! What a coincidence! Ruby Dutcher raised Mack. She died last month, right after we left for the east."

"Well, then it must be you who needs to go through the house, to make sure everything you want is taken out before the work is started there. Mr. Weatherby told Henry the previous owners have until the end of July."

LuAnn's brain began to churn. "I suppose, perhaps, I should go and take a look around. I'm going to need some more furniture for the new house. Maybe I can refinish some of the old standing cupboards from the kitchen and pantry. Sarah, I just had a thought. How would you like to go with me to look at the house . . . say Thursday of this week?" Her eyes danced in anticipation.

"I would love to do that! Why don't you leave Joyce and Jason here to play with my children? I'm sure they aren't anxious to go for another ride yet." She looked inquiringly at the two children who were taking in the conversation. "Would you like to do that? If your mother thinks it's all right."

"Wow! Yeah! Can we have a buggy ride?" Jason wanted to know.

Joyce looked at Susie, who had been listening to the conversation as well. The two girls grabbed one another's hands and, giggling, jumped up and down. Joyce's bare, tanned legs were in stark contrast to Susie's long, blue skirt.

"I imagine Henry can work in a buggy ride for you. It's all set then? I'll check with Martha just to make sure, but I doubt that she will object." Sarah went into the house to consult with her mother-in-law. "She says it's fine with her."

LuAnn picked up two dozen eggs and headed for the car. "I'll be back on Thursday morning, say, eight o'clock." Joyce and Jason waved to the Amish children, and the Volkswagen drove out of the yard.

By Wednesday evening, the bedroom furniture was all painted and varnished. LuAnn stood back and with a sense of pride, admired the accomplishments. With new curtains and bedspreads for each room, the results would be quite acceptable. Even Mack was impressed with the job. "I don't know why you want to go to school to learn this stuff, You're doing OK already."

Sixteen

The little Volkswagen turned sharply into the Yoders' driveway and stopped by the house yard gate. Joyce and Jason popped open the car door and scrambled out. Their bare feet hit the dust of the barnyard, and, with a whoop from Jason, there was an undeclared race to the barn where Grandfather Yoder was harnessing up the buggy horse. Henry and Sarah's three oldest children were helping. In a patient and kindly manner, instructions were being given by the old man as the leather straps were yanked, pulled, and fastened into place by the youngsters. The white-faced, light reddish-brown sorrel stood as still as a statue. There was only an occasional stamp of a hoof and rippling of skin in an attempt to keep the flies off.

Joyce gave up on winning the foot-race, and, with a look of defeat, stopped and turned towards her mother. "Bye, Mom!" With a grin, she was off again . . . jumping, agilely, over piles of horse manure that dotted the dusty ground of the barnyard. "Hi, Susie!" Pecking chickens squawked and fluttered out of the way.

An exuberant Sarah hastened down the path from the house. High black shoes clomped with confidence on the worn dirt path . . . no hesitancy in her step. The long dark-purple skirt and black apron whipped around her slim, strong, legs. A few dampened loose brown curls peeked out from around the edge of the white cap. The cheery face was already moist and pink from the heat of the morning, and her bright blue eyes sparkled. A small black purse was clutched tightly in her right hand. It contained part of her last week's share of the egg money.

She lifted the latch on the yard gate, slid her body through a narrow opening, and carefully locked it. The chickens weren't welcome in there. She leaned into the car. "Good morning, LuAnn! Isn't this wonderful!" Ducking down, she stepped into the Volkswagen. The dress and apron were arranged and smoothed. She looked towards LuAnn, and a mischievous gleam shot from her eyes. Empty hands were held out in front of her as though for the reins. "Where's the horse?" she chirped, and a trill of laughter proceeded the humorous inquisition.

LuAnn blinked, and then catching Sarah's humor, giggled. "Well I guess our horse is behind us. All set? Then, we're on our way!" She released the brake, put the car in gear, and pressed down on the gas pedal. The little bug responded, and they were off. The two mothers, cut loose from their children and other home responsibilities, were going to have a wonderful time. They would both see to that. Anticipation for the day ahead radiated from Sarah's demeanor and was immediately contagious. LuAnn found it very refreshing.

* * *

As the vehicle was propelled along the dirt road, the conversation, naturally, turned to Ruby and the Dutcher place. LuAnn began reminiscing. She spoke slowly and with an apparent degree of thoughtfulness. "It's been nine years since Mack and I lived there. I saw Ruby only once after we moved to Independence. Apparently, she wanted nothing to do with me or the children. She was a very independent person, and never did accept my being there." LuAnn glanced towards Sarah to see if she was listening. Then she continued, "It must have been hard to see a young, healthy woman take her place." Sitting up straighter in the seat with a feeling of satisfaction and a nod, she concluded, "I respected that decision and still harbor no ill feelings."

Then she began to wonder. *How did Sarah manage to maintain a congenial relationship with Martha? They were living in the same house.* So she asked, "Sarah, you seem to be happy with your mother-in-law. Don't you ever have any problems?"

Now LuAnn took closer notice of her passenger. She seemed a bit nervous and was noticeably alert to the speed and maneuvering of the little car. There was a sharp intake of breath on nearly every turn, and the purse was clutched tightly with both hands.

LuAnn let up on the gas pedal and bit her lip. "Or maybe I shouldn't ask. It's really none of my business." There was a long smothering silence . . . and a feeling of discomfort passed between the two.

Finally, Sarah responded, "We Amish find ways to get along, because that is the way God wants it. If our problems become too much, the bishop helps us to find a solution. It works well for the Amish community. Do you believe in God?" Sarah turned and studied the profile of her friend. "Do you have a church, LuAnn?"

LuAnn felt her face flush, and she reluctantly admitted, "We've gone to church very little since leaving Hiawatha. When Joyce and Jason were attending day care at the Presbyterian Church, the children and I attended Sunday School and church occasionally. But, after they started public school, it was easier for me to stay home on Sundays and get the housework caught up. Mack hasn't shown any interest in going. No, we haven't gone to church in a long time, but I do believe God is out there watching over us."

"The man should be the spiritual leader for the family. It would be hard to make decisions without him." Sarah turned away and focused on the fields of tall, green corn flying past the car window. Perhaps enough had been said about that topic.

"Henry and his brothers are very excited about the work they're doing." Graciously, the direction of their conversation was changed. "There will be plenty of lumber for the building we have in mind, and it's of good quality. Henry said he looked inside the house yesterday, and the fruit cupboard in the pantry is in very good condition. The cupboard in the kitchen is very nice, too. If you have room for them in your new house, you should take them."

The refinished bedroom furniture had turned out very well. Perhaps the same thing could be done with those pieces. "I'll bet you're right, Sarah. Well, we'll soon know."

She turned the Volkswagen off the highway and onto the dirt road. In a matter of minutes, they bumped up the short lane leading to the Dutcher place, and lurched to a stop in front of the house. The doors were opened, and they swung hot legs and feet into the open air . . . relieved to be out of the cramped, warm interior of the little car.

The men were hard at work and barely glanced their way. Out in front of the chicken house, Henry and one of his brothers were busy stacking boards ripped from the barn into neat piles. Their dark clothing and bearded silhouettes made it difficult to discern one from the other. Over by the barn, big and burly, John Robey worked with another brother. They were hunched over some boards, pulling out nails. John was the only English man working on the demolition project. He drove the rattly, old, stock truck to the Dutcher place every day. It provided transportation for the Amish men and a means of hauling the lumber home at the end of the day. This afternoon, they would be taking the first load to the Yoder farm.

After the women emerged from the car, Henry and John left their work and strode towards one another. They stopped in the middle of the yard. Their straw hats were tipped close together in what appeared to be a serious conversation. Henry pulled something from his pants pocket and held it out. The sunlight sparkled from whatever it was. The men nodded in agreement. Henry's hand closed tightly around the object. He turned away from John and took quick, long steps towards the two women.

He smiled at Sarah and nodded, acknowledging her presence. Then he gave full attention to LuAnn. "We pulled out the cupboard in the kitchen this morning, and we found these wedged in behind it. They must be yours." Laying on his palm was a tangled accumulation of gold jewelry that haughtily caught light from the sun.

Incredulously, LuAnn stared at the pieces, recognizing them as being real gold and quite expensive. One at a time, they were lifted and carefully examined. There was a wrist watch with a broken crystal, a diamond earring, a necklace with a pearl pendant, and a charm bracelet. The bracelet had only three trinkets on it. Two were hearts. One heart was inscribed *Kate.* The other heart was inscribed *Mack.* The third trinket was a house with *Weatherby Real Estate* inscribed on it.

She began to shake, and she felt sick and weak, as though having been delivered a powerful blow to the stomach. "Yes . . . yes . . . I can't imagine how they got there, but they . . . are . . . mine. Thank you." Like coals too hot to handle, the jewelry was quickly dropped into her purse. Then, mustering up a courageous smile, she started towards the house. "Come on, Sarah. Now, let's see about those cupboards."

Sarah hadn't missed the look of bewilderment that crossed over LuAnn's face and her friend's shaken demeanor. She had the distinct impression that the jewelry wasn't really hers. She had never seen LuAnn wear a bracelet or a necklace, and the earring definitely wasn't something she would choose. She didn't know much about English women's jewelry, but she did know that what Henry found wasn't something LuAnn would likely have. She followed after her into the house, curiosity and concern tickling at her brain.

They looked at the cupboards and through all the rooms. Nine years of dust and dirt covered everything, including the counters and sinks in the kitchen and bath. If there was anything more to be found, it would be by chance when the place was torn down. As they left the house, LuAnn had a request. "Sarah, would you please tell Henry that if he finds anything more, to keep it for me?"

John Robey agreed to transport the two cupboards to the Hanable farm for twenty dollars, and LuAnn paid him in advance. Henry would make certain the man held to his word.

Little by little, the day had turned out to be depressing, and LuAnn wanted so much to keep the trip an enjoyable one. "Sarah, how would you like to drive into Cedar Rapids and have lunch at Bishops? When we come back, we'll stop and see my friend, Francis. I'll bet you haven't ever been in a beauty shop . . . as if you would need one. You must have very beautiful hair under that cap."

* * *

At two o'clock, they pulled up in front of Francis' Beauty Shop. LuAnn hadn't called her since returning from Grafton, so Francis was very surprised to see her, and even more surprised to see the young Amish woman.

"Francis, this is Sarah Yoder. Her husband and his brothers are tearing down the buildings on the Dutcher place. Have you noticed them working over there?"

"Oh, yes! I've been watching what's going on. There's a lot of activity! Joe Weatherby isn't wasting any time getting on with his plans. In fact, he's offered me a great deal of money for my parents' old property . . . where I'm living now," she explained to Sarah. "In fact, his offer is so good that I really can't turn it down. Right now, I'm not sure what I should do. Karen has started her own beauty shop in Cedar Rapids, so I have more than I can handle here by myself. I just may sell it all and live off the money." A satisfied smile confirmed her statement, and scattered wrinkles gave credence to her age. She was resembling Maude more and more each year.

"That sounds good to me . . . if you can get by with it! Maybe you should move to Independence!" The idea appealed to LuAnn, but there was no time for giving the issue further consideration. Francis' next customer came in and immediately started in on her own agenda.

So LuAnn and Sarah crossed the street to say hello to the Cummings at the drug store. Daniel and Becky had enlarged the business two years before, attracting a steady stream of customers. There was little opportunity to give attention to their old employee. Some personal products were purchased, and LuAnn promised to come back another time. As she left the premises, there was a vague feeling of having been intrusive. The passing of time can, of course, change relationships.

The two women walked over to the post office, and the box was checked for anything of importance. Jane and her parents had already written letters. They were placed with the jewelry in her purse to be read later. Her family all questioned Mack's credibility and were making certain she got their letters by sending them to the box in Hiawatha.

Sarah was baffled when LuAnn paid the rent for the next year. Why would a woman have a post office box in another town when her own husband delivered mail?

* * *

During the quiet drive back to Independence, LuAnn contemplated giving Sarah an explanation concerning the jewelry and post office box. If she started talking, all the doubts and fears concerning Mack would be divulged, and, perhaps, Sarah wouldn't really want to know about their personal affairs. So, she began hesitantly. "I hope you won't take what I have to say as a burden on yourself, but I know some things that happened today must seem quite strange . . . " For the remainder of the drive, she articulated the relationship between herself and Mack to Sarah . . . much as she had to Thomas. The details were even more difficult to relate to another woman, especially an Amish woman. Somehow, she felt so inadequate.

Sarah listened, noncommittal, while her busy fingers wove in and out of the apron's folds. Not wanting to interrupt, her eyes stayed on the highway ahead. When the monologue ended, Sarah expressed with assurance, "If you and the children should ever need help, come to Henry and me. We will ask God to help you. We will pray for Mack, too. He needs God's guidance. We are all weak at times." There were many questions she would like to ask, but it wasn't right to interfere in another person's life.

* * *

It was after five o'clock when LuAnn pulled into the driveway. Joyce and Jason smelled like horses and were bubbling over with enthusiasm for the day. On the way home, they begged to go back again before school started.

LuAnn reminded them, "Remember! You're going to be living right out there! You'll be able to ride your bikes up to the Yoders anytime you want to . . . as long as you don't make pests of yourselves. The Yoder children have chores to do. And your father and I just might be finding some for you . . . once we get settled."

* * *

Mack started out the day on a high note. "It's Thursday, July the Third. Tomorrow is Friday . . . July the Fourth. I have Friday, Saturday, and Sunday off. That gives us three full days to get moved out of that old shack and into our new home." He was planning as he drove along and flying high . . . but not for long.

Gravel and dust flew up behind the Lincoln, and then, with the help of a strong southerly wind, settled in on him when the stops were made at the mail boxes. In his haste that morning, the thermos of water and sack lunch were forgotten. His throat felt as parched as a dried noodle, and his stomach as empty as a donut hole. Perspiration soaked his clothing, and dust settled on everything inside the car, including him.

In order to have access to the mailboxes, he sat in the center of the seat. His left arm and leg ached from the strain of reaching the gas pedal, brake and steering wheel. By turning and stretching, he yanked on the lid with his left hand, and thrust the bundles of mail into the box with his right. The opening was missed on two occasions and the mail dropped to the ground. It was necessary to get out of the vehicle. "Damn! More time wasted!"

Nevertheless, he was running a full forty minutes early when he started back to the post office. When he drove past the farmstead, there was a station wagon parked in the yard. "What the hell's going on?" He backed up and pulled in behind it.

The car looked familiar. "Nobody'd better be messin' around my place!" He spoke aloud and stepped from the Lincoln, eyes blazing with impatience and distrust. A woman emerged from the other vehicle. It was Irene White. "What in the hell does she want?" Again, he muttered aloud.

"Why, hello, Mr. Hanable. I'm so glad you stopped in while I'm here." She would make it quick. Apparently, he was upset about something. "I've come to get my sign." She walked through the tall grass and, with considerable effort, pulled the Hope Realty sign from the ground.

When she was walking back to the car, dragging the sign, Mack viewed, with irritation, her steps as being exaggerated knee lifts. "My, but your grass is getting tall! It won't be long until you'll have to make it into hay!" Laughter fell piercingly on his ears.

The comment was taken as a mockery, and he glaringly inquired, "Is there anything else today? I believe all the transactions have been made, and the paperwork is completed. The deed is yet to come, but my lawyer says that is all in order. So, I guess I don't need your services any further." He opened the door of the station wagon, and, with a sweep of his arm, indicated she leave.

With a quizzical expression furrowing her brow, the rear door was opened with a yank and the sign quickly placed inside . . . best not to say anything. In an effort to vent and regain some calm, the door was closed with a vigorous slam. "Sometimes, it doesn't latch properly." Composure restored, she went around to the driver's side where Mack still stood holding the door. A smile was pasted to her lips and directed towards him. She slid into the seat, and got positioned at the wheel. The key was inserted into the ignition. "It's been wonderful doing business with you, Mr. Hanable." The door was closed with a resounding slam.

Mack got into the Lincoln, backed out of the drive, stopped in the middle of the road, and waited for her to leave. He took to muttering again. *Damn woman! She takes my money, takes my time, and tells me how to take care of my property, besides! What business is it of hers if the lawn needs to be mowed?*

Irene drove away slowly and contemplated their encounter. She cautioned a weak wave and headed west, across country to Littleton . . . and back to Waterloo.

* * *

It was still only four-thirty when he pulled into the driveway in Independence. He expected LuAnn to be there, so they could get on with the packing and, possibly, get some boxes moved that evening. When she wasn't there, he began to think about the lawn. Yes, it was in desperate need of mowing. Irene had been right, but he didn't need her to tell him.

There was a lot of lawn to mow out there, so he began to consider the old tractor mower that was used on the Dutcher place. It had been stashed in the back of the garage, accumulating dust, for nine years, because all that was needed for the lawn in town was the little push mower bought used from a neighbor.

Somewhat refreshed, after getting a drink from the hose and splashing water on his face, he decided to see if the tractor mower would even start. With considerable effort, he pushed it out of its confines and into the light of the sun. Sweat drenched his clothes, so he turned on the water spigot for another drink and, this time, ran water over his head.

With a greasy old rag, the accumulation of dust and cobwebs was brushed off the mower. Some gas from a can kept in the garage was poured into the tank, and a can of oil was poured in. With greasy hands, the smarting sweat was wiped away from his eyes. *Gawd, I'm thirsty!* And he went back to the hose and spigot.

The spark plug was examined, and he rummaged through the box of spare parts for a new one to put in. Then he checked the rope for the pull start. It was frayed and needed to be replaced. He dug through the boxes of junk brought from the Dutcher place and found what was needed. After nearly an hour of tinkering, he was ready to give his efforts a try.

* * *

LuAnn pulled into the drive and brought the Volkswagen to a stop within feet of him. Her face radiated happiness as Joyce and Jason chattered about their adventures at the Yoders. It had been a good day for them. They scrambled out of the passenger side and slammed the door before LuAnn even had time to shut off the engine.

With dirty hands on his narrow hips, Jason stood beside his father and looked up at him . . . a miniature reproduction. "Hey Dad, can you guess what we did today?" Mack looked down at his son, and Jason broke into a peel of laughter. His shaggy dark head was humorously tossed back and cocked to one side. He pointed. "Gosh, Dad, you sure look funny. There's dirt all over your face!"

This was the second time today someone had laughed at him, and this time it was his own son. An uncontrollable rage, born of frustration and an empty stomach, took over. With one powerful hand, he grabbed Jason by the back of the neck. "You think I'm funny, do you? Well, let's see what's funny!" With the other hand, he wiped grease and oil from the mower and smeared it all over his face. He repeated this attack three more times, covering the boy's hair and clothes with grime before giving him a shove. "Now get out of my way!"

LuAnn and Joyce stood in stoned silence, neither of them able to move or comprehend the violent reaction Mack directed towards the boy's innocent remark.

Now, he turned on his wife. "Where the hell have you been? I busted my butt to get finished with the route early today so we could have time to get some things moved. I get home, and you aren't even here! A hell of a lot of help you are!" His hand was raised to strike, but when she drew back in fear, it dropped to his side. Grimy fingers curled and uncurled. "I'd better see if I can get this thing started. The lawn needs mowin' real bad out there." His attention was turned back to the machine. "I guess I'm just hungry."

LuAnn ushered the children into the house. "You two get baths and put clean clothes on. You smell like horses!" Then, trying to make light of the grime his father had rubbed on him, she added, "And Jason, you do look funny. Why don't you get yours first?"

LuAnn hurriedly prepared a supper of scrambled eggs with ham, fried potatoes, a loaf of fresh Amish bread from Sarah, peaches and oatmeal cookies. It was nearly ready when some weak sputters and coughs were heard coming from the old lawnmower. In a few more minutes, a shaky rumbling drowned out all other sound. Then, the noise settled into a steady roar. The motor was cut half a dozen times and then started up again. Each time, the reverberation was steadier and more confident.

She looked out the screen door. Mack was standing beside the machine looking satisfied. "I'll need to sharpen the blades after supper, but I think the old critter is going to do the job."

"Can you come in now? It's almost time to eat." LuAnn and the children sat at the table and waited while he went into the bathroom and showered. It was a quiet meal.

Finally, LuAnn broke the silence. "There are boxes packed in the children's rooms. We can take them out to the house this evening, if you want. Do you have plans for hauling the big pieces of furniture?"

"Yeah, yeah, sure. We can take some boxes out this evening. Tomorrow morning Pete Brown is bringing his pickup over. He'll help load and haul the big stuff tomorrow and Sunday." He went back to eating.

* * *

Pete had been their mail carrier ever since moving to Independence. He was one of the few people Mack ever bothered with. He was also the one who confirmed Mack's employment location for Kate Weatherby nine years before. After reports to the post office that Mack was seen fighting with a woman on the city street during deliveries, Pete put two and two together. Whatever the problem was between the two, Pete felt somewhat responsible. After that, he befriended Mack on more than one occasion. There was something about the guy that needed help.

* * *

Wearily, the family loaded up boxes from the children's rooms and boxes from the kitchen, and, using both cars, they drove to the country. LuAnn noticed the FOR SALE sign had been removed. "It looks like Irene White was here today." Everyone pitched in and carried boxes into the new house.

At ten o'clock, the rest of the family crawled into bed, but Mack stayed up for two more hours and sharpened the blades on the mower. There was a lot to do tomorrow.

Seventeen

At four-thirty, the morning of the Fourth of July, a sharp crack of lightning, followed by repeated angry flashes and rumblings of thunder, woke LuAnn. She lay still, not wanting to awaken her husband. But when torrents of rain started splattering against the windows, she slid from the bed and quietly moved around the house lowering the windows against the downpour. In her billowy, thin nightgown, she moved as a ghostly figure flitting from room to room. The children were sleeping peacefully in their beds, oblivious to the storm, cherubs to be cherished. She pushed down the windows in their rooms and lovingly pulled the blankets up over their shoulders. The air had turned cool.

She returned to the bedroom. Mack was still deep in slumber, apparently too tired to be disturbed by the storm. She stood silently watching as his hairy chest rose and fell, rhythmically, with each breath, accompanied by a continuous rumble of snores on the intake. His mouth hung open, and drool oozed from the corner of his mouth to saturate the feather pillow. Deep inside, she longed to feel passionately towards him, but she just couldn't. A lone tear trickled down her cheek and fell on her right breast. From there, it slid into the cleavage.

Again, a brilliant flash of lightning lit up the darkness, and her purse stood illumined starkly on the chair next to the bed. Until then, she had completely forgotten about the jewelry and letters. In the eerie spectacle of shadows and brilliance, fear and apprehension penetrated and magnified her, otherwise, normal senses . . . commensurate with the strikes. He had nearly struck her, and he had treated Jason badly. Apparently, he was losing control again, and something had to be done . . . but what? She took a step towards the bed and studied the dim shape of the man who had been her husband for ten years. Lightning strikes cast a ghastly light on the partially exposed muscular body. Although the body was familiar, the man in it was still a stranger.

Once more, she thought of the heart locket which lay hidden at the bottom of the dresser drawer beneath her underwear. Now, there was even more incriminating "evidence" of her husband's infidelity at the bottom of her purse. She was gripped with an urgency to do something with the accumulation of jewelry. But what?

Perhaps, she should just get rid of it, but the idea ignited a dreadful fear of being left totally helpless. As long as it remained in her possession, there was an unexplainable feeling of having a sense of security. Perhaps, it was a false security, but, somehow, the "evidence" represented a degree of power and control. There was no need to rationalize the feeling. She just knew that to be so.

She opened the dresser drawer and ran a nervous hand beneath the silky apparel . . . at the same time, watching her husband. Sensitive fingers located the box containing the locket, gripped it, and dropped it into the purse with the rest of the jewelry. The purse was clutched tightly as she sat motionless on the chair and searched her brain for a solution. Her head hurt from the trying, as if it were trying to bust wide open. Each beat of her heart pounded forcefully in her ears, and normal breathing seemed very difficult. Finally, she stood up and took a very deep breath. There was no conceivable hiding place in the bedroom. She would have to look elsewhere.

What would Mack's reaction be if he ever found the stash of jewelry? At the very thought, there was an overwhelming sense of panic and a strong temptation to, immediately, dispose of everything into the trash can. Of course, that would be irrational. She already knew that, so she clung passionately to the purse and edged towards the bedroom doorway.

Mack's breaths were still deep and even . . . he was asleep. With bare feet and purse in hand, she crept silently into the living room to find a suitable hiding place. With illumination from the bolts of lightning, her eyes swept over the familiar room. It was immediately evident that no solution to the problem would be found there. Debris from the previous day's packing stuck stubbornly to the bottoms of her feet. With disgust, she wiped them on the carpet and continued the quest into the kitchen.

It was an eerie search, and the creaking of the old floors added to the haunting discomfort. When there wasn't the rumble of thunder and crack of lightning, the ticking of the clocks echoed through the rooms.

The washer and dryer in the utility room were of little consequence. She needed to use the machines, first thing in the morning . . . before they were disconnected. The large box of soap powder was eyed, but it wouldn't do for jewelry to tumble out with grains of detergent.

The stash couldn't be put into the stove. It would rattle around and draw attention. That left only the refrigerator. Mack regularly helped himself to the milk, fruit, and other goodies in the cooling section, but he seldom opened the freezer department for anything other than ice cubes or ice cream.

She opened the door. There were packages of hamburger and chicken wrapped in white paper and sealed with freezer tape. An idea began to take shape. She lifted out one of the smaller packages and critically judged its weight. Then she reached to the bottom of the purse and gathered up the handful of jewelry. The weight was similar, and the solution was found.

With trembling fingers, the smallest package of hamburger was carefully unwrapped. She placed each piece of jewelry into a plastic bag and placed each bag into a container similar to the size and shape of the hamburger. The remaining space was packed with ice cubes. The package was wrapped, sealed, and marked with a small black dot. Good! The package could be identified easily . . . and yet it resembled the others. It was placed into the back of the freezer, and the door was closed. With relief, her tired, shaking body sagged into one of the chairs.

She collapsed at the kitchen table and stared, incredulously, at the chunk of frozen hamburger setting in front of her. Defiantly, the ghost of Kate Weatherby floated around the kitchen. She shook her head to get rid of it. Numbness gradually gave way to acute awareness. She was cold and nauseated from fatigue, but the thin night gown, wet with perspiration, clung seductively to her curves. She tried to pull it free from her skin. Her head hurt, and her hands were shaky and clammy. She folded goose-bumped arms around her shoulders and rubbed vigorously. Exhausted, she bent forward and cushioned her head. A stream of tears trickled down, eventually landing on the table. Fatigued eyes willingly closed, and a fretful sleep followed.

* * *

Kate was with her in a boat, out on the lake, and a storm was pounding down on them. A hand reached up from out of the water and pulled at the side of the craft, rocking it dangerously. Kate fell out, and her screams turned to choked gurgles as she disappeared into the depths below. Now, the hand was reaching for LuAnn, rocking and shaking the boat. She tried to scream, but instead, she sat bolt upright. Mack was shaking her awake.

* * *

"What in hell are you doing out here, LuAnn? We've got work to do! It looks like it stormed last night. At least it's stopped now! I would hate like hell to be moving furniture in the rain." He looked at his wife with an expression of disgust . . . an employee caught napping.

With an exaggerated sigh, he went to the cupboard and took out a box of cereal, a bowl, and a spoon. He set them on the table and went to the refrigerator. "We're almost out of milk. Guess we better wait 'til we're moved before we get anymore, though. No sense in draggin' around a lot of stuff if we don't need to."

He sat down at the table, poured out cereal and milk, and began shoveling and chewing. "Pete's gonna be here any minute. For gawd's sake, LuAnn, go get some clothes on! You can't sit around in that thin nightgown!"

Obediently, she went into the bathroom and splashed cold water on her face. The washcloth was run over clammy arms and legs. Pieces of debris were picked and brushed from her feet. Each leg was lifted, and her feet were washed in the sink. She dried with the only clean towel still hanging there. Fresh deodorant was applied, and her hair was brushed. That would have to do for now.

It was going to be a long day. In an effort to prepare mentally, she began to hum, *Out of my dreams and into your arms . . . I long to fly.* Thomas Maxwell's face floated through memories. She vigorously shook her head and walked down the hallway into the bedroom just as Pete came through the kitchen door.

She dressed in shorts and an old shirt and hurried into the kitchen right after the two men went out the door and to the garage. She watched them through the screen door for a short time. First, they loaded the boxes of tools into the back of the pickup. Then, Pete pulled two boards from the truck box and inclined them against the rear from the bed to the ground. Together, the men shoved the tractor mower up the boards and into the pickup. The loading seemed to be going as planned.

LuAnn began a load of laundry. She had no idea in what order Mack planned to take their household furnishings to the farmstead. But she did know the laundry needed to be done. She went into their bedrooms and woke up Joyce and Jason. It made sense to her to take the furniture from the bedrooms and the living room before taking it from the kitchen. She began making some plans of her own. They could always be changed.

By ten o'clock, the laundry was finished and folded up, put into drawers or boxes, and ready to be moved. Joyce and Jason had been of considerable help with the folding and packing. They couldn't wait to move, so they could get their ponies. At ten-fifteen, Pete Brown came back with the pickup. He was by himself.

"Mack decided he should get his tools put away in the shed out there, and then he wants to get started on the lawn mowing. He says you and I can handle the next load." The big, red-headed man looked at LuAnn almost apologetically, the sweat standing out on his ruddy, freckled face. His grin was friendly and reassuring.

* * *

He was thinking that she was just too small and slim to be lugging heavy boxes. He had always felt rather sorry for her. She didn't seem to be the kind of woman who stuck up for herself very well. That's how he knew, for certain, that the woman who drove the Corvette and was fighting with Mack out in the street couldn't have been his wife.

The witnesses had described her as being nearly as tall as Mack, with dark hair. They said she had a full figure and wore lots of makeup and jewelry. That wasn't LuAnn. Pete always wondered if she knew about the incident. Maybe he would find out.

* * *

"Your husband always has a sense of what he'll do and what he won't do. Right, LuAnn?" He hoped to get her talking. "In fact, sometimes it gets him into trouble down at the post office." He looked to see if she was responding in any way. "I'm glad for your sake and the sake of the kids that he's still around . . . even though he nearly got fired the first week he was here. It was really something when that crazy woman in the Corvette started attacking him right out there in the middle of the street."

He finally had her attention. She stopped peeling potatoes and, keeping her emotions in check, looked at him with blank, expressionless eyes. Her face registered nothing he could read.

"What are you talking about? A woman attacked Mack? Who was she?" LuAnn was certain she already knew, but needed to have Pete tell her. She couldn't look at him while he gave the answer. Instead, she went back to the potato, cutting peelings thick and fast before throwing it into a kettle of water.

"Gosh, maybe you didn't know. I figured Mack would have told you. He said it must be an irate lady he accidentally backed into with his car. He hadn't met her . . . just turned it over to his insurance company . . . nothing but a scratch on her bumper. He didn't ever say a name."

"Did anyone ever say what she looked like?" She kept her eyes on the potatoes. "Just what day was this anyway?"

"Well, it was in June, during Mack's first week on the job. I remember, because I just got back from my vacation. I always leave right after Memorial Day. It was probably about June 11 or 12. Of course, I didn't know him then, so when I heard the story, I thought it was a pretty good one. It's not everybody that gets attacked by a gorgeous brunette in a shiny Corvette. She looked wealthy with lots of makeup and jewelry . . . not the kind of woman we see around here very often. So, the witnesses said, at the time, anyway."

LuAnn finished peeling the potatoes and set the pan on the stove. She had heard enough. Turning the burner to a low setting, she led Pete into the children's bedrooms. "Well, what do you think? Shall we start with the chests of drawers or the dressers?" She was relieved that the package of jewelry was safe in the freezer of the refrigerator. Now, she knew for certain that Mack and Kate had been fighting. Just how violent had the fighting gotten? She could only imagine.

For the next hour, Pete and LuAnn dismantled beds and loaded furniture from Joyce's and Jason's rooms. In an effort to help, the children held open doors and grabbed ahold of corners of furniture. Tonight they would be sleeping in their new bedrooms! When Pete left for the farmstead, he took the children with him. He figured they had a right to help set up the furniture in their new rooms. "It's eleven-thirty now. I don't think you can expect us back before one o'clock . . . if that's OK."

"Certainly, that will give me time to make potato salad and ham sandwiches. That is, if you like potato salad and ham sandwiches."

"That's fine with me! I'm starvin' already. Come on, kids. We've got work to do." Pete backed the pickup out of the drive and drove off down the street.

* * *

When they got out to the Hanable farmstead, Mack was finished with about a third of the mowing. Most of the lawn needed to be passed over twice. Even then, the long grass lay like newly-mown hay. He was irritated to think that Irene was right. Well, it would just have to be raked. No big deal.

He had just put three rakes away in the shed. So, when Pete drove in, he yelled at Joyce and Jason. "Go get two of those rakes from the shed! They're right inside the doorway! You need to earn those ponies! Rake this up while I help Pete unload!"

They knew very little about raking, and were eager to get their rooms set up. So, Joyce objected, "But Dad, Pete said we could help get our rooms in order. We need to tell you how we want them arranged. We can! Can't we, Pete?"

He didn't have an opportunity to answer. Mack took two giant strides towards his daughter and grabbed her by the arm, twisting it behind her. "What did you say? And who are you asking for permission? I'm your father, and I said to get busy and get that grass raked up before I blister your butt! Do you understand?"

He gave her a shove and let loose. She struggled to maintain her balance and fell to one knee. A look of astonishment and fear masked her face. Tears surfaced and were brushed away with a tight fist. Mack turned to Pete, eyes burning with fire. "Let's get that furniture unloaded. I'm hungry as hell." He paused long enough to see that the children were on their way to the shed to get the rakes. "No messin' around either! You hear?"

The furniture was unloaded and carried to the rooms. Then Pete ventured to say, "I think we better wait and set it up later, Mack. LuAnn has dinner waiting for us. I'm hungry as hell, too." Willingly, Mack climbed into the back of the pickup, and the other three got in front. They headed back into town.

* * *

The afternoon dragged on. The rest of the bedroom furniture was loaded and hauled out to the farmstead and set up. The living room furniture was loaded and hauled out to the farmstead and arranged. It looked very sparse in its new surroundings. LuAnn made mental notes of what to do with the new home once they were settled in.

The appliances would be moved the next day, along with the rest of the kitchen furniture. Tonight, they could sleep in their new home, but they would have to drive into town to eat their breakfast.

At six-thirty that evening, Pete made an announcement. "Well folks, I'm finished for the day! I'm taking my family to the Fourth of July celebration in Aurora tonight. They have a damned good one! You'll have to take your family sometime, Mack." He drove off in the pickup.

* * *

After a supper of hamburgers and tomato soup, Mack had something more for the family to do. "We're workin' on the lawn until it gets dark. LuAnn, you can rake, too. There are three rakes out there." They climbed, wearily, into the car and sat back for a short rest before tackling the job.

At ten o'clock, LuAnn and the children went into the house and took baths. They put on night clothes and, wearily, crawled into bed for their first night in the new home. All were sleeping soundly when Mack finally put the mower away.

He showered and then dressed in a pair of old army shorts and a T-shirt. Too uptight to sleep, he went out to the front porch and sat down on the step. In his mind, there was no recognition of the peaceful night, only discontentment.

Why does life have to be so damned hard? How does Pete find the time and energy to take his family out celebrating? It was good of him to help out all day. In fact, he's a damned nice guy. We'll have to invite him and his family out for supper some night . . . after we're all settled. That's what we'll do! We'll invite Pete and his family for supper some night!

With that settled, he went upstairs and crawled into bed with his wife. They hadn't made love in a hellava long time, but he wasn't up to it tonight. He doubted that LuAnn would be open to the idea either, so he turned over and went to sleep.

* * *

By noon Saturday, the appliances had been moved and installed at the Hanable place. All that remained to be done was the cleaning up of the rental property in Independence. LuAnn would do that on Sunday.

Saturday afternoon, she went to the A&P for groceries. Joyce and Jason were still working on the raking. They decided that complaining to their father wasn't a good idea. Besides, they had seen the Amish children raking a good many times. "I guess if we live in the country, we need to get used to the work, huh, Mom?" Jason concluded.

Eighteen

The Lincoln roared out of the yard and east towards town. It needed a new muffler, and everyone within a half mile along the road had to be aware of it. Right now, that was an asset in LuAnn's mind. She was certain Mack was on his way to work. He was complaining about the brakes, too, but that was his problem.

She got out of bed and lifted up the corner of the mattress. The two letters from her family were right where she had put them Saturday evening after making up the bed. There was no time to get to them until now. Besides, it was nice to read her mail in private. It was a personal thing. If, for some reason, she wanted to cry . . . it was nobody else's business. If she wanted to get angry or disgusted and vent a little, well, who was to know?

She flopped back down on the bed and ripped both envelopes open. Quickly, she scanned the contents of both. It was amazing how nearly alike the two letters read: *Mother and Jane have one track minds, and they always harp on the same things.*

> *Please come back to Grafton. We'll help you get on your feet. I just don't trust that husband of yours—why don't you stay with us here in Chicago? You can find a job in a day care or something. How is Mack treating you?—How are the kids doing?—Give Joyce and Jason hugs from all of us.—Love Mom—Love Jane*

Still, there was something consoling in knowing there were those who cared about you. She sighed and crumpled the letters to be disposed of in the burn barrel.

* * *

She walked leisurely around her new home . . . upstairs, downstairs, inside and out, taking in its spaciousness and the bright new paint. Such a lovely place! Room by room, the surroundings were critically scrutinized. The furniture was shabby and didn't begin to fill up the rooms, but she was willing to tolerate that for as long as necessary. However, something was needed to cover the windows. There were rods begging for curtains to be hung.

If she had a sewing machine, perhaps she could make them. That shouldn't be too difficult. Her mother did sewing projects all the time, but she hadn't been interested in learning from her. Now, that bit of stubborn indifference was regretted.

Still, there was no reason why she couldn't learn. Francis or Sarah might be willing to teach her, but she needed a sewing machine, and there was no money for one right now. Perhaps, her mother would be willing to part with hers for a while. When the phone was hooked up tomorrow, she would call and find out.

As soon as Joyce and Jason were up and ready, the rental house in Independence would be checked over to make certain everything was being left in good order. All day Sunday, they had cleaned windows and cupboards and scrubbed and waxed floors. The task had been enormous, and LuAnn had felt more like a robot than a human being. After a while, even the kids had performed mechanically, never issuing a complaint. By Sunday evening, they were all too tired to care about anything except crawling into bed.

The keys would be taken to the landlord this morning. The rent was paid up for the rest of the month, to be sure. However, she wondered if a refund could be negotiated with the man, or she might decide to keep the keys until July 31. With this thought in mind, she had a little leverage in the situation. The money could be used to buy material for curtains. Roy Davis was usually reasonable with her, but he would be repainting the house, no doubt, and that would cost him a considerable amount. But it wouldn't hurt anything to try.

* * *

By the time she drove into Roy Davis' driveway, her strategy was all figured out. He was pulling weeds from the flower beds at the side of the house. "Joyce and Jason, you two stay right here in the Volkswagen!" She wanted no distractions. With a big smile on her face and a spring in her step, she approached the man. "Good morning, Mr. Davis! Your flowers are so beautiful! I don't know how you manage to maintain such lovely flower beds every summer." She held the house keys and rhythmically transferred them from one palm to the other, making sure Mr. Davis noticed.

He paused in his work, straightened up to full height, and wiped his hands on his coveralls. "Good morning, Mrs. Hanable, and what can I do for you today?" The elderly man's face lit up at the mention of his treasured flower beds.

"Well, I guess I'm here to make you an offer." The lines were well-rehearsed, and she hurried on. "You'll be wanting to paint the house now that we're out, I'm sure. We really have more than three weeks to go on our rent. Also . . . we're leaving the swing set. . . . That will be an attraction for new renters. . . . If you want to get into the house to start the painting, so you can have new renters by the first of August, I'm asking for a full refund of the July rent, one hundred and twenty-five dollars."

When she concluded, there was a deep intake of breath. It was always hard to ask for something, and her heart did the Charleston. Embarrassed pink flushed over her cheeks. However, her gaze did not waver. Nonetheless, she wondered what she would really do if he said, "No"? He had always been such a kindly man.

Roy Davis looked at the young woman standing, almost fearfully, in front of him. He remembered her husband's anger when the June's rent was paid. Of course, she was correct. She had a legal right to keep the keys until July 31. She was also correct that it was to his advantage to refund the July payment, if it meant giving him access to the property. It was an easy decision. "Stay right here, Mrs. Hanable . . . I'll write you a check. Should I make it out to you or your husband?"

"To me please." Her eager smile was worth one hundred and twenty-five dollars.

He went into the house and was soon back. He handed her the check. "As far as I'm concerned, I didn't give you a refund . . . OK?" He winked and started back to the flower bed. There was no need to tell that husband of hers!

"Thank you so much, and here's your keys." She thrust them out. "Good luck with your next renters!" She skipped back to the Volkswagen. The transaction had gone better than she could ever have imagined. The money for new curtains was right there in her hand. She drove off to the bank. "Don't you kids tell your dad a thing about this, do you hear? The house needs new curtains, and this is the only way I have to get them." She waved the check in their direction and then slipped it into her purse.

* * *

She hadn't confronted Mack about the finances since getting back from West Virginia. She could wait until the next bank statement came, and that would be most any day now. Even though it was hard to make him realize the necessity, she needed to know how much money he was putting into the household account. Surely, he had thought to have their address changed at the bank and at the post office.

* * *

Mack experienced an inner power surge as he and Pete forwarded the Hanable mail from Pete's delivery route in town to Mack's rural route in the country. This was a bonus that hadn't previously been considered. Now, he would have first access to all the mail sent to their rural route address. Today, there was a J.C. Penney's Fall Catalog, a flyer from the A&P, and two first class letters addressed to 'LuAnn Hanable.' One was from the bank . . . her statement, no doubt. His fingers itched to get into the contents, even though there was never any attempt made to conceal the financial business from him. She always left the statements on the kitchen table, in plain sight, until they were put away in her file box. At tax time . . . it was a damned good thing she was organized. During the remainder of the year, he paid little heed.

The second letter had her parents' return address on the upper left-hand corner. The postmark was Grafton, West Virginia. The envelope bulged from the contents, and curiosity was killing him. He lifted it several times and tapped it nervously against his palm. Reluctantly, it was placed into the mail bag.

Still, his mind wouldn't let it go. What was being sent to his wife? He figured he had a right to know. It just might be something she didn't want him to see . . . something she was keeping from him. That must be it. He glanced over at Pete, who was engrossed in sorting, and then quickly pulled the envelope from the bag and stuck it into the front of his shirt. "Guess I better hit the can before I take off!" His intentions were unnecessarily expressed and excessively loud, as he headed for the door of the men's rest room.

* * *

Pete hadn't missed any of Mack's actions. Interfering with anyone's mail was serious business, even if it's your own spouse's. He would keep an eye on the guy, and should this practice continue, he would have to be reported.

* * *

Inside the restroom, Mack entered one of the stalls and locked the door. He got seated on the stool and pulled the letter from inside his shirt. Without success, he tried to open the flap without tearing up the envelope. That problem could be taken care of after he found out what was in it. There was a letter written by LuAnn's mother and a clipping cut from the front page of the Grafton newspaper. Mack read the headline, and, without any rational reason, his hands began to shake.

REMAINS OF MISSING LOCAL GIRL BELIEVED FOUND IN LAKE

> Acting on a tip from an anonymous caller, the local police conducted a search of a small local lake. Divers found the skeletal remains of a young female believed to be that of Amy Maxwell. She had disappeared in the spring of 1960 while out riding her bicycle. The name and location of the lake are being withheld. A special task force from Charleston has been engaged to conduct any further investigation. The remains would be held in custody of the coroner's office until a positive identification can be made.

He was so shaken that he had a hard time refolding the paper and placing it back into the envelope. He didn't bother to read the letter. He was sure it would contain just more of the same. Why, in hell, would Fern send her daughter such an article? He supposed it was someone she had known, or at least whose parents she had known. It was inconceivable that, after eight years, anyone would come forth with that kind of information.

Reluctantly, he began to get a mental picture of Kate's bones down at the bottom of the lake. Would they be discovered some day, and would someone point their finger at him? Fully aware that he was losing control, he shook his head hard and looked in the restroom mirror. Staring back, was a man with hollow, dark, brooding eyes, and sweat was running down the pinched and ashen mask of a face. Damn it all! Why was he so shaken up? He had put all of that behind him. Hadn't he?

In an effort to calm down, he splashed cold water on his face and arms. That helped. He breathed deeply several times, and once again, he was in control. According to his watch, the other carriers would all be gone by now. The envelope was placed back inside his shirt, and he walked out to where the mail bag was waiting. He pulled the envelope out and slapped some scotch tape over the tattered flap before it was stuck into the bag. LuAnn would assume Fern had torn open the envelope to insert the news article.

To his left, a flicker of movement caught his eye, and Pete came out from behind a filing cabinet. Startled, Mack sprang back and snarled at the other mail carrier, "Hell, man! What are you still doing here? You scared me shitless there for a second!" Then, he guffawed heartily and loudly, but not convincingly.

"I had some unfinished business to take care of . . . just like you . . . I suppose." He gave Mack a steady, unwavering look that left little doubt as to its meaning. Then Pete picked up his mail bag and left. He was already fifteen minutes behind schedule.

* * *

Mack grabbed his bag and headed for the Lincoln. *Damn him! What had he seen?* Well, he would just have to buddy up to Pete a little more. It had always worked in the Army when he found himself in trouble. Most guys are lonely and looking for a friend. So, he reasoned, anyway.

Tomorrow, he would ask Pete to bring his family over for a barbecue on Saturday. That's what people do. That would mean investing in a grill and a picnic table, but what the hell. The family could use it for the rest of the summer. And steaks! He would definitely get steaks! Maybe T-bones! LuAnn and the kids would like that, too! By the time he placed their mail into the box, the rest of the week was all figured out.

* * *

Following the class reunion breakfast, Thomas Maxwell had driven back to Charleston with LuAnn constantly on his mind. If he could have been as mature ten years ago, both of them may have been spared a lot of agony. He still loved her, and was quite certain she still had feelings for him. For sure, their lives hadn't given them much time to think about each other, but he truly believed that once you love someone, you will always love that person. If love comes from God, then real love can never end. God's love never does.

He prayed for the safety of LuAnn, Joyce and Jason. He prayed for Mack, too. Sinners need our prayers the most! And, as always, he prayed for his sister, Amy. She would be eighteen years old now, just the age LuAnn was when he had so clumsily tried to make love to her. He had hurt her! Dear God, what he wouldn't do to take all that back.

* * *

On June 27, a call came into Thomas's office in Charleston, from the Grafton Police Department. It was Chief of Police Mike Richards. "Thomas, I just got an anonymous telephone call from someone . . . who may be a woman. It was hard to tell, because the voice was muffled. Anyway, this person said that we should drag 'dog's lake' if we want to find 'that girl's' body. Then . . . whoever it was just hung up. I don't know of any 'dog's lake.' Do you?" Mike Richards paused and waited for some comment back from his longtime friend and cohort. This conversation was always hard for Thomas, and his deep breaths came through distinctly from the other end of the telephone line.

Then, came his reply, "Thanks, Mike. Something rings a bell there, but I can't tell you what it is right off the cuff. Give me a little time to mull this over, and I'll get back with you, OK? Thanks again!" The line went dead. No time to waste. Another word can always be another lead in any case.

Thomas got out a map of the Grafton area that was drawn up eight years before at the time of Amy's disappearance. His eyes devoured the area roads, highways, lakes and ponds for fifty miles in every direction. Nothing registered with him. He kept repeating aloud, "Dog's lake, dog's lake, dog's lake," until, finally, he heard Eddie Smith, from years before, referring to Katt's Lake as 'dog's lake.' "That's where my daddy always throws all the stray dogs after he shoots 'em. He don't call it Katt's Lake. My daddy calls it 'dog's lake.' "

Thomas was immediately back on the phone to Chief Richards. He recounted everything that was remembered about the man. "Eddie Smith's daddy was one SOB. That much I remember for sure. He knocked around more than one kid who 'struck a wrong note' with him, yours truly, being one of them. I think we may have a good suspect. You better start dragging Katt's Lake. Eddie Smith's the only one that I ever heard refer to the lake in that manner. Just as soon as I hang up, I'm going home to pack. Keep this confidential for as long as you can. OK?"

In less than an hour, Thomas was burning rubber on his way to Grafton. "Amy, honey, I hope your big brother is right this time. We need to put you to rest in a place where you're loved."

* * *

Two hours later, Thomas turned off the county blacktop and headed towards Katt's Lake. About a half mile from the lake, an old trailer house sat off back in the trees. The front yard was overgrown with grass and weeds. Junk was piled up around the rusting old home. The name on the mailbox out front, in bold letters, read SMITH. A scraggly old apple tree was along the fence line. Hard balls of green fruit were hanging from its branches. It was those green apples that had nearly gotten Thomas' arm broken when he was a kid of about six or seven.

He had picked a handful and pelted them as hard as he could against the mailbox. He was enjoying himself immensely when, from out of nowhere, Old Man Smith grabbed his arm and nearly twisted it off. "Them's ain't your apples, boy!" Terrified, he had turned and bitten the old man's arm, nearly losing a few of his loose teeth.

When his grip slackened, Thomas had pulled away and run for all he was worth. He had never told anyone about the incident, because he figured it might get him into trouble. After all, you don't pick other people's apples and then pelt their mailbox with them. What happened hadn't held any significance until now.

* * *

The place seemed deserted, and he wondered if the old man was still living. He would get in touch with Eddie Smith right away and see if he could get him talking. He was a bully and a blunderer, but he liked to talk. Maybe he knew something about the connection between dog's lake and Amy's disappearance. It's for sure somebody did, and Eddie was the only conceivable one. Given Eddie's daddy's reputation, he was a logical suspect.

° ° °

The road wound around for another half mile or so until it stopped abruptly at the edge of the lake, a sandy beach, the only part accessible by car. Thomas got out of the red Firebird and stretched out his long frame. He clasped strong hands behind his head and surveyed the surroundings. It was a small lake, rather beautiful, but seldom used, except by wild water fowl. The shoreline was brushy and full of nettles, ideal for them, but not for man. "Are you in there, Amy?"

The sound of a motor disturbed his thoughts, and a police car pulled up next to the Firebird. It was Chief of Police Mike Richards. The uniformed officer emerged from the vehicle. "Glad you're here, Thomas." The two friends shook hands and then turned towards the lake. "Divers will be going in tomorrow before the waters get churned up and murky. If nothing shows up, we'll start the dragging. Are you ready for this, Thomas . . . if we find Amy's remains?"

He took a deep breath and let it out slowly. "I've never been so ready for anything in my life. My parents and I deserve to know the truth. Then, maybe we can find some comfort when we know Amy is resting in peace." He turned and looked at Mike. "I'll be visiting Eddie Smith this evening. I hope to know a whole lot more by the time the night is over. Right now, I need some time to think. OK?"

"I understand, old friend. I'll see you in the morning." He clapped Thomas on the back, got into the police car, and drove away.

Tears streamed down his face and dropped onto the sand as he knelt along the shore of Katt's Lake and prayed. "Dear Father in Heaven, please give us Amy back." He stood up and tearful eyes mournfully searched the surface of the lake. Such a lonely place. Could something evil have happened here? He sped away and headed for Eddie Smith's home, hoping to find the answer.

° ° °

Eddie wasn't there, but Marlene Hillman and the kids were. When she saw Thomas at the door, she looked relieved, and yet frightened, too. Her right eye had an inch long cut above it, and dark purple bruising surrounded it. Her arms had bruises consistent with having been grasped with a powerful grip. They were all the tell-tale signs of having been the victim of a strong and angry person. He immediately wondered if Marlene had made the anonymous phone call to the police station. "Can you tell me where Eddie is? I would really like to talk to him."

Her eyes averted his inquiring gaze, but she answered, "He's probably with his father. He's in the nursing home at Kingwood. He's not rational anymore; you know. Eddie says he's saying things that could get us all into a lot of trouble." She paused and bit her lip. Then she looked directly at him as though she wanted to go on, but it was apparent that a little encouragement was needed.

"Go on, Marlene," he spoke gently. "Does he ever say anything about 'dog's lake' or about a 'little girl?'" Thomas nodded reassuringly. "You need to tell whatever you know. No harm will come to you and the children, I'll see to that." He looked at the bright eyes of the children staring at him. "Why don't you kids go outside and play on your swing set in the backyard? It looks like a nice one. I'm going to talk with your mother for a while. OK?" They obediently left the kitchen.

"I need to sit down." She pulled a chair out from the table and sank into it. Her hands found a hot pad laying there, and restless fingers started folding, tugging, and creasing. "About a month ago, Eddie's daddy started telling the nursing home aides that he had killed a girl. At first, they thought it was just an old man's ramblings, but when he repeated it time and again, I figured there must be some truth to it. When I heard your testimony at the class reunion, I just knew it had to be your little sister. I went to visit him, something I seldom do, and he told me all about it. He seemed relieved to finally have someone to confess to. Do you want to know what he told me?"

"Yes, Marlene, I do. Please go on." He got up from the chair and filled a glass with water from the sink. He set the glass down and, once more, seated himself at the table across from her. He nodded for her to continue.

"Amy was out riding her bike, and she stopped out in front of the trailer house, by the apple tree. The tree was in full blossom, and she started breaking off branches, I suppose to make a bouquet. Anyway, when the old man saw her, he left the trailer . . . sneaked up behind her . . . grabbed her arm, and twisted it . . . the way he did when kids were out of hand . . . you know. But, this time, Amy's arm snapped. It was broken . . . and she started screaming and crying. He knew he was in real trouble. He figured he would probably be sent to jail. He told her to shut up, but she just kept screaming. So, he clapped his hand over her mouth and held it there . . . for a long time. She finally stopped struggling, and her body went limp. When she fell to the ground, he realized she was dead." A gulp shook her body, and she reached for a dish towel to wipe away the tears.

Taking deep breaths, she continued. "The old man picked Amy up and carried her through the woods . . . across to the lake. There, he undressed her and tied rocks into the legs of her jeans. He used the shirt sleeves to tie the rocks around her waist, and then he dumped her body into a spot . . . about one hundred yards to the right, past the parking area at the end of the road. He said he used a long stick to measure the water . . . to make sure it was plenty deep . . . before dumping her body in." Marlene was sobbing and shaking, but she finished the account. "Then, he went and took her bike back up the road a couple of miles, to where the police found it. He used his shirt to wipe off fingerprints." She wiped her face with the dish towel again and, with a sense of relief, sighed deeply. "That's what he told me."

"Marlene, you're a brave woman for telling me all of this. I need to talk to Eddie tonight. It's obvious to me he's been pounding on you. I'll be here to make certain that doesn't happen again. He'll be spending the night in jail, you can count on that. You might want to stop at the station around eleven in the morning. By then, we'll have some idea about the action we will be taking."

"I'll wait for him right outside . . . if that's all right with you. He won't be coming back in here tonight." He touched her gently on the shoulder. "Why don't you and the kids get to bed now? I'll send them back in," he gave a reassuring nod.

When he got back into the car, Mike was given a call. "Can you come over here to Eddie Smith's? He's been pounding on his wife, and we need to get him into jail and away from her and the kids for the night. He's not home yet, I'm outside waiting for him. I got quite a story from Marlene, too. I'll tell you all about it when you get here. Don't waste any time. OK?"

* * *

Eddie and Mike arrived at the same time. When Eddie saw the Chief of Police drive up and his old classmate waiting for him, he knew Marlene had done some talking. Despite the circumstances, there was an indescribable sense of relief, and he willingly let Chief Richards put the cuffs on.

"This is one helluva situation, huh, Thomas? You know, I saw my old man kill your sister, and I've been too damned scared and ashamed to tell anybody. I was afraid he might do the same thing to me or Ma. Now, here I am pounding on my own woman and kids." He ducked his head and got into the back of the police car. Giant sobs racked his large, boney frame, and a horrible anguish distorted his bullish features.

The next morning, Amy's decomposed body was pulled from Katt's Lake. Her dental records and the broken bone of her right arm left no doubt of the identification. On July 3, 1968, Thomas Maxwell placed his sister's remains into a small, pink, satin-lined casket. Rose buds and baby's breath were strewn over the bones. Her confirmation dress and veil were laid on top, along with her prayer book, tiny gloves, stockings, and shoes. Her favorite doll was placed at the side. The lid was closed. Amy could rest now. A grave was dug along the fence line of the cemetery. An apple tree stood nearby. There would be blossoms in the spring. Mr. and Mrs. Maxwell, Thomas Maxwell, and Father O'Hagan bid the young girl farewell, as tears and incense surrounded the gravesite.

* * *

Old Man Smith died a week later of a massive stroke. His son, Eddie, was exonerated of any wrongdoing in Amy's death. However, therapy and family counseling were a mandatory part of the agreement. A restraining order was issued against Eddie for Marlene and the children until all parties involved agreed to having it lifted at a future date. Thomas headed back to Charleston. After the paperwork was completed, there would be one less missing persons file in the briefcase.

* * *

On Friday, LuAnn received another letter from Fern. This time, the newspaper clipping told of the private graveside service held for Amy Maxwell. She desperately wanted to contact Thomas, but her emotions were already worn thin and she felt very vulnerable. So, instead, she sent five dollars to Fern and asked her to put some pink roses on the grave.

Nineteen

Early Saturday morning, Mack headed for Dayton Hardware. Friday, he had seen a picnic table and grill in the display window on his way to First Federal Savings and Loan. They were just the things he needed to get ready for company that evening. Yesterday he had asked Pete Brown to bring his wife and three kids over for supper. "I'm getting steaks, man! You can't turn me down! We're gonna barbecue 'em . . . outdoors!"

He informed LuAnn of the expected company just before he left to do the shopping. At first, she was not only surprised, but reluctant as well. But then, after giving the plans some thought, she agreed. They needed other people in their lives, especially Mack. "That's a good idea, but how can we be ready for company by this evening?" Mack assured her that he would handle everything, so now he was. He had her list in hand. This was the first company ever to be invited to their home, and he had to make certain the evening would go right. It damned well better! He needed Pete on his side.

They agreed on purchasing the picnic table and grill. That was good. But then, LuAnn had some more ideas. "Don't forget you'll need charcoal briquettes and lighter fluid. And matches . . . some long matches. Steaks? Well . . . maybe some hamburger, too. Or hot dogs. Kids really would rather have hamburgers or hot dogs. Don't forget buns. How about a watermelon? Potato chips would be easier than potato salad. Okay? . . . I'll run over to the Yoders and get some sweet corn. There'll be time to make pies right after dinner. I'll need three large cans of cherry pie filling." She had really gotten into it!

"Shit LuAnn, you'll have to make a list! I can't remember all that stuff! You're sure making a big deal out of this!" He sat down in a chair at the old oak kitchen table, which is now in the dining room along with the cupboard brought from the Dutcher place. He waited impatiently while his wife wrote everything down. His fingers tapped irritatingly on the table. "Why do you women have to make such a big deal out of things?"

"And just how do you think we're supposed to feed five more people, if we don't prepare for them?" Angered by his comment, she was more determined than ever to take advantage of the situation. "I'm adding paper plates . . . and paper cups. We don't have nine decent plates . . . or glasses, in the house! We can make do with the silverware, but plastic forks would help." They were added to the list. "We need long handled utensils for tending the grill, too, like a fork and tongs . . . Pop! We never have pop. Get at least twelve bottles." The list kept growing as she recalled the many cookouts her parents had prepared. Mack's irritation kept growing with each item that was added. Finally, she handed him the paper.

* * *

It was nearly noon by the time he drove back home with all the things on the list. Right after eating, he would start to put the picnic table together. The damn thing was in a box! He hadn't figured how he would transport it home if it hadn't been, but that didn't matter now, anyway. He opened the trunk of the Lincoln. "LuAnn! LuAnn! Come here! Where do you want me to unload this thing? . . . It's in a box!" He bellowed at his wife through the kitchen door.

"Right over there on the back porch! That's closest to the kitchen!" LuAnn yelled back at him as she set dinner on the table. "Come and eat first! Bring in the groceries! I want to chill the watermelon and pop in the refrigerator! We can't leave the meat setting out there in a hot car!"

* * *

Too excited to contain themselves, Joyce and Jason jumped and hopped around their father as he struggled to open the huge carton. Finally, a crowbar from the tool shed was forced under one of the flaps, and with a forceful push and lift, the corrugated cardboard and staples gave way. He viewed the contents with disbelief. So many pieces! How in hell would he ever get that thing together in time to feed company for supper? "LuAnn, come here and look at this damn thing! How's a guy supposed to figure this out? Jason! Joyce! Get the hell out of here! You'd drive a saint crazy!" He backhanded Jason on the side of the head, as he reached to pick up one of the pieces. Then, with clinched fist, he turned on Joyce, but gave the carton a kick instead.

LuAnn came out the kitchen door and very quickly sized up the situation. She looked through the pile of lumber and picked up a large sheet of paper. "Here's the directions. Just give me fifteen minutes to finish up the dishes and get my pies in the oven, and I'll come out and help you." She turned to Jason. "What's the matter? I see tears."

With apprehension, he looked at his father. "Nothing."

"Why don't you kids come with me? I could use some help in the kitchen." She put her hands on their shoulders and led them into the house. It was second nature to keep them out of harm's way when Mack was around.

* * *

At five o'clock, the picnic table and the grill were set up and ready for use. At five-thirty, the Browns drove into the yard. Pete introduced his wife, Connie, and their three children, twelve-year-old Velarie, ten-year-old Victor, and three-year-old Veronica. The two older children, with Pete's eyes, red hair, and freckles, looked at their friends, and smiles lit up their faces. They already knew one another from the school playground. There was no timidity to get over. The Browns had brought a game of Jarts with them, and the four oldest children raced off across the lawn to set it up.

Little Veronica, looking very much like her mother, with auburn hair and green eyes, hid behind her mother's skirts. The women exchanged greetings and took Veronica into the kitchen with them while they finished preparations for supper. To LuAnn's relief, Connie was every bit as amiable as Francis. They chatted as if old friends.

Mack and Pete tended the grill to see that the charcoal reached the right degree of white-hot perfection. They called for the steaks and hot dogs. The meat landed sizzling onto the hot grill, and flames shot up in earnest. "Son of a bitch!" Mack let out an oath and jerked his hand away.

The men said little to one another. After all, they saw each other every day. So, they downed bottles of Coke and watched the meat sputter and smoke. The aroma wafted on the summer air and tantalized their appetites. Pete started to turn the pieces over when a piercing wail came from the front lawn, a sound not unlike the squeal of a stuck hog. The grill was momentarily forgotten, and the women pushed through the kitchen doorway, dragging Veronica with them. "What was that?"

"What in the hell's going on over there?" Mack threw the nearly empty pop bottle down onto the grass and sprang off the porch. In a dozen strides, he was across the lawn to where the kids were playing.

Jason sat on the grass, holding his bare, left, foot and rocking back and forth in syncopation with his sobs. A puncture wound was dripping blood, and his face was screwed up in pain. "What's going on here?" Mack lashed out at him. "Don't you have brains enough to put your shoes on when you're playing a game like this?" He grabbed his arm and yanked him to his feet. His fist was raised to strike when a strong, freckled, hand grabbed his arm from behind.

"I don't think you want to do that! The kid's already learned that lesson." Pete held onto Mack's arm until the grip on Jason was relinquished.

LuAnn put her arm around his waist, and Jason hobbled towards the house. He sat on the porch while the wound was cleansed and covered with a large Band Aid. Connie finished cooking the meat on the grill. The two men sat down on the lawn and watched Velarie and Victor finish up their game. Joyce didn't have the desire to play anymore. She went over to the porch and sat down beside Jason. "I'm sorry I hit you. I didn't mean to."

° ° °

It was a quiet meal, considering there were nine people scrunched around a table meant to seat six. Conversation was cordial. When it came time for the cherry pie, the children took their plates and forks and sat along the edge of the porch. Even Veronica joined them. No longer feeling she was among strangers, she set her plate down and ran out onto the lawn. "See me!" And she commenced to turn somersaults. Her little bottom was raised as high as she could get it, and then she put her head on the ground and flipped over. Her fun and giggles were a welcome relief from the tension . . . and contagious, so the older children finished up their pie and joined her. They all began to show off their acrobatic skills.

When Velarie started doing cartwheels, LuAnn suddenly had a nagging spark of nostalgia. As a cheerleader in high school, she had loved doing them. Perhaps she still could. She got up from the picnic table and sauntered out onto the lawn with the children. Unmindful of anyone watching, she made a short run, took a slight spring, and turned hand over hand, landing lightly on her feet. A look of amazement spread across her damp and flushed face. She did it again and again. What a glorious feeling! Looking around her, everyone else had stopped what they were doing to stare at her. Connie started clapping, and then everyone else joined in, except Mack. He sat at the picnic table and glared at her, muttering, *Damn woman, she's making a spectacle of herself!*

Suddenly embarrassed and fearful of her husband's reaction, she hurried back to the porch and the table. A forced smile covered her discomfort. "Let's get this mess cleaned up. We'll have watermelon after a while." She picked up dirty plates and cups and stacked them together. She went into the kitchen and brought out a garbage bag. The women finished the clean-up job and went into the house.

"Say Mack, how's the old lawnmower working?" Pete wanted to get him away from the women. The men took off across the yard to the tool shed. The children trailed behind at a distance. Velarie picked up Veronica and toted her on her hip.

"I wish Velarie wouldn't do that, it can't be good for her back. But she won't listen to me." Watching from the screen door, Connie let out a deep sigh, more in relief that the previous scene hadn't turned out any worse, than with concern for her daughter. "You know, LuAnn, I would really like to see the rest of your house . . . if you don't mind. I realize you've only been in here for a week, and everything isn't in place yet, but I don't care about that . . . if you don't."

"Well, as you can see . . . there are no curtains up yet. I thought maybe my mother could loan me her sewing machine, but she said *no.* She had a good point, though. How could I get it? She lives in West Virginia, after all." LuAnn giggled nervously and shrugged her shoulders. The women moved from the kitchen into the dining room. "She suggested that I measure the windows and buy the material then send everything to her. She would make the curtains, and we could hope they would fit the windows."

Abruptly, the conversation changed. "LuAnn, wherever did you get this beautiful, old cupboard? It's an antique, isn't it?" Connie touched the cupboard brought from the Dutcher place. A look of awe and reverence shone from her face. "Your oak table and chairs look antique, too. Are you into antiques? These are beautiful pieces."

"You mean the furniture that I've just been 'putting up with,' really has some value? Then, maybe you can tell me about this old fruit cupboard. I put it in the living room, simply to help fill up the space." She led Connie into the next room. "I've washed it up, but I haven't had time to refinish it or anything."

"You don't want to touch it, LuAnn! I know a lot of people who would die of envy if they knew you had these pieces. Two years ago, we took our family vacation out east. That's when I became interested in antiques. Now, I subscribe to a monthly magazine. So, I know what some of these things are worth. What else do you have, for heaven's sake? Show me!"

"Well, we have Mack's old bedroom furniture in our room. This way." The women walked down the hallway. "Everything came from his Aunt Ruby Dutcher's place when we moved to Independence from Hiawatha. It's an old oak bed, and it's not very comfortable, I can tell you that! What do you think?" She waved her hand towards it.

"Well, it's old, all right, and it goes with the other furnishings, but I don't believe the value is significant. I could be wrong, though. What else is there?"

"We're using the other downstairs bedroom for a sort of office. We put his aunt's old desk in here and an old rocker." They entered the next room. "What do you think of the desk?" Each piece being scrutinized was looking better and better to her.

"That's a beautiful old roll-top!" She turned to LuAnn. "Everything is in such wonderful condition! Did Ruby ever have any children? There's hardly a mark on anything!"

"Mack was the only child in the house, except Ruby, herself, when she was growing up. You see, Ruby was Mack's great aunt. His parents deserted him when he was seven years old, and Ruby and Charles Dutcher raised him. Sometimes Mack's behavior, especially towards the children, isn't exactly appropriate, but I understand where he's coming from." She was hoping to make Mack's behavior seem less significant. "Ruby was a very strict disciplinarian, and she gave Mack very little leeway. I'm afraid he's carried her style of discipline over to his own children."

She led Connie down the hallway towards the staircase leading to the second floor. "I'll show you the children's rooms now. I've painted their furniture. We decided it needed a little brightening up, maybe I shouldn't have." She led the way upstairs.

After seeing the furniture and Connie had given her opinion, the women went back down the steps. "I would be happy to help you pick out window coverings. You must have gotten your Penney's catalog this past week. Let's look through it for some ideas." Connie stopped in the living room and tried to visualize what curtains would be appropriate for the windows.

LuAnn went over to the cupboard in the dining room and tugged at the handle on one of the drawers. "I put it in here." The drawer was stubborn, and she gave it several hard and determined jerks. All at once, it came loose and all the way out. The catalog spilled to the floor, and something else came with it. There were fifty dollar bills falling out from somewhere behind the drawer. She stood motionless with her eyes transfixed on the money. The handle of the drawer was still clutched tightly in her hand. In a very small voice, she summoned her guest. "Connie, come here. Do you see what I see? Is that money, or am I hallucinating?"

Connie looked. Her eyes lit up as bright as the charcoal in the grill. A huge grin spread across her face. "That, my dear girl, is money . . . It must have been dear old Aunt Ruby's. Quick! Pick it up before Mack has a chance to see it! You found it, it's yours! Just do what I tell you, LuAnn! I'll explain later." With gusto, she started collecting the bills and thrust them at her bewildered hostess. She reached in behind the drawer glide and discovered still more. These were pressed into LuAnn's hands as well.

Then she pulled out the other drawer, and a similar stash was found. The last of the bills were gathered up before the drawers were shoved back in. It was as if she did this sort of thing every day of her life. LuAnn remained stunned and speechless.

She grabbed the catalog. "Come on, girl! We're gonna buy you some curtains!" Connie took off for the office with LuAnn following obediently behind. She shut the door and locked it. She sat down on the floor in the late rays of the afternoon sun and pulled LuAnn down beside her. "Let's get this counted!" They sat with their legs sprawled out around the crumpled bills. Like an obedient child, LuAnn complied with Connie's demand.

One by one the bills were separated and stacked into piles of ten. When the job was finished, there were forty fifty-dollar bills . . . two thousand dollars. LuAnn finally found her voice and commented nervously. "Connie, I have to tell Mack about this. It's really his money." In spite of the gentle breeze coming through an open window, perspiration stood out on her nose and forehead. The room seemed stifling. "I can't just keep it, can I?" The question was asked in a near whisper.

Connie appeared cool and collected and replied matter-of-factly. "Sure you can, my dear. Mack has been holding out on you for years. I have friends working at First Federal and I know they could get into trouble for divulging this information, but your husband has been socking money away ever since you've lived in Independence. Besides, he just deposited over a hundred thousand from his aunt's estate. There's more I could tell you about him, but I won't right now. Pete and I probably know him better than you do." Connie touched her arm. "You just need to take care of yourself. OK?" She stood up. "Now, where can we put this for safe-keeping?"

LuAnn contemplated the money and her new friend's comments and assertiveness. She knew Connie was right and trusted the woman's intentions. "I know!" She stood up and stepped over the bills. "Wait, right here!" She went into the kitchen and opened the freezer. She took out a package of meat and carefully unwrapped it. A plastic carton was selected and pulled from the bottom of the cupboard. She went back into the room where Connie stood watch at the window, in case anyone approached the house. Thankfully, the men and children were still out investigating the farm and the creek. The money was quickly wrapped and placed in the freezer beside the package of jewelry. "There, how's that?"

Connie watched LuAnn's actions and chortled, "You've got some hard, cold, cash there, my dear . . . whenever you need it!" Her laughter and LuAnn's nervous giggles filled the kitchen. "Now then, if you've got a tape or a yard stick, we can get the windows measured. If we don't have time to go through the catalog this evening, you can have the fun of picking out the curtains yourself. If I was you, I would be getting some matching bedspreads, too."

* * *

LuAnn was writing down the final measurement when they heard the men and children approaching the house. "Isn't that one helluva spot to go fishing back there by that old tree? Hey, Pete . . . kids . . . have some watermelon. It's just waitin' for us right here on the picnic table. LuAnn! We need a knife!" The two women, forever bonded by their little secret, went out and joined the others. The melon was sliced and quickly consumed. Seeds were spit on the ground, and a roll of paper towels was used to wipe the sticky juice from faces, arms, hands, and even legs.

The evening darkness began to set in. The floodlight on the utility pole was turned on, and the first stars appeared. "Damn mosquitoes! Hey, LuAnn, where's that bug spray? The mosquitoes are eating us alive!"

"Never mind, Mack. We've gotta be going. It's late, and the kids have to get up for church in the morning. You ready, Connie? What have you two been doin' while we've been gone?" Pete hadn't really expected an answer, but his wife gave him one.

"Oh, we'll never tell. Will we, LuAnn?" Her wink said a lot. "By the way, do you folks ever go to church? We go to the Catholic church there in town. It means a lot to us." Connie looked directly at Mack and waited for his answer.

"Well, I guess that's just something we never got used to doin' since we've lived here. Maybe we should though, we'll give it some thought. Thanks for coming over." Mack opened the car door on the passenger side and motioned for Connie to get in. He had already heard enough from her. The three children scrambled in from the other side, as their father held the door. Pete got into the driver's seat and started the engine.

"Good night, LuAnn . . . Mack . . . and thanks. That was a mighty good supper. You kids be good now!" Pete turned the car around in the yard and drove out the driveway. Dust rolled up behind and wafted across the front lawn.

"Baths and bed now, kids! Get a move on!" LuAnn headed Jason and Joyce towards the house. "Is your foot doing OK?" It had been a long day and, certainly, not a boring one. It would be wonderful to get under the shower. She smelled of charcoal smoke and perspiration. She was just as sticky and stinky as the rest of the family.

The seeds and juice would need to be hosed down from the porch before the flies took over, but baths and bed were a priority right now. She wished Mack would do the hosing without her telling him to, but he had been giving her some ugly looks. He had even shoved and elbowed her a couple of times when he didn't think Pete or Connie would notice. The cartwheels had upset him. She didn't want to risk angering him further.

When the kids were asleep, she went upstairs to the bathroom so Mack could use the one downstairs. Since the Browns left, he had been sitting out on the back porch amidst the bags of trash and the watermelon mess, swatting mosquitoes. She hoped he would shower pretty soon, so they could go to bed. She was drying her hair when the screen door opened and closed. The sound of the shower soon followed. Thank goodness!

She put on her nightgown and went back down the stairs and through the living room. She stood inside the screen door at the south end of the room and breathed deeply of the night air. The moon, playing hide and seek through the branches of the trees, cast its mystical glow in patches on the front porch. The night breeze blew cool against her skin and gently stirred the leaves of the bridal wreath that drooped over the porch's edge. It looked inviting out there. She opened the screen door and stepped out.

The tranquillity of the night surrounded her. An owl hooted, and somewhere, a night bird was calling to its mate. Crickets chirped in an undisciplined chorus, and the croaking of frogs was heard coming from the direction of the creek. So peaceful. With each stirring of the cool night air, a sensation of floating engulfed her and became intoxicating, as though she was drunk. She wished she could have wings and float away up into the sky with the stars. She was deep in romantic thoughts and feelings when Mack opened the door behind her.

She turned towards the sound, delighted that her husband would join her. But, a look of rage engulfed him. "What in hell are you doing out here? Waiting for your lover? I saw the way Pete looked at you all evening! Then you . . . you showing off with your legs sprawled in the air doing cartwheels! Where're your brains? You were giggling and swingin' your hips, acting like a slut all evening. You're my woman! Do you understand?" Mack grabbed his startled wife by the shoulders and yanked her up. "Just so you don't forget!" He spun her around to face him, relinquished the grip on her left shoulder and pelted her with a sharp blow.

LuAnn's legs buckled under her. Exhaustion, the abrupt assault, and the shock, left her defenseless and as weak as 'Silly Putty.' She lay motionless, not daring to move for fear of further retaliation. She said nothing and felt nothing. Dazed, she couldn't even cry out. Mack stood over her and stared. His breath came in ragged gasps. Then he leapt from the porch, a cornered wild stallion breaking from his confines. He took off running, out the driveway and down the road. His steps thudded off into the distance.

When she felt certain he wasn't returning right away, she cautiously pulled herself to a sitting position. Fingers explored the left side of her face. It was certainly bruised, but there didn't seem to be any bleeding. She grasped the handle of the screen door, pulled up to her feet, and entered the house. Half crawling, she stumbled through the darkness and upstairs to the bathroom.

She locked the door and turned on the light. The reflection in the mirror was the face of a battered woman, not unlike some of the pictures Thomas had shown her. Tears came flooding out and drained away every last bit of her energy. They were washed away with cold water. When she felt strong enough to leave the bathroom, she went down the hallway and slipped into bed with Joyce. She made certain the door to the bedroom was locked.

* * *

Mack ran until he could run no more, then stumbled and fell at the side of the road. He was two miles from the farmstead, out in front of the Yoder home. His body was drenched with perspiration, and his skin crawled. He had an uncontrollable need to scratch all over. There was something under his skin that he had to get rid of. He dug his fists into his eye sockets and rubbed until he ached.

He had just hit someone! He wasn't sure if it was Aunt Ruby or someone else. He looked at his fists. He had always wanted to hit Aunt Ruby. Was it her? No, it couldn't have been. She was already dead. Then who was it? He saw Kate laying on the ground. Blood seeped out from around her hair. She was dead, too. He shook his head, trying to make some sense of the situation.

He looked around and wondered where he was. The farmstead there was so silent, ghostlike, in the dim light of the moon. He stood up and looked at the mailbox on the side of the road. YODER. Yeah, YODER. He was someplace on his mail route. Which way was home? Oh, yes!

Then he remembered who he had struck. It was LuAnn! He wasn't even sure why, but it was LuAnn. Giant sobs racked his frame, so deep, his insides were twisted. He threw up into the ditch. His stomach wretched until there was a taste of blood in his mouth. Tears streamed down his face and mingled with the sweat that dripped from his body. He struggled out of his T-shirt and used it for a handkerchief. He sopped away at his skin. As he rubbed, sand and gravel picked up from the road ground and scratched into his flesh. He didn't feel it.

At one o'clock, he staggered home. To any observer, he appeared very much like a drunkard. After a cold shower, he crawled into bed by himself and didn't even wonder what had become of LuAnn.

Twenty

Sarah Yoder loved Saturday evenings. The week's work was over, and tomorrow was Church Sunday. The aroma of the food she had prepared using the big iron cookstove still hung heavy in the warm, moist air of the kitchen. She could finally let the coals in the firebox cool down. Two chocolate cakes and a large roast beef set on the kitchen counter, covered with dish towels to keep the flies off . . . her contribution to the Church dinner. On the sideboard, cooling off, sat fourteen quarts of canned peaches. Regardless of the intense heat radiating from the stove's surface and oven for the past three hours, there was no better way to get the quality, in roasting and baking, that she desired. Since the stove was heated up anyway, she had decided to do the peaches, too. There was something very satisfying in hearing the ping of the lid, as each jar sealed itself. So, the stifling discomfort of the air in the kitchen had been tolerated all afternoon. Even the slight breeze from the open windows had lent little relief. Her clothing hung limply from her strong, slim body . . . soggy from steam and sweat . . . soiled with chocolate and peach stains.

The Church meeting would be at her sister and brother-in-law's farm, just a mile west as the crow flies, nearly two miles around on the dirt road. The two Yoder brothers' land is joined along the creek that runs zigzagging through the fields at the back of their farms. In hot weather, the women often take the children across the fields and meet at the creek. Away from the sight of the road, they let the little ones splash around in the water wearing only their underwear. The women and the two older girls hitch up their skirts and wade into the cool water up to their thighs. This morning had been such a time. Then, right after the noon meal, the little ones had been ready for a nap, leaving the afternoon free for the women to do their chores.

The three Amish brothers and one of Henry's nephews had been in Hiawatha all day working on the demolition of the Dutcher place. The house was taking considerably longer than they had expected. Since there was a great deal of fine quality wood to be salvaged, they were taking their time. Even the cupboards and sink were worth saving.

Just that morning, Henry had informed Sarah that the job would take them at least until the last of July, and the summer farmwork was becoming a concern for the men. They had taken off three days last week to do Henry's haying. The same consideration would be given to his two brothers in the next weeks. Besides that, the thrashing season was fast approaching, and all the men would have to help during that time. The women had already taken over many of the men's chores at a time when the produce was ready to be canned. Everyone was working long, hard days.

* * *

After eating a supper of vegetable-beef soup and homemade bread, Henry brought the metal tub in from the wash house and set it on the kitchen floor near the big, iron, cookstove. He dipped warm water from the reservoir, and poured it into the tub to a depth of two or three inches. Buckets of cold water were added . . . having been pumped and carried in from the well outside the kitchen door. Pans and kettles were filled and placed on the surface of the stove, to be heated for later use. After refilling the reservoir, he helped the two youngest boys with their baths. In contrast to the hot air of the kitchen, the cooler water in the tub felt refreshingly tepid.

The grimy, sweaty, little bodies splashed and wiggled in an effort to get benefit of every drop of water at the bottom of the tub. The clean smell of P&G soap mingled with the aroma of peaches, roast beef, and chocolate cake. The giggling, squirming youngsters squealed with delight as a pan of clean, cool water was poured over their heads as a final rinse. A good rub with feed sack towels finished off the Saturday night ritual. The little ones were, then, passed on to Sarah for hair combing and preparation for bed.

The three older children were next, and they were expected to be on their own. One at a time, turns were taken . . . girls went first. Pans of warm water were removed from atop the cook stove and added to the bath. Hair and bodies were lathered, and, as with the little boys, the ritual ended with the anointing of clean water being poured over their soapy heads. Henry helped the older boy, and Sarah helped the girls. Susie's longer hair required special attention from her mother. Extra pans of rinse water were necessary to get all the soap removed from the curls.

When all of the children were bathed, Henry clumsily lugged the huge tub out the kitchen door and emptied it off the edge of the porch. Soapy water fanned out over the patch of bare lawn and created a sloppy mud hole for the two pet ducks to waddle through. All chances of grass growing there had been killed out long ago by the many dousings from the bath tub.

After the boys had taken their baths and used the outhouse, they were sent off to bed. Sarah used the damp towels to wipe up puddles from the kitchen floor. A pile of soggy, soiled towels was stacking up near the outside door . . . to be taken to the wash house when all the baths were finished. There was always a large wash to do on Monday morning.

Henry brought the tub back into the kitchen and refilled it, this time for his own use. The six inches or so of water were barely enough to do the job, but by the time he finished, skin had been scrubbed, hair and beard had been shampooed, and pans of cold water had rinsed the soap off. Two towels had been used for the drying off process.

While Henry bathed, Sarah cared for the girls' hair, combing it and braiding it around their heads. It took longer to get Susie's brushed and combed out. The stubborn curliness, like her own, was more difficult to deal with than Mattie's straight, black locks . . . much like her father's.

She was aware of the budding beauty of her older daughter, who was growing up much too quickly. Could it be, that in just a few years, one of the young Amish men would take an interest in her? She secretly prayed it would be a very long time yet. The girls were sent off to bed just before Henry finished with his bath.

After pulling on a clean pair of trousers, he emptied and partially filled the tub, this time for his wife. The kettles and reservoir were filled, and after a trip to the toilet, he went to bed, giving her some personal time.

* * *

Finally, Sarah was alone. She looked forward to this time every evening when the rest of the family was settled down for the night. That morning, she had selected the clothes everyone would wear to church tomorrow. As usual, some of them needed mending. More times than not, the seams she had, so painstakingly, sewn on the garments were ripped and pulled apart. The handmade dresses, trousers, shirts, and jackets just never seemed to fit the way they were supposed to, either.

The family's clothing was often a source of embarrassment, because her sister-in-law and mother-in-law could sew so much better. Hopefully, the seams would hold together long enough to last through church tomorrow. That was always something to pray about.

The accumulation of blacks, blues, greens, and whites were picked up from the chair where they were piled. She flopped them down on the kitchen table, and, with a deep sigh, went to the buffet in the corner of the kitchen to get the sewing basket. After lighting the lamp and positioning it close to the garments, the seams were examined in the dim glow. She threaded a needle, chose the appropriate color thread, and did the necessary repairs.

Saturday evenings were especially gratifying. She could take a leisurely bath and shampoo and dry her hair. There was no one to bother her. When the mending was completed, the clock said ten-thirty. She would take another hour before going to bed. Night clothes and dry towels were laid out on the table, and, with one huff directed into its chimney, the wick of the kerosene lamp was blown out. The moon cast a mellow light through the screen door and the bare windows of the kitchen, providing all the illumination that was needed.

She extracted pins securing the band on the soiled and sodden blue apron she had worn all day. It was lifted over her head, and dropped to the floor. She unhooked the front closure of the burgundy dress and let it fall around her feet. After stepping out of her underwear, each foot was cautiously placed into the tub one at a time. Cold! With hope that the water had managed to absorb the last of the available heat, she reached for the kettles setting on top of the stove. It was poured into the tub around her feet, and she quickly sank down into the lukewarm bath. After enduring the long, hot afternoon, the sensation was glorious. Surely, Bathsheba had never felt so gratified.

Her hair was unbraided, and shampoo and water were poured on. She dug into the itchy scalp with strong, blunt fingernails and scrubbed until it felt truly clean. Soap was lathered all over her body. With vigor, the accumulation of a week's sweat and grime were scrubbed off. Again, the ritual ended with showers of cold water poured from the pan. It cascaded slowly through her hair and flowed intimately over smooth, white shoulders and breasts, carrying the soapy bubbles with it. With eyes closed, she felt caressed.

The briskness of the towels gave feelings of sensuous delight to her whole body. A fresh night gown was pulled on. Then, she started working on her hair. When left down, it cascaded in curls nearly to her waist. It was controlled with the help of the brush, comb and towel. Then, in an effort to get it dry, she stepped out into the warm southerly breeze on the back porch, and in a silent, seductive dance, twirled, lifted, and fanned it out around her . . . a fairy princess at play. A clean, fresh aroma escaped from her flesh, and, despite the fact she had given birth to five children, her body glowed firm and slim. She was ready to go to her husband.

She ascended the stairs to their bedroom. The moon lay its bright glow across the foot of the bed. Henry slept peacefully on top of the sheets. The quilt laying at the bottom of the bed was a wedding gift from her mother. He had pushed it aside. A soft, cool breeze blew in the windows to the south and east, and an owl hooted from someplace nearby. Not yet ready to give up the night, she looked out towards the road.

A dark silhouette moved by the mailbox, drawing her attention. Slowly, her eyes adjusted to the mixture of dark shadows and the brightness of the moon. She watched intently and wondered what the person was doing there. His features weren't clear, but it was a man, fairly tall, with dark hair. There was no beard. Sometimes, the English would break off the Amish' mailboxes or do other destructive things, but an act of vandalism didn't seem to be the intent of this person.

Whoever it was appeared to be in pain. He wildly flailed his arms . . . threw up . . . and, while sitting at the edge of the road, held his head and rocked back and forth. Then, as though seeking help, he stood up and looked directly towards the house. Sarah pulled back from the window. It looked like their mailman! What in the world would Mack Hanable be doing out there this time of night? She watched as he staggered along the road a short distance and then sat down by the ditch again. He seemed to be drunk. Perhaps she should awaken Henry, but he would just tell her, "Never mind the English."

She recalled what LuAnn had told her about Mack. So, she would keep this to herself for now, but Monday, she would drive down to the Hanable place and tell her English friend what she had seen. Besides, there was another good reason for going. Henry had found the other diamond earring and a ruby ring while taking apart the sink. The jewelry was lodged down in the drain. The ring was much too large for her own finger. Curiosity had enticed her to try it on. She was certain that LuAnn could never wear it. Her hands were even smaller than her own. If her English friend tried to say it had belonged to Aunt Ruby, well, she didn't believe that for a minute.

Sarah turned away from the window and noiselessly lay down beside her husband. She gently stroked his beard and chest until he was aroused. With a quiet passion, Henry lost himself in the scent of his wife's hair and body. The cooling air from the open windows whispered around them. The owl hooted its pleasure.

* * *

Once asleep, Mack slept soundly for over four hours. At six-thirty, he awakened and bolted upright in bed. He looked over on LuAnn's side and saw she wasn't there. The evening before came abruptly back at him . . . hitting him like a sledge hammer. He had acted badly . . . very badly. There wasn't any way he could face his wife this morning. He had to get away from there and do some careful thinking.

He found some clean jeans and a T-shirt she had laid on the dresser with the intent that he put them away. A pile of socks was beside them. He never put anything away. "What's the use? I'll just get them out again." He yanked on the T-shirt and hitched up the jeans. The socks were jerked on and his feet pushed into tennis shoes. He located his bill-fold and car keys, stopped long enough to grab his electric shaver from the bathroom and made for the kitchen door. He would relieve himself when he was a safe distance down the road. He didn't know where he was going, but he was going someplace, and right now.

* * *

LuAnn heard the car door slam shut and the rumble of the engine as Mack eased out of the driveway. Then, the roar that followed as he raced away. He still needed a new muffler. She certainly didn't want him around and was relieved to have him gone. Joyce was still sleeping, so she edged out of the bed and tip-toed across the room. The door was unlocked and quietly nudged open. It was doubtful she even knew LuAnn had slept the night with her, and that was just as well.

Halfway down the hall to the bathroom, rubbing sleepy eyes, Jason staggered from the other bedroom. "Mom! Where's Dad going?" Puzzled, he scowled. "What happened to you?" Before she could answer, he spoke accusingly, "Dad hit you, didn't he? Didn't he, Mom? Tell me! Didn't he?" His face twisted painfully, in recognition of some of the same wounds he had received. "How does it feel, Mom? Huh? How does it feel? You always make excuses for him! Now, tell me! How does it feel?"

LuAnn stood rigid . . . unable to move, shocked by Jason's assault and accusations. "I . . . I . . . I fell in the shower last night," she explained weakly, not looking at her son. "Does it show?" She gingerly touched the bruise.

Jason shook his head sorrowfully, and passed by on the way to the bathroom. "You're lying. You always lie to cover up the mean things Dad does. One of these days, he's going to kill all of us!" A sob caught in his throat, and the door to the bathroom slammed shut.

LuAnn bit her lip, and tears came to her eyes. What happened to the promises Mack had made? She assumed he was seeing the psychologist . . . when things got out of hand. Of course, it was easier that way . . . assuming. Confronting him . . . now, that had always been difficult. Jason was right. The things he'd been doing were the very things she told him wouldn't be tolerated. She stared at the closed door to the bathroom.

Slowly and thoughtfully, she went down the stairs and into their bedroom. The bed covers were twisted and bunched, so, he had slept there last night. Then she went into the bathroom and looked at herself in the mirror. The bruise was blackening. A bit of makeup might do the trick. She took a quick shower, hoping it would perk up her spirits. Makeup was gingerly applied, and it really did a pretty good job of covering the damage. It wasn't really very painful, either; she decided. Perhaps what he had done wasn't so bad after all. She dressed in a bright flowered blouse and red skirt, fluffed out her hair, and smiled back at the image in the mirror.

Mack was gone, for now, anyway . . . so what was she going to do? Somehow, she needed to make Jason feel better. What was it Connie had said . . . about their church being important to them? Right! So, now her plan of action was decided. That's what she and the children would be doing today . . . going to church. She looked up the First Presbyterian Church number and made a phone call to see what time the services would be starting. The only service during the summer was at ten o'clock, and they were going to be there.

Joyce complained. "We have to spend half of the day in church?" But she was glad of her mother's determination. She was taking some initiative for a change, and wasn't letting her father's behavior get the best of them. "You know, Jason, we both have friends who go to church there." Jason looked skeptical, but a slim smile touched his lips.

As an added incentive, LuAnn further promised, "After church, we'll go and have breakfast someplace. We'll see what's open. OK? And, do you know what? This afternoon, you can pick out new curtains and bedding for your rooms from the J.C. Penney's catalog. How does that sound? We'll get the order ready, and then we'll take it into town and mail it at the post office!"

She had every intention of depositing the two thousand dollars into her account the first thing Monday. If Mack ever questioned her about such a big deposit, she would just say, "It's mine!" No need to explain anything to him. After last night, she deserved it! "Right now, we need to get the watermelon juice and the seeds hosed off the back porch. Do I have any volunteer helpers?"

* * *

About a mile from home, Mack pulled the Lincoln off to the side of the road. He walked up the driveway leading into a cornfield and relieved himself. After getting back in the car, he turned south at the bend and drove through Independence. He didn't know where he was going, he just drove, not capable of concentrating on anything. Yet, when he was upset, he always drove south, towards Hiawatha.

There was a huge black hole in his stomach that no food could fill, but when he reached Center Point, he stopped at a little café, Mable's Kitchen. It was kind of out of habit, because he had often stopped there on the way to see Aunt Ruby.

This morning, there were just two other people in the café . . . an elderly couple sitting at the far booth. They were eating pancakes with sausage and drinking hot tea. The man nodded at Mack when he came through the door. The bell fastened there jingled a merry note, announcing his presence. He sat down on one of the stools at the counter and looked around.

A shapely, young waitress came through the swinging doors leading into the kitchen. "Good morning! What'll you have today?" She handed him a sticky menu along with an engaging smile as she chewed on a wad of bubble gum. Then, she nonchalantly leaned back on the counter behind her, waiting to take his order. Her ample bosom raised, and the buttons on her pink uniform strained to keep from popping open. It was all Mack could do to concentrate on the menu. Her cheap perfume reeked . . . intoxicating . . . clear across the counter. He didn't remember seeing her before.

"Give me coffee and pancakes . . . and an orange juice." When she reached to take the menu, he grabbed her hand. "Do you have a name?" The touch was exciting.

"Sally . . . Sally Daniels!" She pulled her hand away, but not too fast. There was a mischievous twinkle in her eyes. She chewed slowly and popped a bubble. "I'll be right back with your breakfast." With full, round hips used as leverage, she pushed through the doors.

When she came back ten minutes later with the plate of pancakes and two containers of syrup, her hips, once again, served the same purpose. A roll of silverware, wrapped in a napkin, was slapped down beside the plate, and he reached out to grab her hand again . . . but missed. Another bubble was popped.

He watched every move with appreciation as a mug was filled with coffee and set in front of him. The buttons were begging to be released. Every twist and turn of her body tantalized his need.

Juice was taken from the refrigerator and poured into a large glass. "Did you say large or small juice?" She tipped her head to the side and raised a quizzical eyebrow, waiting for his answer. He gulped. She shrugged her shoulders. "It doesn't really matter. They're both the same size anyway." She laughed melodiously and winked, green eyes sparkling. The juice was placed by the coffee mug, and she did a little curtsy. Her breasts bobbed. *Oh, my lord.* She walked around the counter to check on the elderly couple. His eyes followed hungrily.

Taking a deep breath, he confidently straightened his shoulders and dove into the plate of pancakes. Nothing had tasted so good in a long time, and the hole began to fill up. She liked him. He was certain of that. And, for sure, he wanted to know her better.

He sipped the hot coffee . . . absentmindedly added cream . . . and stirred the brew. Draining the glass of juice, he wiped a hand across his mouth and went back to the pancakes. After sopping up syrup from the plate, he gulped down the last of the coffee. A ten dollar bill was whipped from his billfold and stuck under the mug.

More customers had come into the café, and Sally was hustling around taking orders and delivering food to the booths. Mack brushed up close and whispered in her ear, "What time do you get off?" She was finished at three. "I'll be back!" Her eyes followed him out the door. She picked up the ten spot and, with a coy little smile, stuck it into the pocket of her apron.

° ° °

Despite all reasoning, he headed for the Dutcher place. For years, he had deliberately avoided seeing the construction going on around 'Paradise Lake.' He hadn't wanted to witness the changes . . . convinced that it was of no interest to him. In truth, he stayed away from the lake because of the black moods that arose when even thinking of the place. Hell, even the two cupboards LuAnn brought from the house had set him off.

But today, he was internally driven to be there . . . to confront the demons. They wouldn't leave him alone, so why shouldn't he go? It was time to deal with the past and get on with life. Kate was dead . . . sure, but it hadn't been his fault. There were better things to think about than that bitchy broad! Hell he couldn't even remember what she looked like.

Sally . . . Sally Daniels! Now, that was one to think about. She was a real beauty. A slut, to be sure . . . but a gorgeous one. Red hair . . . tied back with a ribbon hung straight down to her hips. Oh, those hips! And he had never seen breasts trying to pop out of a shirt the way hers did. Eyes . . . he could get lost in those green eyes. The afternoon and evening ahead were going to be exhilarating. He was sure of that. His watch said nine o'clock, so there were six hours to kill. The drive was made slow and easy . . . giving plenty of time to think.

His mind drifted back to LuAnn and the events of the day before. She must have been all right. Hell! He hadn't hit her that hard. After he ran off, she must have gotten up and gone to bed with one of the kids. Besides, she had it coming! Hadn't she pushed him around all day with one demand after another? Anyway, he owed her nothing! Hadn't he been taking care of her for ten years now?

And the kids! Kids are always wanting something or doing something crazy. Why in hell wasn't Jason wearing shoes when he was playing that stupid game? *I spend my money on a decent home for my family. I deserve something out of all this! Don't I?*

° ° °

Mack pulled up at the end of the lane to the Dutcher place. A barricade blocked the road. WEATHERBY CONSTRUCTION was emblazoned in black over the yellow paint. He opened the car door and got out. Curiosity was eating away at him. He stepped over the barricade and took off at a lope up the lane and into the yard. There had been a lot of activity. The ground was rutted from heavy trucks, and nearly all the buildings were torn down. The only thing that remained of the farmstead was the shell of the house.

He trod over the deep tire tracks and stuck his head through the paneless front living-room window. All the floors were torn up. The interior was totally gutted . . . nothing there to look at anymore. His eyes shifted to the east where the lake lay, shimmering in the late morning sun. Houses surrounded it on all sides except to the west where he stood. With the buildings demolished and the weeds and bushes cut down, the view to the lake was wide open. He walked in that direction. Very little of the landscape issued any familiarity. He couldn't even find the path that had once snaked its way from the house yard to the east, around the lake to the north, and into Hiawatha. His intense scrutiny took in the impressiveness of the wealthy community that had grown up around the lake.

So this is 'Paradise Lake!' Each home had a dock built out into the water with at least one boat tied to it. They were all row boats or paddle boats, to be sure. The lake wasn't large enough for motorized craft. On this warm Sunday morning, half a dozen lucky fishermen sat with poles in the water. Spacious lawns, with stone or concrete steps angling to the docks, flanked the waterfront of each of the massive homes. Closed-in porches or balconies offered cool relief on hot days. Every yard was masterfully landscaped with more flowers and shrubs than any one green house could ever boast.

The beauty was hypnotic, and tranquillity dominated the scene, encouraging him to relax. There was no need to look for missing keys or a broken locket anymore. Thankfully, the ghosts seemed to have been demolished and hauled away along with the buildings. He was glad he had come.

Because there was no hurry to leave, he looked for a place to sit down. The sun's mid-summer rays penetrated through his shaggy, unkempt hair to the scalp. He found a seat on a nearby rock and intertwined large, callused fingers over his head to ward off some of the heat.

Reluctantly, his eyes scanned the western shoreline until they fell on the old dock. It had never been torn down, and its rotting boards still jutted up out of the water. In spite of everything, his mind searched the past and calculated the events that had occurred there over nine years before. With a jolt of recollection, he realized the rock on which he was sitting was the very one on which Kate had met her death. He sprang upward, like Jack popping out of his box.

"I didn't mean to frighten you!" came a booming voice from behind him. "Are you interested in some property?"

Mack turned to look directly into the rugged, aging face of Joe Weatherby. His voice faltered, and the blood drained away, leaving his tanned face ashen. Finally, he managed, "I . . . I . . . was just curious. I used to live around here . . . when I was a kid. I happened to be driving by."

"Well, if you're interested, we'll be enlarging the lake eventually, and there will be twelve more lots available either next summer or the summer after. I'm Joe Weatherby, and who did you say you are?" He held out a large rough hand.

Mack reluctantly submitted to the man's powerful grip. Regaining his senses, he doubted very much that Joe Weatherby would ever have heard his name. He would be familiar with 'Ruby Dutcher,' for sure, but 'Mack Hanable,' probably not. No sense in lying to him. "I'm Mack Hanable. Glad to meet you . . . I really must be going. Thanks for letting me look." He walked away and didn't look back, muttered, *Damn bastard! Those Weatherbys can't leave anybody alone!*

* * *

Joe Weatherby's dark, stern eyes penetrated the younger man's back as he walked away. 'Hmm, strange guy there. Not very friendly, but there's something familiar about him. Oh, well, why bother myself with it?' He came into contact with dozens of people every day. Right now, he was more interested in the construction that was about to be started.

As soon as the house was torn down, the heavy equipment would be brought in. The enlargement of the lake would begin about where the house sits and go south to the edge of the yard. The dirt would be bulldozed out and up to provide slope to the lake that would materialize. The last thing that would be done is opening up the Paradise Lake shore on the west, just about where the old dock is situated, letting water from Paradise Lake flood over into the excavated area. He figured the water level would go down significantly, but within a year's time and some good rain and snow fall, the whole lake area would regain its original depth.

The project was important to him. Kate had taken an interest in it before she disappeared. He was doing it for her. The new development would bear her name, KATE'S COVE. He didn't know why it had taken Ruby Dutcher so long to consent to selling him the property. He just hoped his wife would live long enough to see the development completed.

Twenty-one

At ten o'clock Sunday night, LuAnn threw Mack's bed pillow onto the faded and ragged couch in the living room. As an afterthought, an old musty blanket that had been shoved to the back of the linen closet was added to her husband's bedding. If he came home, that was all he was going to get. After the children were asleep, their bedroom doors were locked, and the opener was put on her dresser. No sense in risking the chance that any retaliation would be directed towards Joyce or Jason. She locked her own door and, feeling as secure as possible, went to sleep.

Monday morning, the synchronous twittering of the birds out in the woods awakened her at sunrise. She listened for any movement in the house, and hearing only the tick of the clock hanging on the wall, she unlocked the door and went down the hall to the bathroom. A feeling of uneasiness and apprehension hung over the house. She half expected Mack to come lurching out from one of the doorways.

After completing the morning toilet ritual, she went back to the bedroom, and dressed for the day. The stillness was unnerving, and every step seemed to echo through the house. When she entered the kitchen, it was apparent Mack had eaten the fried chicken left over from supper. The rancid smell filled the room, and the plastic container, bones, skin, and greasy crumbs littered the kitchen counter. Ants were crawling over the mess, busily getting their share. She dumped it into the garbage and wiped off the counter using a soapy dishrag. With a swirl of hot water, ants and crumbs were washed down the drain.

She glanced at the clock. It was already after six. If Mack was going to work, he needed to get ready. Reluctantly, she checked in the living room. The make-shift bed had been found, and he was there asleep, wearing only khaki boxer shorts. Both arms were raised up over the end of the couch, and one leg dangled off the edge to the floor. A sickening, sweet smell saturated the room and consumed her senses. Her stomach knotted and wretched with an unwelcome urge to throw up.

His body appeared pink and slimy . . . sick almost. Had he been drinking? She had never known him to even drink a beer. Deep breaths expanded and contracted the deep, hairy chest, and drool ran from the corner of a half-open mouth . . . saturating the pillow scrunched beneath his head. Dark hair fanned out around a weathered, lax face. He needed a hair cut and a shave. Once, she had thought him handsome, and she still did. Fighting a wave of nausea, tears began to surface and were gulped back.

Perspiration, charged with nerves, stood out on LuAnn's forehead and chin. Standing back at a safe distance, she viewed him and pondered what to do. He needed to wake up, but she couldn't bear to touch him. He was stinky, and, besides that, what would his reaction be to her touch? She wasn't going to take the chance of being belted again.

Of course, the alarm clock! She went into the bedroom and unplugged the cord, replugged it in the outlet nearest the couch, and placed the clock on the floor. The alarm was set to go off in five minutes. Then, she went upstairs and sat down on the landing, where there was a partial view of the living room . . . and waited.

The five minutes seemed like an eternity. She was ready to go back down the stairs to see if the alarm was set properly, when its irritating percussion resonated throughout the living room and up the stairs. The couch springs complained under Mack's weight. There was a drawn-out moan, followed by an oath directed at the alarm clock. She was happy to be only a spectator and at a safe distance. Cursing and stumbling around were followed by a loud thump. "Shit! Almighty!" He must have fallen down. Instincts wanted to help him, but a wiser brain told her to stay right there. After more moans and oaths, the alarm was silenced.

From the perch on the landing, she watched him lurch out of the living room and down the hallway. The bathroom door opened and closed, followed by the gurgle of the flushing stool and the surge of the spraying shower. Five minutes later, the door opened again, and bare feet thudded softly on the carpet down the hallway. In the bedroom, drawers were opened, rummaged through, and slammed shut. Metal hangers danced together on the rod in the closet, followed by more moaning and oaths. He was getting into his clothes. A shoe fell to the floor twice before footsteps were heard going from the bedroom, back down the hallway, and into the kitchen. The refrigerator was opened and closed. The cupboard door squeaked, and there was the sound of liquid being poured, gulped.

There was a scrimmage in the living room as furniture got kicked, and cushions were thrown around. Muttering, "Where in the hell did they go? . . . Damn it all!" Then, thankfully, the soft jingle of keys was heard, and footsteps pounded back through the kitchen. A stool was shoved aside and clattered to the floor. The back screen door got pushed open and left to swing in the early morning breeze. Finally, the engine of the Lincoln caught, and the vehicle roared out the driveway. He was gone.

For several minutes, LuAnn sat placidly, trying to figure out what to do next. The two of them couldn't continue in this manner. Slowly, she got to her feet, descended the stairs and went into the living room. With her body performing like a robot, the cushions were mechanically picked up from the floor, shook, smoothed out, and replaced on the couch. Completely repulsed and numbed by it all, she tried desperately to draw up a sense of compassion for her husband.

However, reality was right there in front of her. The blanket smelled badly and was damp with perspiration. The pillow reeked with the noxious, slimy drool, causing her stomach to wretch once again. With a sigh of resignation, the bedding was wadded together to be washed and dried.

In an effort to rid the room of the sickening odor, the south door leading to the front porch and all the windows were opened to their widest. A fan was brought from the kitchen and directed to blow, at its highest speed, through the living room. Right now, compassion was very hard to come by. Perhaps, she could think better later.

On the way to the basement with the laundry, she closed and hooked the screen door. Already flies were buzzing and crawling all over. Was there no end to Mack's path of destruction? After the laundry was taken care of and she was back in the kitchen, she started swatting them with a vengeance. Their bloody insides were being squashed all over everything. She was ready to burst into tears when there was a light rap at the door. Sarah Yoder stood outside the screen with two egg cartons in her hands and a shy smile on her face. "Good morning, LuAnn. Am I too early?"

Startled from the compulsion to attack something, she managed a quick reply. "Why, Sarah, what a nice surprise!" She looked around the kitchen, laid down the swatter, and shrugged. "I'm afraid my house is a real mess, but do come in. Mack left the screen door open when he left for work this morning, and all the flies in the neighborhood took advantage of the situation." The door was unhooked and held open. A bright smile was forced to welcome her friend and to raise her own sagging spirits. "Would you like a glass of orange juice? I'm just about to have breakfast." She took the eggs. "These are for me? How did you know I needed them? Let me get your dollar before I forget."

She was shaken and needed time to gain some composure. Her stomach was still knotted, and a sob was working its way up from inside. She hurried to the bedroom and took a bill from the top dresser drawer. Seeing her reflection in the mirror, she realized it was too late to cover the bruises with makeup. So, she washed her face with cold water, took several deep breaths, and returned to the kitchen. Without looking at her, the money was handed to Sarah.

A glass of juice was poured for each of them. "Please sit down!" A chair for Sarah was quickly pulled out from the table, and LuAnn took a seat directly across. Sarah had never stopped at the Hanables before, and now LuAnn wanted to keep her. She repeated, "Please sit down!" Suddenly, she was flooded with an overwhelming gratitude and need for the Amish woman's presence. If Sarah left right away, she didn't know what she would do. But Sarah took the seat and deliberately took plenty of time in arranging her skirts. For the next few minutes, they avoided each other's eyes and silently sipped the tangy drink. LuAnn's nerves began to unwind.

Sarah sat at the small, square table with both hands wrapped around the cold glass of juice. The black cap, with the strings untied, sat atop her freshly braided hair. Some of the curls had already begun to escape. In the morning light, her face appeared pale. She had something on her mind, as well.

"LuAnn, I feel that I must tell you what I saw Saturday night . . . around eleven-thirty." She began the narrative slowly. "I was just going to bed, and I heard an owl hoot out towards the road. So, I looked out our bedroom window. I saw Mack out in front of our place, along the side of the road, and he was acting very strangely." She hurried on. "The moon was very bright, so I'm certain it was him."

She paused and took several sips of the juice before continuing. "I remembered some of the things you told me about him. Are you having trouble of some kind?" She glanced nervously at LuAnn and wondered if she had a right to ask such a question. "Perhaps it's none of my business, but it looks to me like he hit you." The timidity had left her voice. "Your face is bruised!" Now, she looked, unwaveringly, at her friend, letting her know that she expected a truthful answer.

LuAnn gingerly touched her cheek and felt around her eye. It would be nearly impossible to lie. The children hadn't believed her 'falling in the bathtub' story. She may as well tell Sarah the truth.

"Yes, Mack hit me. It was Saturday night, and then he took off running and didn't come home until very late." A deep sigh escaped from its lonely confinement down deep in her gut, and a tightness squeezed around her heart. "He must have run as far as your place. I'm sorry he bothered you . . . I slept with Joyce, and he was gone all day yesterday. Last night, he slept on the couch in the living room." There was a need to examine everything, to get all the sordid details out in the open. So, she continued on with the narrative and didn't leave anything out, starting with Saturday and ending as of that morning.

"We haven't even talked about it yet. What would you suggest I do?" With a sense of relief, she got up from the table and started scrambling eggs. She put bread in the toaster. "You'll eat breakfast with me, won't you?" She continued the activities without waiting for an answer.

"The Bishops would take care of the problem in the Amish community. Do you have someone like that to talk to?" Sarah got up from the table and located the plates and silverware. She set the table for the two of them. Both women found it comforting to be busy. By this time, they were both quite hungry, and they finished eating before the issue was pressed further.

"You asked me to give you any jewelry found at the Dutcher place. Well, Henry brought these home Friday. He found them in the drain of the sink." She reached into the apron pocket and handed LuAnn the diamond earring and the ruby ring. "And don't try to tell me they belonged to you or to Mack's aunt!"

"I don't know how they got there, Sarah . . . but I'm certain I know who they belonged to, and, no, it wasn't Ruby Dutcher, and they aren't mine, either." She slipped on the ring, and it was large, even for the middle finger.

What should she do with it? Perhaps it should be put into the freezer with the rest of the jewelry. Again, maybe she should confront Mack with the ring. It would be interesting to see his reaction. However, she didn't want to light the fuse for another explosive attack. With a sense of calmness, both pieces were put in the corner of the counter behind the flour canister. They would be dealt with later.

"I'm so glad you came this morning, Sarah. I really needed someone to talk to."

The Amish woman stood up from the table and pushed the chair back. She smoothed the front of her apron and retied the cap strings.

"Your children must be sleeping late, too. I know mine do on Mondays after Church. Your clock says eight-fifteen, I must get home. Martha won't want to deal with the children by herself this morning. She hasn't been feeling well lately."

She pushed the screen door open and hurried towards the buggy. The green skirts swished around her legs, and bare feet left imprints in the dusty sand of the driveway. The horse was tethered to the fence post near the road. She loosened the reins and climbed up into the buggy seat. With a click of the tongue and a wave of the hand, she was off and down the road.

LuAnn stood on the back porch and watched the buggy until it rolled out of sight. Then she heard the hollow clomping of the horses hooves and the rattle of the steel-clad wheels as it crossed over the Otter Creek bridge. Sarah had such a hard life, and yet she managed it so well. What was wrong with her and Mack that their life was falling apart?

The truth was, they had never really built a life together. Mack always did as he pleased, and she took care of him. She took care of the children, too, to keep them out of his way. The needs of her and the children were rarely communicated to him, unless they, somehow, satisfied his desires, too. She had been afraid to do otherwise.

Yet, where would she be without him? She looked around their new home. He seemed so proud to provide it for them, and she really and truly loved it. Maybe her life wasn't so bad after all. Besides, she couldn't expect to have everything her own way, and feeling sorry for herself didn't help at all.

In a few weeks, she would be starting classes at Hawkeye School of Technology. He wasn't denying her that opportunity, even though he hadn't accepted the decision with enthusiasm. But then, how could he object to her going? She was paying the expenses herself. They would have a good talk when he got home today. Apparently, some issues needed to be aired. Surely, they could work everything out. For some reason, he was just unusually uptight again.

* * *

When Mack got over the shock of getting up to go to work, his mind went back over the events of the day before. That Sally Daniels was really something! She could make a guy forget just about anything that was gnawing at his gut. "She not only has a great ass, but she has great *grass*, too!" He laughed at the queer little joke. Man! He didn't know why he had never tried it before.

Of course, LuAnn would never have permitted marijuana in the house, much less used it. She was no fun at all! Never had been! Always just too damned serious! He supposed it was the family she came from. The Soppees figured their daughter was too good for him. He had always been aware of that. Well, he wasn't going to waste any more time worrying about them. Sally wanted him to come back Friday night, and he sure as hell was going.

* * *

At six o'clock, LuAnn had a roast beef dinner complete with fresh apple pie on the dining room table. She had picked wild Sweet Williams from the ditch in front of the house and arranged them in a fruit jar. They were set in the center. Mack sat down with the family and ate appreciatively. Not a word was spoken by anyone, not even the children. They had been cautioned not to bother their father. Pushing the chair back from the table, he acknowledged, "Good dinner, LuAnn."

Perhaps this was the opening that was needed, so she motioned for the children to leave the room. They left through the living room door, but looked back at their parents with some degree of consternation.

"Mack, we need to talk. We can't go on like this. We need to do something." She made sure the table was between them, as she rapidly began spitting out the rehearsed monologue. She may as well have saved her breath, because he rudely interrupted.

"Woman, I'm doing something right now. You just take care of your job," his arms swept out, indicating their home, "and I'll take care of mine." He tapped a straight pointer finger, determinedly, against his chest like a woodpecker hammering its beak on a rotted tree stump. He threw back his head and swaggered through the kitchen. "I've got things to do!" With finality, the screen door slammed shut.

She followed after him as far as the screen door. To her amazement, he went to the Lincoln and popped open the trunk. He started hauling things out of the vehicle. In a few minutes, he had placed an Army cot, an Army trunk, and a variety of other items from the Army Surplus Store out on the ground.

"Hey Jason, come here and help me with this! Will you?" he bellowed.

Jason came running. "Wow Dad, great! Where did you get this stuff? Where are you taking it? What's it for?" Having gotten, what he figured, was some genuine recognition from his father, his young face beamed with pleasure.

"Stop asking so damned many questions! In the house! Grab ahold!" Mack lifted one end of the cot, and Jason struggled with the other end. "Joyce, we need your help! Get over here!" He may as well include her, too. She was just standing there like a bump on a log with a scowl on her face.

Everything was taken into the downstairs bedroom where the roll-top desk and rocker were the sole occupants. LuAnn kept out of their way and concentrated her efforts on cleaning up the kitchen and dining room and finishing up the dishes. She didn't dare ask what he was doing. She would just have to wait and find out when he was ready to tell her. But, at least, he was including the children.

"Come here a minute, LuAnn." Mack beckoned for her to follow into their bedroom. Apparently, he was about ready to enlighten her, but she was apprehensive and held back, a look of mistrust on her face. "Hell, I'm not going to hurt you. I just want to know if you want the dresser or the chest of drawers. You can have your choice."

"Wh . . . wh . . . what do you mean? What are you talking about? Tell me what's going on. For Heaven's sake, what are you doing?"

"I'm moving into the other bedroom, woman. Can't you see? We don't need each other anymore. You know that! Like I said . . . you take care of the house and the kids . . . feed me right . . . and do my laundry, and I won't bother you anymore. Now, which will it be . . . the dresser or the chest of drawers?"

* * *

He always knew he couldn't live without LuAnn. She took such good care of him. Now, he figured out a way so he wouldn't have to . . . but he could have Sally, too. It would suit them all very well.

Besides, he could never live with Sally! Her homemaking skills were zippo. Even the grilled cheese sandwich she fixed was burned, and the soup tasted like dishwater. Besides that, the trailer house needed a good cleaning. Actually, he had found it a bit distasteful to lay on the soiled sheets. But he had soon forgotten about them. Clean sheets aren't everything! This way he could have the best of both women.

* * *

The chest of drawers was moved into Mack's room. He moved the desk into LuAnn's room. It was full of receipts and things that she knew about. He didn't want to bother himself with any of that business. It was up to her to pay the bills anyway, that's what he gave her money for. Not long ago, she had been bugging him about needing more money, and he had given it to her. So, she should be satisfied for a while, at least.

Joyce and Jason didn't question what was going on. Joyce seemed delighted that her mother would have a room for herself. After all, she did. Jason was impressed with his father's Army gear. As far as they were concerned, the arrangement was logical. The overall aura impregnating the home that evening was one of relief.

LuAnn didn't bother locking the children's bedroom doors, but she still locked her own. Mack went into his room shortly after nine o'clock and shut the door. "Hell, I'm tired!"

* * *

On August 3, Joe Weatherby stood watching as heavy equipment rolled onto the property west of Paradise Lake. This was the beginning. Two years from now, there would be a sign down at the road, KATE'S COVE, and he and his wife would be constructing the first home for themselves. It would be built on the two lots furthest to the west and overlook the cove and the lake. At the present time, Clare's muscular disease was in remission. The doctors expected her to have at least five good years and possibly more. The development of the area would be a balm for her broken spirit. Joe and Clare Weatherby remembered their only child as the light of their lives. All other recollections were always immediately dismissed.

* * *

On August 10, LuAnn began classes at Hawkeye School of Technology. Joyce and Jason spent their days with the Brown family until their school started a week later. Mack spent his week nights at the farmstead. Fridays, after work, he headed for Center Point to spend the night with Sally Daniels. Sometimes, he didn't return home until Sunday, in time for dinner. The Hanable household took on its very own uniqueness.

Mack managed to get to work everyday, and LuAnn managed to keep the bills paid.

Occasionally, he spent time with the children, teaching them how to drive the old lawnmower or taking them to a movie on Sunday afternoon. Twice, he took them fishing back in the woods along the bank of the Otter Creek. The one thing they looked forward to the most was the one thing Mack wouldn't do. He wouldn't buy them ponies as he had promised. "We just don't have time for them." Instead, he bought two calves from the Yoders and put them in the pasture. He showed Joyce and Jason how to care for them and then he left the children on their own. With LuAnn's assistance and advice from the Yoders, the animals managed to survive and thrive. They were named Elvis and Marilyn.

Otter Creek and the woods that had been so important to Mack, quickly lost their appeal. The weeds grew up to astronomical heights, and he didn't want to do the work of cutting them down. Mowing the lawn was job enough. Cockle-burrs and stick-tights clung to every piece of clothing worn when walking through the woods. They even got in a person's hair. Joyce and Jason tried fishing by themselves a few times, but with no one to help them, they quickly became discouraged. During the school year, the children were glad to be picked up by the bus every day. They could see their friends who lived in town.

Part 3

1970

Twenty-two

Students left the classrooms and hurriedly made their ways to the closest exits, leading to the parking lots. Not many of them bothered to exchange greetings or good-byes. It was the last day of classes for the summer, and people seemed to be in a hurry to get away . . . but not everyone. Some students would not be returning in August, and LuAnn was one of them. The graduates tended to linger in the hallways. For nearly two years, the Hawkeye College campus had been like a second home to her . . . more friendly, in many ways, than the house she shared with Mack. They were, probably, the most hectic and hardest years of her life, and, yet, the most gratifying as well.

Now, she was in no hurry. She wanted to soak up every bit of the building's essence before walking out the door. It was very doubtful she would ever be back here again. Plans concerning the future for herself and the children had been formulating for quite some time. In a few weeks, she hoped to realize their fruition.

That evening she would be receiving a Diploma for General Business Management and a Certificate of Merit in the Field of Interior Design. The graduation program was going be held at West High School in Waterloo. She had sent invitations to the people she loved, and they all said they would be there. It was an exciting time.

A graduation announcement was left on the kitchen table for Mack, but he gave no indication of having seen it. He hadn't participated in her life for the past two years, so why should he now? Still, it would be nice to have him sitting with Joyce and Jason.

Taking a final look back down the long hallway, she gave a firm push on the bar of the exit door and walked towards the parking lot. By now, most of the dust from the departing vehicles had settled. A good share of it seemed to have settled on her '65 Ford. To purchase it, she had used a good deal of money from the savings in the Hiawatha State Bank. The little Volkswagen hadn't lasted the first year of driving to classes every day. The winter's ice and snow were more than it could handle.

Mack hadn't even acknowledged her acquisition of a different vehicle, nor even asked how she paid for it. His total disregard for her activities and their finances gave her courage to move what money was left to a safety deposit box in Independence State Bank. Besides, it needed to be immediately accessible to carry out her plan.

* * *

LuAnn had known right away that Mack had a girlfriend . . . and she had even found out her name and where she lived. One Saturday, she and Francis had driven past Sally's trailer, parked behind the sale barn, and Mack's Lincoln was right there. It was beyond their comprehension why he would spend a perfectly good day in that sleazy place when he had an attractive and comfortable home of his own, not to mention two delightful children . . . and a wife.

"You know, LuAnn . . . I think Mack doesn't feel he deserves you, or even Joyce and Jason. It's as though he has to punish himself or something, isn't it?" Francis kept trying to figure him out. "I mean . . . for me . . . *that* would be punishment!" Her finger pointed towards the trailer house.

* * *

As she drove along, LuAnn's mind flitted in many directions. Francis had promised to come to the graduation tonight, and she was bringing Karen with her. Becky and Daniel Cummings wouldn't be there because they had moved to Phoenix, Arizona, just six weeks ago, where they are managing the pharmacy in a K-Mart. Francis had provided this information when the invitation came back to LuAnn marked, *No Forwarding Address.* It seemed that the Cummings family was out of her life forever. Still, LuAnn had many fond memories to cherish.

Pete and Connie Brown would be there with their three children. Their friendship was priceless. For the past two years, whenever LuAnn was in need of a sitter, or anything else for that matter, the Browns volunteered to do what they could. In fact, they would be bringing Joyce and Jason with them tonight, since LuAnn had to be at West High an hour before the program began.

Her watch said three o'clock, so there were still three hours until then. She would go home and relax with a leisurely bath. Special attention would be given to her hair. Two weeks ago, Francis had put in a new perm for the occasion, her graduation gift. She wanted Francis to be pleased with the results, since it was, probably, the last perm she would ever get from her. With a deep sense of nostalgia, they had both remembered the first time LuAnn set foot in her beauty shop, some twelve years before.

Last week, Connie had helped pick out new clothes at Graham's Department Store. She worked there part time now and really enjoyed being of assistance to her friend. There was a new dress hanging in LuAnn's closet, and Joyce and Jason, also, had new clothes. They would be getting ready at the Browns' home.

Pastor Wilkens, his wife, Judy, and three other women from the First Presbyterian Church were planning to attend the graduation exercises. Those five people had provided her, Joyce, and Jason with continuous spiritual guidance. It had been difficult for LuAnn to go to the pastor two years ago, but his acceptance of their situation was remarkably compassionate, loving, and encouraging. She believed his declaration, "God loves you and the children. He loves Mack, too. Everything works out in His time. Have faith." Faith had gotten her this far, and it would take her the rest of the way. She wheeled the Ford into the yard of the Hanable farmstead.

* * *

The morning after the graduation, Saturday, June 21, 1970, Joe Weatherby stood at the bottom of the huge hole . . . nearly half the length and width of Paradise Lake. It had taken the better part of two years to excavate the site for KATE'S COVE. A wall of dirt surrounded him on the north, south, and west, sloping upward to the height of the residences built along Paradise Lake. Load after load of dirt had been dug from the site and hauled away or used for landscaping of the proposed building lots.

Monday, the levee separating Paradise Lake from Kate's Cove would be opened up. The water from the lake would be allowed to seep slowly into the cove. The breach would begin at or near the location of the old dock. Where he stood now would, in time, be the lake's bottom.

The project was progressing satisfactorily, but he still needed to keep on top of things. He decided to stop at Francis Franklin's home to see how she was coming with her preparations for moving. He had purchased the property two years ago, with the option she could live there, rent free, until he needed to begin the excavation of that site. He had told her a month ago that she needed to be out by July first.

* * *

The living room was bare except for a few boxes of old rags and cleaning products. There was no furniture in one bedroom, and the other had only her bed left in it. Clothes and boxes covered the floor. She had sold off nearly everything.

"I think I deserve some new furniture! I've used my folks' old things long enough. I'll have a new apartment, so I need new furniture." This rationalization was made to anyone who was or wasn't interested.

Francis was in the kitchen emptying out drawers when Joe Weatherby knocked at the door. He looked tired. Like her, he wasn't getting any younger. "Have a chair, Mr. Weatherby. I was just about to sit down myself to have some iced tea. Would you like some?" She went to the cupboard and got two glasses. They were set on the table with the two boxes she was using for sorting. One for keeping and the other for throwing away. She was nearly finished with the junk drawer. "I wonder why we keep some things, don't you? At least half of these things were left by my parents. I didn't know what good they were then, and I don't know what good they are now."

Joe Weatherby casually looked at the boxes of junk, and his eyes fell on the box of throw-aways. Laying on top was a set of keys. For some reason, they drew his attention, and he couldn't take his eyes from them. He squinted, bent forward, and looked closer. Surely, he was mistaken. Slowly, he reached over and picked them up . . . cautiously . . . as though they were too hot to touch. Slowly, he examined them . . . not believing what lay in his hands. He turned the gold medallion over and the initials KW struck him in the face. They were the keys to Kate's Corvette. Disbelief overwhelmed him, and his face turned ashen. Afraid to speak out loud, he asked in a hoarse whisper, "Francis, where did you get these keys?"

By now, Francis was fully aware that Joe Weatherby appeared to be in a state of shock. She sat in a chair beside him, grasped his shoulder, and looked into his face. "Mr. Weatherby, what in the world is the matter?" She saw that his eyes were glued to the keys in his hand. What significance might they have? With pain etched on his face, they were held up closer for her to see. She looked from Joe to the keys. Then, she realized, "Oh, my dear God! . . . Those are Kate's initials! They're her keys!" She rose quickly from the chair, brought back a pitcher of iced tea, and poured some into the two glasses. "Here, drink this! This must be a terrible shock for you." She sat back down and sympathetically patted his free hand.

He took a large gulp of the cold liquid. Then, he managed, "Do you have any idea where they came from? How did they get in your drawer? How long have you had them?" The expression on his face was one of total bewilderment.

Francis was just as baffled. "They were here when I moved in. At that time, I cleaned out the junk drawer, and they were in it then. I don't know why I decided to keep them, maybe because Mother did. She usually had a reason for doing things."

There was a long silence, as they each had their own thoughts. Francis sipped the drink and went back to the time of Kate's disappearance. Her mother was not capable of walking any great distance, so where could she have gotten them? Finding them was the only explanation that made any sense.

"I'm willing to bet Mother found them out in the yard. At that time, she seldom went any further. That means Kate was somewhere around here the night she disappeared, doesn't it?"

Joe nodded slowly. "Yes, and that shouldn't surprise me. She was very interested in the Dutcher property, she wanted it so much. It was like a passion to her. Kate could be very determined. You know, once she got something in her head . . . well . . . no one could persuade her otherwise. I'm afraid Clare and I let her carry that trait too far."

Now, tears rolled down his tanned, creased cheeks, and the keys were clenched tightly in a closed fist. With a shudder, he continued, "She always got her way, and this time, it may have killed her." The keys were pressed tightly to his mouth, and he kissed them. "I'll take these with me. Please don't tell anyone about this. I think it's best if Clare doesn't know. She's doing quite well right now, I don't want to upset her. We'll begin construction on our home this fall. I want her to live long enough to enjoy it." He pulled a large, white handkerchief from his pants pocket, wiped his eyes, and blew his nose. Then, he mustered a weak smile.

Francis nodded in agreement. "As you can see, there will be no problem with my being out by July first. Karen and her husband will be moving me on Monday. Most of my furniture will be new, and it will be delivered to my apartment. Give Mrs. Weatherby my regards, and you take care now." She walked him to the door, saw him out, and closed it.

Kate had a passion all right . . . a passion for Mack Hanable. She wondered if LuAnn should be told about the keys. Probably not. Why bother her with anything more? Last night, she was so happy and satisfied with her accomplishments, so why throw cold water on such enthusiasm? Besides, anything concerning Kate Weatherby was Mack's problem, and she wasn't about to make it LuAnn's . . . not at this time. That was for sure!

* * *

Mack was having problems all right, but this time, they were with Sally. She was tired of being his weekend entertainment, and she let him know it. "I'm fed up with giving you my time. Weekends are the only chance I have to get a real relationship going. You'll never marry me. I'm twenty-six years old, and I haven't even had a diamond ring yet." It was late Friday night, and she sat on his lap at the edge of the bed . . . running greasy-smelling fingers through his tangled hair . . . trying for the last time to persuade him to live with her.

She didn't tell him, but, for the past month, the new preacher at the First Day Church had been coming into Mable's Kitchen for breakfast in the morning. Being a bachelor, every single woman, and a few married ones, for twenty miles around, were vying for his attention. Sally figured, *Why not me?* With this thought in mind, she had decided Mack could have one more chance to prove his good intentions.

"Hell! . . . If it's a diamond ring you want . . . I'll get you one! You know I can't leave LuAnn. She could take me for all I've got. Then you wouldn't want me anyway." He started to unbutton the bodice of her uniform.

She stood up and abruptly pushed him backward onto the bed. "Well, then we could at least have a baby. A baby would give me something to do while you're gone. I decided there's gonna be no more marijuana. It ain't good for a baby." She put on the little girl pout that always excited him.

"Then come here, Sally. There's only one way I know of to make a baby." He reached out and grabbed her arm, pulling her down on the bed. "Anything you say, Sweetheart! Anything you say!" He knew full well that a baby wasn't a possibility. He and the doctor had seen to that right after Jason was born.

* * *

He woke up just before sunrise. Without the cloud of reefer smoke hanging in the air, his brain actually worked. He went into the scroungy bathroom to relieve himself. The putrid odor from weeks of neglect nearly choked him. Water was splashed on his face, and fingers were used as a comb. In the mirror, his eyes looked clear for a change. For two years, most Saturday mornings were one big fog that lasted all day. He used the corner of a damp, soiled towel and went back to the bedroom to get into some Army fatigues that were kept there in the closet.

In the kitchen, he pulled a chair away from the table and positioned it where he could see Sally sleeping on the bed. There was some serious thinking to be done. It had been a long time since he had really looked at her. Thoughtfully, he pursed his lips and cocked his head to one side. By his evaluation, her naked body was no longer shapely. Hell, she must have gained twenty or thirty pounds since they met.

Giving her still further scrutiny, he noticed that green eye shadow and black mascara were smeared on both cheeks. Long, red hair was wrapped and plastered in tendrils against her upper body. She reeked of perspiration and cheap perfume. All in all, it was not a pretty sight. Thankfully, her breathing remained deep and regular . . . still asleep.

He got up from the chair and walked to the doorway of the bedroom. Dirty clothes of every description covered the floor, and soiled bedding was yanked about in every direction. Cheap bangles, offered by the discount stores, cluttered the dresser and chest of drawers. A lot of it had been presents from him. Brushes with strands of twisted red hair, dirty combs, and gaudy ribbons were among the rest of the litter. A few reefers were still there. Layers of dust covered everything.

Turning back to the living room and kitchen, the sight and smell of dirty pans and dishes, mixed in with an accumulation of unopened mail and unread papers, sickened him. Love magazines smeared with yellow stains from Corny Curl snacks occupied most of the couch. As he walked across the floor, crumbs and dirt grated under his tennis shoes. He picked up his keys and billfold from the mess on the table and slipped quietly out the door. He wouldn't be coming back.

* * *

He drove south to Hiawatha. The main street of the little town was quiet. No one was out on the street, and only two cars were parked at the curb. He was happy to see a new restaurant located where the drug store had been. He wondered when that change had taken place. There was a sign up in the window, BREAKFAST. Now that was a good idea!

Remodeling was still going on inside, but an elderly couple was there with smiles on their faces and a desire to serve their customers . . . Mack was the first one of the morning. He surveyed the premises and then seated himself in one of the booths. The woman scurried over and handed him a new menu along with a cheerful smile. "Good morning, sir. Would you like coffee?" She picked up a heavy, white mug from the table and held the pot ready to pour.

He nodded and smiled back. That bit of friendly exchange was invigorating, and he wanted the pleasant feeling to continue. Today, time was going to be of no concern. He would relax and drink all the coffee he wanted. There was a lot of thinking to do and issues to sort out. Savoring each morsel, he enjoyed every bite of scrambled eggs, hash browns, and toast. The coffee pot was left at the table, and he drank every drop of it . . . along with a large glass of orange juice. A ten spot was left on the table, and he walked out of the restaurant into the warm and sunny day. It had been months since feeling this good on a Saturday.

He walked down Main Street towards the Trout place. A Ford station wagon was parked out front. The sign on the car door read, WEATHERBY REAL ESTATE AND CONSTRUCTION. That name was going to haunt him forever! There were voices at the front door of the residence, and Joe Weatherby walked out to the vehicle. He seemed intent on his business, whatever it might be. Mack walked across the backyard and up over the landscaped shoreline. He looked down into the basin of Kate's Cove. His gaze was drawn to the old dock. It was still there.

* * *

Inside the house, Francis went back to work. She carried the iced tea glasses to the sink. A flicker of movement through the window drew her attention to the backyard. There was a man dressed in Army fatigues. That wasn't unusual, as a lot of people used her property as an access to viewing the excavation of Kate's Cove. Even before then, the Paradise Lake development had been an attraction for the curious.

She watched as he climbed up the gentle slope of loose dirt. There was something familiar about that gait and stance. At the top of the mound, his silhouette stood straight, with hands on hips . . . military-style, against the blue sky. After ten minutes or so, he turned and loped back down, at times sliding and struggling to maintain his stance. At the edge of the lawn, he sat on the grass and emptied out his shoes. When he came back across the yard, she recognized Mack Hanable. In the recesses of her mind, his presence was filed away, and she went back to sorting junk.

* * *

Mack looked at his watch. He could be home in time to have dinner with LuAnn and the kids. He needed to pay more attention to Joyce and Jason. Hell, he might even get them the ponies they wanted. He climbed into the Lincoln and headed for Independence.

* * *

As soon as Mack pulled away from Sally Daniels' trailer, she jumped out of bed and ran to the bathroom. For ten minutes, she had been 'playing opossum' with her bladder ready to burst. He was gone, and she wasn't going to let him come back! Like Pastor Bronwell said, "God forgives us our sins, as we forgive those who sin against us." And Jesus said, "Go and sin no more." Well, she would forgive Mack, but she wouldn't sin with him anymore.

She looked around the trailer and determined that the place really should be cleaned up. *Really* cleaned up! She wanted to invite Pastor Bronwell over for supper some evening, and she needed to make a good impression. Besides cleaning up the trailer, that would mean learning to cook something, too. There was a lot on her agenda for the weekend. Well, she wouldn't miss Mack's company today. There was plenty to do before church tomorrow, so she better get started. Bent on making a new start, she went into the bedroom and collected the last of the reefers from the top of the dresser. With just a little hesitancy, they were flushed down the toilet stool.

* * *

LuAnn spent the morning going through Joyce's and Jason's closets, sorting out the clothes that were outgrown. One by one, they were placed into paper bags and then loaded into the trunk of the Ford to be taken to the Salvation Army Store. After returning from the graduation program the night before, she had gone through her own closet, sorting and folding items until early morning. She had decided to keep only their clothing that was absolutely necessary. The remainder was placed in the trunk of the car. It was just after eleven o'clock in the morning when the job was finally completed.

"Well, kids, how about going to the A&W for something to eat? We'll drop these bags off, and then we'll go over to the Browns. Mr. and Mrs. Brown and I have some things to discuss. You kids can spend the afternoon at the park." There were no objections, so the house was closed up, and they drove out of the yard.

* * *

Fifteen minutes later, Mack pulled into the driveway expecting to have dinner with his family and to spend the afternoon with them. LuAnn's car wasn't in sight, and the house was shut up tight. The good humor he had been experiencing during the morning suddenly vanished. Muttering, *What in the hell's going on? Nobody's home? Is it too much to expect a meal in my own home?*

The door of the Lincoln was closed with a slam, and he kicked it to make sure. The screen door was yanked open, and he barged into the kitchen. "LuAnn! Joyce! Jason! Where the hell are you?" It was perfectly obvious that no one was home, but there was pleasure in venting anyway.

He stomped over to the refrigerator and rummaged through its contents. Nothing had been cooked, so he looked into the freezer. Hell, he didn't know what to do with anything in there, so he took an apple from the crisper and sank his teeth into it. Then, remembering the huge breakfast eaten earlier in the morning, he realized he wasn't really very hungry anyway.

He rambled through the house as though seeing it for the first time. It was almost two years since he had been in LuAnn's bedroom. The door was wide open. Almost timidly, he entered. It was filled with her essence. Eagerly, his hands ran over the bed and pillow. Then, he opened the closet and smothered his sweaty face in her clean, fresh clothes. She didn't seem to have very many. Nothing like Sally's closet, packed tight with every conceivable color and outfit . . . issuing cheap perfume and perspiration. The items on the dresser were arranged neatly . . . not much there, either. He wondered about the drawers. What does she keep there? One at a time, he pulled them open and rifled through the contents.

At the bottom of the underwear drawer, he found a small plastic bag containing a diamond earring and a ruby ring. "What the hell! Where did these come from?" He put the ring on his little finger. It fit perfectly. At one time, he had selected a ring for Kate that way. But, now, there was no recollection of any ring he had ever bought. The ruby held no significance for him.

He suspected LuAnn's mother had sent it to her, and she never bothered getting it sized. Her time and mind had been so bogged down with all those books she studied, it's a wonder anything else got done. She could have found the earring someplace. It looked like a real diamond, maybe worth keeping. He put the jewelry back and shut the drawer.

He went up the stairs and rummaged through Joyce's and Jason's rooms the same way. He was trying to reconnect with his family and didn't even know it, but there was some degree of comfort in what he was doing. Finally, he went into his own room and collapsed on the bed. Almost instantly, he was asleep.

* * *

When he woke up two hours later, his family still wasn't home, so he drove into town and got a root beer float at the A&W. From there, he went to the Army Surplus Store. He bought a large knife in a sheath and a camouflage helmet. Jason would appreciate these. Hell, maybe Joyce would like them, too, so he bought one more of each. If he could find the old scythe, they could cut down the weeds to make a good path along the creek. Then he could take them fishing.

This time, when he returned home, they were there. He could see LuAnn through the screen door. She was putting groceries away, and the kids were out watering the bull and heifer. He pulled the helmets and knives from the back seat of the car and carried them out to where the kids were taking care of their chores. "Hey guys, see what I got for you!

Here, try them out!" He slapped a helmet on their heads and thrust a knife into their hands.

The children were surprised and rendered speechless. When Joyce realized what had happened, a look of disgust swept over her face. She dropped the knife, yanked off the helmet, threw it to the ground, and ran off to the house, "Mom! Mom!" The kitchen door slammed behind her.

Jason looked apprehensive. "What's this for, Dad? I don't understand."

Mack picked up the two pieces of gear Joyce had dropped and beckoned to Jason. "Come on, and I'll show you." He tugged the helmet on and pulled the knife from its sheath. Brandishing it a few times, he headed for the woods and the nearest patch of weeds. Taking giant swaths with the knife, he commenced to hack away at the plants. "See, like this! Get your knife out! We're cutting our way through the jungle!"

They had to shower before supper. Their clothes were full of sticktights and cockle-burrs. If LuAnn hadn't been so tired, she may have seen some humor in it. Instead, she tried, with disgust, to clean up the clothes while Joyce and Jason did the dishes. One at a time, the nettles were disengaged from their prickly grip. She finally gave up on the socks and threw them away. Mack got out the lawnmower and started in on the lawn. The evening really wasn't going very well.

As soon as the dishes were finished, LuAnn sent Joyce and Jason upstairs to bed. She wanted to be settled in herself before Mack came back into the house. He was acting more peculiar than ever this evening, and she found him looking at her in ways that were very discomforting. She opened the underwear drawer to get a clean pair of pajamas. Someone had, obviously, been in her things. Last night, she had folded and arranged everything as she was sorting out clothes for the Salvation Army. Logic told her that the only one who could have been in there was Mack. The idea was unnerving. She grabbed night clothes and ran down the hallway into the bathroom. The door was locked, and she took a quick shower. She picked up her toiletries and took them back to the bedroom. Again, the door was locked. What was going through Mack's head now? For two years, he had been true to his word and not bothered her. She was grateful for the sound of the lawnmower coming through the window. At least she knew he was still occupied outside.

She lay in bed thinking. As always, she was thankful for the advice and council the Browns had given her that afternoon. For the past two years, they had continually kept one another informed of the situation, and, as of today, they had been made aware of her plans. Only now, matters seemed to be getting worse. As they had kept reminding her, she needed to concentrate, solely, on the children and herself. She intended to do just that. Once again, she mentally ran over the plans she was making. There was no sleep until after the mower was put away and Mack's bedroom door was closed.

Twenty-three

Joe Weatherby spent the remainder of the weekend formulating scenarios in an effort to explain how Kate's keys came to be in Francis Franklin's junk drawer for eleven years. 'What ifs' whirled around, clogging his mind, until his head was ready to explode. He finally settled on a logical explanation and decided to act on it.

Early Monday morning, he parked the company station wagon on Main Street in Hiawatha. He walked across Francis Franklin's backyard and followed the approximate path that had once led around the northwest edge of Paradise Lake. The excavation had changed the landscape considerably, but the fact that the levee was still there, where the path angled to the dock, gave him some semblance of how the terrain had been. He ambled along slowly in the loose dirt, choosing his steps carefully. The once strong and agile body was loosing some of its vigor. Besides, there was much to think about.

If, for some reason, Kate had decided to visit the Paradise Lake site on the night of June 12, 1959, more than likely, she would have approached it through Maude Trout's backyard. In fact, she must have. No doubt, that is where the keys had been found. There was no other explanation for them being in Maude's house.

As he walked along the levee, he tried to imagine what Kate would have done that night. Approaching the old dock, he felt certain she would have walked out onto it. The boards were too rotted to walk out there now . . . and they probably were then, too. But, in the moonlight, she may not have realized the danger. It was conceivable, to him, that she may have broken through the dock and drowned. She was always terrified of water, so, if she had panicked, there was no way she could have saved herself.

He further rationalized that some youths, out having a good time that night, had found her car parked on Main Street. She didn't ever lock the doors, and the spare key was kept in the ash tray . . . not too difficult a place to find it. A yellow Corvette would be too much of a temptation for a bunch of rambunctious kids to pass up. Then, after joy-riding for a while, he figured they must have 'chickened-out' and left it in the vacant lot in southeast Cedar Rapids. They wiped off their fingerprints for fear of getting into trouble and disposed of the spare key in somebody's garbage can. To Joe, the scenario seemed plausible. Satisfied with the rational, he turned back towards Main Street.

Thoughtfully, he ambled back over the levee and through the loose dirt of the slope leading down to Francis's backyard. Like Mack had done on Saturday, he sat down on the edge of the lawn and emptied out his shoes. The early morning sun reflected brightly on something in the grass. Leaning over, he found some change that had fallen from Mack's pocket. He imagined Maude had found the keys in much the same manner. The reflection of the sun had drawn her to them.

Once back in the station wagon, he drove around to the south entrance leading to Kate's Cove. The excavator that would open up the levee was being put in place. "Good morning, Joe! This is the big day you've been waiting for!" The booming voice of Ray Dewey, the foreman of the crew, greeted his boss.

Joe hurried over to inform Ray of the decision he had just made. "Good morning, Ray! I want you to hold up this operation just a bit. There's something that needs to be discussed, just between you and me." Pulling his foreman aside, Joe explained the dilemma. "My daughter's keys were dropped in this location, most likely the night she disappeared . . . eleven years ago. The person who found them was elderly and apparently didn't realize they were of any importance. Anyway, I just got them from this woman's daughter. I have reason to think Kate may have fallen into the lake somewhere around that old dock. If that's so, well . . . I imagine her remains are still there. I'm just telling you what we might find. If your operator would approach the job with a bit of caution, well, I would appreciate it."

Ray Dewey drew his tall, angular body back slightly and, trying not to be obvious, thoughtfully analyzed his boss' demeanor. There were a lot of questions to ask, but this wasn't the time for them. It was apparent Joe was in a state of anxiety. His usual jovial features were tense, and his dark eyes penetrated deeper into his own as each word was spoken. He wondered if the old guy could manage the shock if his daughter's body did surface.

A comforting hand was placed on his boss' shoulder. "Sure, Joe, I understand. I'll see what Jeff suggests we do. OK?" A nod indicated approval. So, he turned and, loping like a deer, covered the distance from the temporary drive, across the rutted tracks, to the operator of the excavator. Jeff was leaning back against the machine, picking breakfast from his teeth, waiting for the 'go-ahead.'

There was a long and intense exchange of information, questions, and opinions between Ray and Jeff. Their conversation was out of earshot, but frequent glances in Joe's direction were disquieting and left him more and more distraught. Finally, Ray was back. "Jeff thinks that if you're pretty darned sure your daughter's body is in there, the police should be here. I'm inclined to agree with him. Is it OK if I go and give them a call?" Without waiting for an answer, he started to turn away.

Joe grabbed the sleeve of Ray's denim work shirt, and, with a twist, pulled it up tight. "No! No! Don't do that! I don't want to be wrong again! I've bothered them with misleading information enough times over the years. They think I'm a foolish old man. If I'm right this time, well, then we can call them. If she's in there, a few more hours won't matter anyway. Go ahead! Get it done!" He released the grip on Ray's shirt.

"Just one request, then, Joe. Go sit over there in my jeep." He pointed to a vehicle sitting on the little knoll off to their right. "It's close enough for you to watch everything that's going on, and I would feel better if you were sitting down. You don't know how you'll react, should we find something." There was compassion in his voice. Ray put his arm around Joe's shoulder and walked up the grassy incline with him. With a show of respect, he was settled into the passenger seat. Joe had treated the crew well over the past fifteen years, so Ray wanted to help him out this time.

The foreman strode back over to the levee where he could watch every move of the excavator. He waved a 'go-ahead' and nodded to Jeff. The roar and whine of the huge machine intensified as the bucket was lowered, and the first bite was taken. The rotten wood of the dock was precisely plucked, ingested, and crunched. Splintered old timbers and boards fell in a mass of confusion . . . resembling a plate of pretzels.

Ray waved, and, again, the machine hungrily lowered its head. This time, it went much deeper. Like a giant water serpent, its jaws opened and groped. Its body trembled as it pushed into the lake bottom. Satisfied with the catch, it slowly raised its head, letting water gush from around its teeth. Its prey was swung over to the levee and dropped precisely within feet of where Ray was standing.

Along with the gravel and silt from the lake bottom, two cement blocks and an accumulation of bones landed at his feet. Ray vigorously waved at Jeff. "Hold everything!"

He sprang off towards the jeep, hoping to ward off Joe before he tried to get a better view. He caught him just before his right foot hit the ground. Bodily, he shoved the man back into the vehicle. "We've got a phone call to make!" He leaped up into the driver's seat and took off before Joe had a chance to object.

Within minutes, the west side of Paradise Lake was roped off with yellow, plastic strips. The coroner's office was called, and the investigative work began. Joe Weatherby conferred with the police department and, thoughtfully, handed them Kate's car keys.

He drove home slowly, wondering how to break the news to Clare. It couldn't be kept from her. By Monday evening, the discovery of a body in Paradise Lake would be plastered all over the TV and newspapers. It would be impossible to keep the news from the media any longer than that.

* * *

After seeing Mack cut across the lawn Saturday morning, Francis had begun to wonder about his relationship with Sally. So, right after lunch, a phone call was made to Mable's Kitchen. The owner had been a friend of hers for years, and it was Mable's knowledge that had directed Francis and LuAnn to drive past Sally's trailer house nearly two years ago. Now, she asked for an update on the affair. "Curiosity is killing me, Mable. What's going on?"

The information she gleaned was passed on to LuAnn. "Mable says Sally has taken a shine to the new preacher there in town. All the single women, and a few married ones, are 'settin' their cap' for him. Sally figures her chances are pretty good, because he comes into the kitchen every day for breakfast. She's even asked to work Saturday mornings again. It looks like Mack's out of the picture."

That explained a lot of things. "He rummaged through the drawers in my bedroom, and he's been looking at me in ways I don't like. He even bought some Army knives, and he has Jason out in the woods with him, 'cutting our way through the jungle,' is how he puts it. Those knives scare me. They're pretty darned sharp! That kind of influence can't be healthy! Can it? Everything concerned with the Army seems to have taken over the thinking in his head."

"Maybe you should step up your plans, LuAnn. The situation

doesn't sound good. Oh, yes! And Joe Weatherby was here just before I saw Mack out back. There was a set of old keys in the junk drawer in the kitchen. Apparently, Mother threw them in there at some time. Joe saw them, and I thought he was going to pass out. They belonged to Kate's Corvette, the one she was driving the night she disappeared. They even have her initials on them. The only thing we could figure is that she dropped them in Mother's backyard that night."

"I'm sure you're right. Then that means Mack was there too. You're right about my leaving, too. As uncomfortable as things are getting around here, the sooner I'm gone, the better."

"Karen and her husband are helping me move this afternoon when they get off work. There's not much left here, just my clothes and some boxes. In a few days, feel free to bring the kids and stay with me. I had a little chat with the Browns Friday evening, after the graduation program. They're a really nice family and are concerned about you, as well. Just remember, if you need help, we're all your friends!"

After the conversation ended, LuAnn went into the bedroom and pulled a large suitcase from the back of the closet. It was filled with winter clothes, ready to be moved. She shoved it in again and pulled out another, as large as the first. This one was empty. Clothes from the hangers, and items from the dresser drawers were folded into the suitcase. It was closed and shoved in beside the other one. What was left could be added in a matter of minutes. The children's winter clothing had been packed as well. As soon as they got up, and breakfast was eaten, the winter clothing would be taken to the Browns and left there.

° ° °

As yet, Joyce and Jason hadn't been told that they would be leaving . . . moving away for good. Children can't keep secrets. So they wouldn't know until they were well on the way to their new home in Huntington, West Virginia.

All of LuAnn's plans were falling into place. There was a job in a furniture store promised to her, and Fern and Clifton Soppee had found a partially furnished duplex for the three of them. "It isn't large, but it has three bedrooms." A check for two months rent had been sent to the leasing company, and they could move in on July 5. That was thirteen days away.

She had planned to leave Independence on July 2. However, circumstances were indicating an earlier departure. Whatever day they left, it would have to be when Mack was working, so they would have a full day's start before he realized they were gone.

° ° °

LuAnn explained the suitcases to the children. "Some of our things need to be mended before school starts this fall. Connie volunteered to look over the clothes in her spare time and do the mending for us. It's just easier if she has them all at once." Joyce and Jason were aware of their mother's dislike for sewing, so the plan seemed logical.

° ° °

Monday afternoon, Henry Yoder drove his buggy into the Hanables' yard. He was there to take Marilyn and Elvis back to the farm. Mack was, once again, promising ponies to Joyce and Jason, so LuAnn had an explanation ready for the children, but she hated the deception. "If your father gets some ponies, we can't keep the cattle anyway."

Tears were blinked back, as Henry haltered the gentle beasts and tied their lead ropes to the rear of the buggy. Obligingly, the animals followed along as he slowly drove from the yard. With sadness etched on their faces, Joyce and Jason watched from the road in front of the house until they were out of sight.

The money the animals brought was enough to cover the first two months' rent on the duplex. It had already been spent. If she had to, the decision to keep it could be defended. After all, she and the children had done all the work in caring for them. Thus, the money should be theirs. Two weeks ago, Mack wouldn't even have missed Elvis and Marilyn, but everything seemed to be a concern for him now.

° ° °

For three days, Mack wondered how to get back with LuAnn. He figured some headway was made with Jason . . . but LuAnn and Joyce still kept their distance. He supposed girls were different . . . Hell! . . . He *knew* they were! Maybe they weren't even worth bothering with. Still, LuAnn's presence aroused his sense of manhood. The dilemma of needing her and yet not wanting to need her was driving him nuts. *Damn it! There was just something about her.*

He stopped at the grocery store and picked out a potted geranium and a box of chocolate-covered cherries . . . a peace offering. Women like flowers. Most of them like candy. Anyway, Sally always appreciated the flowers and candy he gave her. She sure acted like it anyway. Maybe this would help to break the ice with LuAnn.

* * *

It was a quiet supper at the Hanable home. Occasionally, Jason and Mack exchanged a comment about something or other, but LuAnn and Joyce remained quiet. The red geranium set in the center of the table trying to offer a little festivity to the evening. "You like flowers, don't you?" was Mack's attempt at making conversation. She managed a weak smile . . . nothing for him to get excited about. *Can't rush this thing*. He would give her the candy just before going to bed.

Mack and Jason took off for the woods. "If we keep at the weeds, there'll be a decent path to the fallen tree that bridges the banks of the creek. There's a deep hole right there where the catfish grow large enough to keep. You kids haven't ever tasted catfish. LuAnn, I'll bet you haven't either. Well, maybe we can all enjoy some one of these days."

LuAnn started cleaning up the evening meal. The dishes were stacked and ready for washing, when Joyce came into the kitchen from the living room. "Mom, can you come here for a minute? There's something really weird on TV. They've found some bones in Paradise Lake. That's near where Mrs. Franklin lives, isn't it?" LuAnn followed obediently after her daughter. "See, Mom!"

She watched the screen intently as the TV camera swept over the area around the levee separating Paradise Lake from Kate's Cove. The huge excavator set motionless, and a crewman, being interviewed by the reporter, stood next to it. "Well, I just put the bucket down into the lake bottom, and when it came up, there they were."

Jeff didn't say anything about Joe Weatherby's expectations even before he had started digging. That was police business. By this time, the remains had been bagged and removed. The cement blocks and fragments of rope were bagged for evidence and removed from the scene. It appeared that the victim's death was no accident, but he didn't say so. He didn't say anything about the half dozen or more bites he had taken from the lake bottom and deposited on the levee before the police were satisfied, either. The debris would all be examined for evidence as soon as possible.

The camera moved over to Ray Dewey. His account mirrored that of his crewman. He didn't tell the cameras that Joe Weatherby was a witness to the find. They could get that bit of information some other way. He wasn't going to add to the Weatherbys' grief. They needed time to contemplate the discovery. "No, we have no idea whose body it is, or how it got there."

LuAnn knew. She knew more than enough. There was no doubt left that Mack was, in some way, responsible for Kate's death. There was even evidence in the freezer. She turned off the TV. "Thank you for telling me about this, Joyce. Yes, it is weird. Why don't you dry the dishes for me?" There was a need to be near her daughter.

As they worked together in the kitchen, she looked out the window towards the woods. The path to the fishing hole was near completion. What was Mack's real motive for making the fishing hole accessible? An event, early in their marriage, began gnawing away at her subconscious. He had taken her fishing . . . they climbed out on a tree trunk leaning over the water. Something upset him . . . and he nearly knocked her into the lake. She had convinced herself that it was an accident . . . Now, she wasn't so sure.

When she saw Jason emerge from the woods, there was a sigh of relief. Mack was close behind him. Thankfully, the knives were sheathed. If the family could get through the evening without Mack hearing the news, maybe she could figure out a safer arrangement for the children . . . get them away from the house. Their father was bound to react to the news in some manner.

Normally, he paid little attention to the TV. But by tomorrow, the newspapers would be filled with the Paradise Lake discovery. He would find out sometime, some way. What his reaction would be, was anyone's guess. Trying to remain calm, LuAnn turned to her daughter, "Joyce, don't tell your father about what we just saw on the news. He gets so upset over such things, and he grew up around there. Okay?"

"Sure, Mom . . . if you say so." Joyce snapped the dish towel playfully at her mother and went scampering up the stairs to her bedroom. She was so much like Jane, even in disposition.

Jane! Of course, Jane! For the past two years, she had been bugging them to come for another visit. LuAnn's classes had prevented their going until now. She immediately went to the phone and put in a call to the Wright residence. "Please be there, Jane! Please answer your phone!" She looked nervously out the kitchen window to make certain Jason and Mack were still out in the yard. They were out by the cattle shed.

"Hello, Dr. Wright's residence." It was her sister's cheerful voice. Again, LuAnn looked out the window. The guys were still out there but slowly edging towards the house.

"Jane, this is LuAnn. I don't have time to explain, but can I possibly send Joyce and Jason to you tomorrow . . . on the bus? I need you to keep them until I can get there. It may be for more than a week. Just answer 'yes' or 'no.' I'll call you back tomorrow when I get them on the bus."

"Why . . . yes! Does this have anything to do with Mack?"

"Thank you, Jane. I'll tell you more tomorrow." She hung up.

There was one more call to make. Quickly, she dialed. "What time does the earliest bus leave for Chicago tomorrow? . . . Nine-fifteen in the morning . . . Please reserve two tickets for Joyce and Jason Hanable . . . They're children . . . and they will be traveling by themselves. Thank you very much." The thought of sending them off without her, had previously been unsettling, but, this time, she knew God would take care of them.

When she looked out the window, the guys were doing something to the pump that set out in the middle of the barnyard. Thankful for the additional time, she walked into the living room and pulled the plug on the TV. Then, not quite satisfied, she got a knife from the kitchen and hacked away at the wire. If Mack should try to turn the TV on, she could tell him the cord was bad. That was true!

She heard footsteps on the kitchen porch, and the screen door opened. Now to get through the rest of the evening. By nine o'clock, the children were ready for bed and in their rooms reading. LuAnn kept busy in the kitchen, cleaning out the top cupboards, until after ten-fifteen. Mack spent an hour on the porch steps cleaning and sharpening the knives, an activity that was very unnerving. He finally went into the bathroom and showered. Shortly after that, the rumble of snoring came through his bedroom door.

Wearily, LuAnn climbed down from the stool. A box of candy laid on the kitchen table. Mack must have placed it there while her head was in the cupboards. It was unsettling to realize she had been so absorbed with the task that she hadn't noticed his presence. But, the evening had gone well, considering, and, finally, there was an opportunity to relax a bit and prepare for bed. Tomorrow was bound to be a memorable day, and she needed to plan for it well. After locking the bedroom door, sleep came while the list of things to do was running through her mind like a swift-running stream of water eagerly seeking its destination.

Twenty-four

Tuesday morning, June 24, 1970, Chief of Police Mike Richards, picked up the *Charleston Chronicle* and scanned the news. It was the best way he knew to keep abreast of any crime that was happening in the state of West Virginia. Grafton was a pretty quiet town. There hadn't been any crime of consequence since the remains of Amy Maxwell were pulled from Katt's Lake two years before. He vaguely wondered how Thomas Maxwell was doing. He should really call him sometime. Mike scanned his favorite comic strips and then gave the front page and inside page another quick once over. An item, he had previously missed, caught his eye. It had been picked up from an Iowa newspaper.

SKELETAL REMAINS FOUND IN LAKE

> During an excavation project, the skeletal remains of a female were pulled from Paradise Lake, a wealthy residential community near Hiawatha. They are believed to be those of Katherine (Kate) Weatherby, a realtor, who has been missing since June 12, 1959. The case has been re-opened and is under investigation. At the present time, the death is being considered accidental. However, the state crime lab has been asked to conduct an autopsy to rule out the possibility of any criminal cause. Weatherby Real Estate and Construction has been developing the area since 1959. The property was previously owned by Charles and Ruby Dutcher.

Well, now! Mike thought. *This might be of interest to Thomas. Maybe he can get rid of one more of those old Missing Persons files he carries around with him. Guess I'll give him a ring.* He put the call through to Captain Thomas Maxwell of the Charleston Police Department, person-to-person. *He should be there by this time in the morning, but I don't want to talk to anybody else.* The phone rang three times, and then he heard the familiar voice of his longtime friend.

"Thomas, this is Chief Mike Richards! How you doin', buddy?" He didn't give him time to acknowledge the question but, instead, went straight to the issue. "Say, have you read this morning's *Chronicle?* If you haven't, turn to the inside page. There's an item on a body found in a lake in Iowa. I thought you might be interested."

"Give me a minute, Mike." There was a long pause as he located the paper and then the article. He read it through three times before responding. "Interested? You can bet your britches on this one! You remember LuAnn Soppee, don't you? Well, she's connected somehow. Her husband was raised by the Dutchers. Mack Hanable's his name. It was an abusive childhood, and he's repeating the same kind of crap with her and their two children." There was no chance for Mike to interrupt the dialogue. The facts had been mulled over and over in Thomas' mind for a long time. Now, he had a chance to express his view verbally.

So, he went on, "But, LuAnn chooses to defend him, saying he needs love and understanding, and all that stuff we hear every day." Now his voice rose with passion. "He's the guy that got Mary Lou Bailey pregnant before he got LuAnn pregnant and took her off to Iowa with him. I'm out of here, Mike! I'm off to Iowa! Thanks for the tip! I owe you one!"

"Well, old friend, just keep your head on straight in this one. Give me a call when you get back." With a smile of satisfaction, he hung up the phone. All of Grafton was aware that Thomas Maxwell had never gotten over LuAnn. He just hoped the guy wouldn't overreact in his enthusiasm to help her. Sometimes situations can backfire.

* * *

Thomas caught the first plane flying west out of Charleston. He would land in Des Moines at two o'clock that afternoon where a car was waiting for him. Two hours later, he would be in Hiawatha. The first thing he would do is contact Weatherby Real Estate and Construction. They had the most vested interest in the case. Then he would decide just where to go from there.

If nothing else, he would, at least, see LuAnn and the children and make sure they were in no danger. It was hard to predict how Mack would react to the investigation, especially if pressure was put on him. Thomas was, finally, in a position to be of some assistance to the woman he loved, and fervently prayed she would be accepting of it.

* * *

As soon as Mack left for work that morning, LuAnn started preparations for the day. She went into Joyce's bedroom and pulled a large suitcase from the closet. She began taking clothes from the hangers, folding them, and placing them into it. When the closet was emptied out, she began on the dresser drawers. Looking at the clock, she began to throw items into the suitcase without regard to anything but the time. The morning was passing too quickly. It was already seven-thirty.

When the suitcase was nearly full, she gently shook her daughter. "Joyce, wake up! Wake up, Honey! I've talked to your Aunt Jane, and she wants you and Jason to go and stay with them for a while. Isn't that just wonderful?" She smiled brightly. "The bus leaves at nine-fifteen, so we need to leave here in just an hour. The tickets have to be picked up at least half an hour before departure."

Joyce had lain in bed for the past ten minutes with eyes half opened, wondering what her mother was up to. Maybe she was going crazy or something, but, after the plans were explained, no objections were offered. "I've packed most of your things. If there's something more you really want to take, put it in yourself. But do hurry!"

LuAnn went into Jason's bedroom and repeated the procedure. He was immediately reminded, "New horses were bought for your cousins, remember?" He was out of bed and dressed before the drawers were emptied out. "If there's anything that is really important to you, put it in your suitcase. You may be gone for quite some time." She wanted no complaints later about things being left behind.

At eight-thirty, they walked out to the Ford, and the two suitcases were put into the trunk. "But Mom, where's your suitcase? Aren't you going with us?" A tinge of fear was recognized in Joyce's questions, and apprehension shown in her eyes.

LuAnn spoke as confidently as possible. "I'll be coming in a week or so. I have too many things to finish up around here right now, but it is important that you leave today. Don't worry! The Wrights have some special plans for you." She hoped the smile on her lips was more reassuring than the panic she was beginning to feel inside.

"Yeah! Dumdum, we get to ride their new horses." Jason poked his sister with an elbow and made a swipe at her as though brandishing a knife.

Startled by the behavior, LuAnn gripped his shoulders with both hands, and her eyes bore into his. "I expect you both to be good children!" She shook him to make sure the message was getting through.

"The Wright family is good to you, and you can be good to them. Is that understood?" She looked at them both. "What's more, be good to one another!" With a look of determination directed at them both and another shake of Jason's shoulders, her grip was released. She hoped they couldn't see that she was trembling inside.

While driving into town, they met Mack, as he was starting out on the mail route. "Hey, Mom, there's Dad!" Joyce and Jason turned and waved to their father from the back window of the car. He hadn't noticed them. LuAnn was relieved, but there was a moment of intense guilt. She was taking them away from their father. That may be the last time they see him in a very long time . . . if ever again. Then she thought of the alternatives. They could be so much worse.

A half hour later, she was smiling and waving at the children through the bus window. Inside, a deep fear and foreboding agonized her very soul. This was the first time in their lives they wouldn't be under her protection, and Chicago seemed like such a long ways off. She prayed, *God, take care of them.*

Before going back to the farmstead, she stopped at the First Presbyterian Church. She would take a few minutes to explain the situation to Pastor Wilkens. He was very aware of the conflict within the family, but, as yet, she hadn't told him about any plans to leave. When she explained the current situation to him, his reaction to the decision was encouraging. "God gives us choices for a reason. They are not always easy, but He is always with us. Take heart, LuAnn. He will show you the right way. The church will keep you and the children in our prayers."

The phone was ringing when she walked in the kitchen door. It was Connie Brown. Concern resonated in her voice. "LuAnn, where have you been? I've been trying to get a hold of you since before nine o'clock. Pete called me this morning, right after he got to work. He said Mack is really in a strange mood. When he saw the front page of the Cedar Rapids paper this morning, the one he's supposed to deliver today, he kind of freaked out. Pete said he turned pale and just kind of started whimpering like a beaten pup. Then he stuck one of the papers into the front of his shirt and went into the restroom. He didn't come out for a long time. Of course, he was reading the front page! We can be certain of that! Pete waited around in the parking lot to see if he was going to make his route today. Eventually, he came outside with his mail bag, got into the car, and took off." Finally, Connie paused and took a deep breath. Then, she continued, "Have you seen the front page of the paper, LuAnn?"

"No, I haven't seen it yet. Hold on a minute! I'll run out to the box and get our mail." In a few minutes, she was back on the phone. "Mack didn't leave any today. What's in the paper, Connie?" She was already pretty certain of the answer.

"The front page is all about the skeletal remains of a missing woman being found in Paradise Lake. Her name is Kate Weatherby, and there's even a picture of her! LuAnn, does this have anything to do with Mack and the woman that attacked him on the street . . . when he first started delivering here in Independence? The picture sure looks like the person who was described at the time, and when Mack saw it, he certainly reacted in a strange manner."

"I'm sure it does, Connie. Mack is involved in some way. I have no doubt about that! I put the children on the bus to Chicago, so they can stay with my sister. That's why I haven't been home this morning. I saw some of this on the news last night and thought it best if they were gone. I'm getting ready to leave myself . . . right now, in fact. Mack's behavior is just too unsettling to stay here any longer. I need to call Jane, so she'll know what time to pick Joyce and Jason up at the bus depot. I'll be stopping by for our winter clothes just as soon as I get some things packed and in the car. Most of my clothes are in a suitcase already. Gotta go now. I'll see you soon."

The phone call to Jane lasted longer than she wanted it to. It was eleven o'clock before she started packing the last of her clothes into the suitcase. She hurriedly whisked her toiletries into her overnight bag. Then she went to the freezer and got the package of jewelry. She put it into the bag with the toiletries.

One more thing! She rushed up the stairway and quickly slid the curtains from the rods in Joyce's bedroom and folded them together with the bedding. She went into Jason's room and soon had another pile ready. The children deserved the comfort of something familiar in their new home. She took the bundles out to the car and packed them into one side of the trunk.

Back in the house, she swung her purse over her shoulder and picked up the suitcase in one hand and the overnight bag in the other. She was leaving this home, and there was no intention of ever returning. With a feeling of relief, she stepped out into the sun. The luggage was nestled into the trunk with the bedding and curtains. Exhilaration and power filled every pore of her body, and she closed the lid to the trunk with a resounding finality.

With a haze of dust clouding around the Lincoln, Mack drove into the yard. "Are you going someplace, Honey?" He stepped out of the vehicle. "Don't you know it's not nice to leave your husband when he comes home to have dinner with you? Let's go fix us something to eat. What do you say?" He took her arm, and she was forcefully led back into the house. "Where are the kids?" He looked around and stared accusingly.

"They're spending the day with the Browns." It was something they had done many times before, even though he was probably never aware of it. "I was just on my way to get groceries. I'll fix you some soup and a sandwich first though." Then, with trembling hands, she commenced to fry some eggs. She opened a can of tomato soup, added milk, and heated it on one of the burners. Her insides felt as though she had swallowed a stone.

"Gee LuAnn, you're sure nervous today. Something the matter?" He didn't expect an answer. "Of course, there is. You really don't like being around me much . . . do you?" His words were spoken in monotone, emotionless, but his smoldering eyes were kept riveted on her pale, frightened face.

With a deliberate show of gusto, he took a large bite of the sandwich and then slurped soup from the bowl. "Why aren't you eating? You feelin' uncomfortable or somethin'? You know, Sweetheart, we really need to spend more time working on our relationship, getting used to each other again." He looked her up and down to size up her reaction. There didn't seem to be any. The last of the soup was downed, and the remainder of the sandwich was crammed into his mouth.

"Just to make sure you stick around . . . so we can do that . . . I have a little present for you." The chair was slowly pushed away from the table, and he stood up. Keeping his dark and penetrating eyes on LuAnn, he reached casually into the side pocket of his khakis and pulled out two yard-long lengths of clothesline rope. He held them up for her to see. An eerie smile quavered on his lips.

LuAnn started to rise, but strong, callused hands forcefully pushed her back down in the chair. Her strength was no match for his. It would be useless for her to resist. Perhaps, she could reason with him. "What are you doing, Mack? Can't we talk about this? We have all day if you want." She tried to smile, but, instead, choked on the words.

"Well, I guess I better finish out the mail route first. No sense in gettin' people riled up, so they start callin' the post office. When I get back home, if you're good and want to talk, I'll let you loose then." One of the ropes was pulled tightly around her wrists and then through the rungs of the chair back. The other rope was tied around her ankles and then to the legs of the chair. He knew just how to do it, so she couldn't get away. He had worked himself loose from Aunt Ruby's knots a few times, so he knew just how to prevent that from happening. "I'll see you later, Honey." He kissed the top of her head and patted her shoulder. The screen door slammed, and the Lincoln sped away.

Thankfully, he hadn't covered her mouth. At least breathing was no problem, but no one could hear her if she did scream. The house was too far away from the road. She struggled for a moment to get free of the ropes, but that was useless. It seemed best to remain as calm as possible, because there was one strong possibility that help would soon be arriving. Connie was expecting her, and she was aware of Mack's emotional state. If she didn't show up at the Browns' soon, hopefully, Connie would come looking for her. So, right now, it was best to save her strength and try to get her head cleared. She prayed for a plan to come to mind in case Mack returned before anyone else had a chance to find her.

In answer to her prayer, a small, frightened voice was heard outside on the kitchen porch, and a light rap was heard on the screen door. "LuAnn . . . LuAnn . . . are you home? Are you all right?" Praise God! It was Sarah. In the early afternoon light, her silhouette wafted in the doorway and cast a welcome shadow across the kitchen floor.

"Oh Sarah, come in! I'm so glad to see you! Please help me!"

When Sarah entered the kitchen, her breath caught, and she stared at LuAnn in utter amazement. "What happened? Did Mack do this to you? What can I do?" With tears running down her cheeks and hands shaking, she tried to undo the knots.

"Use a knife, Sarah. Over there in the second drawer. Yes, Mack did this." Her voice caught. "Something has really upset him, and he's being very irrational. Apparently, he's even sicker than I realized." Her hands worked loose as the ropes were cut. "Whatever brought you here?"

"Well, we didn't get our Cedar Rapids paper today. Susie was at the mailbox when Mack came by our place, but when she asked him about it, he said there wasn't any. However, a whole stack lay right on the front seat beside him. He got really angry when she pointed them out and asked for one. He just took off. A while later, we saw him go back past our place. He never does that, so we wondered what he was doing. We were concerned for you and the children and rightfully so."

LuAnn was freed from the last of the ropes. "We both must go right now, Sarah, before Mack returns! I'm leaving here, and it will be a long time before I ever come back. I sent Joyce and Jason on the bus to my sister's in Chicago this morning. I'll write to you as soon as I get settled. Good-bye, Sarah, and may God bless you and your family." There was a tight embrace, and she gave her friend a gentle shove towards the door. "Now, go!" She followed after, out into the yard, and watched as Sarah ran barefoot over to the buggy, climbed up into the seat, and urged the horse out the driveway and up the road. LuAnn got into her own vehicle and the two women drove off in opposite directions.

* * *

She had to hurry. With a stop at the bank, her accounts were closed out, and the money and documents from the safety deposit box were placed securely into her purse. She could leave no forwarding address. The tellers exchanged curious glances, but they complied with the requests.

The next stop was the Browns. The suitcases containing winter clothes were placed into the back seat. While they were being loaded, Connie was quickly told about the events of the past two hours. "God sent Sarah to me. I have no doubt about that."

Connie placed the last suitcase into the car and slammed the door. "Pete will try to forward any mail that comes to the post office for you to your parents' address. Are you starting to Chicago today?"

"No, I have a package to deliver to the Cedar Rapids Police Station first. If I can use your phone, I'll call Francis Franklin and stay with her tonight. I don't think Mack will do anything to draw attention to himself right now. If I need to stay there for a few days, I'll be all right. It would be foolish for him to try anything else." She called Francis, and then, for the third time that day, said good-bye to friends.

It was shortly after four o'clock when the apartment complex was located, and Francis was anxiously waiting for her guest by the front entrance. Connie had called ahead with this advice, "If she doesn't show up by five o'clock, call the police station."

The two women fixed and ate supper while listening to Roger Williams tapes. The idea was that the music would help LuAnn to relax, but it didn't work. Too much of concern was racing through her cluttered mind, and she scarcely heard the melodies being played. Then, at six o'clock a call was put in to the Wrights' residence. "Jane, did Joyce and Jason get there all right?"

"They're just fine. Right now, they're out by the stables getting acquainted with the new horses." Finally, this news brought a sense of relief. After watching a Hop-a-Long Cassidy movie on TV, the guest room was made up, and the night was spent peacefully.

* * *

When Mack drove into the yard at five o'clock that evening, LuAnn's missing car was the first indication that his plans were not going to materialize. Expressionless, he walked through the house. All three closets were empty. Even the curtains and bedding were gone from the children's rooms. He knew LuAnn had no intention of coming back. In the kitchen, he picked up the severed pieces of rope and the knife that had done the work. Someone had cut her free. He hadn't counted on that. After being examined, the rope was casually dropped on the table.

He walked into his room and picked up one of the knives laying at the foot of the bed. He pulled it from its sheath and brandished it. Then he walked into LuAnn's bedroom and commenced to cut up the curtains and bedding. His powerful slashes were slow, calculated, and methodical. His eyes were cold and lifeless. There was no perspiration on his brow. There was no emotion or effort given to produce it. His eyes scanned the room. He nodded in appreciation for what he had just accomplished, and then he walked slowly up the stairs and into each of his children's rooms. The only things left there to slice up were the mattresses. He scored them as though he were cutting a giant loaf cake. Again, he nodded in appreciation for what he had done, turned, and walked back down the stairs. For all purposes, he had just put an end to his family.

In the kitchen, he found the box of matches used to light the grill. He picked up the pieces of rope from the table, carried them outside, and put them into the burn barrel, setting out by the pasture fence. Then he ambled over to the Lincoln and opened the door on the passenger side. He picked up the stack of undelivered newspapers that lay on the front seat. These were carried over to the burn barrel and dropped to the ground.

He pulled the front page loose . . . intently stared back at Kate

Weatherby's picture . . . crumpled it, and struck a match. Igniting the paper, he dropped the flames into the burn barrel. One by one . . . sheet by sheet, slowly and methodically, he added fuel from the stack of newspapers. Each time Kate's picture appeared, he stared back before crumpling it and adding it to the flames. In desperation, he was trying to rid himself of her memory once and for all.

A car turned into the driveway, pulled up, and stopped beside the Lincoln. Mack didn't bother to look up from his job at hand, or, perhaps, his mind was so far away that he didn't even hear it. Three men got out and walked across the yard to where he stood. One of the men was Pete Brown. The other two, he didn't know.

Pete did the introductions. "Mack, this is Pastor Wilkens from the First Presbyterian Church. LuAnn has known him for several years now." Mack did not acknowledge the pastor's extended hand.

"LuAnn stopped by the church this morning. She thought you might appreciate a visit from me this evening. I see you have been busy cleaning things up." He nodded towards the barrel. Bits of charred paper and smoke soared upward and then wafted off towards the pasture.

* * *

When Pete had returned home from work that afternoon, Connie told him about Mack's assault on LuAnn and that she and the children had left. The Browns had become acquainted with Pastor Wilkens and his wife the night of LuAnn's graduation. They felt the pastor was a logical person to contact.

After a discussion of the events, the two men decided Mack was in need of help from someone. They contacted the county sheriff and told him as much as they knew. Perhaps a psychological evaluation was in order. LuAnn and the children may be gone and safe now, but that didn't mean he wouldn't eventually hurt someone else.

* * *

Pete turned to the other man, who was a bit beyond middle-aged, on the short side in height, and wearing a rather shabby, faded blue uniform. It was filled out rather well with a paunchy stomach that fell over the belt line and broad shoulders that strained at the back of the shirt. "Mack, this is Sheriff Reilly. I think he has a few questions to ask you."

The sheriff stepped forward to take over.

"What kind of questions? I ain't done nothin'." There was no emotion in Mack's voice, nor on his face.

"Well, do you suppose we could go into the house and do our talking?" Sheriff Reilly was curious about what was being burned. He started leading the way across the back yard, hoping Mack would follow along. He did, and they all clomped across the porch and filed into the kitchen.

"Nice house you got here, Mack." The sheriff tried to put him at ease. "Mind if I use your john before we sit down? You guys go ahead and make yourselves comfortable. I'll just take whatever chair's left when I get back." He patted Mack's shoulder companionably. "You just stay put. I'll find it."

Sheriff Reilly left the kitchen and ambled down the hallway until he came to the bathroom. He opened and closed the door, but he didn't go in. Instead, he tiptoed down the hall to the bedrooms. The carpeting muffled his steps. The first room was full of Army stuff. Two knives laid on the bed. One was sheathed. The blade of the other shone brightly in the late afternoon sunlight that was streaming in through the window. He shook his head in bewilderment. *Who would want to hang onto that kind of stuff?* Some thirty years ago, he had been more than glad to get out of the Army himself.

He continued on down the hallway and pushed the door open to the second bedroom. *Holy shit! What's this?* The curtains and bedding were in shreds. *I'll bet somebody's damn glad they weren't in that bed!* Relieved that the family was gone, but enraged with the carnage, he strode heavily back down the hallway and took three steps at a time to get to the upstairs. His breath came in deep gulps, but he didn't waste any time finding the other bedrooms. The scored mattresses gave him goose bumps.

When he entered the kitchen, Mack eyed the sheriff . . . waiting for the bomb to fall. He had heard the man lumbering his way down the hallway and then up the stairs. Now, all his actions of the day had been found out. In the first place, no doubt, LuAnn had told on him and sent them scurrying out there. Now this, on the pretense of everyone being friendly. "Did you find the john all right?" he asked in a surly manner.

With a grim look on his face, the sheriff nodded to Pete and Pastor Wilkens. Then he addressed Mack, "It looks like you got pretty excited about something today. Those bedrooms are a real mess. You better let me put these on before you hurt somebody real bad." He grabbed Mack's wrists and slapped on the handcuffs. "We need to find a different place for you to stay tonight. We can have our little conversation down at the station. You must have a lot on your mind that needs to be talked about."

Twenty-five

Mack was taken to the county jail and booked for disorderly conduct. He could be held for twenty-four hours. Before heading for home and his family, Pete Brown placed his hands over Mack's, cuffs and all. "I'll see you at the post office in the morning. You've got a good job there, and you've been a loyal employee. Don't mess it up." He gave the new prisoner an encouraging, though forced, smile, patted his shoulder, and left the station. Outside, in the humid night air, the tensions of the day exploded in one single syllable. "SHIT!"

Sheriff Reilly had no way of holding Mack without a formal complaint of assault filed by LuAnn. Pete Brown, Pastor Wilkens, nor himself, wanted to drag her into the situation again. She was gone. The three of them knew where she was, but Mack didn't. They wanted to keep it that way, and their efforts would be directed to that purpose. The cell door was closed carefully with an effort to minimize the clang of metal against metal. It was hoped that the occupant would gain some control over his nerves and emotions before morning.

"I'm going to leave you for a while, Mack. Pastor Wilkens will be sitting right here in this chair if you need someone to talk to." The sheriff pulled a straight-back, wooden chair to within four foot of the steel bars. "I'll drive out to your place and make sure the house is closed up for the night. If you want, I can bring you some clean clothes. You're smelling like that burn barrel of yours. We don't want you to miss making your route tomorrow. OK?" The guy needed something to look forward to in the morning. Mack voiced no objection, so Sheriff Reilly headed back out to the farmstead. He would look around again before closing up the house. He hoped there wouldn't be anymore surprises.

* * *

"I'll sit right here, Mack. If there is anything you want to talk about, I'll listen. No hurry, take your time. Sometimes it takes a while to get our heads on straight, so we can make sense out of our recollections." Pastor

Wilkens slid his bony, angular body down in the chair, crossed his ankles, closed his eyes, and waited. This was nothing new. He had been in this situation before. His bald head shone from the dim light on the ceiling above. His gray jacket lay open, exposing a white shirt open at the collar. Folded hands with nicely manicured nails and a plain gold wedding band finished the picture. He was certainly no one to fear.

The scent of charred paper slowly escaped from the fibers of Mack's clothing and mingled with the musty smells of the urinal, mattress, and cement. He sat on the edge of the cot and ran restless fingers through his tangled, bushy hair. He needed a hair cut, but personal appearance hadn't been considered important for quite some time. A deep, irregular rasping from way down inside his guts was the only sound heard for the next twenty minutes. It's awfully hard to breathe when there's an overwhelming need to cry, but you don't know how.

"I would have killed her, you know." The silence was broken. "If she hadn't been cut loose, I would have killed her. Who cut the ropes anyway? Was it Connie Brown when she brought the kids home?" He looked at Pastor Wilkens for the first time since the steel door had clanged shut.

"You don't need to know that, Mack. Just be glad that somebody did. Otherwise, you would be sitting here with a murder charge against you, and a wonderful woman would be dead. Would killing your wife really make you feel better? What about Joyce and Jason, would you have killed them, too?" Pastor Wilkens struggled to keep a steady voice. What could have happened was inconceivable.

"You just don't know how it is, man!" Emotions were beginning to rise. "Women have never been any good for me!" He sprang up from the cot and grabbed the bars on the cell door. "They all want something, and when I can't give it to them, they get all bent out of shape!" Pastor Wilkens made no response.

Resigned to the circumstances, his hands dropped in a show of helplessness, and he went back to sit on the cot. After a brief period of silence, he started in again. "Even Sally! We were doing pretty good until she wanted a baby. I don't know what to do with kids! They're just a pain in the butt for me!"

Stillness, once again, dominated the cell. Mack sat hunched over with tight fists curled beneath a strong, square chin . . . and his elbows were supported by muscular thighs clad in the usual Army fatigues. Pastor Wilkins sat and waited.

"I guess I can't blame Aunt Ruby for the way she treated me."

Resignation crept into his voice, and the tone turned into a whine. "I was a bad kid sometimes, and she didn't like kids either! If I wasn't good, she tied me to a chair, and sometimes I didn't know how to be good." The tone of his voice became excited and raised to a higher decibel. "Sometimes, I didn't get to eat . . . because I was late for supper. At least, I didn't do that to my kids. Mostly, I guess, because LuAnn wouldn't let me." The monologue trailed off to a near whisper.

"Do you think she should have let you treat the children in that manner?"

"No, no, I only tied them up once, and she took the kids and left that time. She made me promise to leave them alone. I even saw a shrink for a while. Most of the time we did just fine after that." The palms of his hands beat a nervous rhythm on his knees.

"What do you think, Mack? Are you happy with LuAnn and the kids, or would you do better without them?" He hoped the right door was opened and waited for the answer.

"Do you want to know the truth, Preacher?" Once again, the bars were gripped with gorilla-like hands. The eyes of a confused, caged animal looked piercingly into Pastor Wilken's passive face. "Well . . . do you?"

"The truth is always the best . . . I've found." A slight shuffle in the chair was meant to indicate attention was being given to the conversation. He dared not show too great an interest, or the confession could come to an abrupt halt. This ability, to learn to listen objectively, was gleaned from years of experience.

"Well . . . then . . . the truth is . . . Sally Daniels was good for me . . . real good for me. With her, I didn't ever have to prove anything. Just one problem though . . . well . . . two, actually. She couldn't cook worth a damn, and her trailer was more like a pigsty." He hurried on. "I put up with it though. I figured if she could put up with me . . . married and all . . . well . . . I could put up with her faults. That's fair, right?" He seemed to be nearing euphoria.

"That sounds fair enough to me." God could be the judge of that. "Maybe you and Sally should talk over your problems. You know . . . there are homemaking classes offered at the high school sometimes . . . or over at Hawkeye College. You two should think about that. Do something that would benefit both of you." Efforts to direct Mack's thinking away from LuAnn and the children were beginning to work.

"Sally says she doesn't want anything more to do with me." Again, there was the whine in his voice, as the grip on the bars was relinquished. A look of defeat covered his face, and he sat down on the cot again.

"Well, women have been known to change their minds." He wasn't about to give up. "Why don't you give it some consideration? You just might be surprised."

He unfolded from the chair and stretched his arms high over head. A big yawn indicated his intentions. "I'll be back first thing in the morning. You and I can have some breakfast, and then I'll ride along on your mail route. It must get kind of lonely out there sometimes." He went to the security door and rapped on the window. "Good-night, now. I'll see you in the morning. Get some sleep." The door was opened by the attending officer, and he went home.

Mack lay down on the cot. A weak smile crossed his lips. Maybe it wasn't too late for him and Sally after all. He would give it some thought. Right now, he sure felt tired.

* * *

Thomas Maxwell decided to contact Joe Weatherby, not as an officer of the law, but as a concerned citizen who could identify with the pain he and his wife were going through. When he reached the outskirts of Cedar Rapids, he pulled the rented Chrysler up to a telephone booth. The ravaged pages of Ma Bell's directory, miraculously, still contained the number he needed. He dialed the company's office and asked to speak to Joe himself. It was immediately apparent that the calls to Mr. Weatherby were being screened.

"Please tell him I'm acting only in, what I consider to be, the best interest of him and his wife. Two years ago, the remains of my sister were pulled from a lake in West Virginia. I know a little bit of what they're going through. Also, I may have some knowledge of the circumstances surrounding his daughter's disappearance. Ask him if the name Mack Hanable means anything to him." Thomas spelled out his claim for consideration as precisely as possible. "If he wants to contact me, I'll be staying at the Howard Johnson Motel, room 208, on Marion Road. I'm heading there right now. Give me thirty minutes." He hung up and put the car in drive.

He scarcely had time to claim the room and use the john when there was a resounding knock at the door. The man standing there was quickly scrutinized. He would demand anyone's attention. Although on the upper side of middle age, his body was brawny, neatly groomed and attired. The cut of his clothes and the meticulous styling of his hair spoke 'money.' A wedding band encrusted with half a dozen karat diamonds encircled the ring finger of his left hand. A huge ruby adorned the middle finger of his right hand. Weatherby Real Estate and Construction had done well over the past thirty years.

"I'm Joe Weatherby. My secretary gave me your message. I hope we're not wasting each other's time." His voice was direct and booming with assurance, while his gaze was a mixture of apprehension and hopefulness. Usually such a 'lead' meant someone would try to hit him for money. This time, however, the name 'Mack Hanable' had peeked his interest. It was somehow familiar. The call just might hold some merit. So, here he was, once more, trying to put closure to his daughter's untimely disappearance.

"Thank you for coming, Mr. Weatherby. I think you'll be glad you did. Please come in." The motel room door was opened to its widest, giving his visitor a clear view of the interior. He wanted to relieve any anxiety the man may have about entering. "In case your secretary didn't get my name, I'm Thomas Maxwell." He held out a strong hand. Joe always had respect for a firm handshake. A small step had been taken towards breaking the tension between them. "Please, have a seat over there." Thomas nodded, turned away briefly, and closed the door.

Joe pulled a straight-back chair away from the small, round table in the corner. He situated himself in a position where the entire room was visible and hung his left arm at the edge of the table. His right hand slid casually down into his pant's pocket.

Thomas knew there was a good possibility that the man carried a small handgun. So, the first thing he did was place his police ID and badge on the table. "I'm not here to work as a law enforcement officer. I'm here to help as a friend. But these are my credentials." He picked up the briefcase containing the files on missing persons and placed it on the other side of the table. He sat down and popped the case open.

"Since my sister's disappearance in 1960, I've kept a file on missing persons cases. Amy's body was found in a lake two years ago. We were able to put her remains to rest in a decent burial. I know how important closure is for the family of such victims. When I saw the article in the *Charleston Chronicle* concerning your daughter's death, well, the circumstances were similar, so I decided to offer my help . . . that is if you want it." He reached into the briefcase and laid papers covering the case of Kathryn (Kate) Weatherby in front of Joe. He waited, giving the man time for everything to sink in.

Joe continued to search through the papers, looking for anything that might be new. The only thing that struck him, as such, was the name Mack Hanable penciled along the margin. "My secretary said you mentioned the name Mack Hanable. The name is familiar, but I can't remember how. What can you tell me about him?"

"Mack is married to an old friend of mine, LuAnn Soppee. We went to high school together. She met him when he was in the Army stationed in West Virginia. Two years ago, at our ten-year class reunion, she talked about him to some length. He was raised by Charles and Ruby Dutcher. They owned the property you're developing. Isn't that right?" Thomas didn't wait for an answer but continued on.

"The Dutchers were abusive to Mack. He, in turn, has been abusive to his own family. He and LuAnn lived with Ruby the first year they were married. Then, Ruby moved into an apartment, and the Hanables moved to Independence. LuAnn took it on herself to keep peace in the family. But, there seems to be a history of Mack having trouble with other women. Maybe Kate was one of them, and the situation got out of hand." Now, Thomas waited for some kind of comment from Joe.

Joe stared at the papers without really seeing them. The stillness in the room began to close in, and his breathing quickened. It was his turn to contribute information if the circumstances leading up to Kate's death were to be examined and exposed. With a deep breath, he began to search for the truth. For the first time in his life, he would take an honest look at who his daughter was. In a low, gruff voice, tempered with sorrow, he began. A cough cleared his throat.

"Kate had a lot of men. Some of them were married. Some of them weren't. Each time a new man came into her life, she assured her mother and myself that he was 'the one.' We wanted to believe her, and we turned our eyes away from the truth. Families were left broken, and jobs were lost. After she got what she wanted, it didn't matter anymore. She was just never satisfied."

With some effort, he got up from the chair. "Are there any cups in there?" indicating the bathroom. "I need a drink of water." Without waiting for an answer, he went to find one. The top cup was lifted from the stack and unwrapped. Then, the cold water was turned on and let run for a very long time. The cup was filled to overflowing, and its contents drank down in two gulps. He splashed water on his face, dried with a towel, and went back to sit down at the table again.

"Men weren't the only ones she tried to destroy. She insisted that I fire one of my best realtors, Irene White. Kate made it look like Irene embezzled some funds. I knew better, but I still let it happen. By then, I'll admit . . . even I was afraid of her." Once Joe opened up, the truth couldn't be stopped.

"You wonder if Mack Hanable could have been one of her men? In all probability, he was. A young man used to accompany Ruby to church. I figured his name was Dutcher, too. Are you telling me that his name is Hanable?"

"Yes, Ruby was Mack's great-aunt. His own parents deserted him when he was seven years old. Nobody else seemed to want him, so the Dutchers took him. He's gone through a lot of emotional abuse, as well as physical abuse."

Thomas needed someone to supply information that put Mack and Kate together. Apparently, Joe knew nothing of their relationship. "You mentioned an Irene White. Perhaps we should talk to her. Chances are, if Kate was determined to get her fired, there must have been a pretty good reason."

"I'm afraid the only reason was Kate's jealousy. She couldn't let another woman do better or get more. Her mother and I had spoiled her. We just loved her too much, I suppose, and we didn't know any other way to show it. We made sure she got everything that pleased her when she was growing up. Then when she was an adult, there wasn't any way to satisfy her." Joe shrugged in resignation. "I do owe Irene an apology, though. I've never felt right about what happened."

Here was an opening. "Suppose we contact Irene? You can offer your apologies, and I can ask some questions. I hope she's still around this area."

"As far as I know, she's still working with Hope Realty in Waterloo. I got her a position there when she left us."

"Well, Mr. Weatherby, why don't you call her first thing in the morning? That's a good place for us to start." He stood up and stretched. With a direction to take, he was ready for some food and shut-eye.

"About my wife, Thomas, I don't think Clare could stand the truth. We don't need to tell her any of this. She isn't well. Agnes Smith is her nurse-companion. So far, we've managed to keep the discovery of the remains from her. Of course, she must be told as soon as the police investigation is over."

"Where are the police in their investigation?"

"The autopsy findings will most likely be in sometime tomorrow. When they said there were two gold fillings in the bottom molars, well, I knew it was her. Of course, they are being checked with her dental records. The condition of the skull indicates some kind of trauma. That much, they've told me." Joe held out his hand. "Thank you for taking an interest. I'll give you a call by nine o'clock tomorrow morning. It would be good to see Irene again. Good-night."

After taking a cool shower and having dinner in the motel's dining room, Thomas expected to catch up on some much-needed sleep. Instead, he found his mind going over the day's events. How was LuAnn handling the news? Even more importantly, how was Mack handling it? After plumping the pillow for the tenth time, he turned the table lamp back on and reached for the brief case. He had paper clipped LuAnn's address and telephone number to the pocket on the inside. He put in a call. The phone rang a dozen times. There was no answer. Apparently, no one was home. Without having any luck, he put the call in three more times and finally gave up at midnight. He hoped there was a logical explanation.

Twenty-six

The cadenced shriek of a siren resonated above the normal growling, snarling, and beeping flow of early morning traffic. It gradually dissipated into the western city limits only to be followed by the wailful call of an ambulance. LuAnn lay still and listened. Waking up in the city was quite different than waking up in the country. There, the morning was embraced by silence with only the occasional barking of a dog or the crowing of a rooster . . . sounds broadcast on the breeze flowing from the nearest neighbors. The roar of a garbage truck echoed down the streets. When it slowed down, the noise was accentuated by the reverberating clang of galvanized cans and lids. Bright sunlight touched the cracks left between the drawn curtains. It was time to get up.

The clock on the dresser said eight o'clock. She stretched, luxuriating in the smoothness of the new cotton percale bedding. It had been laundered in the fragile scent of Lily of the Valley, Francis' favorite. The room was furnished with an Early American style. The softness of Wedgwood blue harmonized with the dusty rose, pinks, and creams, creating a haven in which one could languish without feeling guilt. She was seduced to stay longer, even turn over and go back to sleep, but the call of the bathroom was greater. The covers were thrown back, and, with determination, her feet were placed firmly on the floor. The day had to start sometime.

When Francis heard the stool flush in the bathroom, she started preparing breakfast. She had already called Connie Brown to see how the events of the day before had culminated. The two women agreed, LuAnn should be spared any details . . . at least until a time when she was less vulnerable. A half hour later, breakfast was placed on the table. They took each other's hands and bowed in gratitude. "Heavenly Father, we thank you for keeping LuAnn, Jason, and Joyce in Your loving care. Bless these gifts before us and all those around us. In Jesus' Name, we pray. Amen." Even though Mack needed their prayers too, by Francis' calculations . . . it was best not to mention his name right now.

"Thank you, Francis." Tears began to surface. She was bombarded with a mixture of emotions. Each surfaced as it chose, and it was impossible to be selective. As soon as breakfast was over, she would call Jane to make certain the children were still doing OK. Right now, the savory smell of breakfast was tantalizing, so she picked up the fork and began eating the bacon and eggs. "Oh my, this is good!" One hunger was being satisfied.

The call was made, and she was, again, informed that everything was "going great." When the phone was hung up, an unwelcome surge of jealousy flooded over her . . . no doubt left over from childhood. Her big sister had something else she wanted, . . . her children! The feeling was irrational, and she hated it.

What fault was that of Jane's? Here she was, again, thinking she deserved something different. Envy and stubbornness were partly to blame for the predicament she was in. The situation would take some time to resolve, and she may as well accept that. It was time to grow up and assume responsibility. Her decision, alone, had put her with Francis and had put the children in Chicago. The feeling towards Jane should be one of gratitude. She kept scolding herself, and, eventually, the irritation passed. A feeling of thankfulness took its place.

The phone rang, and Francis answered with a cheerful, "Hello."

It was Detective Patrick O'Hagan of the Cedar Rapids Police Department. "Good morning, Mrs. Franklin. Lovely day, don't you think?" He didn't expect an answer and continued, "Joe Weatherby was in this morning to talk about a set of car keys. He said they belonged to his daughter's Corvette . . . missing since her apparent death. They've been in your possession, I understand." Now, he paused and waited for a comment.

What was he implying? Taken off guard, she stammered. "Yes . . . yes . . . that's correct, but I hope you realize . . . they have no relevance . . . as far as I'm concerned." For the first time, it occurred that suspicion could be directed her way. Of course, the idea was ludicrous, but perhaps the police would view the situation differently.

"We understand that, Mrs. Franklin, but we need a statement from you . . . some information. If you could come down to the station later this morning, say eleven o'clock, we would appreciate it."

"Yes! Yes, of course! You can count on it. I'll be there!" She hung up the phone and turned to LuAnn. "Joe Weatherby gave the car keys we found to the police. They need a statement from me. I told them eleven o'clock, at the station, would be fine. You can decide whether you want to go along with me or not."

"Yes, I'll go. I have something to give them, too." She went into the bedroom and pulled the package of 'meat' from the overnight bag . . . then rummaged through the suitcase and found the plastic bag containing the diamond earring and ruby ring. The freezer package sloshed with water from the melted ice cubes, so the plastic carton was carefully unwrapped and drained off into the sink. The array of jewelry was placed on a dish towel, and she sat down at the table.

Each piece was reviewed. LuAnn considered it critical to articulate all that she knew about them to the officers precisely. They had all been found on the Dutcher property. She had found the heart locket with the broken chain outside by the barn. Henry Yoder had found the wrist watch, one diamond earring, the necklace with a pearl pendant, and the charm bracelet behind the cupboard in the kitchen. He had found the other diamond earring and the ruby ring in the drain of the sink.

Without comment, Francis watched as each piece was picked up and examined a multitude of times. She wondered what was going through LuAnn's mind. Hopefully, she would follow through with her intentions. No sense in wondering about that now, though. "I'll be ready to leave at ten-thirty. That gives us just a little more than an hour." She bustled off to the bedroom to get ready.

The jewelry was scooped up and, unceremoniously, dumped back into the plastic container. It was thrust into the bottom of LuAnn's purse. She took a deep breath and slowly let the air out through her mouth. There would be a tremendous sense of relief in getting rid of it. She nodded as though in agreement with herself. Then she patted the leather bag with gratitude, as one might pat an obedient child.

With confidence and determination, she entered the guest room and began preparing for the morning. She chose the black pant suit and white blouse. In spite of the warm weather, it was important to appear professional and in charge. She did not want to present herself as a blubbering, rejected, and jealous wife. At times, that may have been true, but not anymore. Her hair was smoothed with the curling iron and then sprayed into place. Makeup was applied artistically. Not wanting to appear sleazy, only a light touch was used. Pumps were retrieved from the suitcase, even though sandals would have been more comfortable. She pushed her feet into them. Actually, she liked the feel they gave being dressed up. Pearl earrings were clipped on. Then, with her purse and its contents in hand, she was ready to face the Cedar Rapids Police Department.

* * *

Irene White was willing to meet with Joe Weatherby and Thomas Maxwell that morning. When the men were told she had handled the purchase of the Hanable farmstead, they agreed to meet in Independence. They would drive out to the place together.

Thomas didn't know what would be gained by going there with Joe and Irene, but he had to do something. No one answered the phone again this morning. In spite of the many rational reasons for this, none of them was satisfactory. He needed to see just why for himself.

By ten-thirty, the three sat, quietly, at a booth in the Lunch Box Café drinking coffee and eating cinnamon rolls. Finally, Joe broke the silence. Coffee was sipped, and his throat was cleared with an exaggerated cough. His face began to redden with embarrassment. "Irene, I owe you an apology. I didn't ever tell you, but I knew you hadn't done anything illegal with the company. My misdirected conduct, to protect Kate, was very wrong. I know she's the one that took the money, not you. Shamefully, I let you take the blame." His eyes were cast down looking at the cup of coffee, grasped by both hands, sitting in front of him. "Can you forgive me?"

"Joe, I've never held it against you. Actually, I've been doing very well with Hope Realty." The engaging smile and confident persona gave credibility to this declaration. "Is there anything I can do for you? You said you have some questions for me." Her bright and alert green eyes scanned the faces of the two men. Like a hungry cat waiting at a mouse hole, she seldom missed any flicker of emotion or movement.

Thomas took his cue. "We would like you to tell us anything you know about Mack Hanable. What's he like from your point of view? Has he made any kind of impression, good or bad? That sort of thing."

Her lips pursed in thought, and a look of amusement flitted across the strong, attractive features of her face. "Well, in fact, he is a man that made an impression on me every time I saw him. The first time was at the realtor's convention in Des Moines. That was the spring before Kate disappeared. He kind of stood out. You know, he didn't seem classy enough for Kate. She was always dressed so . . . so . . . expensively . . . almost gaudily. I'm sorry, Joe, but that was my impression." Her eyes shifted to meet his.

"When I saw them together, she was being very adamant that Mack buy her a charm bracelet. He was shaking his head, 'no,' and trying to get away from the salesman, but she wouldn't take 'no' for an answer. The two were beginning to create an uncomfortable scene. Finally, Mack pulled a hundred dollar bill out of a very worn billfold and handed it over. As soon as the transaction was completed, Kate didn't even put the bracelet on. Instead, with a sarcastic smile of satisfaction on her face, she just threw it into the bottom of her purse and walked off. Mack had to run to catch up with her."

Joe had experienced such clashes with her himself. He hunched forward and riveted his eyes back on the coffee cup. If he could crawl into a hole, he would. Thomas wrote notes on a small pad pulled from his shirt pocket.

Irene continued. "The next time I saw him, he had called me about seeing the property east of Otterville. That was the easiest sale I've ever made! We spent maybe an hour going through the house, and then he handed me a check for twenty-five thousand dollars. The remainder was paid in just a few days. He didn't even inquire about the taxes, utilities, flooding possibilities, or anything most people would want to know . . . but, why should I argue? His money was good! It came from you, Joe . . . right? It came from your purchase of the Dutcher place."

"Yes, yes. I'm sure that it did. Ruby died in May or June of 1968."

"Was that the last time you saw him. When the ownership of the property was turned over?" Thomas pressed for more information.

"No, I saw him once more after that. I stopped at the farmstead to pick up my sign. He pulled into the yard right behind me. I made a stupid remark about having to make hay out of his lawn, the grass had gotten so long. I laughed trying to make a joke of it. As soon as I put the sign in my trunk, he yanked the car door open for me to get in and as much as told me to leave and not come back." She spread out her hands and shrugged. "I guess he didn't like my sense of humor." Her eyes sparkled, and a little chuckle came from her throat.

"Well guys, I'm ready to go if you are." She gracefully slid from the booth. The pale blue suit stunningly graced her slim hips and other body curves. The color was a perfect accent to her reddish-blond hair, green eyes, and fair complexion. "You can follow me. I'll just leave from out there when we're finished with our business." She was totally aware of the appreciative gawking of the two men who walked behind her.

* * *

Fifteen minutes later, the two vehicles pulled up at the side of the road out in front of the farmstead. Irene preferred to park at a safe distance from the house, and she didn't get out of the station wagon. For a brief time, the three of them sat there taking in the place. From all appearances, no one was around. Finally, Thomas couldn't stand to wait any longer, so he pushed open the door and stepped out from behind the wheel. "Well, I'm not sitting here!" The car door was closed with an impatient slam.

He jogged around the gate post and continued up the drive to the porch outside the kitchen door. With a clenched fist, he knocked. No response. He knocked harder. Still, no response. He tried the door. It opened. In his experience, rural homes were seldom locked. He turned and waved to his companions, to let them know his intentions, and entered the kitchen.

All four chairs were pushed away from the table. It appeared that at least four people had been sitting there recently. Two bowls were setting towards the center of the table, as though they had been pushed out of the way. They had contained tomato soup. One was empty. Cracker crumbs were scattered around. A spoon set in the bowl. The other bowl was still half filled with soup. It was beginning to smell spoiled. A spoon had fallen to the floor. LuAnn would never have left the kitchen this way . . . if she had a choice.

He proceeded into the dining room. There was nothing amiss. The living room was not disturbed. The first door down the hallway stood open. The bath showed little indication that a woman and children lived in the house. The counter was cleaned off. A few soiled towels laid on the floor.

He pushed open the first bedroom door. The place looked like a mini Army surplus store. The cot in the corner of the room had been slept on. Mack's room, no doubt. The guy must miss his 'good old Army days.'

The next door was closed. With a degree of apprehension, he turned the knob and pushed it open. He was not prepared for the shambled condition of the room. Mid-day light shown through the tattered curtains onto the ravaged bed, creating a Halloweenish nightmare. The sight sent him reeling against the door frame, and his hands clutched for support. Without knowing what was happening, he pounded his forehead against the frame . . . bruising and cutting. With eyes closed tightly against the scene, he prayed fervently. *God, don't let it be!* Slowly and agonizingly, his senses returned. With held breath, he was forced to look again. His eyes swept around the room. Then he breathed. There was no odor of death, no blood, and no body. Relief swept over him.

Not yet convinced, he ran down the hall and rocketed up the stairs. Again, there were no signs that anyone had recently used the bathroom. The soiled towels on the floor were dry.

One at a time, he opened the bedroom doors. All of the curtains and bedding were gone from the rooms, as though the occupants were preparing to move. The mattresses were cut into rectangular sections. The condition of the bedrooms was bazaar, but, again, relief swept through him. There was no blood and no bodies . . . Outside? . . . He plummeted down the stairs and out the kitchen door . . . colliding with Sheriff Reilly.

"Whoa! there, fella! Nothing to worry about!" The sheriff grabbed him by the sleeve and held on. "LuAnn and the children are safely tucked away. I've been talking to Joe Weatherby and Irene White for the past five minutes . . . so I know what your mission is all about." He relinquished the grip on Thomas' sleeve. "Steady, now!"

"I came to take some pictures of the bedrooms. Then, I'm going to dispose of everything out there in the burn barrel." He pointed to the backyard. "There's no sense in having Mack return to the shambles he created. Yeah, he did this, but there's nothing that says a guy can't cut up his furnishings. However, it's in everybody's best interest if he's allowed to forget about this. He can't be retained for another night, unless LuAnn files a complaint. I think you'll agree that we don't want to bring her back for that." The grip was relinquished. "It's OK with Mack for me to clean up the place. That's good thinking on his part. Wouldn't you agree?"

Dazed and bewildered, Thomas sat down on the edge of the porch and collapsed against a supporting column. "You say LuAnn and the children are safe? Do you know where they are? No one has answered the phone here since I began calling last night. What in hell has gone on in there?" His fingers ran anxiously through his straight, brown hair leaving it spiked, in a comical sort of way, at the top of his head. "Give me some sort of explanation, will you?"

The sheriff reached over and, with a fatherly touch and a little chuckle, smoothed down Thomas' hair. "Well, Mack got a little excited when he discovered LuAnn and the kids had left him. As you can see, he cut the place up pretty good, but we have the situation under control. He spent last night in the county jail. I took the damned knives he used down to the station. They're two, big, ugly things . . . bought at the Army Surplus Store . . . machetes, I guess. Pastor Wilkens is spending the day with him on the mail route. He knows all about the situation. LuAnn confided in him on a regular basis over the past two years." He headed towards the kitchen doorway.

"I need to take some pictures." He held up a small, black camera with a flash attachment. "Then, if you can lend me a hand, we'll drag out those mattresses and get 'em burned. They can be pretty damned heavy." The sheriff opened the screen door and motioned for Thomas to follow. "You can even hang around and meet the guy if you want."

"I'll help you with the mattresses. Then, I want to go. I'll delay the privilege of meeting Mr. Hanable until another day, if you don't mind. I'm not in the best mood right now. You didn't tell me where LuAnn and the kids are." Thomas followed the sheriff back into the house.

"Well, she went to stay with Francis somebody, a friend in Cedar Rapids. I think Joe Weatherby knows her. He seems to, anyway." Pictures of the downstairs bedroom were taken, and, together, they carried the tattered mattress down the hallway and out through the kitchen door. After another ten minutes, all three mattresses were piled out by the burn-barrel and ready to be torched.

Thomas walked, thoughtfully, back to the rented Chrysler. The sheriff had given Joe and Irene a briefing of LuAnn and the children's whereabouts. They were leaning against Irene's dusty, old, white station wagon discussing the information. To the west a buggy rattled over the bridge and was driven to the entrance of the driveway where the horse was brought to an abrupt halt.

A young Amish woman stepped down and walked hesitantly towards them. "Excuse me, but do you know if LuAnn is all right?" Curls escaped from under the black cap. Her voice was soft, almost apologetic, and her smooth cheeks were flushed with apprehension and embarrassment.

Thomas approached her a short distance from the buggy. "Do you know LuAnn?" Finally, someone to make a real connection with, and maybe she knew something that no one else seemed willing to tell him.

"Oh yes, and I have been so worried about her!" Fearfully, her eyes took in the three vehicles . . . one of which was the sheriff's car. "You see . . . I stopped here yesterday . . . about this time . . . and found her tied up to a chair in the kitchen. I cut her loose, and we both left. I would like to know if she got safely to her friend's home in Cedar Rapids."

LuAnn had told him about an Amish woman who accompanied her on their trip east two years ago. Her name was very Amish. Sarah . . . it was. Yes . . . Sarah . . . Yoder. "Are you Sarah Yoder?"

The question flustered her. "Yes, but how would you know?" The pink of her cheeks deepened.

"LuAnn spoke of you when I saw her in West Virginia two years ago. And, yes, I'm told she's safe with Francis Franklin right now. I hadn't heard of her being tied to a chair! Mack did that to her?" The condition of the house was beginning to make sense. She had left in a hurry, and Mack wasn't too pleased about it.

"Yes, I'm afraid he did. I'm so thankful I found her. Mack is our mail carrier, and he has been acting very strangely. I was glad to see another man with him today. Well, thank you, and if you see LuAnn . . . tell her . . . tell her . . . tell her, I love her." Tears welled up and she turned to go.

Thomas hurried up beside her. "Sarah! I can never thank you enough for what you've done. Perhaps I'll be contacting you again. That is, if I may, and I'm sure that LuAnn loves you, too." Here was an angel, indeed.

"We live up the road two miles, but my husband would rather not get involved with the English. I hope you understand. However, if I can help LuAnn, let me know." She climbed into the buggy and arranged her skirt. Tongue was clicked in cheek, and the reins were flipped. With a curt nod, she drove from the yard. Tears of thankfulness cascaded down her cheeks, as the buggy rumbled back over the bridge. She would miss her friend.

"This has certainly been an eventful day!" Irene held out a well-manicured hand. "It has been nice meeting you, Thomas Maxwell. If there is anything more I can do for you, give me a call." She turned to Joe and, again, offered her hand. "It has been nice seeing an old friend. I hope the investigation goes well. Perhaps, we'll cross paths again sometime." With a warm smile directed at the two men, she drove off.

"Well, Joe, how about getting something to eat at the Lunch Box Café? Then, we'll head back to Cedar Rapids. I want to get Irene's notes copied over and add what Sarah told me to my accounts." He blasted the horn at Sheriff Reilly as he threw a pile of shredded curtains on top of the flaming mattresses. Those memories were too painful to keep.

"Suppose we stop down at the Cedar Rapids Police Station as soon as we get back and see how their investigation is coming? I'll get Francis Franklin's address and telephone number. God willing . . . I'll see LuAnn this evening."

"The plate lunch special today is meat loaf. Did you notice that, Thomas?"

"Meat loaf, you say? I could sure go for some meat loaf. Lunch is on me!"

Twenty-seven

Two things were utmost in Sally's mind. She intended to clean up the trailer house and lose weight. She had read someplace, in one of the magazines, that the best way to slim down was to do housework in the nude. That way, every time you passed by a mirror, there was a reminder, of the excess weight being reflected back at you. It made sense to her, so she brushed out her long, red hair, popped a chaw of bubble gum into her mouth, and started in on the cleaning. Lady Godiva would have been jealous. The swinging mane clung to her damp shoulders and breasts in a most seductive way. And, it was true! Every time she passed by a mirror, the extra twenty pounds glared back at her. There was no denying the extra weight. The idea was going to work!

All weekend, bags of garbage piled up outside the trailer's door. By Sunday evening, every cupboard and drawer was cleaned out. The piles of magazines and papers were sorted, ripped up, and dumped. The floors were swept, scrubbed, and vacuumed. Sinks, tile, and counter-tops discovered a new life beneath layers of grease and grime. Wads of bubble gum were scraped off from beneath the table and under the bed. She even took down all the curtains and washed the windows. Monday after work, she would drive into Cedar Rapids and buy new window coverings . . . and a bed-spread. Most importantly, a scale would be purchased and placed in the kitchen near the refrigerator, as a constant reminder. How else would she know when the twenty pounds were shed?

Intent on getting the trailer all cleaned up, she was willing to miss the church service on Sunday morning. So, when Pastor Bronwell arrived at Mable's Kitchen for breakfast on Monday, she was ready to offer an invitation to supper. She filled his usual order of coffee and orange juice and, last of all, placed the plate of eggs, ham, and toast on the table. Then, smiling seductively, she slid into the booth, facing him. A new perfume, Enticement, issued from her skin and permeated the air surrounding them.

Folding her hands piously on the table, she leaned towards the preacher and began her approach. "I'll just bet you get tired of eating here all the time, don't you?" She smiled sweetly and batted her long mascara-laden eyelashes. "Maybe you would like to try my cooking sometime." She had clipped out a bunch of recipes before disposing of the magazines. Some of them appeared to be easy enough. "I've got some new recipes to try out . . . if you're willing." She began to feel uncomfortable and could feel the blood slowly creeping up her neck and into her cheeks. Beads of perspiration were accumulating on her forehead. A paper napkin was yanked from the dispenser and used to blot them. Pastor Bronwell hadn't, as yet, looked up from the plate of food. "Say, tomorrow around six o'clock? Unless, of course, you're busy," she hurriedly added.

The pastor was well aware, over the past few weeks, that Sally was looking at him seductively. It was quite obvious to him that she had something more intimate than waiting on his table in mind. He considered their relationship strictly platonic, and so, to be prepared, he had run such a scenario through his mind several times. The rejection of her offer was going to be much easier than he thought. Her culinary skills were a running joke at Mable's. Sometimes, he even felt remorse for the ribbing she got. Now, he used this advantageously.

He was able to look up from eating breakfast and make an honest and heartfelt response. "Sally, your offer is most gracious, considering the lack of knowledge and skill you have in the area of cooking. However, I have a much better idea. My fiancee will be coming on Friday. She loves to cook, and I'm certain she would be delighted to have you eat with us. She can give you a little instruction at the same time." With a sense of caring and compassion, he looked directly into her eyes and waited for an answer. "What do you say?" he smiled warmly.

This wasn't the response she was hoping for. Her eyes dropped to the table top, and the smile faded . . . replaced by a little-girl pout. Her stomach knotted up, and tears, impatient to surface, were pushing at her eyelids. She had worked so hard all weekend, and for what? Heat from embarrassment flooded her whole body. There was an undeniable stupidity in thinking that he could be interested in her. Her normally pinkish complexion turned a deep red. The sick feeling was accompanied by a flood of heat, and sweat seeped from every pore. Stammering, she didn't know how else to answer him. "Th . . . th . . . thank you, p . . . p . . . pastor, that sounds j . . . j . . . just wonderful. When do you w . . . w . . . want me there?"

* * *

Three calls came into the Cedar Rapids Police Station on Wednesday. Each person had a similar story to relate. They all lived on Third Avenue northeast in Independence and had seen the picture of Kate Weatherby on the front page of Tuesday's *Cedar Rapids Gazette.* They were all certain this woman was out in front of their homes eleven years ago. She had been part of a memorable scene.

After bringing her fancy car to a skidding stop, crossways in the street, she ran after their mail carrier, screamed obscene names, and attacked him. The man put his hands up in self-defense, but the woman kept at it. Then apparently, he said something that calmed her down. Anyway, she got back into the car and drove away.

A few days later, her picture appeared in the paper as 'missing.' At the time, no one gave any particular relevance to the event. For many years after that, the mail carrier did his job without incident. No one ever filed complaints against him. But now, the discovery of the woman's body and her picture, once again appearing in the paper, gave them a different perspective. Perhaps the two occurrences were related. Yes, they would give statements if the police wanted them to. Their mail carrier at that time was Mack Hanable.

* * *

The autopsy report came into the office shortly after two o'clock. Cause of death was stated as, "Severe trauma to the back of the skull caused by a blow or fall." The weapon would have been heavy and broad based. A large rock could have caused such a fracture. Because there were no rocks in the lake, where the body was discovered, the death blow would have been administered while the victim was on the shore. The two cement blocks and the fragments of rope were most likely the reason why the body never surfaced. The investigation would proceed as a homicide.

All of the evidence acquired, so far, pointed solely in the direction of Mack Hanable. The jewelry his wife relinquished, and her statements concerning their relationship, were particularly incriminating. There was enough to bring him in for questioning. A call was put into the office of the Buchanan County sheriff.

* * *

Joe and Thomas were brought up to date. Thomas was given Francis Franklin's telephone number and address. There was no need to be too impatient. There was time to go back to the motel and get a shower and shave. He should do that, if he wanted to make a good impression . . . no sense in looking like a bum. Besides, the smell of cigarette smoke at the police station reeked from his clothes.

After dinner, he would call Francis to ask if LuAnn would be willing to see him. No doubt, the past several days had been very stressful. He didn't want to add to her discomfort in anyway. Besides, in the past two years, they had made no direct contact with one another. He was aware that Fern had put flowers on Amy's grave . . . at LuAnn's request. The consideration had touched him deeply.

Would she be receptive of him now? He began to have doubts. However, love and concern kept nagging, pushing him to follow through with his intentions. After all, they had brought him there in the first place.

The phone rang three times before Francis answered. He was ready to hang up and drive over to the apartment. He would sit outside there and wait if necessary. "Hello, Mrs. Franklin, I'm a friend of LuAnn's. How is she doing?"

"She seems to be doing fine, considering everything she's been through lately. She just stepped into the shower. Who did you say is calling?"

"This is an old friend from West Virginia . . . Thomas Maxwell. Do you think she's up to having some company this evening?"

"Are you the police officer from Charleston? Detective O'Hagan mentioned your name when I was at the station this morning." She was trying to remember.

"Of course, and he said you're a friend of LuAnn's!" *Was it Thomas that LuAnn had cried over so many years ago?* She was inclined to think it was.

"If tomorrow would be better, I can wait until then." In spite of the earlier resolve, he was beginning to back down.

"Oh! No, no! LuAnn could do with seeing a familiar face. Old friends are often the best. Give us another half hour. Should I tell her you're coming, or would you rather surprise her?"

"I'll let you decide that. I'll be there at . . . eight-fifteen!" He hung up.

Francis smiled. She recognized passion in a man's voice. Thomas Maxwell's interest in LuAnn was more than as a friend.

* * *

LuAnn stepped from the shower . . . her hair dripping. A towel was taken from the chrome bar and wrapped around her. Her hair was dried and curled with no consideration given to the time. The past days had been eventful enough. There was no place to go tonight, no need to hurry. She could enjoy Francis' company and maybe listen to those tapes again.

A pink satin robe was pulled on, and she padded, barefoot, back to the guest room. The bed covers were thrown back. It would be wonderful to crawl in right now. The light scent of Lily of the Valley would soothe away the last tangle in her nerves. Then, Francis knocked on the bedroom door.

"LuAnn, I got a call from the police station. One of the officers is stopping by. He has a few more questions for us." Somehow, LuAnn should be prepared for the expected company. "He'll be here any minute."

With a sigh, she obligingly pulled on a pair of flowered lounging pajamas and applied a touch of lipstick. As she left the guest room, Francis went into her own bedroom and closed the door. There was a light knock. She expected Francis to let the officer in, but the bedroom door remained closed. The knock became more demanding. Reluctantly, she padded down the hallway and through the living room. The distorted image seen through the peephole was of no help, so the door was opened.

"Hello, LuAnn." Thomas's voice caught, and all reservations crumbled.

"Thomas?" Her voice was a whisper. Her knees buckled, and she fell into a pair of strong, eager arms.

They clung to one another as their bodies rocked with years of unexpressed emotion and desire. Tears washed away the agony of separation. He picked her up and carried her to the davenport. No words were necessary, as he kissed her sweet-smelling hair, her cheeks, and her lips. There would be time for words later. He lightly caressed the slim body, willing his strength into her. She wasn't going to get away from him ever again. He held her protectively, and eventually, they slept.

At some point in the night, LuAnn separated herself from Thomas' embrace. Without disturbing him, she kissed his forehead, and stumbled into the guest room. She pulled the covers up and smiled contentedly. Dreams of tomorrow mingled with the scent of Lily of the Valley.

* * *

Mack sat on the kitchen porch steps with Pete Brown on one side and Sheriff Reilly on the other. For the past two hours, he had related every aspect of his life to the two men. His relationship with Kate Weatherby was described in detail, as nervous fingers raked through his dark hair in rhythm with the pain of confession. Occasionally, a tear was wiped away from his cheek. The back of his shirt clung with perspiration. When there was no more to say, deep sobs escaped from his guts. He lay back on the porch and stared up at the roof. Water still dripped from the leaves and bushes, due to an early evening shower. It seemed as though the whole world was crying. Pete handed him a handkerchief to mop up the tears and blow his nose.

"What you're saying is that Kate's death was a result of you trying to defend yourself? Then, you'll have to tell the Cedar Rapids police the same things you told us. But, it seems to me, you were only acting in self-defense. Of course, your actions following her death weren't very smart. You'll need to get yourself a lawyer. Do you have anyone in mind?" Sheriff Reilly was preparing Mack for what was ahead.

A car from the Cedar Rapids Police Department pulled into the yard. Two officers stepped out. The sheriff went out to meet them. The older of the officers presented their business. "Sheriff Reilly, we have a warrant to bring Mackenzie Hanable into the station for questioning in the death of Katherine Weatherby." His eyes shifted from Pete to Mack.

Mack stepped forward. "That's me." He held out his hands to accept the cuffs. There was no more fight left.

The younger officer read him his rights. He was put into the rear seat, and the car disappeared down the dirt road.

* * *

Thursday morning, the phone rang in Francis' apartment, arousing one very sleepy person. It took Thomas a few minutes to remember where he had spent the night. Then he heard Francis say, "Yes, he's here.

He slept on my davenport in the living room. Just a minute, I'll see if he's awake yet." A middle-aged woman with graying, reddish-brown hair and a big smile came from the kitchen. "Good morning, Thomas I hope you had a good night." Her eyes sparkled knowingly. "Joe Weatherby would like to speak with you."

Thomas returned her smile, a bit sheepishly, and went into the kitchen to see what was on Joe's mind so early in the morning. "Mack Hanable was brought in last night. I requested that you and I be present during the interrogation this morning. I hope it's all right that I spoke for you, too."

"Of course . . . it's time I met this guy. What time are we looking at? I'll be there!" He hung up the phone and turned to Francis. "I guess you've already figured out that I'm Thomas Maxwell, LuAnn's friend." He held out his hand.

"The bathroom is down the hallway. You better get in there before LuAnn does. Sometimes, a woman can take a while." He may as well get used to the idea.

The door to the guest room was slightly ajar. He pushed it open further and his sense of being was filled, completely, with the view of LuAnn laying curled up like a child. So small . . . so tender . . . and so tough! Her breathing was deep and even.

He smiled contentedly, pulled the door shut, and found the bathroom. After preparing for the morning, he found Francis in the kitchen. "I need to leave right now. Tell LuAnn I'll be back as soon as possible. Don't let her get away. OK?" He felt his pockets for keys and billfold and left.

* * *

A variety of donuts, along with a pot of coffee and two coffee cups, were set on a table for Joe and Thomas. They would view the proceedings from an adjacent room without being observed. Sheriff Reilly had contacted a lawyer. So now, Mack, his lawyer, Osgood Morris, and Detective Patrick O'Hagan sat around the table in the interrogation room. A tape recorder was placed on the table, and Mack began his narration.

* * *

Three hours later, he was finished, and all questions were answered. Joe and Thomas sat thoughtfully, neither of them quite sure of what, if anything, was left to be said. Joe broke the silence first. "I think it's only fitting that we get the man some psychological help. Surely, that can be requested as part of the deal. He certainly isn't guilty of murder. I may not have said that eleven years ago, but when the truth hits a person in the eyes, well, you better see it."

* * *

The only charges brought against Mack were for illegally disposing of a body. These charges would be dropped after completing mandatory sessions with a psychiatrist . . . if the therapy was successful. He must, also, give LuAnn a divorce and not seek custody or visitation rights with the children, Joyce and Jason. In return, LuAnn would seek no alimony or child support. Mack gratefully accepted all these conditions.

* * *

On Monday, June 30, 1970, Thomas loaded luggage into LuAnn's car. After nearly twelve years, she was ready to leave Iowa. He would drive separately in his rented Chrysler and accompany her to Chicago. Together, they would pick up the children and drive on to Huntington. He would help them get settled into their new home before going on to Charleston. He not only hoped to make the drive safer for them, but he would try to help LuAnn answer some of the questions Joyce and Jason were bound to ask.

* * *

When Sally read the coverage of the story in the Sunday edition of the *Cedar Rapids Gazette,* she was stricken by how desperately Mack must need her. She called every hour until she finally reached him Monday evening. "Macky, I'm so sorry for all you've been through! As a friend, I should be there. Is it okay if I come and see you? Just remember though, I can't stay all night. Under the circumstances, that wouldn't be the right thing to do . . . Do you think?"

* * *

Kate's remains were laid to rest, with only Joe, Clare, and Pastor Yokum present. The diamonds and emeralds on Clare's fingers glistened in the sun as she placed a wrinkled hand on her daughter's coffin . . . bidding good-bye. Joe helped his wife back to the hearse, and it slowly made its way down the winding drive and out of the cemetery.

An hour later, Joe watched as the levee between Paradise Lake and Kate's Cove was opened up, and the water began to seek its level.